Case Studies in Contemporary Criticism

JOSEPH CONRAD

Heart of Darkness

Case Studies in Contemporary Criticism

SERIES EDITOR: Ross C Murfin

Charlotte Brontë, *Jane Eyre*
EDITED BY Beth Newman, Southern Methodist University

Emily Brontë, *Wuthering Heights*
EDITED BY Linda H. Peterson, Yale University

Geoffrey Chaucer, *The Wife of Bath*
EDITED BY Peter G. Beidler, Lehigh University

Kate Chopin, *The Awakening*
EDITED BY Nancy A. Walker, Vanderbilt University

Joseph Conrad, *Heart of Darkness*, Second Edition
EDITED BY Ross C Murfin, University of Miami

Charles Dickens, *Great Expectations*
EDITED BY Janice Carlisle, Tulane University

Nathaniel Hawthorne, *The Scarlet Letter*
EDITED BY Ross C Murfin, University of Miami

Henry James, *The Turn of the Screw*
EDITED BY Peter G. Beidler, Lehigh University

James Joyce, *The Dead*
EDITED BY Daniel R. Schwarz, Cornell University

James Joyce, *A Portrait of the Artist as a Young Man*
EDITED BY R. B. Kershner, University of Florida

William Shakespeare, *Hamlet*
EDITED BY Susanne L. Wofford, University of Wisconsin–Madison

Mary Shelley, *Frankenstein*
EDITED BY Johanna M. Smith, University of Texas at Arlington

Jonathan Swift, *Gulliver's Travels*
EDITED BY Christopher Fox, University of Notre Dame

Edith Wharton, *The House of Mirth*
EDITED BY Shari Benstock, University of Miami

Case Studies in Contemporary Criticism

SERIES EDITOR: Ross C Murfin, *Southern Methodist University*

JOSEPH CONRAD
Heart of Darkness

Complete, Authoritative Text with
Biographical and Historical Contexts,
Critical History, and Essays from
Five Contemporary Critical Perspectives

SECOND EDITION

EDITED BY

Ross C Murfin
Southern Methodist University

Bedford/St. Martin's
BOSTON ◆ NEW YORK

For Bedford/St. Martin's
President and Publisher: Charles H. Christensen
General Manager and Associate Publisher: Joan E. Feinberg
Managing Editor: Elizabeth M. Schaaf
Developmental Editor: Stephen A. Scipione
Editorial Assistant: Mark Reimold
Production Editor: Karen S. Baart
Copyeditor: Nancy Bell Scott
Text Design: Sandra Rigney, The Book Department
Cover Design: Richard Emery Design, Inc.
Cover Art: Cotton and silk wrapper (Asante peoples, Ghana). Photograph by Franko Khoury. National Museum of African Art, Eliot Elisofon Archives, Smithsonian Institution.

Library of Congress Catalog Card Number: 95–80800
Copyright © 1996 by BEDFORD BOOKS

Manufactured in the United States of America.

5   4
p   o   n   m

For information, write: Bedford/St. Martin's
75 Arlington Street, Boston, MA 02116 (617-399-4000)

ISBN: 0–312–11491–5 (paperback)
ISBN: 0–312–15901–3 (hardcover)

Published and distributed outside North America by:

MACMILLAN PRESS LTD.
Houndmills, Basingstoke, Hampshire RG21 2XS and London
Companies and representatives throughout the world.

ISBN: 0–333–65707–1

Acknowledgments

About the Series

Volumes in the Case Studies in Contemporary Criticism series provide college students with an entrée into the current critical and theoretical ferment in literary studies. Each volume reprints the complete text of a classic literary work and presents critical essays that approach the work from different theoretical perspectives, together with the editors' introductions to both the literary work and the critics' theoretical perspectives.

The volume editor of each Case Study has selected and prepared an authoritative text of the classic work, written an introduction to the work's biographical and historical contexts, and surveyed the critical responses to the work since its initial publication. Thus situated biographically, historically, and critically, the work is examined in five critical essays, each representing a theoretical perspective of importance to contemporary literary studies. These essays, prepared especially for undergraduates, show theory in praxis; whether written by established scholars or exceptional young critics, they demonstrate how current theoretical approaches can generate compelling readings of great literature.

As series editor, I have prepared introductions, with bibliographies, to the theoretical perspectives represented in the five critical essays. Each introduction presents the principal concepts of a particular theory in their historical context and discusses the major figures and

key works that have influenced their formulation. It is my hope that
these introductions will reveal to students that effective criticism is informed by a set of coherent assumptions, and will encourage them to
recognize and examine their own assumptions about literature. After
each introduction, a selective bibliography presents a partially anno-
tated list of important works from the literature of the particular theoretical perspective, including the most recent and readily available edi-
tions and translations of the works cited in the introduction. Finally, I
have compiled a glossary of key terms that recur in these volumes and
in the discourse of contemporary theory and criticism. We hope that
the Case Studies in Contemporary Criticism series will reaffirm the
richness of its literary works, even as it introduces invigorating new
ways to mine their apparently inexhaustible wealth.

Ross C Murfin
Series Editor
University of Miami

About This Volume

Part One of this volume reprints the text of *Heart of Darkness* from the 1921 Heinemann edition of Conrad's *Collected Works* — the last version of the text that Conrad approved.

Part Two includes five contemporary critical essays on *Heart of Darkness*, representing reader-response, deconstructionist, feminist and gender, new historicist, and cultural approaches to Conrad's most famous tale. Three of the essays — reader-response, feminist and gender, and new historicist — were specifically written for this edition.

New to This Edition

I undertook a second edition to make this Case Study of *Heart of Darkness* a more useful and current resource for introducing students to the latest trends in contemporary criticism. Both the reader-response and the cultural essays are new, reflecting recent developments in those fields of theory. The feminist essay of the first edition has been revised to encompass a more contemporary gender perspective, and the new historicist essay has been updated. All of the introductions and bibliographies to the critical approaches have been significantly revised. The critical history now extends well into the 1990s, and also discusses Chinua Achebe's "An Image of Africa: Conrad's

Heart of Darkness," which has been so influential in recent postcolonial and cultural investigations of Conrad's work.

Acknowledgments

I am indebted to those whose comments have improved the introductions to the critical approaches: Shari Benstock, Patrick Brantlinger, Janice Carlisle, Steven Mailloux, J. Hillis Miller, Margot Norris, and Brook Thomas. I am deeply grateful to the authors of the critical essays, especially Peter J. Rabinowitz for his new reader-response essay, and Johanna Smith and Brook Thomas for the revisions of their respective essays from the first edition of this Case Study. I continue to appreciate the exemplary help of the people at Bedford Books, especially Chuck Christensen, Joan Feinberg, Steve Scipione, Elizabeth Schaaf, Karen Baart, Laura Arcari, and Mark Reimold. At the University of Miami, I would like to thank my staff assistant, Tracy Helenbrook, for her extraordinary competence, diligence, and good cheer. Patricia Woodward tutored me on the subject of gender studies and helped me develop the bibliography in that area. This book is dedicated to Supryia Ray, whose research habits, editorial acumen, debating skills, and unfailing, friendly support made it possible for me to revise and update the introductions to all five critical approaches represented in this volume.

Contents

About the Series   v

About This Volume   vii

PART ONE
Heart of Darkness:
The Complete Text

Introduction: Biographical and Historical Contexts   3

The Complete Text   17

PART TWO
Heart of Darkness:
A Case Study in Contemporary Criticism

A Critical History of *Heart of Darkness*   99

Reader-Response Criticism and *Heart of Darkness*   115

What Is Reader-Response Criticism?   115
Reader-Response Criticism: A Selected Bibliography   127

A Reader-Response Perspective:
  PETER J. RABINOWITZ, Reader Response, Reader Responsibility:
  Heart of Darkness and the Politics of Displacement   131

Feminist and Gender Criticism and *Heart of Darkness*   148

What Are Feminist and Gender Criticism?   148
Feminist and Gender Criticism: A Selected Bibliography   162
A Feminist and Gender Perspective:
  JOHANNA M. SMITH, "Too Beautiful Altogether": Ideologies
  of Gender and Empire in *Heart of Darkness*   169

Deconstruction and *Heart of Darkness*   185

What Is Deconstruction?   185
Deconstruction: A Selected Bibliography   201
A Deconstructive Perspective:
  J. HILLIS MILLER, *Heart of Darkness* Revisited   206

The New Historicism and *Heart of Darkness*   221

What Is the New Historicism?   221
The New Historicism: A Selected Bibliography   233
A New Historicist Perspective:
  BROOK THOMAS, Preserving and Keeping Order by Killing Time
  in *Heart of Darkness*   239

Cultural Criticism and *Heart of Darkness*   258

What Is Cultural Criticism?   258
Cultural Criticism: A Selected Bibliography   272
A Cultural Perspective:
  PATRICK BRANTLINGER, *Heart of Darkness:* Anti-Imperialism,
  Racism, or Impressionism?   277

Glossary of Critical and Theoretical Terms   299

About the Contributors   313

Case Studies in Contemporary Criticism

JOSEPH CONRAD

Heart of Darkness

PART ONE

Heart of Darkness: The Complete Text

Introduction:
Biographical and
Historical Contexts

Polish, not English, was the language Joseph Conrad grew up speaking. English wasn't even his second language: French was. The fact that Conrad achieved fame in his third language is testimony to his genius — genius that could be contained neither by linguistic barriers nor by national boundaries. Early political persecution and exile failed to stifle it; even the loss of family and deep personal unhappiness could only restrain it temporarily.

Conrad was christened Josef Konrad Nalecz Korzeniowski. Both his mother, Ewa, and his father, Apollo, were descended from wealthy Polish families. Born in 1857 — "in the 85th year of Muscovite Oppression," as his father put it — Josef found himself, from childhood on, a person without a country. In 1772 Poland had been divided up among Russia, Prussia, and Austria, only to be redivided in 1793 and 1795.

Thus, although Conrad was born into the landed gentry of Polish culture (in what had become a western Russian province), his childhood years were full of uncertainty. His headstrong, talented father, a poet and translator of French and English literature, was dedicated to the cause of Polish independence from Russia. Just before a Polish uprising was quelled in 1863, Apollo was arrested and exiled to the village of Vologda, hundreds of miles north of Moscow.

The trip to Vologda nearly killed young Josef, and the brutal winters there hastened the demise of both his parents. Ewa died of tuberculosis in 1865, her despairing husband shortly thereafter, in 1869. Josef, who was but twelve years old, was adopted by his mother's uncle, an at once firm but indulgent gentleman named Tadeusz Bobrowski.

Uncle Tadeusz cared well for his orphaned nephew, sending him first to school in Krakow, later to Geneva with a tutor. But the young Conrad could adjust neither to the rigors of school life nor to the personal attentions of his private teacher, who continually tried to reform his pupil's romantic views on life and the world. Finally, the exasperated Josef persuaded his Uncle Tadeusz to let him join the French merchant navy.

The four years following were more adventure-filled, but apparently no more satisfying, than the earlier, teenage years. Conrad sailed to the West Indies and Venezuela, squandered a small fortune, lost in love, got involved in a gun-running venture for the Carlists (who were seeking to seize the throne of Spain for Carlos de Bourbon), and attempted suicide in 1878. That same year, French immigration authorities prevented him from continuing as a sailor on merchant marine vessels.

This last turn of events seems in the long run to have been a fortunate one, since Conrad was to sail for the next sixteen years on British ships and to become a British subject in 1887. Conrad's metamorphosis from a French sailor to an English one caused him to master the language in which he would ultimately choose to write his novels. The greatest of these — including *Heart of Darkness, Lord Jim, Nostromo, The Secret Agent,* and *Victory* — have been, almost since their publication, ranked with the most powerful and poetic novels ever written in English.

Like other geniuses, Conrad had a way of turning disadvantage into advantage. He made unconventional, poetic use of a language he was forced to master by circumstance. A lesser talent would have been blunted by twenty trying years of life on deck; Conrad transformed his experiences into art.

From his years in the East and West Indies, he gained the atmosphere as well as the insights into human nature that he was to draw upon while writing works from *Almayer's Folly* (published in 1895, when Conrad was in his thirties) to *The Rescue* (published in 1920, four years before Conrad's death).

But it was not only in the East and West Indies that Conrad came by the store of experiences that were later to be metamorphosed into art. Indeed, the voyage that seems to have had the greatest impact on Conrad's life and art was not by sea at all — or at least the most memorable part of the trip was not. That was the expedition that saw Conrad far up the Congo River on a rusty steamboat with a shrill whistle.

Conrad had begun writing *Almayer's Folly*, his first novel, in 1889, just before commencing the trip up to Stanley (now Boyoma) Falls in 1890. In spite of the near-torturous nature of the journey, he managed to make continual progress on the book while en route. The trip from Boma to Stanley Falls and back was one of the last Conrad ever made as a sailor. It marked, in a sense, the beginning of a brief but crucial period of his life, a period that came to an end in 1894, the year his beloved Uncle Tadeusz died. For it was then that Conrad decided to devote himself to writing full time. Shortly after making that decision, he was to marry Jessie George. The troubled Pole without a clear-cut family, nationality, language, love, or even calling in life was now Joseph Conrad, a British subject, husband, and writer.

Present-day Zaire, one of the largest nations in Africa, was known as the Belgian Congo from 1908 until 1960, when it gained its independence. The Congo visited by Conrad and by the narrator of *Heart of Darkness* was officially called "L'État Indépendent du Congo" (customarily if roughly translated into English as "the Congo Free State"). But Belgian the Congo was, from 1885 on, thanks to a conference called in Berlin in 1884 by Otto von Bismarck, first chancellor of the newly formed German Empire.

Not that Belgium had opened up the Congo to European exploration, exploitation, and development. The celebrated Scot Dr. David Livingstone had gone there in 1856, to be "found" by the Americanized Welshman Henry Morton Stanley in 1871. Livingstone and Stanley, moreover, had been preceded by Portuguese, Dutch, and French pioneers. In fact, until 1876, King Leopold II of Belgium had merely sat back and watched with interest. In that year, though, this ambitious and notoriously immoral monarch of a nation less than fifty years old made his first move. He organized a meeting in Brussels to discuss a plan "to open to civilization the only part of our globe where Christianity has not yet penetrated and to pierce the darkness which envelops the entire population" (Hennessy 13).

Bismarck, who had gradually come to realize that no nation would win anything if all were drawn into a territorial, theological, or trade war, eventually called his own conference in Berlin. To the surprise of astute political forecasters throughout the Western world, Bismarck's

1884 convention resulted in a decision to make the Congo the personal property of Leopold II. All the king had to do was guarantee that all nations would be permitted to trade freely there, that taxes and tariffs would not be collected, and that nations would not be granted monopolies on particular items of trade. Leopold, who ended up shirking most of his commitments, controlled the Congo until he died in 1908. In a will written in 1889, he bequeathed the territory to Belgium in exchange for a government loan of 150 million francs.

Thus, the Congo had been all but Belgian since long before 1908. And it had been ruled by a tyrant whose promise to bring civilization to Africa had turned out to be little more than a cruel joke. Leopold had divided the country into sixteen districts, each governed by a commissioner who rendered the local chiefs impotent. Some of these officials went on to build personal fortunes by collecting taxes from the natives, and since few of the natives had anything to give but their labor, the commissioners were, in effect, slaveholders, and the Congolese were slaves in all but name. Leopold, in turn, received a portion of all profits made by his administrators, so it was in his interest to make sure that when Africans rebelled against the sentries who guarded them while they worked out their taxes, they be taught a swift and brutal lesson.

Reports of atrocities were drifting back to Europe within a few years after Leopold had been granted proprietorship. Baptist missionaries duped by the king's stated goal of Christianizing the Congo were among the first to cry foul. But the Congo was far from Europe, and the damning reports from scattered missionaries were relatively few and far between. And anyway, people wondered in Europe, wasn't it inevitable that the lives of some Africans would be lost? When natives rebelled, weren't the sentries merely protecting themselves, or at worst doing their duty? King Leopold assured his people that their "agents" were "profoundly reluctant to use force." However, he explained, unfortunate incidents were bound to happen, since many of the sentries were "wretched negroes" with "sanguinary habits" recruited from the local population, natives who were, in other words, prone to turn viciously on their own people (Burrows 286).

Many of the station managers and traders that Leopold refers to as his agents were drawn from the ranks of the Belgian army, and by 1890 they had, with Leopold's blessing, given the lie to their king's promise that the Congo would be a free-trade territory. Ivory, the most valuable commodity, had become a Belgian monopoly; non-Belgian traders caught carrying it could be summarily shot, either by Leopold's army-trained representatives or by their sentries. Among these sentries were natives "freed" from their black slaveowners and offered "protection" by the white invaders. They had to work seven years for their new master, wherever he chose to send them, for whatever wages he sought to bestow, and in whatever conditions he saw fit to provide.

Why did Conrad go to such a place? Since the mid 1870s, he had been sailing the high seas, mainly on English ships. Why would he want to ride a leaky Belgian steamboat upriver into the troubled heart of Africa when the open seas led to a whole world of places whose names surely conjured up more images of romance and adventure?

Part of the answer can perhaps be found in Conrad's late essay "Geography and Some Explorers," in which he recalls that, as an adolescent, he had been particularly fascinated by stories of polar explorers. Of Leopold McClintock's book *The Voyage of the "Fox" in the Arctic Seas* (1859), Conrad writes: "There could hardly have been imagined a better book for letting in the breath of the stern romance of polar exploration. . . . The great spirit of the realities of the story sent me off on the romantic explorations of my inner self" ("Geography" 16–17).

Another, complementary explanation of why Conrad wanted to visit King Leopold's troubled Congo may lie in the same essay, in the paragraphs that tell of a lifelong fascination with maps. By age thirteen, he recalls, he was "addicted" to "map-gazing," much as other people become hooked on star-gazing. "And it was Africa," Conrad writes, "the Continent out of which the Romans used to say some new thing was always coming," that seemed particularly fascinating. So much of that continent was unknown and unexplored that maps of whole regions of it would be covered by "exciting spaces of white paper." Thus, owing to its "regions unknown," the "heart of Africa" as represented by maps was "white and big" ("Geography" 19–20).

At about the age of sixteen, Conrad made a public commitment to travel someday to unknown Africa. "One day," he recalls, "putting my finger on a spot in the very middle of the then white heart of Africa, I declared that some day I would go there" ("Geography" 24). Long before he was sixteen and even before he read *The Voyage of the "Fox" in the Arctic Seas,* though, Conrad had expressed his intention to do what he finally did in 1890 on the steamer *Roi des Belges.* In his late, autobiographical retrospective entitled *Some Reminiscences,* Conrad claims that the decision was made during childhood:

It was in 1868, when I was nine years old or thereabouts, that while looking at a map of Africa of the time and putting my finger on the blank space then representing the unsolved mystery of the continent, I said to myself with absolute assurance and an amazing audacity which are no longer in my character now: "When I grow up I shall go there." (41)

Conrad then says that he gave that proclamation no further thought until, more than twenty years later, the opportunity to travel up the Congo River to Stanley Falls actually presented itself. For Stanley Falls was the very spot on the map he had pointed at in 1868: "the blankest of blank spaces on the earth's figured surface" (*Reminiscences* 41).

These various personal records suggest that Conrad decided to go to the Congo for several closely related reasons. In part because the interior of Africa had been represented by cartographers as a mysterious white blankness, and in part because tales of polar exploration had equated white blankness with the unknown and explorers of the white wilderness with true heroism, Conrad associated the Congo with the unknown and equated a voyage there with the most important, heroic kind of voyage. Tales of seamen wandering the South Pacific were tales of the "acquisitive spirit," of those urged on by "the desire of trade . . . or loot," whereas the "aims" of the polar explorers were "as pure as the air of those high latitudes" ("Geography" 14). If mere stories of such men sent Conrad "off on . . . explorations of [his] inner self," how much more he was likely to learn about his own nature and human nature in general by traveling into the great expanse of white that lay beyond the colored, mapped areas of Africa.

There is an obvious irony in Conrad's implicit association of the unknown Congo, hot and humid home of a dark race, with whiteness and the arctic. Another irony emerges as we read Conrad's novel set in the Congo: the aims of several white "explorers" portrayed in it were morally black as pitch — not at all like the "pure" aims of arctic wayfarers in search of the Northwest Passage. So obvious are these ironies that they were, obviously, intended.

Still, we must remember that the Conrad who wrote not *Heart of Whiteness* but, rather, *Heart of Darkness* — the Conrad who still later penned *Some Reminiscences* and the essay on maps and explorers — was an older and wiser Conrad than the young man who set sail from France on the sixth of May, 1890, for the Congolese coast. Conrad could not have known until he actually experienced the Congo just how much its "explorers" were prompted by the desire for "loot." The Congo was supposed to be a relatively free, peaceable state, open to all traders and therefore free not only of the murderous violence but also of the slavery found in so many other areas of the world. Conrad had to discover, personally, just how false that supposition was. In seeing how easily Europeans who set forth in ships to enlighten and civilize can corrupt and destroy, Conrad came to a profound realization about human nature: whiteness and light may turn out to be blackness and darkness, and blackness and darkness may be relatively pure. In learning that hard lesson, Conrad also discovered something profound about himself: that it was as a writer, not as a merchant sailor, that he wanted to explore the world — especially the inner world of "civilized" humanity.[1] Thus, even though Conrad could not have been prepared to find what he found in the Congo by white spaces on a map, tales of polar exploration, or accounts of the Congo Free State that amounted to a king's whitewash, he did, in a sense, find in the Congo exactly what, as a schoolboy, he had somehow sensed he would find: the mysterious unknown, self-knowledge, and even, it seems fair to say, his destiny.

There were, of course, practical reasons why Conrad decided to go to the Congo. Fated though it seems he was by the promise he had made in childhood to go there, drawn as he was to the idea of discovering something about himself while voyaging into uncharted territory, Conrad was also attracted to the Congo because it promised a much-needed source of financial support (Conrad had used up his inheritance by the age of twenty-one) and because there, it seemed, he would be not just a sailor but a captain. He had briefly served as master of an Australian vessel, but it was not until 1886 that he had passed the examination qualifying him for a commission certified by the British Board of Trade.

In 1889 Conrad approached Albert Thys, managing director of the Société Anonyme Belge pour le Commerce du Haut-Congo, in the hope that Thys could procure him a position commanding a steamer plying the Congo River. But Conrad also looked into other positions that, had they materialized, would have sent him back to the West Indies as a captain. Neither destination beckoned immediately; Thys had nothing to offer, perhaps because Conrad wanted a long-term commitment. "A short visit would not be worth the trouble and

---

[1]Frederick Karl develops this idea in *Joseph Conrad: The Three Lives* (New York: Farrar, 1979). I am indebted to Karl not only for this idea but also for bringing together illuminating excerpts from Conrad's letters and diary, some of which are quoted below.

expense of leaving [Europe] for," he remarked to Thys in a letter dated December 27, 1889 (Karl 276).

With no immediate prospects, Conrad decided to visit Uncle Tadeusz in the Ukraine, then to return to England by way of Brussels, where he hoped not only to reassert his interest in a Congo command but also to visit with his "Aunt" Marguerite and "Uncle" Aleksander Poradowska. (Uncle Aleksander was actually Conrad's cousin; Aunt Marguerite, a writer of novels and short stories, was related to Conrad only by marriage.) Hearing that Aleksander was ill and failing fast, Conrad changed his plans and went to Brussels first. He arrived on February 5, 1890; two days later his cousin died. Although Conrad was soon to enter a close relationship and correspondence with Marguerite, he left her before her husband was buried, traveling to Warsaw, then to Lublin, and finally to Kazimierowka, where he stayed with Uncle Tadeusz for two months.

In spite of Tadeusz's attempt to discourage him from his interest in a Congo command, Conrad returned to Brussels on April 26, 1890. There he learned that a steamer captain named Freiesleben had died in the Congo and that a command was available. Actually, Conrad's turn in luck was due to far more than the death of the ship's captain; Aunt Marguerite had, with Conrad's permission, used her considerable influence on several important men involved in the colonization effort, including Thys. After signing with Thys, Conrad headed for a French port, from which he shipped for Boma, the main port of entry to the Congo.

Conrad wrote letters back to Marguerite Poradowska, so we have a fair idea of what his journey to the heart of the "Haut-Congo" was like — or at least the first, easiest part of his journey. He was working on *Almayer's Folly* and thinking constantly of his "aunt," who seems to have been not only a mother figure but also a woman whose image raised romantic possibilities in his mind. ("You have endowed my life with new interest, new affection," he tells her in a letter mailed from Libreville [Karl 285].) Conrad arrived at his destination on June 12, after an interminable-seeming sea voyage down the African coast. The trip, from Bordeaux to Boma on the *Ville de Maceio*, had taken more than a month.

Forty miles from Boma, in Matadi, Conrad met Roger Casement, who had come to the Congo Free State thinking that he would abolish the slave trade carried on by Arabs in the area and establish a railway that would link the coastal region with Stanley (now Malebo) Pool, where the Congo River becomes navigable and stays navigable all the way inland to Stanley (Boyoma) Falls. When he met Conrad in the spring of 1890, Casement was beginning the railway project, as yet unaware (like Conrad) that many of King Leopold's men were using the natives as slave labor. Conrad shared a room with Casement for almost a month, at the end of which he began the overland journey made arduous by the lack of a railway and fresh water, and by the presence of what turned out to be three virtual plagues: heat, mosquitoes, and one of Leopold's agents, Prosper Harou.

The trip to Stanley Pool had to be made by foot: "Not an ass here," Conrad joked in a letter to Marguerite, "except your very humble servant" (Karl 289). But there were other things to see along the way, not beasts of burden but evidence that men and women were being treated worse than animals. Conrad kept a diary in which he recorded these sights and sounds: "Saw at a camp place the dead body of a Backongo. Shot? Horrid smell" [July 3]. "Saw another dead body lying by the path in an attitude of meditative repose. . . . At night when the moon rose heard shouts and drumming in distant villages. Passed a bad night" [July 4].

Agent Harou, apparently, passed a worse one: "H. lame and not in very good form," Conrad wrote in his diary on July 25. "Passed a skeleton tied up to a post," Conrad was to write some days later; "put [Harou] in hammock" (Karl 290–92).

Harou's crippling lameness made the trip more difficult for everyone, but it was far from the most disappointing development to try Conrad's spirits during the thirty-six-day trip that ended on August 2. On July 29, Conrad met a man named Louette who was transporting another sick agent back in the direction of Boma. From Louette Conrad learned that the steamer he had been hired to command now lay sunk on the bottom of the river. Having come all the way from Belgium to captain *The Florida,* Conrad suddenly learned that he would be shipping upriver not as a captain but as a sailor on the *Roi des Belges.*

Rather miraculously, Conrad had continually been writing *Almayer's Folly* while making the torturous overland trek. Although work had proceeded fitfully, something definite had been accomplished. The loss of a command was a serious blow to Conrad and may have made him prefer the slow progress of writing to the unpredictable vagaries besetting a would-be captain. Certainly, the period commencing just before Conrad's arrival at Kinshasa marked the beginning of a period of disillusionment — with Africa, with life on deck, with colonial trade, and with white European agents running trading stations throughout the Congo. Conrad seems to have particularly disliked Camille Delcommune, the manager of the station at Kinshasa, whom he later called "a common ivory dealer with base instincts" (Karl 294). To Conrad's dismay, Delcommune decided to make the trip on the *Roi des Belges* all the way to the Inner Station at Stanley Falls, where an agent named Klein lay desperately ill. That four-week trip and the return downriver to Kinshasa with the corpse of Klein seem not only to have cured Conrad's weakness for life aboard ship but also to have very nearly robbed him of all taste for life in general. "Everything here is repellent to me," he wrote to Marguerite once the round trip had been completed. "Men and things, but above all men" (Karl 294).

Conrad, who wished to leave Africa as quickly as possible, got out of his contract with the Société Anonyme Belge pour le Commerce du Haut-Congo. A terrible case of dysentery that he had picked up on his journey turned out to be an adequate excuse. Perhaps fearing that it wouldn't be adequate, Conrad had written Brussels to ask Marguerite to inform Albert Thys that the Société had failed to live up to its terms: a command had been promised, whereas in fact Conrad had served only as mate, except for a brief period during the return trip, when Captain L. R. Koch was even sicker than Conrad was.

What Conrad couldn't wriggle out of was his Congo experience; it seems to permeate *Heart of Darkness,* even though the novel wasn't begun for almost a decade following its author's departure from Africa. Some of the parallels between *Heart of Darkness* and Conrad's Congo adventure are so obvious that it may be tempting to think of the novel as thinly veiled autobiography.

It may be tempting, but it may also be treacherous, for reasons that have perhaps been best articulated by formalist critics. A work of art, formalists would argue, is not undigested experience; rather, it is characterized by *form.* That characteristic form is to be discovered by finding the patterns and relationships that exist within the work itself, not the connections that may seem to exist between the work and its author's life story.

Still, even formalists would not have us be unaware of those connections. For one thing, we have to know that connections exist before we can affirm or deny their ultimate significance. For another, knowing the biographical background of a text helps us to better appreciate the text's *difference;* that is, the shape it has been given by the artist's imagination. And there is still another reason to become aware of the parallels between Conrad's Congo experience and Marlow's. With such an awareness comes the possibility of deciding that the formalist view is too narrow, too limiting.

To summarize the parallels briefly: Marlow, the novel's protagonist and narrator, tells his listeners about his childhood passion for maps and about his declared intention to go, someday, to the blank heart of Africa. He describes how, years later, he signed up for a Congo command in the office of a "great man" — "pale plumpness in a frock-coat" — after receiving some behind-the-scenes help from "an aunt, a dear enthusiastic soul." Whereas Conrad got his command due to the death of a captain named Freiesleben, Marlow is signed on shortly after the demise of the unlucky Captain Fresleven.

Marlow's description of his sea voyage down the African coast ("Every day looked the same") reads like Conrad's diary, and his description of an overland journey from a company station not far from the African coast to the "Central Station" repeats many of Conrad's experiences in traveling from Matadi to Kinshasa, by Stanley Pool. Heat and mosquitoes and the lack of water are mentioned, as is "a white companion" who becomes so sick with fever that he has to be "carried in a hammock slung under a pole." A corpse like the one Conrad was shocked to see while on his overland trek turns up in *Heart of Darkness:* "Can't say I saw any road or any upkeep," Marlow recalls, "unless the body of a middle-aged negro, with a bullet hole in the forehead, upon which I absolutely stumbled . . . may be considered as a permanent improvement."

Marlow, like Conrad, learns that an accident has befallen the steamer that he was to have commanded; like Conrad he journeys up-river to retrieve a sick agent who dies on board shortly after being rescued. And Marlow is accompanied on his travels by a man who must have been modeled on Camille Delcommune, the station manager at Kinshasa whom Conrad referred to as "a common ivory dealer with base instincts." (Marlow calls the manager of the Central Station, who accompanies him upriver to the Inner Station, "a common trader" with "no learning and no intelligence.")

But the differences between Conrad's experiences and those of Charlie Marlow are as striking as the similarities. To begin with, there is the matter of Marlow himself, a thoroughly English Everyman — not a Polish intellectual who happens to be a sailor, too. Marlow is a recognizable kind of guy, one perfectly capable of joking that a corpse may be a road improvement, and one made more than a little uncomfortable by the efforts made in his behalf by his aunt: "Would you believe it?" he asks the other men listening to his story, "I, Charlie Marlow, set the women to work — to get a job."

Other differences abound. The "great man" who hires Marlow is not named Thys — in fact, no names are given for Marlow's aunt, the station manager modeled on Delcommune, or the "white companion" who becomes sick and has to be carried much as Prosper Harou became lame and unable to walk. The ship Marlow travels upriver on is left similarly unnamed, as is the "Company" that Conrad knew as the Société Anonyme Belge pour le Commerce du Haut-Congo. No character in the novel bears more than a passing resemblance to Roger Casement, whom Conrad stayed with in Matadi. Whereas Conrad didn't get to captain a ship, thanks to the damage done to his intended vessel, Marlow waits months for rivets and repairs that eventually allow him to command his steamboat. Marlow retrieves Kurtz only to have him die on his ship; Anton Klein was the name of the agent who died on Conrad's ship. But whereas all we know about Klein is that he had fallen ill near Stanley Falls, Kurtz is a marvelously mysterious imaginative creation, a kind of Everyman, like Marlow ("All Europe contributed to the making of Kurtz," Marlow says, when the matter of his lineage comes up), but a mythological demon figure as well. Critics have often compared him to Faust and to Satan.

Kurtz is, then, someone who exceeds the dimensions of anyone Conrad met in the Congo, just as the Africa in *Heart of Darkness* is far more than a continent — it has universal dimensions. There are minor characters, too, who testify to Conrad's ability not just to transcribe reality but to invent a world full of powerful significances. In the area that corresponds to the place where Conrad met Casement, Marlow meets a wonderfully sleazy accountant whom he describes as a "hairdresser's dummy." There is a station manager modeled after Delcommune, but his agent, characterized as a "papier-mâché Mephistopheles," seems to be pure invention. Even more fascinating is the Russian mindlessly loyal to the murderous Kurtz, a harlequin figure "covered with patches all over, with bright patches, blue, red, and yellow — patches on the back, patches on the front, patches on elbows, on knees; coloured binding around his jacket, scarlet edging at the bottom of his trousers." These characters are not part of any diary or historical record; rather, they are masterful touches in a great work of novelistic art.

Not all of the artfulness of *Heart of Darkness* is to be found in its characters. Part of the creative complexity of the work lies in the form Conrad's narrative takes; that is to say, in the way the story is told.

After all, we are not told the tale of a trip to Africa by an omniscient, authorial narrator. Instead, we find ourselves reading a story within a story. We must learn about Kurtz and the harlequin, the hairdresser's dummy and the Eldorado Explorers, from a nameless, anonymous source, a man who repeats the tale he says Charlie Marlow told him and four other men one night sitting on a cruising yawl anchored in the Thames River.

Thus, part of the meaning of the story is the way we learn about "reality" through other people's accounts of it, many of which are, themselves, twice-told tales. Part of the meaning of the novel, too, is the possibly unreliable nature of our teachers; Marlow is the source of our story, but he is also a character within the story we read, and a flawed one at that. Marlow's macho comments about women and his insensitive reaction to the "dead negro" with a "bullet hole in his forehead" cause us to refocus our critical attention, to shift it from the story being retold, to the storyteller whose supposedly autobiographical yarn is being repeated.

Because we occasionally judge Marlow negatively, we find ourselves having to take certain passages ironically, and the ironic distance that we experience between ourselves and our narrator is another important difference between a novel like *Heart of Darkness* and a diary or a history book. Irony, after all, makes possible a complex form of humor in which we find ourselves laughing at as well as with the chronicler. It is irony, too, that causes us to apprehend something profound about the human self: namely, its capacity to understand or "see through" others while remaining self-destructively ignorant about its own identity. We see what Marlow shows us, but we also see Marlow, and one of the things about him we can see is his blindness to his own nature.

Marlow interrupts the story he tells to the Lawyer, the Accountant, the Chief of Companies, and the person who retells his story to put it this way: "Of course in this you fellows see more than I could then. You see me, whom you know. . . ." What he fails to mention is that his listeners "see" different things, for the Marlow known to each of them is surely different from the one known to all the others. We, as readers, enjoy the same privilege — and suffer the same predicament — as Marlow's auditors. What we "see in" the story depends on the nature and extent of our knowledge. Knowledge of Conrad's life may lead us to "see" Marlow's story as Conrad's own. Further knowledge — of formalist theory, for instance — may cause us to decide that Marlow is, after all, an artificial construct: a narrator, and an unreliable one at that. But there is still more to know about Conrad and his times — for example, the kind of knowledge that psychoanalytic, feminist, and new-historicist critics would bring to bear. And there is more, too, to see in literary art than formalist theorists have seen in it. Deconstructors, for instance, would make us aware not of the definite form of a text but, rather, of its surprisingly contradictory elements. Reader-response critics might argue that a work of art is what we make of it. Each of these ways of knowing (which are explored in Part Two of this edition) causes us to see more in Marlow's story than the Lawyer, the Accountant, or the Chief of Companies did — perhaps even more than Conrad did. But one thing is sure: each of these ways of knowing brings a different kind of light and color to *Heart of Darkness*.

WORKS CITED

Burrows, Guy. *The Land of the Pigmies*. London: Pearson, 1898.

Conrad, Joseph. "Geography and Some Explorers." *Last Essays*. Ed. Richard Curle. London: Dent, 1926.

———. *Some Reminiscences*. London: Eveleigh Nash, 1912.

Hennessy, Maurice. *Congo: A Brief History and Appraisal*. New York: Praeger, 1961.

Karl, Frederick. *Joseph Conrad: The Three Lives*. New York: Farrar, 1979.

Heart of Darkness

I

The _Nellie_, a cruising yawl, swung to her anchor without a flutter of the sails, and was at rest. The flood had made, the wind was nearly calm, and being bound down the river, the only thing for it was to come to and wait for the turn of the tide.

The sea-reach of the Thames stretched before us like the beginning of an interminable waterway. In the offing the sea and the sky were welded together without a joint, and in the luminous space the tanned sails of the barges drifting up with the tide seemed to stand still in red clusters of canvas sharply peaked, with gleams of varnished sprits. A haze rested on the low shores that ran out to sea in vanishing flatness. The air was dark above Gravesend,° and farther back still seemed condensed into a mournful gloom, brooding motionless over the biggest, and the greatest, town on earth.

The Director of Companies was our captain and our host. We four affectionately watched his back as he stood in the bows looking to seaward. On the whole river there was nothing that looked half so nautical. He resembled a pilot, which to a seaman is trustworthiness personified. It was difficult to realise his work was not out there in the luminous estuary, but behind him, within the brooding gloom.

Gravesend: A town on the Thames estuary.

Between us there was, as I have already said somewhere, the bond of the sea. Besides holding our hearts together through long periods of separation, it had the effect of making us tolerant of each other's yarns — and even convictions. The Lawyer — the best of old fellows — had, because of his many years and many virtues, the only cushion on deck, and was lying on the only rug. The Accountant had brought out already a box of dominoes, and was toying architecturally with the bones. Marlow sat cross-legged right aft, leaning against the mizzenmast. He had sunken cheeks, a yellow complexion, a straight back, an ascetic aspect, and, with his arms dropped, the palms of hands outwards, resembled an idol. The Director, satisfied the anchor had good hold, made his way aft and sat down amongst us. We exchanged a few words lazily. Afterwards there was silence on board the yacht. For some reason or other we did not begin that game of dominoes. We felt meditative, and fit for nothing but placid staring. The day was ending in a serenity of still and exquisite brilliance. The water shone pacifically; the sky, without a speck, was a benign immensity of unstained light; the very mist on the Essex marshes was like a gauzy and radiant fabric, hung from the wooded rises inland, and draping the low shores in diaphanous folds. Only the gloom to the west, brooding over the upper reaches, became more sombre every minute, as if angered by the approach of the sun.

And at last, in its curved and imperceptible fall, the sun sank low, and from glowing white changed to a dull red without rays and without heat, as if about to go out suddenly, stricken to death by the touch of that gloom brooding over a crowd of men.

Forthwith a change came over the waters, and the serenity became less brilliant but more profound. The old river in its broad reach rested unruffled at the decline of day, after ages of good service done to the race that peopled its banks, spread out in the tranquil dignity of a waterway leading to the uttermost ends of the earth. We looked at the venerable stream not in the vivid flush of a short day that comes and departs for ever, but in the august light of abiding memories. And indeed nothing is easier for a man who has, as the phrase goes, "followed the sea" with reverence and affection, than to evoke the great spirit of the past upon the lower reaches of the Thames. The tidal current runs to and fro in its unceasing service, crowded with memories of men and ships it has borne to the rest of home or to the battles of the sea. It had known and served all the men of whom the nation is proud, from Sir Francis Drake to Sir John Franklin, knights all, titled and untitled — the great knights-errant of the sea. It had borne all the ships whose names are like jewels flashing in the night of time, from the *Golden Hind* returning with her round flanks full of treasure, to be visited by the Queen's Highness and thus pass out of the gigantic tale, to the *Erebus* and *Terror,* bound on other conquests — and that never returned. It had known the ships and the men. They had sailed from Deptford, from Greenwich, from Erith — the adventurers and the settlers; kings' ships and the ships of men on 'Change; captains, admirals, the dark "interlopers" of the Eastern trade, and the commissioned "generals" of East India fleets.° Hunters for gold or pursuers of fame, they all had gone out on that stream, bearing the sword, and often the torch, messengers of the might within the land, bearers of spark from the sacred fire. What greatness had not floated on the ebb of that river into the mystery of an unknown earth! . . . The dreams of men, the seed of commonwealths, the germs of empires.

The sun set; the dusk fell on the stream, and lights began to appear along the shore. The Chapman lighthouse, a three-legged thing erect on a mud-flat, shone strongly. Lights of ships moved in the fairway — a great stir of lights going up and going down. And farther west on the upper reaches the place of the monstrous town was still marked ominously on the sky, a brooding gloom in sunshine, a lurid glare under the stars.

"And this also," said Marlow suddenly, "has been one of the dark places of the earth."

He was the only man of us who still "followed the sea." The worst that could be said of him was that he did not represent his class. He was a seaman, but he was a wanderer too, while most seamen lead, if one may so express it, a sedentary life. Their minds are of the stay-at-home order, and their home is always with them — the ship; and so is their country — the sea. One ship is very much like another, and the sea is always the same. In the immutability of their surroundings the foreign shores, the foreign faces, the changing immensity of life, glide past, veiled not by a sense of mystery but by a slightly disdainful ignorance; for there is nothing mysterious to a seaman unless it be the sea itself, which is the mistress of his existence and as inscrutable as Destiny. For the rest, after his hours of work, a casual stroll or a casual spree on shore suffices to unfold for him the secret of a whole continent, and generally he finds the secret not worth knowing. The yarns

Sir Francis Drake . . . fleets: Drake (c. 1540–1596) commanded the *Golden Hind,* and Sir John Franklin (1786–1847) led the ships *Erebus* and *Terror* on an ill-fated expedition to find the Northwest Passage. Deptford, Greenwich, and Erith are ports between London and Gravesend.

of seamen have a direct simplicity, the whole meaning of which lies within the shell of a cracked nut. But Marlow was not typical (if his propensity to spin yarns be excepted), and to him the meaning of an episode was not inside like a kernel but outside, enveloping the tale which brought it out only as a glow brings out a haze, in the likeness of one of these misty halos that sometimes are made visible by the spectral illumination of moonshine.

His remark did not seem at all surprising. It was just like Marlow. It was accepted in silence. No one took the trouble to grunt even; and presently he said, very slow:

"I was thinking of very old times, when the Romans first came here, nineteen hundred years ago — the other day. . . . Light came out of this river since — you say Knights? Yes; but it is like a running blaze on a plain, like a flash of lightning in the clouds. We live in the flicker — may it last as long as the old earth keeps rolling! But darkness was here yesterday. Imagine the feelings of a commander of fine — what d'ye call 'em? — trireme in the Mediterranean, ordered suddenly to the north; run overland across the Gauls in a hurry; put in charge of one of these craft the legionaries — a wonderful lot of handy men they must have been too — used to build, apparently by the hundred, in a month or two, if we may believe what we read. Imagine him here — the very end of the world, a sea the colour of lead, a sky the colour of smoke, a kind of ship about as rigid as a concertina — and going up this river with stores, or orders, or what you like. Sandbanks, marshes, forests, savages — precious little to eat fit for a civilised man, nothing but Thames water to drink. No Falernian wine° here, no going ashore. Here and there a military camp lost in a wilderness, like a needle in a bundle of hay — cold, fog, tempests, disease, exile, and death — death skulking in the air, in the water, in the bush. They must have been dying like flies here. Oh yes — he did it. Did it very well, too, no doubt, and without thinking much about it either, except afterwards to brag of what he had gone through in his time, perhaps. They were men enough to face the darkness. And perhaps he was cheered by keeping his eye on a chance of promotion to the fleet at Ravenna by and by, if he had good friends in Rome and survived the awful climate. Or think of a decent young citizen in a toga — perhaps too much dice, you know — coming out here in the train of some prefect, or tax-gatherer, or trader, even, to mend his fortunes. Land in a

---

Falernian wine: Wine celebrated by the Latin poet Horace (65 B.C.–8 B.C.).

swamp, march through the woods, and in some inland post feel the savagery, the utter savagery, had closed round him — all that mysterious life of the wilderness that stirs in the forest, in the jungles, in the hearts of wild men. There's no initiation either into such mysteries. He has to live in the midst of the incomprehensible, which is also detestable. And it has a fascination, too, that goes to work upon him. The fascination of the abomination — you know. Imagine the growing regrets, the longing to escape, the powerless disgust, the surrender, the hate."

He paused.

"Mind," he began again, lifting one arm from the elbow, the palm of the hand outwards, so that, with his legs folded before him, he had the pose of a Buddha preaching in European clothes and without a lotus-flower — "Mind, none of us would feel exactly like this. What saves us is efficiency — the devotion to efficiency. But these chaps were not much account, really. They were no colonists; their administration was merely a squeeze, and nothing more, I suspect. They were conquerors, and for that you want only brute force — nothing to boast of, when you have it, since your strength is just an accident arising from the weakness of others. They grabbed what they could get for the sake of what was to be got. It was just robbery with violence, aggravated murder on a great scale, and men going at it blind — as is very proper for those who tackle a darkness. The conquest of the earth, which mostly means the taking it away from those who have a different complexion or slightly flatter noses than ourselves, is not a pretty thing when you look into it too much. What redeems it is the idea only. An idea at the back of it; not a sentimental pretence but an idea; and an unselfish belief in the idea — something you can set up, and bow down before, and offer a sacrifice to. . . ."

He broke off. Flames glided in the river, small green flames, red flames, white flames, pursuing, overtaking, joining, crossing each other — then separating slowly or hastily. The traffic of the great city went on in the deepening night upon the sleepless river. We looked on, waiting patiently — there was nothing else to do till the end of the flood; but it was only after a long silence, when he said, in a hesitating voice, "I suppose you fellows remember I did once turn fresh-water sailor for a bit," that we knew we were fated, before the ebb began to run, to hear about one of Marlow's inconclusive experiences.

"I don't want to bother you much with what happened to me personally," he began, showing in this remark the weakness of many tellers of tales who seem so often unaware of what their audience would best like to hear; "yet to understand the effect of it on me you ought to know how I got out there, what I saw, how I went up that river to the place where I first met the poor chap. It was the farthest point of navigation and the culminating point of my experience. It seemed somehow to throw a kind of light on everything about me — and into my thoughts. It was sombre enough too — and pitiful — not extraordinary in any way — not very clear either. No, not very clear. And yet it seemed to throw a kind of light.

"I had then, as you remember, just returned to London after a lot of Indian Ocean, Pacific, China Seas — a regular dose of the East — six years or so, and I was loafing about, hindering you fellows in your work and invading your homes, just as though I had got a heavenly mission to civilise you. It was very fine for a time, but after a bit I did get tired of resting. Then I began to look for a ship — I should think the hardest work on earth. But the ships wouldn't even look at me. And I got tired of that game too.

"Now when I was a little chap I had a passion for maps. I would look for hours at South America, or Africa, or Australia, and lose my-self in all the glories of exploration. At that time there were many blank spaces on the earth, and when I saw one that looked particularly inviting on a map (but they all look that) I would put my finger on it and say, When I grow up I will go there. The North Pole was one of these places, I remember. Well, I haven't been there yet, and shall not try now. The glamour's off. Other places were scattered about the Equator, and in every sort of latitude all over the two hemispheres. I have been in some of them, and . . . well, we won't talk about that. But there was one yet — the biggest, the most blank, so to speak — that I had a hankering after.

"True, by this time it was not a blank space any more. It had got filled since my boyhood with rivers and lakes and names. It had ceased to be a blank space of delightful mystery — a white patch for a boy to dream gloriously over. It had become a place of darkness. But there was in it one river especially, a mighty big river, that you could see on the map, resembling an immense snake uncoiled, with its head in the sea, its body at rest curving afar over a vast country, and its tail lost in the depths of the land. And as I looked at the map of it in a shop-window it fascinated me as a snake would a bird — a silly little bird. Then I remembered there was a big concern, a Company for trade on that river. Dash it all! I thought to myself, they can't trade without using some kind of craft on that lot of fresh water — steamboats! Why shouldn't I try to get charge of one? I went on along Fleet Street,° but could not shake off the idea. The snake had charmed me.

"You understand it was a Continental concern, that Trading Society; but I have a lot of relations living on the Continent, because it's cheap and not so nasty as it looks, they say.

"I am sorry to own I began to worry them. This was already a fresh departure for me. I was not used to get things that way, you know. I always went my own road and on my own legs where I had a mind to go. I wouldn't have believed it of myself; but, then — you see — I felt somehow I must get there by hook or by crook. So I worried them. The men said, 'My dear fellow,' and did nothing. Then — would you believe it? — I tried the women. I, Charlie Marlow, set the women to work — to get a job. Heavens! Well, you see, the notion drove me. I had an aunt, a dear enthusiastic soul. She wrote: 'It will be delightful. I am ready to do anything, anything for you. It is a glorious idea. I know the wife of a very high personage in the Administration, and also a man who has lots of influence with,' etc. etc. She was determined to make no end of fuss to get me appointed skipper of a river steamboat, if such was my fancy.

"I got my appointment — of course; and I got it very quick. It appears the Company had received news that one of their captains had been killed in a scuffle with the natives. This was my chance, and it made me the more anxious to go. It was only months and months afterwards, when I made the attempt to recover what was left of the body, that I heard the original quarrel arose from a misunderstanding about some hens. Yes, two black hens. Fresleven — that was the fellow's name, a Dane — thought himself wronged somehow in the bargain, so he went ashore and started to hammer the chief of the village with a stick. Oh, it didn't surprise me in the least to hear this, and at the same time to be told that Fresleven was the gentlest, quietest creature that ever walked on two legs. No doubt he was; but he had been a couple of years already out there engaged in the noble cause, you know, and he probably felt the need at last of asserting his self-respect in some way. Therefore he whacked the old nigger mercilessly, while a big crowd of his people watched him, thunderstruck, till some man — I was told the chief's son — in desperation at hearing the old chap yell, made a tentative jab with a spear at the white man — and of course it went quite easy between the shoulder-blades. Then the whole population cleared into the forest, expecting all kinds of

Fleet Street: A major street in London known for business and journalism.

calamities to happen, while, on the other hand, the steamer Fresleven commanded left also in a bad panic, in charge of the engineer, I believe. Afterwards nobody seemed to trouble much about Fresleven's remains, till I got out and stepped into his shoes. I couldn't let it rest, though; but when an opportunity offered at last to meet my predecessor, the grass growing through his ribs was tall enough to hide his bones. They were all there. The supernatural being had not been touched after he fell. And the village was deserted, the huts gaped black, rotting, all askew within the fallen enclosures. A calamity had come to it, sure enough. The people had vanished. Mad terror had scattered them, men, women, and children, through the bush, and they had never returned. What became of the hens I don't know either. I should think the cause of progress got them, anyhow. However, through this glorious affair I got my appointment, before I had fairly begun to hope for it.

"I flew around like mad to get ready, and before forty-eight hours I was crossing the Channel to show myself to my employers, and sign the contract. In a very few hours I arrived in a city that always makes me think of a whited sepulchre. Prejudice no doubt. I had no difficulty in finding the Company's offices. It was the biggest thing in the town, and everybody I met was full of it. They were going to run an oversea empire, and make no end of coin by trade.

"A narrow and deserted street in deep shadow, high houses, innumerable windows with venetian blinds, a dead silence, grass sprouting between the stones, imposing carriage archways right and left, immense double doors standing ponderously ajar. I slipped through one of these cracks, went up a swept and ungarnished staircase, as arid as a desert, and opened the first door I came to. Two women, one fat and the other slim, sat on straw-bottomed chairs, knitting black wool. The slim one got up and walked straight at me — still knitting with downcast eyes — and only just as I began to think of getting out of her way, as you would for a somnambulist, stood still, and looked up. Her dress was as plain as an umbrella-cover, and she turned round without a word and preceded me into a waiting-room. I gave my name, and looked about. Deal table in the middle, plain chairs all round the walls, on one end a large shining map, marked with all the colours of a rainbow. There was a vast amount of red — good to see at any time, because one knows that some real work is done in there, a deuce of a lot of blue, a little green, smears of orange, and, on the East Coast, a purple patch, to show where the jolly pioneers of progress drink the jolly lager-beer. However, I wasn't going into any of these. I was going into the yellow. Dead in the centre. And the river was there — fascinating — deadly — like a snake. Ough! A door opened, a white-haired secretarial head, but wearing a compassionate expression, appeared, and a skinny forefinger beckoned me into the sanctuary. Its light was dim, and a heavy writing-desk squatted in the middle. From behind that structure came out an impression of pale plumpness in a frockcoat. The great man himself. He was five feet six, I should judge, and had his grip on the handle-end of ever so many millions. He shook hands, I fancy, murmured vaguely, was satisfied with my French. *Bon voyage.*

"In about forty-five seconds I found myself again in the waiting-room with the compassionate secretary, who, full of desolation and sympathy, made me sign some document. I believe I undertook amongst other things not to disclose any trade secrets. Well, I am not going to.

"I began to feel slightly uneasy. You know I am not used to such ceremonies, and there was something ominous in the atmosphere. It was just as though I had been let into some conspiracy — I don't know — something not quite right; and I was glad to get out. In the outer room the two women knitted black wool feverishly. People were arriving, and the younger one was walking back and forth introducing them. The old one sat on her chair. Her flat cloth slippers were propped up on a foot-warmer, and a cat reposed on her lap. She wore a starched white affair on her head, had a wart on one cheek, and silver-rimmed spectacles hung on the tip of her nose. She glanced at me above the glasses. The swift and indifferent placidity of that look troubled me. Two youths with foolish and cheery countenances were being piloted over, and she threw at them the same quick glance of unconcerned wisdom. She seemed to know all about them and about me too. An eerie feeling came over me. She seemed uncanny and fateful. Often far away there I thought of these two, guarding the door of Darkness, knitting black wool as for a warm pall, one introducing, introducing continuously to the unknown, the other scrutinising the cheery and foolish faces with unconcerned old eyes. *Ave!* Old knitter of black wool. *Morituri te salutant.*° Not many of those she looked at ever saw her again — not half, by a long way.

"There was yet a visit to the doctor. 'A simple formality,' assured me the secretary, with an air of taking an immense part in all my sorrows. Accordingly a young chap wearing his hat over the left eyebrow,

---

Ave! . . . *Morituri te salutant:* "Greetings! . . . We who are about to die salute you."

some clerk I suppose — there must have been clerks in the business, though the house was as still as a house in a city of the dead — came from somewhere upstairs, and led me forth. He was shabby and care-less, with ink-stains on the sleeves of his jacket, and his cravat was large and billowy, under a chin shaped like the toe of an old boot. It was a little too early for the doctor, so I proposed a drink, and thereupon he developed a vein of joviality. As we sat over our vermuths he glorified the Company's business, and by and by I expressed casually my sur-prise at him not going out there. He became very cool and collected all at once. 'I am not such a fool as I look, quoth Plato to his dis-ciples,' he said sententiously, emptied his glass with great resolution, and we rose.

"The old doctor felt my pulse, evidently thinking of something else the while. 'Good, good for there,' he mumbled, and then with a certain eagerness asked me whether I would let him measure my head. Rather surprised, I said Yes, when he produced a thing like callipers and got the dimensions back and front and every way, taking notes carefully. He was an unshaven little man in a threadbare coat like a gaberdine, with his feet in slippers, and I thought him a harmless fool. 'I always ask leave, in the interests of science, to measure the crania of those going out there,' he said. 'And when they come back too?' I asked. 'Oh, I never see them,' he remarked; 'and, moreover, the changes take place inside, you know.' He smiled, as if at some quiet joke. 'So you are going out there. Famous. Interesting too.' He gave me a searching glance, and made another note. 'Ever any madness in your family?' he asked, in matter-of-fact tone. I felt very annoyed. 'Is that question in the interests of science too?' 'It would be,' he said, without taking notice of my irritation, 'interesting for science to watch the mental changes of individuals, on the spot, but . . .' 'Are you an alienist?'° I interrupted. 'Every doctor should be — a little,' answered that original imperturbably. 'I have a little theory which you Messieurs who go out there must help me to prove. This is my share in the advantages my country shall reap from the possession of such a mag-nificent dependency. The mere wealth I leave to others. Pardon my questions, but you are the first Englishman coming under my observa-tion . . .' I hastened to assure him I was not in the least typical. 'If I were,' said I, 'I wouldn't be talking like this with you.' 'What you say is rather profound, and probably erroneous,' he said, with a laugh. 'Avoid irritation more than exposure to the sun. Adieu. How do you

alienist: A doctor concerned with psychological disturbances.

English say, eh? Good-bye. Ah! Good-bye. Adieu. In the tropics one must before everything keep calm.' . . . He lifted a warning fore-finger. . . . *Du calme, du calme. Adieu.'*

"One thing more remained to do — say goodbye to my excellent aunt. I found her triumphant. I had a cup of tea — the last decent cup of tea for many days — and in a room that most soothingly looked just as you would expect a lady's drawing-room to look, we had a long quiet chat by the fireside. In the course of these confidences it became quite plain to me I had been represented to the wife of the high digni-tary, and goodness knows to how many more people besides, as an ex-ceptional and gifted creature — a piece of good fortune for the Com-pany — a man you don't get hold of every day. Good Heavens! and I was going to take charge of a two-penny-halfpenny river-steamboat with a penny whistle attached! It appeared, however, I was also one of the Workers, with a capital — you know. Something like an emissary of light, something like a lower sort of apostle. There had been a lot of such rot let loose in print and talk just about that time, and the excel-lent woman, living right in the rush of all that humbug, got carried off her feet. She talked about 'weaning those ignorant millions from their horrid ways,' till, upon my word, she made me quite uncomfortable. I ventured to hint that the Company was run for profit.

"'You forget, dear Charlie, that the labourer is worthy of his hire,' she said brightly. It's queer how out of touch with truth women are. They live in a world of their own, and there had never been anything like it, and never can be. It is too beautiful altogether, and if they were to set it up it would go to pieces before the first sunset. Some con-founded fact we men have been living contentedly with ever since the day of creation would start up and knock the whole thing over.

"After this I got embraced, told to wear flannel, be sure to write often, and so on — and I left. In the street — I don't know why — a queer feeling came to me that I was an impostor. Odd thing that I, who used to clear out for any part of the world at twenty-four hours' notice, with less thought than most men give to the crossing of a street, had a moment — I won't say of hesitation, but of startled pause, before this commonplace affair. The best way I can explain it to you is by saying that, for a second or two, I felt as though, instead of going to the centre of a continent, I were about to set off for the cen-tre of the earth.

"I left in a French steamer, and she called in every blamed port they have out there, for, as far as I could see, the sole purpose of land-ing soldiers and custom-house officers. I watched the coast. Watching a coast as it slips by the ship is like thinking about an enigma. There it is before you — smiling, frowning, inviting, grand, mean, insipid, or savage, and always mute with an air of whispering, Come and find out. This one was almost featureless, as if still in the making, with an aspect of monotonous grimness. The edge of a colossal jungle, so dark green as to be almost black, fringed with white surf, ran straight, like a ruled line, far, far away along a blue sea whose glitter was blurred by a creeping mist. The sun was fierce, the land seemed to glisten and drip with steam. Here and there greyish-whitish specks showed up clustered inside the white surf, with a flag flying above them perhaps — settlements some centuries old, and still no bigger than pin-heads on the untouched expanse of their background. We pounded along, stopped, landed soldiers; went on, landed custom-house clerks to levy toll in what looked like a God-forsaken wilderness, with a tin shed and a flag-pole lost in it; landed more soldiers — to take care of the custom-house clerks presumably. Some, I heard, got drowned in the surf; but whether they did or not, nobody seemed particularly to care. They were just flung out there, and on we went. Every day the coast looked the same, as though we had not moved; but we passed various places — trading places — with names like Gran' Bassam, Little Popo; names that seemed to belong to some sordid farce acted in front of a sinister back-cloth. The idleness of a passenger, my isolation amongst all these men with whom I had no point of contact, the oily and languid sea, the uniform sombreness of the coast, seemed to keep me away from the truth of things, within the toil of a mournful and senseless delusion. The voice of the surf heard now and then was a positive pleasure, like the speech of a brother. It was something natural, that had its reason, that had a meaning. Now and then a boat from the shore gave one a momentary contact with reality. It was paddled by black fellows. You could see from afar the white of their eyeballs glistening. They shouted, sang; their bodies streamed with perspiration; they had faces like grotesque masks — these chaps; but they had bone, muscle, a wild vitality, an intense energy of movement, that was as natural and true as the surf along their coast. They wanted no excuse for being there. They were a great comfort to look at. For a time I would feel I belonged still to a world of straightforward facts; but the feeling would not last long. Something would turn up to scare it away. Once, I remember, we came upon a man-of-war anchored off the coast. There wasn't even a shed there, and she was shelling the bush. It appears the French had one of their wars going on thereabouts. Her ensign dropped limp like a rag; the muzzles of the long six-inch guns stuck out all over the low hull; the greasy, slimy swell swung her up lazily and let her down, swaying her thin masts. In the empty immensity of earth, sky, and water, there she was, incomprehensible, firing into a continent. Pop, would go one of the six-inch guns; a small flame would dart and vanish, a little white smoke would disappear, a tiny projectile would give a feeble screech — and nothing happened. Nothing could happen. There was a touch of insanity in the proceeding, a sense of lugubrious drollery in the sight; and it was not dissipated by somebody on board assuring me earnestly there was a camp of natives — he called them enemies! — hidden out of sight somewhere.

"We gave her her letters (I heard the men in that lonely ship were dying of fever at the rate of three a day) and went on. We called at some more places with farcical names, where the merry dance of death and trade goes on in a still and earthy atmosphere as of an overheated catacomb; all along the formless coast bordered by dangerous surf, as if Nature herself had tried to ward off intruders; in and out of rivers, streams of death in life, whose banks were rotting into mud, whose waters, thickened into slime, invaded the contorted mangroves, that seemed to writhe at us in the extremity of an impotent despair. Nowhere did we stop long enough to get a particularised impression, but the general sense of vague and oppressive wonder grew upon me. It was like a weary pilgrimage amongst hints for nightmares.

"It was upward of thirty days before I saw the mouth of the big river. We anchored off the seat of the government. But my work would not begin till some two hundred miles farther on. So as soon as I could I made a start for a place thirty miles higher up.

"I had my passage on a little sea-going steamer. Her captain was a Swede, and knowing me for a seaman, invited me on the bridge. He was a young man, lean, fair, and morose, with lanky hair and a shuffling gait. As we left the miserable little wharf, he tossed his head contemptuously at the shore. 'Been living there?' he asked. I said, 'Yes.' 'Fine lot these government chaps — are they not?' he went on, speaking English with great precision and considerable bitterness. 'It is funny what some people will do for a few francs a month. I wonder what becomes of that kind when it goes up country?' I said to him I expected to see that soon. 'So-o-o!' he exclaimed. He shuffled athwart, keeping one eye ahead vigilantly. 'Don't be too sure,' he continued. 'The other day I took up a man who hanged himself on the road. He was a Swede, too.' 'Hanged himself! Why, in God's name?' I cried. He kept on looking out watchfully. 'Who knows? The sun too much for him, or the country perhaps.'

"At last we opened a reach. A rocky cliff appeared, mounds of turned-up earth by the shore, houses on a hill, others with iron roofs, amongst a waste of excavations, or hanging to the declivity. A continuous noise of the rapids above hovered over this scene of inhabited devastation. A lot of people, mostly black and naked, moved about like ants. A jetty projected into the river. A blinding sunlight drowned all this at times in a sudden recrudescence of glare. 'There's your Company's station,' said the Swede, pointing to three wooden barrack-like structures on the rocky slope. 'I will send your things up. Four boxes did you say? So. Farewell.'

"I came upon a boiler wallowing in the grass, then found a path leading up the hill. It turned aside for the boulders, and also for an undersized railway truck lying there on its back with its wheels in the air. One was off. The thing looked as dead as the carcass of some animal. I came upon more pieces of decaying machinery, a stack of rusty rails. To the left a clump of trees made a shady spot, where dark things seemed to stir feebly. I blinked, the path was steep. A horn tooted to the right and I saw the black people run. A heavy and dull detonation shook the ground, a puff of smoke came out of the cliff, and that was all. No change appeared on the face of the rock. They were building a railway. The cliff was not in the way or anything; but this objectless blasting was all the work going on.

"A slight clinking behind me made me turn my head. Six black men advanced in a file, toiling up the path. They walked erect and slow, balancing small baskets full of earth on their heads, and the clink kept time with their footsteps. Black rags were wound round their loins, and the short ends behind waggled to and fro like tails. I could see every rib, the joints of their limbs were like knots in a rope; each had an iron collar on his neck, and all were connected together with a chain whose bights swung between them, rhythmically clinking. Another report from the cliff made me think suddenly of that ship of war I had seen firing into a continent. It was the same kind of ominous voice; but these men could by no stretch of imagination be called enemies. They were called criminals, and the outraged law, like the bursting shells, had come to them, an insoluble mystery from the sea. All their meagre breasts panted together, the violently dilated nostrils quivered, the eyes stared stonily uphill. They passed me within six inches, without a glance, with that complete, deathlike indifference of unhappy savages. Behind this raw matter one of the reclaimed, the product of the new forces at work, strolled despondently, carrying a rifle by its middle. He had a uniform jacket with one button off, and seeing a white man on the path, hoisted his weapon to his shoulder with alacrity. This was simple prudence, white men being so much alike at a distance that he could not tell who I might be. He was speedily reassured, and with a large, white, rascally grin, and a glance at his charge, seemed to take me into partnership in his exalted trust. After all, I also was a part of the great cause of these high and just proceedings.

"Instead of going up, I turned and descended to the left. My idea was to let that chain-gang get out of sight before I climbed the hill. You know I am not particularly tender; I've had to strike and to fend off. I've had to resist and to attack sometimes — that's only one way of resisting — without counting the exact cost, according to the demands of such sort of life as I had blundered into. I've seen the devil of violence, and the devil of greed, and the devil of hot desire; but, by all the stars! these were strong, lusty, red-eyed devils, that swayed and drove men — men, I tell you. But as I stood on this hillside, I foresaw that in the blinding sunshine of that land I would become acquainted with a flabby, pretending, weak-eyed devil of a rapacious and pitiless folly. How insidious he could be, too, I was only to find out several months later and a thousand miles farther. For a moment I stood appalled, as though by a warning. Finally I descended the hill, obliquely, towards the trees I had seen.

"I avoided a vast artificial hole somebody had been digging on the slope, the purpose of which I found it impossible to divine. It wasn't a quarry or a sandpit, anyhow. It was just a hole. It might have been connected with the philanthropic desire of giving the criminals something to do. I don't know. Then I nearly fell into a very narrow ravine almost no more than a scar in the hillside. I discovered that a lot of imported drainage-pipes for the settlement had been tumbled in there. There wasn't one that was not broken. It was a wanton smashup. At last I got under the trees. My purpose was to stroll into the shade for a moment; but no sooner within than it seemed to me I had stepped into the gloomy circle of some Inferno. The rapids were near, and an uninterrupted, uniform, headlong, rushing noise filled the mournful stillness of the grove, where not a breath stirred, not a leaf moved, with a mysterious sound — as though the tearing pace of the launched earth had suddenly become audible.

"Black shapes crouched, lay, sat between the trees, leaning against the trunks, clinging to the earth, half coming out, half effaced within the dim light, in all the attitudes of pain, abandonment, and despair. Another mine on the cliff went off, followed by a slight shudder of the soil under my feet. The work was going on. The work! And this was the place where some of the helpers had withdrawn to die.

"They were dying slowly — it was very clear. They were not enemies, they were not criminals, they were nothing earthly now — nothing but black shadows of disease and starvation, lying confusedly in the greenish gloom. Brought from all the recesses of the coast in all the legality of time contracts, lost in uncongenial surroundings, fed on unfamiliar food, they sickened, became inefficient, and were then allowed to crawl away and rest. These moribund shapes were free as air — and nearly as thin. I began to distinguish the gleam of the eyes under the trees. Then, glancing down, I saw a face near my hand. The black bones reclined at full length with one shoulder against the tree, and slowly the eyelids rose and the sunken eyes looked up at me, enormous and vacant, a kind of blind, white flicker in the depths of the orbs, which died out slowly. The man seemed young — almost a boy — but you know with them it's hard to tell. I found nothing else to do but to offer him one of my good Swede's ship's biscuits I had in my pocket. The fingers closed slowly on it and held — there was no other movement and no other glance. He had tied a bit of white worsted round his neck — Why? Where did he get it? Was it a badge — an ornament — a charm — a propitiatory act? Was there any idea at all connected with it? It looked startling round his black neck, this bit of white thread from beyond the seas.

"Near the same tree two more bundles of acute angles sat with their legs drawn up. One, with his chin propped on his knees, stared at nothing, in an intolerable and appalling manner: his brother phantom rested its forehead, as if overcome with a great weariness; and all about others were scattered in every pose of contorted collapse, as in some picture of a massacre or a pestilence. While I stood horror-struck, one of these creatures rose to his hands and knees, and went off on all-fours towards the river to drink. He lapped out of his hand, then sat up in the sunlight, crossing his shins in front of him, and after a time let his woolly head fall on his breastbone.

"I didn't want any more loitering in the shade, and I made haste towards the station. When near the buildings I met a white man, in such an unexpected elegance of get-up that in the first moment I took him for a sort of vision. I saw a high starched collar, white cuffs, a light alpaca jacket, snowy trousers, a clean necktie, and varnished boots. No hat. Hair parted, brushed, oiled, under a green-lined parasol held in a big white hand. He was amazing, and had a pen-holder behind his ear.

"I shook hands with this miracle, and I learned he was the Company's chief accountant, and that all the book-keeping was done at this station. He had come out for a moment, he said, 'to get a breath of fresh air.' The expression sounded wonderfully odd, with its suggestion of sedentary desk-life. I wouldn't have mentioned the fellow to you at all, only it was from his lips that I first heard the name of the man who is so indissolubly connected with the memories of that time. Moreover, I respected the fellow. Yes; I respected his collars, his vast cuffs, his brushed hair. His appearance was certainly that of a hairdresser's dummy; but in the great demoralisation of the land he kept up his appearance. That's backbone. His starched collars and got-up shirt-fronts were achievements of character. He had been out nearly three years; and, later, I could not help asking him how he managed to sport such linen. He had just the faintest blush, and said modestly, 'I've been teaching one of the native women about the station. It was difficult. She had a distaste for the work.' Thus this man had verily accomplished something. And he was devoted to his books, which were in apple-pie order.

"Everything else in the station was in a muddle, — heads, things, buildings. Strings of dusty niggers with splay feet arrived and departed; a stream of manufactured goods, rubbishy cottons, beads, and brass-wire set into the depths of darkness, and in return came a precious trickle of ivory.

"I had to wait in the station for ten days — an eternity. I lived in a hut in the yard, but to be out of the chaos I would sometimes get into the accountant's office. It was built of horizontal planks, and so badly put together that, as he bent over his high desk, he was barred from neck to heels with narrow strips of sunlight. There was no need to open the big shutter to see. It was hot there too; big flies buzzed fiendishly and did not sting, but stabbed. I sat generally on the floor, while, of faultless appearance (and even slightly scented), perching on a high stool, he wrote, he wrote. Sometimes he stood up for exercise. When a truckle-bed with a sick man (some invalided agent from up-country) was put in there, he exhibited a gentle annoyance. 'The groans of this sick person,' he said, 'distract my attention. And without that it is extremely difficult to guard against clerical errors in this climate.'

"One day he remarked, without lifting his head, 'In the interior you will no doubt meet Mr. Kurtz.' On my asking who Mr. Kurtz was, he said he was a first-class agent; and seeing my disappointment at this information, he added slowly, laying down his pen, 'He is a very remarkable person.' Further questions elicited from him that Mr. Kurtz was at present in charge of a trading-post, a very important one, in the true ivory-country, at 'the very bottom of there. Sends in as much ivory as all the others put together . . .' He began to write again. The sick man was too ill to groan. The flies buzzed in a great peace.

"Suddenly there was a growing murmur of voices and a great tramping of feet. A caravan had come in. A violent babble of uncouth sounds burst out on the other side of the planks. All the carriers were speaking together, and in the midst of the uproar the lamentable voice of the chief agent was heard 'giving it up' tearfully for the twentieth time that day. . . . He rose slowly. 'What a frightful row,' he said. He crossed the room gently to look at the sick man, and returning, said to me, 'He does not hear.' 'What! Dead?' I asked, startled. 'No, not yet,' he answered, with great composure. Then, alluding with a toss of the head to the tumult in the station-yard, 'When one has got to make correct entries, one comes to hate those savages — hate them to death.' He remained thoughtful for a moment. 'When you see Mr. Kurtz,' he went on, 'tell him for me that everything here' — he glanced at the desk — 'is very satisfactory. I don't like to write to him — with those messengers of ours you never know who may get hold of your letter — at that Central Station.' He stared at me for a moment with his mild, bulging eyes. 'Oh, he will go far, very far,' he began again. 'He will be a somebody in the Administration before long. They, above — the Council in Europe, you know — mean him to be.'

"He turned to his work. The noise outside had ceased, and presently in going out I stopped at the door. In the steady buzz of flies the homeward-bound agent was lying flushed and insensible; the other, bent over his books, was making correct entries of perfectly correct transactions; and fifty feet below the doorstep I could see the still tree-tops of the grove of death.

"Next day I left that station at last, with a caravan of sixty men, for a two-hundred-mile tramp.

"No use telling you much about that. Paths, paths, everywhere; a stamped-in network of paths spreading over the empty land, through long grass, through burnt grass, through thickets, down and up chilly ravines, up and down stony hills ablaze with heat; and a solitude, a solitude, nobody, not a hut. The population had cleared out a long time ago. Well, if a lot of mysterious niggers armed with all kinds of fearful weapons suddenly took to travelling on the road between Deal and Gravesend, catching the yokels right and left to carry heavy loads for them, I fancy every farm and cottage thereabouts would get empty very soon. Only here the dwellings were gone too. Still, I passed through several abandoned villages. There's something pathetically childish in the ruins of grass walls. Day after day, with the stamp and shuffle of sixty pair of bare feet behind me, each pair under a 60-lb. load. Camp, cook, sleep; strike camp, march. Now and then a carrier dead in harness, at rest in the long grass near the path, with an empty water-gourd and his long staff lying by his side. A great silence around and above. Perhaps on some quiet night the tremor of far-off drums, sinking, swelling, a tremor vast, faint; a sound weird, appealing, suggestive, and wild — and perhaps with as profound a meaning as the sound of bells in a Christian country. Once a white man in an unbuttoned uniform, camping on the path with an armed escort of lank Zanzibaris,° very hospitable and festive — not to say drunk. Was looking after the upkeep of the road, he declared. Can't say I saw any road or any upkeep, unless the body of a middle-aged negro, with a bullet-hole in the forehead, upon which I absolutely stumbled three miles farther on, may be considered a permanent improvement. I had a white companion too, not a bad chap, but rather too fleshy and with the exasperating habit of fainting on the hot hillsides, miles away from the least bit of shade and water. Annoying, you know, to hold your own coat like a parasol over a man's head while he is coming to. I couldn't help asking him once what he meant by coming there at all. 'To make money, of course. What do you think?' he said scornfully. Then he got fever, and had to be carried in a hammock slung under a pole. As he weighed sixteen stone° I had no end of rows with the carriers. They jibbed, ran away, sneaked off with their loads in the night — quite a mutiny. So, one evening, I made a speech in English with gestures, not one of which was lost to the sixty pairs of eyes before me, and the next morning I started the hammock off in front all right. An hour afterwards I came upon the whole concern wrecked in a bush — man, hammock, groans, blankets, horrors. The heavy pole had skinned his poor nose. He was very anxious for me to kill somebody, but there wasn't the shadow of a carrier near. I remembered the old doctor — 'It would be interesting for science to watch the mental changes to individuals, on the spot.' I felt I was becoming scientifically interesting. However, all that is to no purpose. On the fifteenth day I came in sight of the big river again, and hobbled into the Central Station. It was on a back water surrounded by scrub and forest, with a

---

Zanzibaris: Mercenaries from the African Zanzibar nation.
sixteen stone: 224 pounds.

pretty border of smelly mud on one side, and on the three others enclosed by a crazy fence of rushes. A neglected gap was all the gate it had, and the first glance at the place was enough to let you see the flabby devil was running that show. White men with long staves in their hands appeared languidly from amongst the buildings, strolling up to take a look at me, and then retired out of sight somewhere. One of them, a stout, excitable chap with black moustaches, informed me with great volubility and many digressions, as soon as I told him who I was, that my steamer was at the bottom of the river. I was thunderstruck. What, how, why? Oh, it was 'all right.' The 'manager himself' was there. All quite correct. 'Everybody had behaved splendidly! splendidly!' — 'You must,' he said in agitation, 'go and see the general manager at once. He is waiting!'

"I did not see the real significance of that wreck at once. I fancy I see it now, but I am not sure — not at all. Certainly the affair was too stupid — when I think of it — to be altogether natural. Still . . . But at the moment it presented itself simply as a confounded nuisance. The steamer was sunk. They had started two days before in a sudden hurry up the river with the manager on board, in charge of some volunteer skipper, and before they had been out three hours they tore the bottom out of her on stones, and she sank near the south bank. I asked myself what I was to do there, now my boat was lost. As a matter of fact, I had plenty to do in fishing my command out of the river. I had to set about it the very next day. That, and the repairs when I brought the pieces to the station, took some months.

"My first interview with the manager was curious. He did not ask me to sit down after my twenty-mile walk that morning. He was commonplace in complexion, in feature, in manners, and in voice. He was of middle size and of ordinary build. His eyes, of the usual blue, were perhaps remarkably cold, and he certainly could make his glance fall on one as trenchant and heavy as an axe. But even at these times the rest of his person seemed to disclaim the intention. Otherwise there was only an indefinable, faint expression of his lips, something stealthy — a smile — not a smile — I remember it, but I can't explain. It was unconscious, this smile was, though just after he had said something it got intensified for an instant. It came at the end of his speeches like a seal applied to the words to make the meaning of the commonest phrase appear absolutely inscrutable. He was a common trader, from his youth up employed in these parts — nothing more. He was obeyed, yet he inspired neither love nor fear, nor even respect. He inspired uneasiness. That was it! Uneasiness. Not a definite mistrust —

just uneasiness — nothing more. You have no idea how effective such a . . . a . . . faculty can be. He had no genius for organising, for initiative, or for order even. That was evident in such things as the deplorable state of the station. He had no learning, and no intelligence. His position had come to him — why? Perhaps because he was never ill . . . He had served three terms of three years out there . . . Because triumphant health in the general rout of constitutions is a kind of power in itself. When he went home on leave he rioted on a large scale — pompously. Jack ashore — with a difference — in externals only. This one could gather from his casual talk. He originated nothing, he could keep the routine going — that's all. But he was great. He was great by this little thing that it was impossible to tell what could control such a man. He never gave that secret away. Perhaps there was nothing within him. Such a suspicion made one pause — for out there there were no external checks. Once when various tropical diseases had laid low almost every 'agent' in the station, he was heard to say, 'Men who come out here should have no entrails.' He sealed the utterance with that smile of his, as though it had been a door opening into a darkness he had in his keeping. You fancied you had seen things — but the seal was on. When annoyed at meal-times by the constant quarrels of the white men about precedence, he ordered an immense round table to be made, for which a special house had to be built. This was the station's mess-room. Where he sat was the first place — the rest were nowhere. One felt this to be his unalterable conviction. He was neither civil nor uncivil. He was quiet. He allowed his 'boy' — an overfed young negro from the coast — to treat the white men, under his very eyes, with provoking insolence.

"He began to speak as soon as he saw me. I had been very long on the road. He could not wait. Had to start without me. The up-river stations had to be relieved. There had been so many delays already that he did not know who was dead and who was alive, and how they got on — and so on, and so on. He paid no attention to my explanations, and, playing with a stick of sealing-wax, repeated several times that the situation was 'very grave, very grave.' There were rumours that a very important station was in jeopardy, and its chief, Mr. Kurtz, was ill. Hoped it was not true. Mr. Kurtz was . . . I felt weary and irritable. Hang Kurtz, I thought. I interrupted him by saying I had heard of Mr. Kurtz on the coast. 'Ah! So they talk of him down there,' he murmured to himself. Then he began again, assuring me Mr. Kurtz was the best agent he had, an exceptional man, of the greatest importance to the Company; therefore I could understand his anxiety. He was, he said, 'very, very uneasy.' Certainly he fidgeted on his chair a good deal, exclaimed, 'Ah, Mr. Kurtz!' broke the stick of sealing-wax and seemed dumbfounded by the accident. Next thing he wanted to know 'how long it would take to' . . . I interrupted him again. Being hungry, you know, and kept on my feet too, I was getting savage. 'How can I tell?' I said. 'I haven't even seen the wreck yet — some months, no doubt.' All this talk seemed to me so futile. 'Some months,' he said. 'Well, let us say three months before we can make a start. Yes. That ought to do the affair.' I flung out of his hut (he lived all alone in a clay hut with a sort of verandah) muttering to myself my opinion of him. He was a chattering idiot. Afterwards I took it back when it was borne in upon me startlingly with what extreme nicety he had estimated the time requisite for the 'affair.'

"I went to work the next day, turning, so to speak, my back on that station. In that way only it seemed to me I could keep my hold on the redeeming facts of life. Still, one must look about sometimes; and then I saw this station, these men strolling aimlessly about in the sunshine of the yard. I asked myself sometimes what it all meant. They wandered here and there with their absurd long staves in their hands, like a lot of faithless pilgrims bewitched inside a rotten fence. The word 'ivory' rang in the air, was whispered, was sighed. You would think they were praying to it. A taint of imbecile rapacity blew through it all, like a whiff from some corpse. By Jove! I've never seen anything so unreal in my life. And outside, the silent wilderness surrounding this cleared speck on the earth struck me as something great and invincible, like evil or truth, waiting patiently for the passing away of this fantastic invasion.

"Oh, those months! Well, never mind. Various things happened. One evening a grass shed full of calico, cotton prints, beads, and I don't know what else, burst into a blaze so suddenly that you would have thought the earth had opened to let an avenging fire consume all that trash. I was smoking my pipe quietly by my dismantled steamer, and saw them all cutting capers in the light, with their arms lifted high, when the stout man with moustaches came tearing down to the river, a tin pail in his hand, assured me that everybody was 'behaving splendidly, splendidly,' dipped about a quart of water and tore back again. I noticed there was a hole in the bottom of his pail.

"I strolled up. There was no hurry. You see the thing had gone off like a box of matches. It had been hopeless from the very first. The flame had leaped high, driven everybody back, lighted up everything — and collapsed. The shed was already a heap of embers glowing fiercely.

A nigger was being beaten near by. They said he had caused the fire in some way; be that as it may, he was screeching most horribly. I saw him, later, for several days, sitting in a bit of shade looking very sick and trying to recover himself: afterwards he arose and went out — and the wilderness without a sound took him into its bosom again. As I approached the glow from the dark I found myself at the back of two men, talking. I heard the name of Kurtz pronounced, then the words 'take advantage of this unfortunate accident.' One of the men was the manager. I wished him a good evening. 'Did you ever see anything like it — eh? it is incredible,' he said, and walked off. The other man remained. He was a first-class agent, young, gentlemanly, a bit re-served, with a forked little beard and a hooked nose. He was stand-offish with the other agents, and they on their side said he was the manager's spy upon them. As to me, I had hardly ever spoken to him before. We got into talk, and by and by we strolled away from the hiss-ing ruins. Then he asked me to his room, which was in the main build-ing of the station. He struck a match, and I perceived that this young aristocrat had not only a silver-mounted dressing-case but also a whole candle all to himself. Just at that time the manager was the only man supposed to have any right to candles. Native mats covered the clay walls; a collection of spears, assegais,° shields, knives, was hung up in trophies. The business entrusted to this fellow was the making of bricks — so I had been informed; but there wasn't a fragment of a brick anywhere in the station, and he had been there more than a year — waiting. It seems he could not make bricks without something, I don't know what — straw maybe. Anyway, it could not be found there, and as it was not likely to be sent from Europe, it did not appear clear to me what he was waiting for. An act of special creation perhaps. However, they were all waiting — all the sixteen or twenty pilgrims of them — for something; and upon my word it did not seem an uncon-genial occupation, from the way they took it, though the only thing that ever came to them was disease — as far as I could see. They be-guiled the time by backbiting and intriguing against each other in a foolish kind of way. There was an air of plotting about that station, but nothing came of it, of course. It was as unreal as everything else — as the philanthropic pretence of the whole concern, as their talk, as their government, as their show of work. The only real feeling was a desire to get appointed to a trading-post where ivory was to be had, so that they could earn percentages. They intrigued and slandered and

assegais: Thin spears designed to be thrown.

hated each other only on that account — but as to effectually lifting a little finger — oh no. By Heavens! there is something after all in the world allowing one man to steal a horse while another must not look at a halter. Steal a horse straight out. Very well. He has done it. Perhaps he can ride. But there is a way of looking at a halter that would provoke the most charitable of saints into a kick.

"I had no idea why he wanted to be sociable, but as we chatted in there it suddenly occurred to me the fellow was trying to get at something — in fact, pumping me. He alluded constantly to Europe, to the people I was supposed to know there — putting leading questions as to my acquaintances in the sepulchral city, and so on. His little eyes glittered like mica discs — with curiosity — though he tried to keep up a bit of superciliousness. At first I was astonished, but very soon I became awfully curious to see what he would find out from me. I couldn't possibly imagine what I had in me to make it worth his while. It was very pretty to see how he baffled himself, for in truth my body was full only of chills, and my head had nothing in it but that wretched steamboat business. It was evident he took me for a perfectly shameless prevaricator. At last he got angry, and, to conceal a movement of furious annoyance, he yawned. I rose. Then I noticed a small sketch in oils, on a panel, representing a woman, draped and blindfolded, carrying a lighted torch. The background was sombre — almost black. The movement of the woman was stately, and the effect of the torchlight on the face was sinister.

"It arrested me, and he stood by civilly, holding an empty half-pint champagne bottle (medical comforts) with the candle stuck in it. To my question he said Mr. Kurtz had painted this — in this very station more than a year ago — while waiting for means to go to his trading-post. 'Tell me, pray,' said I, 'who is this Mr. Kurtz?'

"'The chief of the Inner Station,' he answered in a short tone, looking away. 'Much obliged,' I said, laughing. 'And you are the brickmaker of the Central Station. Every one knows that.' He was silent for a while. 'He is a prodigy,' he said at last. 'He is an emissary of pity, and science, and progress, and devil knows what else. We want,' he began to declaim suddenly, 'for the guidance of the cause entrusted to us by Europe, so to speak, higher intelligence, wide sympathies, a singleness of purpose.' 'Who says that?' I asked. 'Lots of them,' he replied. 'Some even write that; and so he comes here, a special being, as you ought to know.' 'Why ought I to know?' I interrupted, really surprised. He paid no attention. 'Yes. To-day he is chief of the best station, next year he will be assistant-manager, two years

more and . . . but I daresay you know what he will be in two years'
time. You are of the new gang — the gang of virtue. The same people
who sent him specially also recommended you. Oh, don't say no. I've
my own eyes to trust.' Light dawned upon me. My dear aunt's influential acquaintances were producing an unexpected effect upon that
young man. I nearly burst into a laugh. 'Do you read the Company's
confidential correspondence?' I asked. He hadn't a word to say. It was
great fun. 'When Mr. Kurtz,' I continued severely, 'is General Manager, you won't have the opportunity.'

"He blew the candle out suddenly, and we went outside. The
moon had risen. Black figures strolled about listlessly, pouring water
on the glow, whence proceeded a sound of hissing; steam ascended in
the moonlight; the beaten nigger groaned somewhere. 'What a row
the brute makes!' said the indefatigable man with the moustaches, appearing near us. 'Serve him right. Transgression — punishment —
bang! Pitiless, pitiless. That's the only way. This will prevent all confla-
grations for the future. I was just telling the manager . . .' He noticed
my companion, and became crestfallen all at once. 'Not in bed yet,' he
said, with a kind of servile heartiness; 'it's so natural. Ha! Danger —
agitation.' He vanished. I went on to the river-side, and the other followed me. I heard a scathing murmur at my ear, 'Heaps of muffs —
go to.' The pilgrims could be seen in knots gesticulating, discussing.
Several had still their staves in their hands. I verily believe they took
these sticks to bed with them. Beyond the fence the forest stood up
spectrally in the moonlight, and through the dim stir, through the
faint sounds of that lamentable courtyard, the silence of the land went
home to one's very heart — its mystery, its greatness, the amazing reality of its concealed life. The hurt nigger moaned feebly somewhere
near by, and then fetched a deep sigh that made me mend my pace
away from there. I felt a hand introducing itself under my arm. 'My
dear sir,' said the fellow, 'I don't want to be misunderstood, and especially by you, who will see Mr. Kurtz long before I can have that pleasure. I wouldn't like him to get a false idea of my disposition. . . .'

"I let him run on, this papier-mâché Mephistopheles, and it
seemed to me that if I tried I could poke my forefinger through him,
and would find nothing inside but a little loose dirt, maybe. He, don't
you see, had been planning to be assistant-manager by and by under
the present man, and I could see that the coming of that Kurtz had
upset them both not a little. He talked precipitately, and I did not try
to stop him. I had my shoulders against the wreck of my steamer,
hauled up on the slope like a carcass of some big river animal. The

smell of mud, of primeval mud, by Jove! was in my nostrils, the high stillness of primeval forest was before my eyes; there were shiny patches on the black creek. The moon had spread over everything a thin layer of silver — over the rank grass, over the mud, upon the wall of matted vegetation standing higher than the wall of a temple, over the great river I could see through a sombre gap glittering, glittering, as it flowed broadly by without a murmur. All this was great, expectant, mute, while the man jabbered about himself. I wondered whether the stillness on the face of the immensity looking at us two were meant as an appeal or as a menace. What were we who had strayed in here? Could we handle that dumb thing, or would it handle us? I felt how big, how confoundedly big, was that thing that couldn't talk and perhaps was deaf as well. What was in there? I could see a little ivory coming out from there, and I had heard Mr. Kurtz was in there. I had heard enough about it too — God knows! Yet somehow it didn't bring any image with it — no more than if I had been told an angel or a fiend was in there. I believed it in the same way one of you might believe there are inhabitants in the planet Mars. I knew once a Scotch sailmaker who was certain, dead sure, there were people in Mars. If you asked him for some idea how they looked and behaved, he would get shy and mutter something about 'walking on all-fours.' If you as much as smiled, he would — though a man of sixty — offer to fight you. I would not have gone so far as to fight for Kurtz, but I went for him near enough to a lie. You know I hate, detest, and can't bear a lie, not because I am straighter than the rest of us, but simply because it appals me. There is a taint of death, a flavour of mortality in lies — which is exactly what I hate and detest in the world — what I want to forget. It makes me miserable and sick, like biting something rotten would do. Temperament, I suppose. Well, I went near enough to it by letting the young fool there believe anything he liked to imagine as to my influence in Europe. I became in an instant as much of a pretence as the rest of the bewitched pilgrims. This simply because I had a notion it somehow would be of help to that Kurtz whom at the time I did not see — you understand. He was just a word for me. I did not see the man in the name any more than you do. Do you see him? Do you see the story? Do you see anything? It seems to me I am trying to tell you a dream — making a vain attempt, because no relation of a dream can convey the dream-sensation, that commingling of absurdity, surprise, and bewilderment in a tremor of struggling revolt, that notion of being captured by the incredible which is of the very essence of dreams. . . ."

He was silent for a while.

"... No, it is impossible; it is impossible to convey the life-sensation of any given epoch of one's existence — that which makes its truth, its meaning — its subtle and penetrating essence. It is impossible. We live, as we dream — alone. . . ."

He paused again as if reflecting, then added:

"Of course in this you fellows see more than I could then. You see me, whom you know. . . ."

It had become so pitch dark that we listeners could hardly see one another. For a long time already he, sitting apart, had been no more to us than a voice. There was not a word from anybody. The others might have been asleep, but I was awake. I listened, I listened on the watch for the sentence, for the word, that would give me the clue to the faint uneasiness inspired by this narrative that seemed to shape itself without human lips in the heavy night-air of the river.

"... Yes — I let him run on," Marlow began again, "and think what he pleased about the powers that were behind me. I did! And there was nothing behind me! There was nothing but that wretched, old, mangled steamboat I was leaning against, while he talked fluently about 'the necessity for every man to get on.' 'And when one comes out here, you conceive, it is not to gaze at the moon.' Mr. Kurtz was a 'universal genius,' but even a genius would find it easier to work with 'adequate tools — intelligent men.' He did not make bricks — why, there was a physical impossibility in the way   as I was well aware; and if he did secretarial work for the manager, it was because 'no sensible man rejects wantonly the confidence of his superiors.' Did I see it? I saw it. What more did I want? What I really wanted was rivets, by Heaven! Rivets. To get on with the work — to stop the hole. Rivets I wanted. There were cases of them down at the coast — cases — piled up — burst — split! You kicked a loose rivet at every second step in that station yard on the hillside. Rivets had rolled into the grove of death. You could fill your pockets with rivets for the trouble of stooping down — and there wasn't one rivet to be found where it was wanted. We had plates that would do, but nothing to fasten them with. And every week the messenger, a lone negro, letter-bag on shoulder and staff in hand, left our station for the coast. And several times a week a coast caravan came in with trade goods — ghastly glazed calico that made you shudder only to look at it, glass beads value about a penny a quart, confounded spotted cotton handkerchiefs. And no rivets. Three carriers could have brought all that was wanted to set that steamboat afloat.

"He was becoming confidential now, but I fancy my unresponsive

attitude must have exasperated him at last, for he judged it necessary
to inform me he feared neither God nor devil, let alone any mere man.
I said I could see that very well, but what I wanted was a certain quantity of rivets — and rivets were what really Mr. Kurtz wanted, if he had
only known it. Now letters went to the coast every week. . . . 'My dear
sir,' he cried, 'I write from dictation.' I demanded rivets. There was a
way — for an intelligent man. He changed his manner; became very
cold, and suddenly began to talk about a hippopotamus; wondered
whether sleeping on board the steamer (I stuck to my salvage night
and day) I wasn't disturbed. There was an old hippo that had the bad
habit of getting out on the bank and roaming at night over the station
grounds. The pilgrims used to turn out in a body and empty every rifle
they could lay hands on at him. Some even had sat up o' nights for
him. All this energy was wasted, though. 'That animal has a charmed
life,' he said; 'but you can say this only of brutes in this country. No
man — you apprehend me? — no man here bears a charmed life.' He
stood there for a moment in the moonlight with his delicate hooked
nose set a little askew, and his mica eyes glittering without a wink,
then, with a curt Good-night, he strode off. I could see he was disturbed and considerably puzzled, which made me feel more hopeful
than I had been for days. It was a great comfort to turn from that chap
to my influential friend, the battered, twisted, ruined, tin-pot steamboat. I clambered on board. She rang under my feet like an empty
Huntley & Palmer biscuit-tin kicked along a gutter; she was nothing
so solid in make, and rather less pretty in shape, but I had expended
enough hard work on her to make me love her. No influential friend
would have served me better. She had given me a chance to come out
a bit — to find out what I could do. No, I don't like work. I had
rather laze about and think of all the fine things that can be done. I
don't like work — no man does — but I like what is in the work —
the chance to find yourself. Your own reality — for yourself, not for
others — what no other man can ever know. They can only see the
mere show, and never can tell what it really means.

"I was not surprised to see somebody sitting aft, on the deck, with
his legs dangling over the mud. You see I rather chummed with the
few mechanics there were in that station, whom the other pilgrims
naturally despised — on account of their imperfect manners, I suppose. This was the foreman — a boiler-maker by trade — a good
worker. He was a lank, bony, yellow-faced man, with big intense eyes.
His aspect was worried, and his head was as bald as the palm of my
hand; but his hair in falling seemed to have stuck to his chin, and had

prospered in the new locality, for his beard hung down to his waist. He was a widower with six young children (he had left them in charge of a sister of his to come out there), and the passion of his life was pigeon-flying. He was an enthusiast and a connoisseur. He would rave about pigeons. After work hours he used sometimes to come over from his hut for a talk about his children and his pigeons; at work, when he had to crawl in the mud under the bottom of the steamboat, he would tie up that beard of his in a kind of white serviette° he brought for the purpose. It had loops to go over his ears. In the evening he could be seen squatted on the bank rinsing that wrapper in the creek with great care, then spreading it solemnly on a bush to dry.

"I slapped him on the back and shouted 'We shall have rivets!' He scrambled to his feet exclaiming 'No! Rivets!' as though he couldn't believe his ears. Then in a low voice, 'You . . . eh?' I don't know why we behaved like lunatics. I put my finger to the side of my nose and nodded mysteriously. 'Good for you!' he cried, snapped his fingers above his head, lifting one foot. I tried a jig. We capered on the iron deck. A frightful clatter came out of that hulk, and the virgin forest on the other bank of the creek sent it back in a thundering roll upon the sleeping station. It must have made some of the pilgrims sit up in their hovels. A dark figure obscured the lighted doorway of the manager's hut, vanished, then, a second or so after, the doorway itself vanished too. We stopped, and the silence driven away by the stamping of our feet flowed back again from the recesses of the land. The great wall of vegetation, an exuberant and entangled mass of trunks, branches, leaves, boughs, festoons, motionless in the moonlight, was like a rioting invasion of soundless life, a rolling wave of plants, piled up, crested, ready to topple over the creek, to sweep every little man of us out of his little existence. And it moved not. A deadened burst of mighty splashes and snorts reached us from afar, as though an ichthyosaurus° had been taking a bath of glitter in the great river. 'After all,' said the boiler-maker in a reasonable tone, 'why shouldn't we get the rivets?' Why not, indeed! I did not know of any reason why we shouldn't. 'They'll come in three weeks,' I said confidently.

"But they didn't. Instead of rivets there came an invasion, an infliction, a visitation. It came in sections during the next three weeks, each section headed by a donkey carrying a white man in new clothes and tan shoes, bowing from that elevation right and left to the

serviette: Napkin.
ichthyosaurus: Giant prehistoric reptile.

impressed pilgrims. A quarrelsome band of footsore sulky niggers trod on the heels of the donkey; a lot of tents, camp-stools, tin boxes, white cases, brown bales would be shot down in the courtyard, and the air of mystery would deepen a little over the muddle of the station. Five such instalments came, with their absurd air of disorderly flight with the loot of innumerable outfit shops and provision stores, that, one would think, they were lugging, after a raid, into the wilderness for equitable division. It was an inextricable mess of things decent in themselves but that human folly made look like the spoils of thieving.

"This devoted band called itself the Eldorado Exploring Expedition, and I believe they were sworn to secrecy. Their talk, however, was the talk of sordid buccaneers: it was reckless without hardihood, greedy without audacity, and cruel without courage; there was not an atom of foresight or of serious intention in the whole batch of them, and they did not seem aware these things are wanted for the work of the world. To tear treasure out of the bowels of the land was their desire, with no more moral purpose at the back of it than there is in burglars breaking into a safe. Who paid the expenses of the noble enterprise I don't know; but the uncle of our manager was leader of that lot.

"In exterior he resembled a butcher in a poor neighbourhood, and his eyes had a look of sleepy cunning. He carried his fat paunch with ostentation on his short legs, and during the time his gang infested the station spoke to no one but his nephew. You could see these two roaming about all day long with their heads close together in an everlasting confab.

"I had given up worrying myself about the rivets. One's capacity for that kind of folly is more limited than you would suppose. I said Hang! — and let things slide. I had plenty of time for meditation, and now and then I would give some thought to Kurtz. I wasn't very interested in him. No. Still, I was curious to see whether this man, who had come out equipped with moral ideas of some sort, would climb to the top after all, and how he would set about his work when there."

II

"One evening as I was lying flat on the deck of my steamboat, I heard voices approaching — and there were the nephew and the uncle strolling along the bank. I laid my head on my arm again, and had nearly lost myself in a doze, when somebody said in my ear, as it were: 'I am as harmless as a little child, but I don't like to be dictated to. Am

I the manager — or am I not? I was ordered to send him there. It's incredible.' . . . I became aware that the two were standing on the shore alongside the forepart of the steamboat, just below my head. I did not move; it did not occur to me to move: I was sleepy. 'It *is* unpleasant,' grunted the uncle. 'He has asked the Administration to be sent there,' said the other, 'with the idea of showing what he could do; and I was instructed accordingly. Look at the influence that man must have. Is it not frightful?' They both agreed it was frightful, then made several bizarre remarks: 'Make rain and fine weather — one man — the Council — by the nose' — bits of absurd sentences that got the better of my drowsiness, so that I had pretty near the whole of my wits about me when the uncle said, 'The climate may do away with this difficulty for you. Is he alone there?' 'Yes,' answered the manager; 'he sent his assistant down the river with a note to me in these terms: "Clear this poor devil out of the country, and don't bother sending more of that sort. I had rather be alone than have the kind of men you can dispose of with me." It was more than a year ago. Can you imagine such impudence?' 'Anything since then?' asked the other hoarsely. 'Ivory,' jerked the nephew; 'lots of it — prime sort — lots — most annoying, from him.' 'And with that?' questioned the heavy rumble. 'Invoice,' was the reply fired out, so to speak. Then silence. They had been talking about Kurtz.

"I was broad awake by this time, but, lying perfectly at ease, remained still, having no inducement to change my position. 'How did that ivory come all this way?' growled the elder man, who seemed very vexed. The other explained that it had come with a fleet of canoes in charge of an English half-caste clerk Kurtz had with him; that Kurtz apparently intended to return himself, the station being by that time bare of goods and stores, but after coming three hundred miles, had suddenly decided to go back, which he started to do alone in a small dugout with four paddlers, leaving the half-caste to continue down the river with the ivory. The two fellows there seemed astounded at anybody attempting such a thing. They were at a loss for an adequate motive. As for me, I seemed to see Kurtz for the first time. It was a distinct glimpse: the dugout, four paddling savages, and the lone white man turning his back suddenly on the headquarters, on relief, on thoughts of home — perhaps; setting his face towards the depths of the wilderness, towards his empty and desolate station. I did not know the motive. Perhaps he was just simply a fine fellow who stuck to his work for its own sake. His name, you understand, had not been pronounced once. He was 'that man.' The half-caste, who, as far as I

could see, had conducted a difficult trip with great prudence and
pluck, was invariably alluded to as 'that scoundrel.' The 'scoundrel'
had reported that the 'man' had been very ill — had recovered imper-
fectly. . . . The two below me moved away then a few paces, and
strolled back and forth at some little distance. I heard: 'Military
post — doctor — two hundred miles — quite alone now — unavoidable delays — nine months — no news — strange rumours.' They approached again, just as the manager was saying, 'No one, as far as I
know, unless a species of wandering trader — a pestilential fellow,
snapping ivory from the natives.' Who was it they were talking about
now? I gathered in snatches that this was some man supposed to be in
Kurtz's district, and of whom the manager did not approve. 'We will
not be free from unfair competition till one of these fellows is hanged
for an example,' he said. 'Certainly,' grunted the other; 'get him
hanged! Why not? Anything — anything can be done in this country.
That's what I say; nobody here, you understand, *here* can endanger
your position. And why? You stand the climate — you outlast them
all. The danger is in Europe; but there before I left I took care to —— '
They moved off and whispered, then their voices rose again. 'The extraordinary series of delays is not my fault. I did my possible.' The fat
man sighed, 'Very sad.' 'And the pestiferous absurdity of his talk,' continued the other; 'he bothered me enough when he was here. "Each
station should be like a beacon on the road towards better things, a
centre for trade of course, but also for humanising, improving, in-
structing." Conceive you — that ass! And he wants to be manager!
No, it's —— ' Here he got choked by excessive indignation, and I
lifted my head the least bit. I was surprised to see how near they
were — right under me. I could have spat upon their hats. They were
looking on the ground, absorbed in thought. The manager was
switching his leg with a slender twig: his sagacious relative lifted his
head. 'You have been well since you came out this time?' he asked.
The other gave a start. 'Who? I? Oh! Like a charm — like a charm. But
the rest — oh, my goodness! All sick. They die so quick, too, that I
haven't the time to send them out of the country — it's incredible.'
'H'm. Just so,' grunted the uncle. 'Ah! my boy, trust to this — I say,
trust to this.' I saw him extend his short flipper of an arm for a gesture
that took in the forest, the creek, the mud, the river — seemed to
beckon with a dishonouring flourish before the sunlit face of the land
a treacherous appeal to the lurking death, to the hidden evil, to the
profound darkness of its heart. It was so startling that I leaped to my
feet and looked back at the edge of the forest, as though I had ex-

pected an answer of some sort to that black display of confidence. You know the foolish notions that come to one sometimes. The high stillness confronted these two figures with its ominous patience, waiting for the passing away of a fantastic invasion.

"They swore aloud together — out of sheer fright, I believe — then, pretending not to know anything of my existence, turned back to the station. The sun was low; and leaning forward side by side, they seemed to be tugging painfully uphill their two ridiculous shadows of unequal length, that trailed behind them slowly over the tall grass without bending a single blade.

"In a few days the Eldorado Expedition went into the patient wilderness, that closed upon it as the sea closes over a diver. Long afterwards the news came that all the donkeys were dead. I know nothing as to the fate of the less valuable animals. They, no doubt, like the rest of us, found what they deserved. I did not inquire. I was then rather excited at the prospect of meeting Kurtz very soon. When I say very soon I mean it comparatively. It was just two months from the day we left the creek when we came to the bank below Kurtz's station.

"Going up that river was like travelling back to the earliest beginnings of the world, when vegetation rioted on the earth and the big trees were kings. An empty stream, a great silence, and impenetrable forest. The air was warm, thick, heavy, sluggish. There was no joy in the brilliance of sunshine. The long stretches of the waterway ran on, deserted, into the gloom of overshadowed distances. On silvery sandbanks hippos and alligators sunned themselves side by side. The broadening waters flowed through a mob of wooded islands; you lost your way on that river as you would in a desert, and butted all day long against shoals, trying to find the channel, till you thought yourself bewitched and cut off for ever from everything you had known once — somewhere — far away — in another existence perhaps. There were moments when one's past came back to one, as it will sometimes when you have not a moment to spare to yourself; but it came in the shape of an unrestful and noisy dream, remembered with wonder amongst the overwhelming realities of this strange world of plants, and water, and silence. And this stillness of life did not in the least resemble a peace. It was the stillness of an implacable force brooding over an inscrutable intention. It looked at you with a vengeful aspect. I got used to it afterwards; I did not see it any more; I had no time. I had to keep guessing at the channel; I had to discern, mostly by inspiration, the signs of hidden banks; I watched for sunken stones; I was learning to clap my teeth smartly before my heart flew out, when I shaved by a

fluke some infernal sly old snag that would have ripped the life out of
the tin-pot steamboat and drowned all the pilgrims; I had to keep a
look-out for the signs of dead wood we could cut up in the night for
the next day's steaming. When you have to attend to things of that
sort, to the mere incidents of the surface, the reality — the reality, I
tell you — fades. The inner truth is hidden — luckily, luckily. But I
felt it all the same; I felt often its mysterious stillness watching me at
my monkey tricks, just as it watches you fellows performing on your
respective tight-ropes for — what is it? half a crown a tumble ——"

"Try to be civil, Marlow," growled a voice, and I knew there was
at least one listener awake besides myself.

"I beg your pardon. I forgot the heartache which makes up the
rest of the price. And indeed what does the price matter, if the trick be
well done? You do your tricks very well. And I didn't do badly either,
since I managed not to sink that steamboat on my first trip. It's a wonder to me yet. Imagine a blindfolded man set to drive a van over a bad
road. I sweated and shivered over that business considerably, I can tell
you. After all, for a seaman, to scrape the bottom of the thing that's
supposed to float all the time under his care is the unpardonable sin.
No one may know of it, but you never forget the thump — eh? A
blow on the very heart. You remember it, you dream of it, you wake
up at night and think of it — years after — and go hot and cold all
over. I don't pretend to say that steamboat floated all the time. More
than once she had to wade for a bit, with twenty cannibals splashing
around and pushing. We had enlisted some of these chaps on the way
for a crew. Fine fellows — cannibals — in their place. They were men
one could work with, and I am grateful to them. And, after all, they
did not eat each other before my face: they had brought along a provision of hippo-meat which went rotten, and made the mystery of the
wilderness stink in my nostrils. Phoo! I can sniff it now. I had the
manager on board and three or four pilgrims with their staves — all
complete. Sometimes we came upon a station close by the bank, clinging to the skirts of the unknown, and the white men rushing out of a
tumble-down hovel, with great gestures of joy and surprise and welcome, seemed very strange — had the appearance of being held there
captive by a spell. The word 'ivory' would ring in the air for a while —
and on we went again into the silence, along empty reaches, round the
still bends, between the high walls of our winding way, reverberating
in hollow claps the ponderous beat of the stern-wheel. Trees, trees,
millions of trees, massive, immense, running up high; and at their foot,
hugging the bank against the stream, crept the little begrimed steam-

boat, like a sluggish beetle crawling on the floor of a lofty portico. It made you feel very small, very lost, and yet it was not altogether depressing, that feeling. After all, if you were small, the grimy beetle crawled on — which was just what you wanted it to do. Where the pilgrims imagined it crawled to I don't know. To some place where they expected to get something, I bet! For me it crawled towards Kurtz — exclusively; but when the steam-pipes started leaking we crawled very slow. The reaches opened before us and closed behind, as if the forest had stepped leisurely across the water to bar the way for our return. We penetrated deeper and deeper into the heart of darkness. It was very quiet there. At night sometimes the roll of drums behind the curtain of trees would run up the river and remain sustained faintly, as if hovering in the air high over our heads, till the first break of day. Whether it meant war, peace, or prayer we could not tell. The dawns were heralded by the descent of a chill stillness; the woodcutters slept, their fires burned low; the snapping of a twig would make you start. We were wanderers on a prehistoric earth, on an earth that wore the aspect of an unknown planet. We could have fancied ourselves the first of men taking possession of an accursed inheritance, to be subdued at the cost of profound anguish and of excessive toil. But suddenly, as we struggled round a bend, there would be a glimpse of rush walls, of peaked grass-roofs, a burst of yells, a whirl of black limbs, a mass of hands clapping, of feet stamping, of bodies swaying, of eyes rolling, under the droop of heavy and motionless foliage. The steamer toiled along slowly on the edge of a black and incomprehensible frenzy. The prehistoric man was cursing us, praying to us, welcoming us — who could tell? We were cut off from the comprehension of our surroundings; we glided past like phantoms, wondering and secretly appalled, as sane men would be before an enthusiastic outbreak in a madhouse. We could not understand because we were too far and could not remember, because we were travelling in the night of first ages, of those ages that are gone, leaving hardly a sign — and no memories.

"The earth seemed unearthly. We are accustomed to look upon the shackled form of a conquered monster, but there — there you could look at a thing monstrous and free. It was unearthly, and the men were —— No, they were not inhuman. Well, you know, that was the worst of it — this suspicion of their not being inhuman. It would come slowly to one. They howled and leaped, and spun, and made horrid faces; but what thrilled you was just the thought of their humanity — like yours — the thought of your remote kinship with this wild and passionate uproar. Ugly. Yes, it was ugly enough; but if you

were man enough you would admit to yourself that there was in you
just the faintest trace of a response to the terrible frankness of that
noise, a dim suspicion of there being a meaning in it which you — you
so remote from the night of first ages — could comprehend. And why
not? The mind of man is capable of anything — because everything is
in it, all the past as well as all the future. What was there after all? Joy,
fear, sorrow, devotion, valour, rage — who can tell? — but truth —
truth stripped of its cloak of time. Let the fool gape and shudder —
the man knows, and can look on without a wink. But he must at least
be as much of a man as these on the shore. He must meet that truth
with his own true stuff — with his own inborn strength. Principles?
Principles won't do. Acquisitions, clothes, pretty rags — rags that
would fly off at the first good shake. No; you want a deliberate belief.
An appeal to me in this fiendish row — is there? Very well; I hear; I
admit, but I have a voice too, and for good or evil mine is the speech
that cannot be silenced. Of course, a fool, what with sheer fright and
fine sentiments, is always safe. Who's that grunting? You wonder I
didn't go ashore for a howl and a dance? Well, no — I didn't. Fine
sentiments, you say? Fine sentiments be hanged! I had no time. I had
to mess about with white-lead and strips of woollen blanket helping to
put bandages on those leaky steam-pipes — I tell you. I had to watch
the steering, and circumvent those snags, and get the tin-pot along by
hook or by crook. There was surface-truth enough in these things to
save a wiser man. And between whiles I had to look after the savage
who was fireman. He was an improved specimen; he could fire up a
vertical boiler. He was there below me, and, upon my word, to look at
him was as edifying as seeing a dog in a parody of breeches and a
feather hat, walking on his hind legs. A few months of training had
done for that really fine chap. He squinted at the steam-gauge and at
the water-gauge with an evident effort of intrepidity — and he had
filed teeth too, the poor devil, and the wool of his pate shaved into
queer patterns, and three ornamental scars on each of his cheeks. He
ought to have been clapping his hands and stamping his feet on the
bank, instead of which he was hard at work, a thrall to strange witch-
craft, full of improving knowledge. He was useful because he had been
instructed; and what he knew was this — that should the water in that
transparent thing disappear, the evil spirit inside the boiler would get
angry through the greatness of his thirst, and take a terrible vengeance.
So he sweated and fired up and watched the glass fearfully (with an
impromptu charm, made of rags, tied to his arm, and a piece of polished bone, as big as a watch, stuck flatways through his lower lip),

while the wooded banks slipped past us slowly, the short noise was left behind, the interminable miles of silence — and we crept on, towards Kurtz. But the snags were thick, the water was treacherous and shallow, the boiler seemed indeed to have a sulky devil in it, and thus neither that fireman nor I had any time to peer into our creepy thoughts.

"Some fifty miles below the Inner Station we came upon a hut of reeds, an inclined and melancholy pole, with the unrecognisable tatters of what had been a flag of some sort flying from it, and a neatly stacked wood-pile. This was unexpected. We came to the bank, and on the stack of firewood found a flat piece of board with some faded pencil-writing on it. When deciphered it said: 'Wood for you. Hurry up. Approach cautiously.' There was a signature, but it was illegible — not Kurtz — a much longer word. Hurry up. Where? Up the river? 'Approach cautiously.' We had not done so. But the warning could not have been meant for the place where it could be only found after approach. Something was wrong above. But what — and how much? That was the question. We commented adversely upon the imbecility of that telegraphic style. The bush around said nothing, and would not let us look very far, either. A torn curtain of red twill hung in the doorway of the hut, and flapped sadly in our faces. The dwelling was dismantled; but we could see a white man had lived there not very long ago. There remained a rude table — a plank on two posts; a heap of rubbish reposed in a dark corner, and by the door I picked up a book. It had lost its covers, and the pages had been thumbed into a state of extremely dirty softness; but the back had been lovingly stitched afresh with white cotton thread, which looked clean yet. It was an extraordinary find. Its title was, *An Inquiry into some Points of Seamanship*, by a man Towser, Towson — some such name — Master in His Majesty's Navy. The matter looked dreary reading enough, with illustrative diagrams and repulsive tables of figures, and the copy was sixty years old. I handled this amazing antiquity with the greatest possible tenderness, lest it should dissolve in my hands. Within, Towson or Towser was inquiring earnestly into the breaking strain of ships' chains and tackle, and other such matters. Not a very enthralling book; but at the first glance you could see there a singleness of intention, an honest concern for the right way of going to work, which made these humble pages, thought out so many years ago, luminous with another than a professional light. The simple old sailor, with his talk of chains and purchases, made me forget the jungle and the pilgrims in a delicious sensation of having come upon something unmistakably real. Such a book being there was wonderful enough; but still more astounding were the notes pencilled in the margin, and plainly referring to the text. I couldn't believe my eyes! They were in cipher! Yes, it looked like cipher. Fancy a man lugging with him a book of that description into this nowhere and studying it — and making notes — in cipher at that! It was an extravagant mystery.

"I had been dimly aware for some time of a worrying noise, and when I lifted my eyes I saw the wood-pile was gone, and the manager, aided by all the pilgrims, was shouting at me from the river-side. I slipped the book into my pocket. I assure you to leave off reading was like tearing myself away from the shelter of an old and solid friendship.

"I started the lame engine ahead. 'It must be this miserable trader — this intruder,' exclaimed the manager, looking back malevolently at the place we had left. 'He must be English,' I said. 'It will not save him from getting into trouble if he is not careful,' muttered the manager darkly. I observed with assumed innocence that no man was safe from trouble in this world.

"The current was more rapid now, the steamer seemed at her last gasp, the stern-wheel flopped languidly, and I caught myself listening on the tiptoe for the next beat of the float, for in sober truth I expected the wretched thing to give up every moment. It was like watching the last flickers of a life. But still we crawled. Sometimes I would pick out a tree a little way ahead to measure our progress towards Kurtz by, but I lost it invariably before we got abreast. To keep the eyes so long on one thing was too much for human patience. The manager displayed a beautiful resignation. I fretted and fumed and took to arguing with myself whether or no I would talk openly with Kurtz; but before I could come to any conclusion it occurred to me that my speech or my silence, indeed any action of mine, would be a mere futility. What did it matter what any one knew or ignored? What did it matter who was manager? One gets sometimes such a flash of insight. The essentials of this affair lay deep under the surface, beyond my reach, and beyond my power of meddling.

"Towards the evening of the second day we judged ourselves about eight miles from Kurtz's station. I wanted to push on; but the manager looked grave, and told me the navigation up there was so dangerous that it would be advisable, the sun being very low already, to wait where we were till next morning. Moreover, he pointed out that if the warning to approach cautiously were to be followed, we must approach in daylight — not at dusk, or in the dark. This was sensible enough. Eight miles meant nearly three hours' steaming for us, and I could also see suspicious ripples at the upper end of the reach.

Nevertheless, I was annoyed beyond expression at the delay, and most
unreasonably too, since one more night could not matter much after
so many months. As we had plenty of wood, and caution was the
word, I brought up in the middle of the stream. The reach was narrow, straight, with high sides like a railway cutting. The dusk came
gliding into it long before the sun had set. The current ran smooth
and swift, but a dumb immobility sat on the banks. The living trees,
lashed together by the creepers and every living bush of the undergrowth, might have been changed into stone, even to the slenderest
twig, to the lightest leaf. It was not sleep — it seemed unnatural, like a
state of trance. Not the faintest sound of any kind could be heard. You
looked on amazed, and began to suspect yourself of being deaf —
then the night came suddenly, and struck you blind as well. About
three in the morning some large fish leaped, and the loud splash made
me jump as though a gun had been fired. When the sun rose there was
a white fog, very warm and clammy, and more blinding than the
night. It did not shift or drive; it was just there, standing all round you
like something solid. At eight or nine, perhaps, it lifted as a shutter
lifts. We had a glimpse of the towering multitude of trees, of the immense matted jungle, with the blazing little ball of the sun hanging
over it — all perfectly still — and then the white shutter came down
again, smoothly, as if sliding in greased grooves. I ordered the chain,
which we had begun to heave in, to be paid out again. Before it
stopped running with a muffled rattle, a cry, a very loud cry, as of infinite desolation, soared slowly in the opaque air. It ceased. A complaining clamour, modulated in savage discords, filled our ears. The sheer
unexpectedness of it made my hair stir under my cap. I don't know
how it struck the others: to me it seemed as though the mist itself had
screamed, so suddenly, and apparently from all sides at once, did this
tumultuous and mournful uproar arise. It culminated in a hurried outbreak of almost intolerably excessive shrieking, which stopped short,
leaving us stiffened in a variety of silly attitudes, and obstinately listening to the nearly as appalling and excessive silence. 'Good God! What
is the meaning —— ?' stammered at my elbow one of the pilgrims —
a little fat man, with sandy hair and red whiskers, who wore side-spring
boots, and pink pyjamas tucked into his socks. Two others remained
open-mouthed a whole minute, then dashed into the little cabin, to
rush out incontinently and stand darting scared glances, with Winchesters at 'ready' in their hands. What we could see was just the steamer
we were on, her outlines blurred as though she had been on the point
of dissolving, and a misty strip of water, perhaps two feet broad,

around her — and that was all. The rest of the world was nowhere, as far as our eyes and ears were concerned. Just nowhere. Gone, disappeared; swept off without leaving a whisper or a shadow behind.

"I went forward, and ordered the chain to be hauled in short, so as to be ready to trip the anchor and move the steamboat at once if necessary. 'Will they attack?' whispered an awed voice. 'We will all be butchered in this fog,' murmured another. The faces twitched with the strain, the hands trembled slightly, the eyes forgot to wink. It was very curious to see the contrast of expressions of the white men and of the black fellows of our crew, who were as much strangers to that part of the river as we, though their homes were only eight hundred miles away. The whites, of course greatly discomposed, had besides a curious look of being painfully shocked by such an outrageous row. The others had an alert, naturally interested expression; but their faces were essentially quiet, even those of the one or two who grinned as they hauled at the chain. Several exchanged short, grunting phrases, which seemed to settle the matter to their satisfaction. Their head-man, a young, broad-chested black, severely draped in dark-blue fringed cloths, with fierce nostrils and his hair all done up artfully in oily ringlets, stood near me. 'Aha!' I said, just for good fellowship's sake. 'Catch 'im,' he snapped, with a bloodshot widening of his eyes and a flash of sharp teeth — 'catch 'im. Give 'im to us.' 'To you, eh?' I asked; 'what would you do with them?' 'Eat 'im!' he said curtly, and, leaning his elbow on the rail, looked out into the fog in a dignified and profoundly pensive attitude. I would no doubt have been properly horrified, had it not occurred to me that he and his chaps must be very hungry: that they must have been growing increasingly hungry for at least this month past. They had been engaged for six months (I don't think a single one of them had any clear idea of time, as we at the end of countless ages have. They still belonged to the beginnings of time — had no inherited experience to teach them, as it were), and of course, as long as there was a piece of paper written over in accordance with some farcical law or other made down the river, it didn't enter anybody's head to trouble how they would live. Certainly they had brought with them some rotten hippo-meat, which couldn't have lasted very long, anyway, even if the pilgrims hadn't, in the midst of a shocking hullabaloo, thrown a considerable quantity of it overboard. It looked like a high-handed proceeding; but it was really a case of legitimate self-defence. You can't breathe dead hippo waking, sleeping, and eating, and at the same time keep your precarious grip on existence. Besides that, they had given them every week three pieces of brass wire, each about nine inches long; and the theory was they were to buy their provisions with that currency in river-side villages. You can see how *that* worked. There were either no villages, or the people were hostile, or the director, who like the rest of us fed out of tins, with an occasional old he-goat thrown in, didn't want to stop the steamer for some more or less recondite reason. So, unless they swallowed the wire itself, or made loops of it to snare the fishes with, I don't see what good their extravagant salary could be to them. I must say it was paid with a regularity worthy of a large and honourable trading company. For the rest, the only thing to eat — though it didn't look eatable in the least — I saw in their possession was a few lumps of some stuff like half-cooked dough, of a dirty lavender colour, they kept wrapped in leaves, and now and then swallowed a piece of, but so small that it seemed done more for the look of the thing than for any serious purpose of sustenance. Why in the name of all the gnawing devils of hunger they didn't go for us — they were thirty to five — and have a good tuck-in for once, amazes me now when I think of it. They were big powerful men, with not much capacity to weigh the consequences, with courage, with strength, even yet, though their skins were no longer glossy and their muscles no longer hard. And I saw that something restraining, one of those human secrets that baffle probability, had come into play there. I looked at them with a swift quickening of interest — not because it occurred to me I might be eaten by them before very long, though I own to you that just then I perceived — in a new light, as it were — how unwholesome the pilgrims looked, and I hoped, yes, I positively hoped, that my aspect was not so — what shall I say? — so — unappetising: a touch of fantastic vanity which fitted well with the dream-sensation that pervaded all my days at that time. Perhaps I had a little fever too. One can't live with one's finger everlastingly on one's pulse. I had often 'a little fever,' or a little touch of other things — the playful paw-strokes of the wilderness, the preliminary trifling before the more serious onslaught which came in due course. Yes; I looked at them as you would on any human being, with a curiosity of their impulses, motives, capacities, weaknesses, when brought to the test of an inexorable physical necessity. Restraint! What possible restraint? Was it superstition, disgust, patience, fear — or some kind of primitive honour? No fear can stand up to hunger, no patience can wear it out, disgust simply does not exist where hunger is; and as to superstition, beliefs, and what you may call principles, they are less than chaff in a breeze. Don't you know the devilry of lingering starvation, its exasperating torment, its black thoughts, its sombre and brooding ferocity? Well, I do. It takes a man all his inborn strength to fight hunger properly. It's really easier to face bereavement, dishonour, and the perdition of one's soul — than this kind of prolonged hunger. Sad, but true. And these chaps too had no earthly reason for any kind of scruple. Restraint! I would just as soon have expected restraint from a hyena prowling amongst the corpses of a battlefield. But there was the fact facing me — the fact dazzling, to be seen, like the foam on the depths of the sea, like a ripple on an unfathomable enigma, a mystery greater — when I thought of it — than the curious, inexplicable note of desperate grief in this savage clamour that had swept by us on the river-bank, behind the blind whiteness of the fog.

"Two pilgrims were quarrelling in hurried whispers as to which bank. 'Left.' 'No, no; how can you? Right, right, of course.' 'It is very serious,' said the manager's voice behind me; 'I would be desolated if anything should happen to Mr. Kurtz before we came up.' I looked at him, and had not the slightest doubt he was sincere. He was just the kind of man who would wish to preserve appearances. That was his restraint. But when he muttered something about going on at once, I did not even take the trouble to answer him. I knew, and he knew, that it was impossible. Were we to let go our hold of the bottom, we would be absolutely in the air — in space. We wouldn't be able to tell where we were going to — whether up or down stream, or across — till we fetched against one bank or the other — and then we wouldn't know at first which it was. Of course I made no move. I had no mind for a smash-up. You couldn't imagine a more deadly place for a shipwreck. Whether drowned at once or not, we were sure to perish speedily in one way or another. 'I authorise you to take all the risks,' he said, after a short silence. 'I refuse to take any,' I said shortly; which was just the answer he expected, though its tone might have surprised him. 'Well, I must defer to your judgment. You are captain,' he said, with marked civility. I turned my shoulder to him in sign of my appreciation, and looked into the fog. How long would it last? It was the most hopeless look-out. The approach to this Kurtz grubbing for ivory in the wretched bush was beset by as many dangers as though he had been an enchanted princess sleeping in a fabulous castle. 'Will they attack, do you think?" asked the manager, in a confidential tone.

"I did not think they would attack, for several obvious reasons. The thick fog was one. If they left the bank in their canoes they would get lost in it, as we would be if we attempted to move. Still, I had also judged the jungle of both banks quite impenetrable — and yet eyes were in it, eyes that had seen us. The river-side bushes were certainly very thick; but the undergrowth behind was evidently penetrable.

However, during the short lift I had seen no canoes anywhere in the reach — certainly not abreast of the steamer. But what made the idea of attack inconceivable to me was the nature of the noise — of the cries we had heard. They had not the fierce character boding of immediate hostile intention. Unexpected, wild, and violent as they had been, they had given me an irresistible impression of sorrow. The glimpse of the steamboat had for some reason filled those savages with unrestrained grief. The danger, if any, I expounded, was from our proximity to a great human passion let loose. Even extreme grief may ultimately vent itself in violence — but more generally takes the form of apathy. . . .

"You should have seen the pilgrims stare! They had no heart to grin, or even to revile me; but I believe they thought me gone mad — with fright, maybe. I delivered a regular lecture. My dear boys, it was no good bothering. Keep a look-out? Well, you may guess I watched the fog for the signs of lifting as a cat watches a mouse; but for anything else our eyes were of no more use to us than if we had been buried miles deep in a heap of cotton-wool. It felt like it too — choking, warm, stifling. Besides, all I said, though it sounded extravagant, was absolutely true to fact. What we afterwards alluded to as an attack was really an attempt at repulse. The action was very far from being aggressive — it was not even defensive, in the usual sense: it was undertaken under the stress of desperation, and in its essence was purely protective.

"It developed itself, I should say, two hours after the fog lifted, and its commencement was at a spot, roughly speaking, about a mile and a half below Kurtz's station. We had just floundered and flopped round a bend, when I saw an islet, a mere grassy hummock of bright green, in the middle of the stream. It was the only thing of the kind; but as we opened the reach more, I perceived it was the head of a long sandbank, or rather of a chain of shallow patches stretching down the middle of the river. They were discoloured, just awash, and the whole lot was seen just under the water, exactly as a man's backbone is seen running down the middle of his back under the skin. Now, as far as I did see, I could go to the right or to the left of this. I didn't know either channel, of course. The banks looked pretty well alike, the depth appeared the same; but as I had been informed the station was on the west side, I naturally headed for the western passage.

"No sooner had we fairly entered it than I became aware it was much narrower than I had supposed. To the left of us there was the long uninterrupted shoal, and to the right a high steep bank heavily overgrown with bushes. Above the bush the trees stood in serried ranks. The twigs overhung the current thickly, and from distance to distance a large limb of some tree projected rigidly over the stream. It was then well on in the afternoon, the face of the forest was gloomy, and a broad strip of shadow had already fallen on the water. In this shadow we steamed up — very slowly, as you may imagine. I sheered her well inshore — the water being deepest near the bank, as the sounding-pole informed me.

"One of my hungry and forbearing friends was sounding in the bows just below me. This steamboat was exactly like a decked scow. On the deck there were two little teak-wood houses, with doors and windows. The boiler was in the fore-end, and the machinery right astern. Over the whole there was a light roof, supported on stanchions. The funnel projected through that roof, and in front of the funnel a small cabin built of light planks served for a pilot-house. It contained a couch, two camp-stools, a loaded Martini-Henry leaning in one corner, a tiny table, and the steering-wheel. It had a wide door in front and a broad shutter at each side. All these were always thrown open, of course. I spent my days perched up there on the extreme fore-end of that roof, before the door. At night I slept, or tried to, on the couch. An athletic black belonging to some coast tribe, and educated by my poor predecessor, was the helmsman. He sported a pair of brass earrings, wore a blue cloth wrapper from the waist to the ankles, and thought all the world of himself. He was the most unstable kind of fool I had ever seen. He steered with no end of a swagger while you were by; but if he lost sight of you, he became instantly the prey of an abject funk, and would let that cripple of a steamboat get the upper hand of him in a minute.

"I was looking down at the sounding-pole, and feeling much annoyed to see at each try a little more of it stick out of that river, when I saw my poleman give up the business suddenly, and stretch himself flat on the deck, without even taking the trouble to haul his pole in. He kept hold on it though, and it trailed in the water. At the same time the fireman, whom I could also see below me, sat down abruptly before his furnace and ducked his head. I was amazed. Then I had to look at the river mighty quick, because there was a snag in the fairway. Sticks, little sticks, were flying about — thick: they were whizzing before my nose, dropping below me, striking behind me against my pilot-house. All this time the river, the shore, the woods, were very quiet — perfectly quiet. I could only hear the heavy splashing thump of the stern-wheel and the patter of these things. We cleared the snag clumsily. Arrows, by Jove! We were being shot at! I stepped in quickly to close the shutter on the land-side. That fool-helmsman, his hands on the spokes, was lifting his knees high, stamping his feet, champing his mouth, like a reined-in horse. Confound him! And we were staggering within ten feet of the bank. I had to lean right out to swing the heavy shutter, and I saw a face amongst the leaves on the level with my own, looking at me very fierce and steady; and then suddenly, as though a veil had been removed from my eyes, I made out, deep in the tangled gloom, naked breasts, arms, legs, glaring eyes — the bush was swarming with human limbs in movement, glistening, of bronze colour. The twigs shook, swayed, and rustled, the arrows flew out of them, and then the shutter came to. 'Steer her straight,' I said to the helmsman. He held his head rigid, face forward; but his eyes rolled, he kept on lifting and setting down his feet gently, his mouth foamed a little. 'Keep quiet!' I said in a fury. I might just as well have ordered a tree not to sway in the wind. I darted out. Below me there was a great scuffle of feet on the iron deck; confused exclamations; a voice screamed, 'Can you turn back?' I caught sight of a V-shaped ripple on the water ahead. What? Another snag! A fusillade burst out under my feet. The pilgrims had opened with their Winchesters, and were simply squirting lead into that bush. A deuce of a lot of smoke came up and drove slowly forward. I swore at it. Now I couldn't see the ripple or the snag either. I stood in the doorway, peering, and the arrows came in swarms. They might have been poisoned, but they looked as though they wouldn't kill a cat. The bush began to howl. Our woodcutters raised a warlike whoop; the report of a rifle just at my back deafened me. I glanced over my shoulder, and the pilot-house was yet full of noise and smoke when I made a dash at the wheel. The fool-nigger had dropped everything, to throw the shutter open and let off that Martini-Henry. He stood before the wide opening, glaring, and I yelled at him to come back, while I straightened the sudden twist out of that steamboat. There was no room to turn even if I had wanted to, the snag was somewhere very near ahead in that confounded smoke, there was no time to lose, so I just crowded her into the bank — right into the bank, where I knew the water was deep.

"We tore slowly along the overhanging bushes in a whirl of broken twigs and flying leaves. The fusillade below stopped short, as I had foreseen it would when the squirts got empty. I threw my head back to a glinting whiz that traversed the pilot-house, in at one shutter-hole and out at the other. Looking past that mad helmsman, who was shaking the empty rifle and yelling at the shore, I saw vague forms of men running bent double, leaping, gliding, distinct, incomplete, evanescent.

Something big appeared in the air before the shutter, the rifle went
overboard, and the man stepped back swiftly, looked at me over his
shoulder in an extraordinary, profound, familiar manner, and fell upon
my feet. The side of his head hit the wheel twice, and the end of what
appeared a long cane clattered round and knocked over a little camp-
stool. It looked as though after wrenching that thing from somebody
ashore he had lost his balance in the effort. The thin smoke had blown
away, we were clear of the snag, and looking ahead I could see that in
another hundred yards or so I would be free to sheer off, away from
the bank; but my feet felt so very warm and set that I had to look
down. The man had rolled on his back and stared straight up at me;
both his hands clutched that cane. It was the shaft of a spear that, either thrown or lunged through the opening, had caught him in the
side just below the ribs; the blade had gone in out of sight, after making a frightful gash; my shoes were full; a pool of blood lay very still,
gleaming dark-red under the wheel; his eyes shone with an amazing
lustre. The fusillade burst out again. He looked at me anxiously, grip-
ping the spear like something precious, with an air of being afraid I
would try to take it away from him. I had to make an effort to free my
eyes from his gaze and attend to the steering. With one hand I felt
above my head for the line of the steam whistle, and jerked out screech
after screech hurriedly. The tumult of angry and warlike yells was
checked instantly, and then from the depths of the woods went out
such a tremulous and prolonged wail of mournful fear and utter despair as may be imagined to follow the flight of the last hope from the
earth. There was a great commotion in the bush; the shower of arrows
stopped, a few dropping shots rang out sharply — then silence, in
which the languid beat of the sternwheel came plainly to my ears. I put
the helm hard a-starboard at the moment when the pilgrim in pink pyjamas, very hot and agitated, appeared in the doorway. 'The manager
sends me —— ' he began in an official tone, and stopped short. 'Good
God!' he said, glaring at the wounded man.

"We two whites stood over him, and his lustrous and inquiring
glance enveloped us both. I declare it looked as though he would
presently put to us some question in a understandable language; but
he died without uttering a sound, without moving a limb, without
twitching a muscle. Only in the very last moment, as though in response to some sign we could not see, to some whisper we could not
hear, he frowned heavily, and that frown gave to his black death-mask
an inconceivably sombre, brooding, and menacing expression. The
lustre of inquiring glance faded swiftly into vacant glassiness. 'Can you

steer?' I asked the agent eagerly. He looked very dubious; but I made a grab at his arm, and he understood at once I meant him to steer whether or no. To tell you the truth, I was morbidly anxious to change my shoes and socks. 'He is dead,' murmured the fellow, immensely impressed. 'No doubt about it,' said I, tugging like mad at the shoe-laces. 'And by the way, I suppose Mr. Kurtz is dead as well by this time.'

"For the moment that was the dominant thought. There was a sense of extreme disappointment, as though I had found out I had been striving after something altogether without a substance. I couldn't have been more disgusted if I had travelled all this way for the sole purpose of talking with Mr. Kurtz. Talking with . . . I flung one shoe overboard, and became aware that that was exactly what I had been looking forward to — a talk with Kurtz. I made the strange discovery that I had never imagined him as doing, you know, but as discoursing. I didn't say to myself, 'Now I will never see him' or 'Now I will never shake him by the hand,' but, 'Now I will never hear him.' The man presented himself as a voice. Not of course that I did not connect him with some sort of action. Hadn't I been told in all the tones of jealousy and admiration that he had collected, bartered, swindled, or stolen more ivory than all the other agents together? That was not the point. The point was in his being a gifted creature, and that of all his gifts the one that stood out preeminently, that carried with it a sense of real presence, was his ability to talk, his words — the gift of expression, the bewildering, the illuminating, the most exalted and the most contemptible, the pulsating stream of light, or the deceitful flow from the heart of an impenetrable darkness.

"The other shoe went flying unto the devil-god of that river. I thought, By Jove! it's all over. We are too late; he has vanished — the gift has vanished, by means of some spear, arrow, or club. I will never hear that chap speak after all — and my sorrow had a startling extravagance of emotion, even such as I had noticed in the howling sorrow of these savages in the bush. I couldn't have felt more of lonely desolation somehow, had I been robbed of a belief or had missed my destiny in life. . . . Why do you sigh in this beastly way, somebody? Absurd? Well, absurd. Good Lord! mustn't a man ever —— Here, give me some tobacco." . . .

There was a pause of profound stillness, then a match flared, and Marlow's lean face appeared, worn, hollow, with downward folds and dropped eyelids, with an aspect of concentrated attention; and as he took vigorous draws at his pipe, it seemed to retreat and advance out of the night in the regular flicker of the tiny flame. The match went out.

"Absurd!" he cried. "This is the worst of trying to tell . . . Here you all are, each moored with two good addresses, like a hulk with two anchors, a butcher round one corner, a policeman round another, excellent appetites, and temperature normal — you hear — normal from year's end to year's end. And you say, Absurd! Absurd be — exploded! Absurd! My dear boys, what can you expect from a man who out of sheer nervousness had just flung overboard a pair of new shoes? Now I think of it, it is amazing I did not shed tears. I am, upon the whole, proud of my fortitude. I was cut to the quick at the idea of having lost the inestimable privilege of listening to the gifted Kurtz. Of course I was wrong. The privilege was waiting for me. Oh yes, I heard more than enough. And I was right, too. A voice. He was very little more than a voice. And I heard — him — it — this voice — other voices — all of them were so little more than voices — and the memory of that time itself lingers around me, impalpable, like a dying vibration of one immense jabber, silly, atrocious, sordid, savage, or simply mean, without any kind of sense. Voices, voices — even the girl herself — now —— "

He went silent for a long time.

"I laid the ghost of his gifts at last with a lie," he began suddenly. "Girl! What? Did I mention a girl? Oh, she is out of it — completely. They — the women I mean — are out of it — should be out of it. We must help them to stay in that beautiful world of their own, lest ours gets worse. Oh, she had to be out of it. You should have heard the disinterred body of Mr. Kurtz saying, 'My Intended.' You would have perceived directly then how completely she was out of it. And the lofty frontal bone of Mr. Kurtz! They say the hair goes on growing sometimes, but this — ah — specimen was impressively bald. The wilderness had patted him on the head, and, behold, it was like a ball — an ivory ball; it had caressed him, and — lo! — he had withered; it had taken him, loved him, embraced him, got into his veins, consumed his flesh, and sealed his soul to its own by the inconceivable ceremonies of some devilish initiation. He was its spoiled and pampered favourite. Ivory? I should think so. Heaps of it, stacks of it. The old mud shanty was bursting with it. You would think there was not a single tusk left either above or below the ground in the whole country. 'Mostly fossil,' the manager had remarked disparagingly. It was no more fossil than I am; but they call it fossil when it is dug up. It appears these niggers do bury the tusks sometimes — but evidently they couldn't bury this parcel deep enough to save the gifted Mr. Kurtz from his fate. We filled the steamboat with it, and had to pile a lot on the deck. Thus he could see and enjoy as long as he could see, because the appreciation of this favour had remained with him to the last. You should have heard him say, 'My ivory.' Oh yes, I heard him. 'My Intended, my ivory, my station, my river, my —— ' everything belonged to him. It made me hold my breath in expectation of hearing the wilderness burst into a prodigious peal of laughter that would shake the fixed stars in their places. Everything belonged to him — but that was a trifle. The thing was to know what he belonged to, how many powers of darkness claimed him for their own. That was the reflection that made you creepy all over. It was impossible — it was not good for one either — trying to imagine. He had taken a high seat amongst the devils of the land — I mean literally. You can't understand. How could you? — with solid pavement under your feet, surrounded by kind neighbours ready to cheer you or to fall on you, stepping delicately between the butcher and the policeman, in the holy terror of scandal and gallows and lunatic asylums — how can you imagine what particular region of the first ages a man's untrammelled feet may take him into by the way of solitude — utter solitude without a policeman — by the way of silence — utter silence, where no warning voice of a kind neighbour can be heard whispering of public opinion? These little things make all the great difference. When they are gone you must fall back upon your own innate strength, upon your own capacity for faithfulness. Of course you may be too much of a fool to go wrong — too dull even to know you are being assaulted by the powers of darkness. I take it, no fool ever made a bargain for his soul with the devil: the fool is too much of a fool, or the devil too much of a devil — I don't know which. Or you may be such a thunderingly exalted creature as to be altogether deaf and blind to anything but heavenly sights and sounds. Then the earth for you is only a standing place — and whether to be like this is your loss or your gain I won't pretend to say. But most of us are neither one nor the other. The earth for us is a place to live in, where we must put up with sights, with sounds, with smells, too, by Jove! — breathe dead hippo, so to speak, and not be contaminated. And there, don't you see? your strength comes in, the faith in your ability for the digging of unostentatious holes to bury the stuff in — your power of devotion, not to yourself, but to an obscure, back-breaking business. And that's difficult enough. Mind, I am not trying to excuse or even explain — I am trying to account to myself for — for — Mr. Kurtz — for the shade of Mr. Kurtz. This initiated

wraith from the back of Nowhere honoured me with its amazing confidence before it vanished altogether. This was because it could speak
English to me. The original Kurtz had been educated partly in England, and — as he was good enough to say himself — his sympathies
were in the right place. His mother was half-English, his father was
half-French. All Europe contributed to the making of Kurtz; and by
and by I learned that, most appropriately, the International Society for
the Suppression of Savage Customs had entrusted him with the making of a report, for its future guidance. And he had written it too. I've
seen it. I've read it. It was eloquent, vibrating with eloquence, but too
high-strung, I think. Seventeen pages of close writing he had found
time for! But this must have been before his — let us say — nerves
went wrong, and caused him to preside at certain midnight dances
ending with unspeakable rites, which — as far as I reluctantly gathered from what I heard at various times — were offered up to him —
do you understand? — to Mr. Kurtz himself. But it was a beautiful
piece of writing. The opening paragraph, however, in the light of later
information, strikes me now as ominous. He began with the argument
that we whites, from the point of development we had arrived at,
'must necessarily appear to them [savages] in the nature of supernatural beings — we approach them with the might as of a deity,' and so
on, and so on. 'By the simple exercise of our will we can exert a power
for good practically unbounded,' etc. etc. From that point he soared
and took me with him. The peroration was magnificent, though difficult to remember, you know. It gave me the notion of an exotic Immensity ruled by an august Benevolence. It made me tingle with enthusiasm. This was the unbounded power of eloquence — of words —
of burning noble words. There were no practical hints to interrupt the
magic current of phrases, unless a kind of note at the foot of the last
page, scrawled evidently much later, in an unsteady hand, may be regarded as the exposition of a method. It was very simple, and at the
end of that moving appeal to every altruistic sentiment it blazed at
you, luminous and terrifying, like a flash of lightning in a serene sky:
'Exterminate all the brutes!' The curious part was that he had apparently forgotten all about that valuable postscriptum, because, later on,
when he in a sense came to himself, he repeatedly entreated me to take
good care of 'my pamphlet' (he called it), as it was sure to have in the
future a good influence upon his career. I had full information about
all these things, and, besides, as it turned out, I was to have the care of
his memory. I've done enough for it to give me the indisputable right
to lay it, if I choose, for an everlasting rest in the dust-bin of progress,

amongst all the sweepings and, figuratively speaking, all the dead cats of civilisation. But then, you see, I can't choose. He won't be forgotten. Whatever he was, he was not common. He had the power to charm or frighten rudimentary souls into an aggravated witch-dance in his honour; he could also fill the small souls of the pilgrims with bitter misgivings: he had one devoted friend at least, and he had conquered one soul in the world that was neither rudimentary nor tainted with self-seeking. No; I can't forget him, though I am not prepared to affirm the fellow was exactly worth the life we lost in getting to him. I missed my late helmsman awfully — I missed him even while his body was still lying in the pilot-house. Perhaps you will think it passing strange this regret for a savage who was no more account than a grain of sand in a black Sahara. Well, don't you see, he had done something, he had steered; for months I had him at my back — a help — an instrument. It was a kind of partnership. He steered for me — I had to look after him, I worried about his deficiencies, and thus a subtle bond had been created, of which I only became aware when it was suddenly broken. And the intimate profundity of that look he gave me when he received his hurt remains to this day in my memory — like a claim of distant kinship affirmed in a supreme moment.

"Poor fool! If he had only left that shutter alone. He had no restraint, no restraint — just like Kurtz — a tree swayed by the wind. As soon as I had put on a dry pair of slippers, I dragged him out, after first jerking the spear out of his side, which operation I confess I performed with my eyes shut tight. His heels leaped together over the little doorstep; his shoulders were pressed to my breast; I hugged him from behind desperately. Oh! he was heavy, heavy; heavier than any man on earth, I should imagine. Then without more ado I tipped him overboard. The current snatched him as though he had been a wisp of grass, and I saw the body roll over twice before I lost sight of it for ever. All the pilgrims and the manager were then congregated on the awning-deck about the pilot-house, chattering at each other like a flock of excited magpies, and there was a scandalised murmur at my heartless promptitude. What they wanted to keep that body hanging about for I can't guess. Embalm it, maybe. But I had also heard another, and a very ominous, murmur on the deck below. My friends the wood-cutters were likewise scandalised, and with a better show of reason — though I admit that the reason itself was quite inadmissible. Oh, quite! I had made up my mind that if my late helmsman was to be eaten, the fishes alone should have him. He had been a very second-rate helmsman while alive, but now he was dead he might have

become a first-class temptation, and possibly cause some startling
trouble. Besides, I was anxious to take the wheel, the man in pink pyjamas showing himself a hopeless duffer at the business.

"This I did directly the simple funeral was over. We were going
half-speed, keeping right in the middle of the stream, and I listened to
the talk about me. They had given up Kurtz, they had given up the
station; Kurtz was dead, and the station had been burnt — and so on,
and so on. The red-haired pilgrim was beside himself with the thought
that at least poor Kurtz had been properly revenged. 'Say! We must
have made a glorious slaughter of them in the bush. Eh? What do you
think? Say?' He positively danced, the bloodthirsty little gingery beg-
gar. And he had nearly fainted when he saw the wounded man! I
could not help saying, 'You made a glorious lot of smoke, anyhow.' I
had seen, from the way the tops of the bushes rustled and flew, that almost all the shots had gone too high. You can't hit anything unless
you take aim and fire from the shoulder; but these chaps fired from the
hip with their eyes shut. The retreat, I maintained — and I was
right — was caused by the screeching of the steam-whistle. Upon this
they forgot Kurtz, and began to howl at me with indignant protests.

"The manager stood by the wheel murmuring confidentially about
the necessity of getting well away down the river before dark at all
events, when I saw in the distance a clearing on the river-side and the
outlines of some sort of building. 'What's this?' I asked. He clapped
his hands in wonder. 'The station!' he cried. I edged in at once, still
going half-speed.

"Through my glasses I saw the slope of a hill interspersed with rare
trees and perfectly free from undergrowth. A long decaying building
on the summit was half buried in the high grass; the large holes in the
peaked roof gaped black from afar; the jungle and the woods made a
background. There was no enclosure or fence of any kind; but there
had been one apparently, for near the house half a dozen slim posts remained in a row, roughly trimmed, and with their upper ends orna-
mented with round carved balls. The rails, or whatever there had been
between, had disappeared. Of course the forest surrounded all that.
The river-bank was clear, and on the water side I saw a white man
under a hat like a cart-wheel beckoning persistently with his whole
arm. Examining the edge of the forest above and below, I was almost
certain I could see movements — human forms gliding here and there.
I steamed past prudently, then stopped the engines and let her drift
down. The man on the shore began to shout, urging us to land. 'We
have been attacked,' screamed the manager. 'I know — I know. It's all

right,' yelled back the other, as cheerful as you please. 'Come along.
It's all right. I am glad.'

"His aspect reminded me of something I had seen — something
funny I had seen somewhere, As I manœuvred to get alongside, I was
asking myself, 'What does this fellow look like?' Suddenly I got it. He
looked like a harlequin. His clothes had been made of some stuff that
was brown holland probably, but it was covered with patches all over,
with bright patches, blue, red, and yellow — patches on the back,
patches on the front, patches on elbows, on knees; coloured binding
round his jacket, scarlet edging at the bottom of his trousers; and the
sunshine made him look extremely gay and wonderfully neat withal,
because you could see how beautifully all this patching had been done.
A beardless, boyish face, very fair, no features to speak of, nose peel-
ing, little blue eyes, smiles and frowns chasing each other over that
open countenance like sunshine and shadow on a wind-swept plain.
'Look out, captain!' he cried; 'there's a snag lodged in here last night.'
What! Another snag? I confess I swore shamefully. I had nearly holed
my cripple, to finish off that charming trip. The harlequin on the bank
turned his little pug-nose up to me. 'You English?' he asked, all smiles.
'Are you?' I shouted from the wheel. The smiles vanished, and he
shook his head as if sorry for my disappointment. Then he brightened
up. 'Never mind!' he cried encouragingly. 'Are we in time?' I asked.
'He is up there,' he replied, with a toss of the head up the hill, and becoming gloomy all of a sudden. His face was like the autumn sky,
overcast one moment and bright the next.

"When the manager, escorted by the pilgrims, all of them armed
to the teeth, had gone to the house, this chap came on board. 'I say, I
don't like this. These natives are in the bush,' I said. He assured me
earnestly it was all right. 'They are simple people,' he added; 'well, I
am glad you came. It took me all my time to keep them off.' 'But you
said it was all right,' I cried. 'Oh, they meant no harm,' he said; and as
I stared he corrected himself, 'Not exactly.' Then vivaciously, 'My
faith, your pilot-house wants a clean-up!' In the next breath he advised
me to keep enough steam on the boiler to blow the whistle in case of
any trouble. 'One good screech will do more for you than all your
rifles. They are simple people,' he repeated. He rattled away at such a
rate he quite overwhelmed me. He seemed to be trying to make up for
lots of silence, and actually hinted, laughing, that such was the case.
'Don't you talk with Mr. Kurtz?' I said. 'You don't talk with that
man — you listen to him,' he exclaimed with severe exaltation. 'But
now —— ' He waved his arm, and in the twinkling of an eye was in

the uttermost depths of despondency. In a moment he came up again with a jump, possessed himself of both my hands, shook them continuously, while he gabbled: 'Brother sailor . . . honour . . . pleasure . . . delight . . . introduce myself . . . Russian . . . son of an archpriest . . . Government of Tambov . . . What? Tobacco! English tobacco; the excellent English tobacco! Now, that's brotherly. Smoke? Where's a sailor that does not smoke?'

"The pipe soothed him, and gradually I made out he had run away from school, had gone to sea in a Russian ship; ran away again; served some time in English ships; was now reconciled with the arch-priest. He made a point of that. 'But when one is young one must see things, gather experience, ideas; enlarge the mind.' 'Here!' I interrupted. 'You can never tell! Here I met Mr. Kurtz,' he said, youthfully solemn and reproachful. I held my tongue after that. It appears he had persuaded a Dutch trading-house on the coast to fit him out with stores and goods, and had started for the interior with a light heart, and no more idea of what would happen to him than a baby. He had been wandering about that river for nearly two years alone, cut off from everybody and everything. 'I am not so young as I look. I am twenty-five,' he said. 'At first old Van Shuyten would tell me to go to the devil,' he narrated with keen enjoyment; 'but I stuck to him, and talked and talked, till at last he got afraid I would talk the hind-leg off his favourite dog, so he gave me some cheap things and a few guns, and told me he hoped he would never see my face again. Good old Dutchman, Van Shuyten. I sent him one small lot of ivory a year ago, so that he can't call me a little thief when I get back. I hope he got it. And for the rest, I don't care. I had some wood stacked for you. That was my old house. Did you see?'

"I gave him Towson's book. He made as though he would kiss me, but restrained himself. 'The only book I had left, and I thought I had lost it,' he said, looking at it ecstatically. 'So many accidents happen to a man going about alone, you know. Canoes get upset sometimes — and sometimes you've got to clear out so quick when the people get angry.' He thumbed the pages. 'You made notes in Russian?' I asked. He nodded. 'I thought they were written in cipher,' I said. He laughed, then became serious. 'I had lots of trouble to keep these people off,' he said. 'Did they want to kill you?' I asked. 'Oh no!' he cried, and checked himself. 'Why did they attack us?' I pursued. He hesitated, then said shamefacedly, 'They don't want him to go.' 'Don't they?' I said curiously. He nodded a nod full of mystery and wisdom. 'I tell you,' he cried, 'this man has enlarged my mind.'

He opened his arms wide, staring at me with his little blue eyes that were perfectly round."

III

"I looked at him, lost in astonishment. There he was before me, in motley, as though he had absconded from a troupe of mimes, enthusiastic, fabulous. His very existence was improbable, inexplicable, and altogether bewildering. He was an insoluble problem. It was inconceivable how he had existed, how he had succeeded in getting so far, how he had managed to remain — why he did not instantly disappear. 'I went a little farther,' he said, 'then still a little farther — till I had gone so far that I don't know how I'll ever get back. Never mind. Plenty time. I can manage. You take Kurtz away quick — quick — I tell you.' The glamour of youth enveloped his parti-coloured rags, his destitution, his loneliness, the essential desolation of his futile wanderings. For months — for years - his life hadn't been worth a day's purchase; and there he was gallantly, thoughtlessly alive, to all appearance indestructible solely by the virtue of his few years and of his unreflecting audacity. I was seduced into something like admiration — like envy. Glamour urged him on, glamour kept him unscathed. He surely wanted nothing from the wilderness but space to breathe in and to push on through. His need was to exist, and to move onwards at the greatest possible risk, and with a maximum of privation. If the absolutely pure, uncalculating, unpractical spirit of adventure had ever ruled a human being, it ruled this be-patched youth. I almost envied him the possession of this modest and clear flame. It seemed to have consumed all thought of self so completely, that, even while he was talking to you, you forgot that it was he — the man before your eyes — who had gone through these things. I did not envy him his devotion to Kurtz, though. He had not meditated over it. It came to him, and he accepted it with a sort of eager fatalism. I must say that to me it appeared about the most dangerous thing in every way he had come upon so far.

"They had come together unavoidably, like two ships becalmed near each other, and lay rubbing sides at last. I suppose Kurtz wanted an audience, because on a certain occasion, when encamped in the forest, they had talked all night, or more probably Kurtz had talked. 'We talked of everything,' he said, quite transported at the recollection. 'I forgot there was such a thing as sleep. The night did not seem to last an hour. Everything! Everything! . . . Of love too.' 'Ah, he talked to

you of love!' I said, much amused. 'It isn't what you think,' he cried,
almost passionately. 'It was in general. He made me see things —
things.'

"He threw his arms up. We were on deck at the time, and the
head-man of my wood-cutters, lounging near by, turned upon him his
heavy and glittering eyes. I looked around, and I don't know why, but
I assure you that never, never before, did this land, this river, this
jungle, the very arch of this blazing sky, appear to me so hopeless and
so dark, so impenetrable to human thought, so pitiless to human
weakness. 'And, ever since, you have been with him, of course?' I said.

"On the contrary. It appears their intercourse had been very much
broken by various causes. He had, as he informed me proudly, managed to nurse Kurtz through two illnesses (he alluded to it as you
would to some risky feat), but as a rule Kurtz wandered alone, far in
the depths of the forest. 'Very often coming to this station, I had to
wait days and days before he would turn up,' he said. 'Ah, it was worth
waiting for! — sometimes.' 'What was he doing? exploring or what?' I
asked. 'Oh yes, of course'; he had discovered lots of villages, a lake
too — he did not know exactly in what direction; it was dangerous to
inquire too much — but mostly his expeditions had been for ivory.
'But he had no goods to trade with by that time,' I objected. 'There's
a good lot of cartridges left even yet,' he answered, looking away. 'To
speak plainly, he raided the country,' I said. He nodded. 'Not alone,
surely!' He muttered something about the villages round that lake.
'Kurtz got the tribe to follow him, did he?' I suggested. He fidgeted a
little. 'They adored him,' he said. The tone of these words was so extraordinary that I looked at him searchingly. It was curious to see his
mingled eagerness and reluctance to speak of Kurtz. The man filled his
life, occupied his thoughts, swayed his emotions. 'What can you expect?' he burst out; 'he came to them with thunder and lightning, you
know — and they had never seen anything like it — and very terrible.
He could be very terrible. You can't judge Mr. Kurtz as you would an
ordinary man. No, no, no! Now — just to give you an idea — I don't
mind telling you, he wanted to shoot me too one day — but I don't
judge him.' 'Shoot you!' I cried. 'What for?' 'Well, I had a small lot of
ivory the chief of that village near my house gave me. You see I used
to shoot game for them. Well, he wanted it, and wouldn't hear reason.
He declared he would shoot me unless I gave him the ivory and then
cleared out of the country, because he could do so, and had a fancy for
it, and there was nothing on earth to prevent him killing whom he
jolly well pleased. And it was true too. I gave him the ivory. What did I

care! But I didn't clear out. No, no. I couldn't leave him. I had to be careful, of course, till we got friendly again for a time. He had his second illness then. Afterwards I had to keep out of the way; but I didn't mind. He was living for the most part in those villages on the lake. When he came down to the river, sometimes he would take to me, and sometimes it was better for me to be careful. This man suffered too much. He hated all this, and somehow he couldn't get away. When I had a chance I begged him to try and leave while there was time; I offered to go back with him. And he would say yes, and then he would remain; go off on another ivory hunt; disappear for weeks; forget himself amongst these people — forget himself — you know.' 'Why! he's mad,' I said. He protested indignantly. Mr. Kurtz couldn't be mad. If I had heard him talk, only two days ago, I wouldn't dare hint at such a thing. . . . I had taken up my binoculars while we talked, and was looking at the shore, sweeping the limit of the forest at each side and at the back of the house. The consciousness of there being people in that bush, so silent, so quiet — as silent and quiet as the ruined house on the hill — made me uneasy. There was no sign on the face of nature of this amazing tale that was not so much told as suggested to me in desolate exclamations, completed by shrugs, in interrupted phrases, in hints ending in deep sighs. The woods were unmoved, like a mask — heavy, like the closed door of a prison — they looked with their air of hidden knowledge, of patient expectation, of unapproachable silence. The Russian was explaining to me that it was only lately that Mr. Kurtz had come down to the river, bringing along with him all the fighting men of that lake tribe. He had been absent for several months — getting himself adored, I suppose — and had come down unexpectedly, with the intention to all appearance of making a raid either across the river or down stream. Evidently the appetite for more ivory had got the better of the — what shall I say? — less material aspirations. However, he had got much worse suddenly. 'I heard he was lying helpless, and so I came up — took my chance,' said the Russian. 'Oh, he is bad, very bad.' I directed my glass to the house. There were no signs of life, but there were the ruined roof, the long mud wall peeping above the grass, with three little square window-holes, no two of the same size; all this brought within reach of my hand, as it were. And then I made a brusque movement, and one of the remaining posts of that vanished fence leaped up in the field of my glass. You remember I told you I had been struck at the distance by certain attempts at ornamentation, rather remarkable in the ruinous aspect of the place. Now I had suddenly a nearer view, and its first result was to make me throw my head back as if before a blow. Then I went carefully from post to post with my glass, and I saw my mistake. These round knobs were not ornamental but symbolic; they were expressive and puzzling, striking and disturbing — food for thought and also for vultures if there had been any looking down from the sky; but at all events for such ants as were industrious enough to ascend the pole. They would have been even more impressive, those heads on the stakes, if their faces had not been turned to the house. Only one, the first I had made out, was facing my way. I was not so shocked as you may think. The start back I had given was really nothing but a movement of surprise. I had expected to see a knob of wood there, you know. I returned deliberately to the first I had seen — and there it was, black, dried, sunken, with closed eyelids — a head that seemed to sleep at the top of that pole, and, with the shrunken dry lips showing a narrow white line of the teeth, was smiling too, smiling continuously at some endless and jocose dream of that eternal slumber.

"I am not disclosing any trade secrets. In fact the manager said afterwards that Mr. Kurtz's methods had ruined the district. I have no opinion on that point, but I want you clearly to understand that there was nothing exactly profitable in these heads being there. They only showed that Mr. Kurtz lacked restraint in the gratification of his various lusts, that there was something wanting in him — some small matter which, when the pressing need arose, could not be found under his magnificent eloquence. Whether he knew of this deficiency himself I can't say. I think the knowledge came to him at last — only at the very last. But the wilderness had found him out early, and had taken on him a terrible vengeance for the fantastic invasion. I think it had whispered to him things about himself which he did not know, things of which he had no conception till he took counsel with this great solitude — and the whisper had proved irresistibly fascinating. It echoed loudly within him because he was hollow at the core. . . . I put down the glass, and the head that had appeared near enough to be spoken to seemed at once to have leaped away from me into inaccessible distance.

"The admirer of Mr. Kurtz was a bit crestfallen. In a hurried, indistinct voice he began to assure me he had not dared to take these — say, symbols — down. He was not afraid of the natives; they would not stir till Mr. Kurtz gave the word. His ascendancy was extraordinary. The camps of these people surrounded the place, and the chiefs came every day to see him. They would crawl . . . 'I don't want to know anything of the ceremonies used when approaching Mr. Kurtz,'

I shouted. Curious, this feeling that came over me that such details would be more intolerable than those heads drying on the stakes under Mr. Kurtz's windows. After all, that was only a savage sight, while I seemed at one bound to have been transported into some lightless region of subtle horrors, where pure, uncomplicated savagery was a positive relief, being something that had a right to exist — obviously — in the sunshine. The young man looked at me with surprise. I suppose it did not occur to him that Mr. Kurtz was no idol of mine. He forgot I hadn't heard any of these splendid monologues on, what was it? on love, justice, conduct of life — or what not. If it had come to crawling before Mr. Kurtz, he crawled as much as the veriest savage of them all. I had no idea of the conditions, he said: these heads were the heads of rebels. I shocked him excessively by laughing. Rebels! What would be the next definition I was to hear? There had been enemies, criminals, workers — and these were rebels. Those rebellious heads looked very subdued to me on their sticks. 'You don't know how such a life tries a man like Kurtz,' cried Kurtz's last disciple. 'Well, and you?' I said. 'I! I! I am a simple man. I have no great thoughts. I want nothing from anybody. How can you compare me to . . . ?' His feelings were too much for speech, and suddenly he broke down. 'I don't understand,' he groaned. 'I've been doing my best to keep him alive, and that's enough. I had no hand in all this. I have no abilities. There hasn't been a drop of medicine or a mouthful of invalid food for months here. He was shamefully abandoned. A man like this, with such ideas. Shamefully! Shamefully! I — I — haven't slept for the last ten nights. . . .'

"His voice lost itself in the calm of the evening. The long shadows of the forests had slipped downhill while we talked, had gone far beyond the ruined hovel, beyond the symbolic row of stakes. All this was in the gloom, while we down there were yet in the sunshine, and the stretch of the river abreast of the clearing glittered in a still and dazzling splendour, with a murky and overshadowed bend above and below. Not a living soul was seen on the shore. The bushes did not rustle.

"Suddenly round the corner of the house a group of men appeared, as though they had come up from the ground. They waded waist-deep in the grass, in a compact body, bearing an improvised stretcher in their midst. Instantly, in the emptiness of the landscape, a cry arose whose shrillness pierced the still air like a sharp arrow flying straight to the very heart of the land; and, as if by enchantment, streams of human beings — of naked human beings — with spears in their hands, with bows, with shields, with wild glances and savage movements, were poured into the clearing by the dark-faced and pensive forest. The bushes shook, the grass swayed for a time, and then everything stood still in attentive immobility.

"'Now, if he does not say the right thing to them we are all done for,' said the Russian at my elbow. The knot of men with the stretcher had stopped too, half-way to the steamer, as if petrified. I saw the man on the stretcher sit up, lank and with an uplifted arm, above the shoulders of the bearers. 'Let us hope that the man who can talk so well of love in general will find some particular reason to spare us this time,' I said. I resented bitterly the absurd danger of our situation, as if to be at the mercy of that atrocious phantom had been a dishonouring necessity. I could not hear a sound, but through my glasses I saw the thin arm extended commandingly, the lower jaw moving, the eyes of that apparition shining darkly far in its bony head that nodded with grotesque jerks. Kurtz — Kirtz — that means 'short' in German — don't it? Well, the name was as true as everything else in his life — and death. He looked at least seven feet long. His covering had fallen off, and his body emerged from it pitiful and appalling as from a winding-sheet. I could see the cage of his ribs all astir, the bones of his arm waving. It was as though an animated image of death carved out of old ivory had been shaking its hand with menaces at a motionless crowd of men made of dark and glittering bronze. I saw him open his mouth wide — it gave him a weirdly voracious aspect, as though he had wanted to swallow all the air, all the earth, all the men before him. A deep voice reached me faintly. He must have been shouting. He fell back suddenly. The stretcher shook as the bearers staggered forward again, and almost at the same time I noticed that the crowd of savages was vanishing without any perceptible movement of retreat, as if the forest that had ejected these beings so suddenly had drawn them in again as the breath is drawn in a long aspiration.

"Some of the pilgrims behind the stretcher carried his arms — two shot-guns, a heavy rifle, and a light revolver-carbine — the thunderbolts of that pitiful Jupiter. The manager bent over him murmuring as he walked beside his head. They laid him down in one of the little cabins — just a room for a bed-place and a camp-stool or two, you know. We had brought his belated correspondence, and a lot of torn envelopes and open letters littered his bed. His hand roamed feebly amongst these papers. I was struck by the fire of his eyes and the composed languor of his expression. It was not so much the exhaustion of disease. He did not seem in pain. This shadow looked satiated and calm, as though for the moment it had had its fill of all the emotions.

"He rustled one of the letters, and looking straight in my face said, 'I am glad.' Somebody had been writing to him about me. These special recommendations were turning up again. The volume of tone he emitted without effort, almost without the trouble of moving his lips, amazed me. A voice! a voice! It was grave, profound, vibrating, while the man did not seem capable of a whisper. However, he had enough strength in him — factitious no doubt — to very nearly make an end of us, as you shall hear directly.

"The manager appeared silently in the doorway; I stepped out at once and he drew the curtain after me. The Russian, eyed curiously by the pilgrims, was staring at the shore. I followed the direction of his glance.

"Dark human shapes could be made out in the distance, flitting indistinctly against the gloomy border of the forest, and near the river two bronze figures, leaning on tall spears, stood in the sunlight under fantastic head-dresses of spotted skins, warlike and still in statuesque repose. And from right to left along the lighted shore moved a wild and gorgeous apparition of a woman.

"She walked with measured steps, draped in striped and fringed cloths, treading the earth proudly, with a slight jingle and flash of barbarous ornaments. She carried her head high; her hair was done in the shape of a helmet; she had brass leggings to the knee, brass wire gauntlets to the elbow, a crimson spot on her tawny cheek, innumerable necklaces of glass beads on her neck; bizarre things, charms, gifts of witch-men, that hung about her, glittered and trembled at every step. She must have had the value of several elephant tusks upon her. She was savage and superb, wild-eyed and magnificent; there was something ominous and stately in her deliberate progress. And in the hush that had fallen suddenly upon the whole sorrowful land, the immense wilderness, the colossal body of the fecund and mysterious life seemed to look at her, pensive, as though it has been looking at the image of its own tenebrous and passionate soul.

"She came abreast of the steamer, stood still, and faced us. Her long shadow fell to the water's edge. Her face had a tragic and fierce aspect of wild sorrow and of dumb pain mingled with the fear of some struggling, half-shaped resolve. She stood looking at us without a stir, and like the wilderness itself, with an air of brooding over an inscrutable purpose. A whole minute passed, and then she made a step forward. There was a low jingle, a glint of yellow metal, a sway of fringed draperies, and she stopped as if her heart had failed her. The young fellow by my side growled. The pilgrims murmured at my back.

She looked at us all as if her life had depended upon the unswerving steadiness of her glance. Suddenly she opened her bared arms and threw them up rigid above her head, as though in an uncontrollable desire to touch the sky, and at the same time the swift shadows darted out on the earth, swept around on the river, gathering the steamer in a shadowy embrace. A formidable silence hung over the scene.

"She turned away slowly, walked on, following the bank, and passed into the bushes to the left. Once only her eyes gleamed back at us in the dusk of the thickets before she disappeared.

"'If she had offered to come aboard I really think I would have tried to shoot her,' said the man of patches nervously. 'I had been risking my life every day for the last fortnight to keep her out of the house. She got in one day and kicked up a row about those miserable rags I picked up in the storeroom to mend my clothes with. I wasn't decent. At least it must have been that, for she talked like a fury to Kurtz for an hour, pointing at me now and then. I don't understand the dialect of this tribe. Luckily for me, I fancy Kurtz felt too ill that day to care, or there would have been mischief. I don't understand. . . . No — it's too much for me. Ah, well, it's all over now.'

"At this moment I heard Kurtz's deep voice behind the curtain: 'Save me! — save the ivory, you mean. Don't tell me. Save *me!* Why, I've had to save you. You are interrupting my plans now. Sick! Sick! Not so sick as you would like to believe. Never mind. I'll carry my ideas out yet — I will return. I'll show you what can be done. You with your little peddling notions — you are interfering with me. I will return. I . . . '

"The manager came out. He did me the honour to take me under the arm and lead me aside. 'He is very low, very low,' he said. He considered it necessary to sigh, but neglected to be consistently sorrowful. 'We have done all we could for him — haven't we? But there is no disguising the fact, Mr. Kurtz has done more harm than good to the Company. He did not see the time was not ripe for vigorous action. Cautiously, cautiously — that's my principle. We must be cautious yet. The district is closed to us for a time. Deplorable! Upon the whole, the trade will suffer. I don't deny there is a remarkable quantity of ivory — mostly fossil. We must save it, at all events — but look how precarious the position is — and why? Because the method is unsound.' 'Do you,' said I, looking at the shore, 'call it "unsound method"?' 'Without doubt,' he exclaimed hotly. 'Don't you?' . . . 'No method at all,' I murmured after a while. 'Exactly,' he exulted. 'I anticipated this. Shows a complete want of judgment. It is my duty to point it out in the proper quarter.' 'Oh,' said I, 'that fellow — what's his name? — the brickmaker, will make a readable report for you.' He appeared confounded for a moment. It seemed to me I had never breathed an atmosphere so vile, and I turned mentally to Kurtz for relief — positively for relief. 'Nevertheless, I think Mr. Kurtz is a remarkable man,' I said with emphasis. He started, dropped on me a cold heavy glance, said very quietly, 'He *was*,' and turned his back on me. My hour of favour was over; I found myself lumped along with Kurtz as a partisan of methods for which the time was not ripe: I was unsound! Ah! but it was something to have at least a choice of nightmares.

"I had turned to the wilderness really, not to Mr. Kurtz, who, I was ready to admit, was as good as buried. And for a moment it seemed to me as if I also were buried in a vast grave full of unspeakable secrets. I felt an intolerable weight oppressing my breast, the smell of the damp earth, the unseen presence of victorious corruption, the darkness of an impenetrable night. . . . The Russian tapped me on the shoulder. I heard him mumbling and stammering something about 'brother seaman — couldn't conceal — knowledge of matters that would affect Mr. Kurtz's reputation.' I waited. For him evidently Mr. Kurtz was not in his grave; I suspect that for him Mr. Kurtz was one of the immortals. 'Well!' said I at last, 'speak out. As it happens, I am Mr. Kurtz's friend — in a way.'

"He stated with a good deal of formality that had we not been 'of the same profession,' he would have kept the matter to himself without regard to consequences. He suspected 'there was an active ill-will towards him on the part of these white men that —— ' 'You are right,' I said, remembering a certain conversation I had overheard. 'The manager thinks you ought to be hanged.' He showed a concern at this intelligence which amused me at first. 'I had better get out of the way quietly,' he said earnestly. 'I can do no more for Kurtz now, and they would soon find some excuse. What's to stop them? There's a military post three hundred miles from here.' 'Well, upon my word,' said I, 'perhaps you had better go if you have any friends amongst the savages near by.' 'Plenty,' he said. 'They are simple people — and I want nothing, you know.' He stood biting his lip, then: 'I don't want any harm to happen to these whites here, but of course I was thinking of Mr. Kurtz's reputation — but you are a brother seaman and —— ' 'All right,' said I, after a time. 'Mr. Kurtz's reputation is safe with me.' I did not know how truly I spoke.

"He informed me, lowering his voice, that it was Kurtz who had ordered the attack to be made on the steamer. 'He hated sometimes the idea of being taken away — and then again . . . But I don't understand these matters. I am a simple man. He thought it would scare you away — that you would give it up, thinking him dead. I could not stop him. Oh, I had an awful time of it this last month.' 'Very well,' I said. 'He is all right now.' 'Y-e-e-es,' he muttered, not very convinced apparently. 'Thanks,' said I; 'I shall keep my eyes open.' 'But quiet — eh?' he urged anxiously. 'It would be awful for his reputation if anybody here —— ' I promised a complete discretion with great gravity. 'I have a canoe and three black fellows waiting not very far. I am off. Could you give me a few Martini-Henry cartridges?' I could, and did, with proper secrecy. He helped himself, with a wink at me, to a handful of my tobacco. 'Between sailors — you know — good English tobacco.' At the door of the pilot-house he turned round — 'I say, haven't you a pair of shoes you could spare?' He raised one leg. 'Look.' The soles were tied with knotted strings sandal-wise under his bare feet. I rooted out an old pair, at which he looked with admiration before tucking it under his left arm. One of his pockets (bright red) was bulging with cartridges, from the other (dark blue) peeped 'Towson's Inquiry,' etc. etc. He seemed to think himself excellently well equipped for a renewed encounter with the wilderness. 'Ah! I'll never, never meet such a man again. You ought to have heard him recite poetry — his own too it was, he told me. Poetry!' He rolled his eyes at the recollection of these delights. 'Oh, he enlarged my mind!' 'Goodbye,' said I. He shook hands and vanished in the night. Sometimes I ask myself whether I had ever really seen him — whether it was possible to meet such a phenomenon! . . .

"When I woke up shortly after midnight his warning came to my mind with its hint of danger that seemed, in the starred darkness, real enough to make me get up for the purpose of having a look round. On the hill a big fire burned, illuminating fitfully a crooked corner of the station-house. One of the agents with a picket of a few of our blacks, armed for the purpose, was keeping guard over the ivory; but deep within the forest, red gleams that wavered, that seemed to sink and rise from the ground amongst confused columnar shapes of intense blackness, showed the exact position of the camp where Mr. Kurtz's adorers were keeping their uneasy vigil. The monotonous beating of a big drum filled the air with muffled shocks and a lingering vibration. A steady droning sound of many men chanting each to himself some weird incantation came out from the black, flat wall of the woods as the humming of bees comes out of a hive, and had a strange narcotic effect upon my half-awake senses. I believe I dozed off leaning over the rail, till an abrupt burst of yells, an overwhelming outbreak of a pent-up and mysterious frenzy, woke me up in a bewildered wonder. It was cut short all at once, and the low droning went on with an effect of audible and soothing silence. I glanced casually into the little cabin. A light was burning within, but Mr. Kurtz was not there.

"I think I would have raised an outcry if I had believed my eyes. But I didn't believe them at first — the thing seemed so impossible. The fact is, I was completely unnerved by a sheer blank fright, pure abstract terror, unconnected with any distinct shape of physical danger. What made this emotion so overpowering was — how shall I define it? — the moral shock I received, as if something altogether monstrous, intolerable to thought and odious to the soul, had been thrust upon me unexpectedly. This lasted of course the merest fraction of a second, and then the usual sense of commonplace, deadly danger, the possibility of a sudden onslaught and massacre, or something of the kind, which I saw impending, was positively welcome and composing. It pacified me, in fact, so much, that I did not raise an alarm.

"There was an agent buttoned up inside an ulster and sleeping on a chair on deck within three feet of me. The yells had not awakened him; he snored very slightly; I left him to his slumbers and leaped ashore. I did not betray Mr. Kurtz — It was ordered I should never betray him — it was written I should be loyal to the nightmare of my choice. I was anxious to deal with this shadow by myself alone — and to this day I don't know why I was so jealous of sharing with any one the peculiar blackness of that experience.

"As soon as I got on the bank I saw a trail — a broad trail through the grass. I remember the exultation with which I said to myself, 'He can't walk — he is crawling on all-fours — I've got him.' The grass was wet with dew. I strode rapidly with clenched fists. I fancy I had some vague notion of falling upon him and giving him a drubbing. I don't know. I had some imbecile thoughts. The knitting old woman with the cat obtruded herself upon my memory as a most improper person to be sitting at the other end of such an affair. I saw a row of pilgrims squirting lead in the air out of Winchesters held to the hip. I thought I would never get back to the steamer, and imagined myself living alone and unarmed in the woods to an advanced age. Such silly things — you know. And I remember I confounded the beat of the drum with the beating of my heart, and was pleased at its calm regularity.

"I kept to the track though — then stopped to listen. The night was very clear; a dark blue space, sparkling with dew and starlight, in which black things stood very still. I thought I could see a kind of motion ahead of me. I was strangely cocksure of everything that night. I actually left the track and ran in a wide semicircle (I verily believe chuckling to myself) so as to get in front of that stir, of that motion I had seen — if indeed I had seen anything. I was circumventing Kurtz as though it had been a boyish game.

"I came upon him, and, if he had not heard me coming, I would have fallen over him too, but he got up in time. He rose, unsteady, long, pale, indistinct, like a vapour exhaled by the earth, and swayed slightly, misty and silent before me; while at my back the fires loomed between the trees, and the murmur of many voices issued from the forest. I had cut him off cleverly; but when actually confronting him I seemed to come to my senses, I saw the danger in its right proportion. It was by no means over yet. Suppose he began to shout? Though he could hardly stand, there was still plenty of vigour in his voice. 'Go away — hide yourself,' he said, in that profound tone. It was very awful. I glanced back. We were within thirty yards from the nearest fire. A black figure stood up, strode on long black legs, waving long black arms, across the glow. It had horns — antelope horns, I think — on its head. Some sorcerer, some witch-man, no doubt: it looked fiend-like enough. 'Do you know what you are doing?' I whispered. 'Perfectly,' he answered, raising his voice for that single word: it sounded to me far off and yet loud, like a hail through a speaking-trumpet. If he makes a row we are lost, I thought to myself. This clearly was not a case for fisticuffs, even apart from the very natural aversion I had to beat that Shadow — this wandering and tormented thing. 'You will be lost,' I said — 'utterly lost.' One gets sometimes such a flash of inspiration, you know. I did say the right thing, though indeed he could not have been more irretrievably lost than he was at this very moment, when the foundations of our intimacy were being laid — to endure — to endure — even to the end — even beyond.

"'I had immense plans,' he muttered irresolutely. 'Yes,' said I; 'but if you try to shout I'll smash your head with —— ' There was not a stick or a stone near. 'I will throttle you for good,' I corrected myself. 'I was on the threshold of great things,' he pleaded, in a voice of longing, with a wistfulness of tone that made my blood run cold. 'And now for this stupid scoundrel —— ' 'Your success in Europe is assured in any case,' I affirmed steadily. I did not want to have the throttling of him, you understand — and indeed it would have been very little use for any practical purpose. I tried to break the spell — the heavy, mute spell of the wilderness — that seemed to draw him to its pitiless breast by the awakening of forgotten and brutal instincts, by the memory of gratified and monstrous passions. This alone, I was convinced, had driven him out to the edge of the forest, to the bush, towards the gleam of fires, the throb of drums, the drone of weird incantations; this alone had beguiled his unlawful soul beyond the bounds of permitted aspirations. And, don't you see, the terror of the position was not in being knocked on the head — though I had a very lively sense of that danger too — but in this, that I had to deal with a being to whom I could not appeal in the name of anything high or low. I had, even like the niggers, to invoke him — himself — his own exalted and incredible degradation. There was nothing either above or below him, and I knew it. He had kicked himself loose of the earth. Confound the man! he had kicked the very earth to pieces. He was alone, and I before him did not know whether I stood on the ground or floated in the air. I've been telling you what we said — repeating the phrases we pronounced — but what's the good? They were common everyday words — the familiar, vague sounds exchanged on every waking day of life. But what of that? They had behind them, to my mind, the terrific suggestiveness of words heard in dreams, of phrases spoken in nightmares. Soul! If anybody had ever struggled with a soul, I am the man. And I wasn't arguing with a lunatic either. Believe me or not, his intelligence was perfectly clear — concentrated, it is true, upon himself with horrible intensity, yet clear; and therein was my only chance — barring, of course, the killing him there and then, which wasn't so good, on account of unavoidable noise. But his soul was mad. Being alone in the wilderness, it had looked within itself, and, by Heavens! I tell you, it had gone mad. I had — for my sins, I suppose, to go through the ordeal of looking into it myself. No eloquence could have been so withering to one's belief in mankind as his final burst of sincerity. He struggled with himself too. I saw it — I heard it. I saw the inconceivable mystery of a soul that knew no restraint, no faith, and no fear, yet struggling blindly with itself. I kept my head pretty well; but when I had him at last stretched on the couch, I wiped my forehead, while my legs shook under me as though I had carried half a ton on my back down that hill. And yet I had only supported him, his bony arm clasped round my neck — and he was not much heavier than a child.

"When next day we left at noon, the crowd, of whose presence behind the curtain of trees I had been acutely conscious all the time, flowed out of the woods again, filled the clearing, covered the slope with a mass of naked, breathing, quivering, bronze bodies. I steamed up a bit, then swung downstream, and two thousand eyes followed the evolutions of the splashing, thumping, fierce river-demon beating the water with its terrible tail and breathing black smoke into the air. In front of the first rank, along the river, three men, plastered with bright red earth from head to foot, strutted to and fro restlessly. When we came abreast again, they faced the river, stamped their feet, nodded their horned heads, swayed their scarlet bodies; they shook towards the fierce river-demon a bunch of black feathers, a mangy skin with a pendent tail — something that looked like a dried gourd; they shouted periodically together strings of amazing words that resembled no sounds of human language; and the deep murmurs of the crowd, interrupted suddenly, were like the responses of some satanic litany.

"We had carried Kurtz into the pilot-house: there was more air there. Lying on the couch, he stared through the open shutter. There was an eddy in the mass of human bodies, and the woman with helmeted head and tawny cheeks rushed out to the very brink of the stream. She put out her hands, shouted something, and all that wild mob took up the shout in a roaring chorus of articulated, rapid, breathless utterance.

"'Do you understand this?' I asked.

"He kept on looking out past me with fiery, longing eyes, with a mingled expression of wistfulness and hate. He made no answer, but I saw a smile, a smile of indefinable meaning, appear on his colourless lips that a moment after twitched convulsively. 'Do I not?' he said slowly, gasping, as if the words had been torn out of him by a supernatural power.

"I pulled the string of the whistle, and I did this because I saw the pilgrims on deck getting out their rifles with an air of anticipating a jolly lark. At the sudden screech there was a movement of abject terror through that wedged mass of bodies. 'Don't! don't you frighten them away,' cried some one on deck disconsolately. I pulled the string time after time. They broke and ran, they leaped, they crouched, they swerved, they dodged the flying terror of the sound. The three red chaps had fallen flat, face down on the shore, as though they had been shot dead. Only the barbarous and superb woman did not so much as flinch, and stretched tragically her bare arms after us over the sombre and glittering river.

"And then that imbecile crowd down on the deck started their little fun, and I could see nothing more for smoke.

"The brown current ran swiftly out of the heart of darkness, bearing us down towards the sea with twice the speed of our upward progress; and Kurtz's life was running swiftly too, ebbing, ebbing out of his heart into the sea of inexorable time. The manager was very placid, he had no vital anxieties now, he took us both in with a comprehensive and satisfied glance: the 'affair' had come off as well as could be wished. I saw the time approaching when I would be left alone of the party of 'unsound method.' The pilgrims looked upon me with disfavour. I was, so to speak, numbered with the dead. It is strange how I accepted this unforeseen partnership, this choice of nightmares forced upon me in the tenebrous land invaded by these mean and greedy phantoms.

"Kurtz discoursed. A voice! a voice! It rang deep to the very last. It survived his strength to hide in the magnificent folds of eloquence the barren darkness of his heart. Oh, he struggled! he struggled! The wastes of his weary brain were haunted by shadowy images now — images of wealth and fame revolving obsequiously round his unextinguishable gift of noble and lofty expression. My Intended, my station, my career, my ideas — these were the subjects for the occasional utterances of elevated sentiments. The shade of the original Kurtz frequented the bedside of the hollow sham, whose fate it was to be buried presently in the mould of primeval earth. But both the diabolic love and the unearthly hate of the mysteries it had penetrated fought for the possession of that soul satiated with primitive emotions, avid of lying fame, of sham distinction, of all the appearances of success and power.

"Sometimes he was contemptibly childish. He desired to have kings meet him at railway stations on his return from some ghastly Nowhere, where he intended to accomplish great things. 'You show them you have in you something that is really profitable, and then there will be no limits to the recognition of your ability,' he would say. 'Of course you must take care of the motives — right motives — always.' The long reaches that were like one and the same reach, monotonous bends that were exactly alike, slipped past the steamer with their multitude of secular trees looking patiently after this grimy fragment of another world, the forerunner of change, of conquest, of trade, of massacres, of blessings. I looked ahead — piloting. 'Close the shutter,' said Kurtz suddenly one day; 'I can't bear to look at this.' I did so. There was a silence. 'Oh, but I will wring your heart yet!' he cried at the invisible wilderness.

"We broke down — as I had expected — and had to lie up for repairs at the head of an island. This delay was the first thing that shook

Kurtz's confidence. One morning he gave me a packet of papers and a photograph — the lot tied together with a shoe-string. 'Keep this for me,' he said. 'This noxious fool' (meaning the manager) 'is capable of prying into my boxes when I am not looking.' In the afternoon I saw him. He was lying on his back with closed eyes, and I withdrew quietly, but I heard him mutter, 'Live rightly, die, die . . . ' I listened. There was nothing more. Was he rehearsing some speech in his sleep, or was it a fragment of a phrase from some newspaper article? He had been writing for the papers and meant to do so again, 'for the furthering of my ideas. It's a duty.'

"His was an impenetrable darkness. I looked at him as you peer down at a man who is lying at the bottom of a precipice where the sun never shines. But I had not much time to give him, because I was helping the engine-driver to take to pieces the leaky cylinders, to straighten a bent connecting-rod, and in other such matters. I lived in an infernal mess of rust, filings, nuts, bolts, spanners, hammers, ratchet-drills — things I abominate, because I don't get on with them. I tended the little forge we fortunately had aboard; I toiled wearily in a wretched scrap-heap — unless I had the shakes too bad to stand.

"One evening coming in with a candle I was startled to hear him say a little tremulously, 'I am lying here in the dark waiting for death.' The light was within a foot of his eyes. I forced myself to murmur, 'Oh, nonsense!' and stood over him as if transfixed.

"Anything approaching the change that came over his features I have never seen before, and hope never to see again. Oh, I wasn't touched. I was fascinated. It was as though a veil had been rent. I saw on that ivory face the expression of sombre pride, of ruthless power, of craven terror — of an intense and hopeless despair. Did he live his life again in every detail of desire, temptation, and surrender during that supreme moment of complete knowledge? He cried in a whisper at some image, at some vision — he cried out twice, a cry that was no more than a breath:

"'The horror! The horror!'

"I blew the candle out and left the cabin. The pilgrims were dining in the mess-room, and I took my place opposite the manager, who lifted his eyes to give me a questioning glance, which I successfully ignored. He leaned back, serene, with that peculiar smile of his sealing the unexpressed depths of his meanness. A continuous shower of small flies steamed upon the lamp, upon the cloth, upon our hands and faces. Suddenly the manager's boy put his insolent black head in the doorway, and said in a tone of scathing contempt:

"'Mistah Kurtz — he dead.'

"All the pilgrims rushed out to see. I remained, and went on with my dinner. I believe I was considered brutally callous. However, I did not eat much. There was a lamp in there — light, don't you know — and outside it was so beastly, beastly dark. I went no more near the remarkable man who had pronounced a judgment upon the adventures of his soul on this earth. The voice was gone. What else had been there? But I am of course aware that next day the pilgrims buried something in a muddy hole.

"And then they very nearly buried me.

"However, as you see, I did not go to join Kurtz there and then. I did not. I remained to dream the nightmare out to the end, and to show my loyalty to Kurtz once more. Destiny. My destiny! Droll thing life is — that mysterious arrangement of merciless logic for a futile purpose. The most you can hope from it is some knowledge of yourself — that comes too late — a crop of unextinguishable regrets. I have wrestled with death. It is the most unexciting contest you can imagine. It takes place in an impalpable greyness, with nothing underfoot, with nothing around, without spectators, without clamour, without glory, without the great desire of victory, without the great fear of defeat, in a sickly atmosphere of tepid scepticism, without much belief in your own right, and still less in that of your adversary. If such is the form of ultimate wisdom, then life is a greater riddle than some of us think it to be. I was within a hair's-breadth of the last opportunity for pronouncement, and I found with humiliation that probably I would have nothing to say. This is the reason why I affirm that Kurtz was a remarkable man. He had something to say. He said it. Since I had peeped over the edge myself, I understand better the meaning of his stare, that could not see the flame of the candle, but was wide enough to embrace the whole universe, piercing enough to penetrate all the hearts that beat in the darkness. He had summed up — he had judged. 'The horror!' He was a remarkable man. After all, this was the expression of some sort of belief; it had candour, it had conviction, it had a vibrating note of revolt in its whisper, it had the appalling face of a glimpsed truth — the strange commingling of desire and hate. And it is not my own extremity I remember best — a vision of greyness without form filled with physical pain, and a careless contempt for the evanescence of all things — even of this pain itself. No! It is his extremity that I seem to have lived through. True, he had made that last stride, he had stepped over the edge, while I had been permitted to draw back my hesitating foot. And perhaps in this is the whole difference; perhaps all the wisdom, and all truth, and all sincerity, are just compressed into that inappreciable moment of time in which we step over the threshold of the invisible. Perhaps! I like to think my summing-up would not have been a word of careless contempt. Better his cry — much better. It was an affirmation, a moral victory paid for by innumerable defeats, by abominable terrors, by abominable satisfactions. But it was a victory! That is why I have remained loyal to Kurtz to the last, and even beyond, when a long time after I heard once more, not his own voice, but the echo of his magnificent eloquence thrown to me from a soul as translucently pure as a cliff of crystal.

"No, they did not bury me, though there is a period of time which I remember mistily, with a shuddering wonder, like a passage through some inconceivable world that had no hope in it and no desire. I found myself back in the sepulchral city resenting the sight of people hurrying through the streets to filch a little money from each other, to devour their infamous cookery, to gulp their unwholesome beer, to dream their insignificant and silly dreams. They trespassed upon my thoughts. They were intruders whose knowledge of life was to me an irritating pretence, because I felt so sure they could not possibly know the things I knew. Their bearing, which was simply the bearing of commonplace individuals going about their business in the assurance of perfect safety, was offensive to me like the outrageous flauntings of folly in the face of a danger it is unable to comprehend. I had no particular desire to enlighten them, but I had some difficulty in restraining myself from laughing in their faces, so full of stupid importance. I daresay I was not very well at that time. I tottered about the streets — there were various affairs to settle — grinning bitterly at perfectly respectable persons. I admit my behavior was inexcusable, but then my temperature was seldom normal in these days. My dear aunt's endeavours to 'nurse up my strength' seemed altogether beside the mark. It was not my strength that wanted nursing, it was my imagination that wanted soothing. I kept the bundle of papers given me by Kurtz, not knowing exactly what to do with it. His mother had died lately, watched over, as I was told, by his Intended. A clean-shaved man, with an official manner and wearing gold-rimmed spectacles, called on me one day and made inquiries, at first circuitous, afterwards suavely pressing, about what he was pleased to denominate certain 'documents.' I was not surprised, because I had had two rows with the manager on that subject out there. I had refused to give up the smallest scrap out of that package, and I took the same attitude with the spectacled man. He became darkly menacing at last, and with much heat argued that the Company had the right to every bit of information about its 'territories.' And, said he, 'Mr. Kurtz's knowledge of unexplored regions must have been necessarily extensive and peculiar — owing to his great abilities and to the deplorable circumstances in which he had been placed: therefore —— ' I assured him Mr. Kurtz's knowledge, however extensive, did not bear upon the problems of commerce or administration. He invoked then the name of science. 'It would be an incalculable loss if,' etc. etc. I offered him the report of the 'Suppression of Savage Customs,' with the postscriptum torn off. He took it up eagerly, but ended by sniffing at it with an air of contempt. 'This is not what we had a right to expect,' he remarked. 'Expect nothing else,' I said. 'There are only private letters.' He withdrew upon some threat of legal proceedings, and I saw him no more; but another fellow, calling himself Kurtz's cousin, appeared two days later, and was anxious to hear all the details about his dear relative's last moments. Incidentally he gave me to understand that Kurtz had been essentially a great musician. 'There was the making of an immense success,' said the man, who was an organist, I believe, with lank grey hair flowing over a greasy coat-collar. I had no reason to doubt his statement; and to this day I am unable to say what was Kurtz's profession, whether he ever had any — which was the greatest of his talents. I had taken him for a painter who wrote for the papers, or else for a journalist who could paint — but even the cousin (who took snuff during the interview) could not tell me what he had been — exactly. He was a universal genius — on that point I agreed with the old chap, who thereupon blew his nose noisily into a large cotton handkerchief and withdrew in senile agitation, bearing off some family letters and memoranda without importance. Ultimately a journalist anxious to know something of the fate of his 'dear colleague' turned up. This visitor informed me Kurtz's proper sphere ought to have been politics 'on the popular side.' He had furry straight eyebrows, bristly hair cropped short, an eyeglass on a broad ribbon, and, becoming expansive, confessed his opinion that Kurtz really couldn't write a bit — 'but Heavens! how that man could talk! He electrified large meetings. He had faith — don't you see? — he had the faith. He could get himself to believe anything — anything. He would have been a splendid leader of an extreme party.' 'What party?' I asked. 'Any party,' answered the other. 'He was an — an — extremist.' Did I not think so? I assented. Did I know, he asked, with a sudden flash of curiosity, 'what it was that had induced him to go out there?' 'Yes,' said I, and forthwith handed him the famous Report for publication, if he thought fit. He glanced through it hurriedly, mumbling all the time, judged 'it would do,' and took himself off with this plunder.

"Thus I was left at last with a slim packet of letters and the girl's portrait. She struck me as beautiful — I mean she had a beautiful expression. I know that the sunlight can be made to lie too, yet one felt that no manipulation of light and pose could have conveyed the delicate shade of truthfulness upon those features. She seemed ready to listen without mental reservation, without suspicion, without a thought for herself. I concluded I would go and give her back her portrait and those letters myself. Curiosity? Yes; and also some other feeling perhaps. All that had been Kurtz's had passed out of my hands: his soul, his body, his station, his plans, his ivory, his career. There remained only his memory and his Intended — and I wanted to give that up too to the past, in a way — to surrender personally all that remained of him with me to that oblivion which is the last word of our common fate. I don't defend myself. I had no clear perception of what it was I really wanted. Perhaps it was an impulse of unconscious loyalty, or the fulfillment of one of those ironic necessities that lurk in the facts of human existence. I don't know. I can't tell. But I went.

"I thought his memory was like the other memories of the dead that accumulate in every man's life — a vague impress on the brain of shadows that had fallen on it in their swift and final passage; but before the high and ponderous door, between the tall houses of a street as still and decorous as a well-kept alley in a cemetery, I had a vision of him on the stretcher, opening his mouth voraciously, as if to devour all the earth with all its mankind. He lived then before me; he lived as much as he had ever lived — a shadow insatiable of splendid appearances, of frightful realities; a shadow darker than the shadow of the night, and draped nobly in the folds of a gorgeous eloquence. The vision seemed to enter the house with me — the stretcher, the phantom-bearers, the wild crowd of obedient worshippers, the gloom of the forests, the glitter of the reach between the murky bends, the beat of the drum, regular and muffled like the beating of a heart — the heart of a conquering darkness. It was a moment of triumph for the wilderness, an invading and vengeful rush which, it seemed to me, I would have to keep back alone for the salvation of another soul. And the memory of what I had heard him say afar there, with the horned shapes stirring at my back, in the glow of fires, within the patient woods, those broken phrases came back to me, were heard again in their ominous and terrifying simplicity. I remembered his abject pleading, his abject threats, the colossal scale of his vile desires, the meanness, the torment, the tempestuous anguish of his soul. And later on I seemed to see his collected languid manner, when he said one day, 'This lot of ivory now is really mine. The Company did not pay for it. I collected it myself at a very great personal risk. I am afraid they will try to claim it as theirs though. H'm. It is a difficult case. What do you think I ought to do — resist? Eh? I want no more than justice.' . . . He wanted no more than justice — no more than justice. I rang the bell before a mahogany door on the first floor, and while I waited he seemed to stare at me out of the glassy panel — stare with that wide and immense stare embracing, condemning, loathing all the universe. I seemed to hear the whispered cry, 'The horror! The horror!'

"The dusk was falling. I had to wait in a lofty drawing-room with three long windows from floor to ceiling that were like three luminous and bedraped columns. The bent gilt legs and backs of the furniture shone in indistinct curves. The tall marble fireplace had a cold and monumental whiteness. A grand piano stood massively in a corner; with dark gleams on the flat surfaces like a sombre and polished sarcophagus. A high door opened — closed. I rose.

"She came forward, all in black, with a pale head, floating towards me in the dusk. She was in mourning. It was more than a year since his death, more than a year since the news came; she seemed as though she would remember and mourn for ever. She took both my hands in hers and murmured, 'I had heard you were coming.' I noticed she was not very young — I mean not girlish. She had a mature capacity for fidelity, for belief, for suffering. The room seemed to have grown darker, as if all the sad light of the cloudy evening had taken refuge on her forehead. This fair hair, this pale visage, this pure brow, seemed surrounded by an ashy halo from which the dark eyes looked out at me. Their glance was guileless, profound, confident, and trustful. She carried her sorrowful head as though she were proud of that sorrow, as though she would say, I — I alone know how to mourn for him as he deserves. But while we were still shaking hands, such a look of awful desolation came upon her face that I perceived she was one of those creatures that are not the play-things of Time. For her he had died only yesterday. And, by Jove! the impression was so powerful that for me too he seemed to have died only yesterday — nay, this very minute. I saw her and him in the same instant of time — his death and her sorrow — I saw her sorrow in the very moment of his death. Do you understand? I saw them together — I heard them together. She had said, with a deep catch of the breath, 'I have survived'; while my strained ears seemed to hear distinctly, mingled with her tone of de-spairing regret, the summing-up whisper of his eternal condemnation. I asked myself what I was doing there, with a sensation of panic in my heart as though I had blundered into a place of cruel and absurd mys-teries not fit for a human being to behold. She motioned me to a chair. We sat down. I laid the packet gently on the little table, and she put her hand over it. . . . 'You knew him well,' she murmured, after a moment of mourning silence.

"'Intimacy grows quickly out there,' I said. 'I knew him as well as it is possible for one man to know another.'

"'And you admired him,' she said. 'It was impossible to know him and not to admire him. Was it?'

"'He was a remarkable man,' I said unsteadily. Then before the ap-pealing fixity of her gaze, that seemed to watch for more words on my lips, I went on, 'It was impossible not to —— '

"'Love him,' she finished eagerly, silencing me into an appalled dumbness. 'How true! how true! But when you think that no one knew him so well as I! I had all his noble confidence. I knew him best.'

"'You knew him best,' I repeated. And perhaps she did. But with every word spoken the room was growing darker, and only her fore-head, smooth and white, remained illumined by the unextinguishable light of belief and love.

"'You were his friend,' she went on. 'His friend,' she repeated, a little louder. 'You must have been, if he had given you this, and sent you to me. I feel I can speak to you — and oh! I must speak. I want you — you who have heard his last words — to know I have been wor-thy of him. . . . It is not pride. . . . Yes! I am proud to know I under-stood him better than any one on earth — he told me so himself. And since his mother died I have had no one — no one — to — to —— '

"I listened. The darkness deepened. I was not even sure whether he had given me the right bundle. I rather suspect he wanted me to take care of another batch of his papers which, after his death, I saw the manager examining under the lamp. And the girl talked, easing her pain in the certitude of my sympathy; she talked as thirsty men drink. I had heard that her engagement with Kurtz had been disapproved by her people. He wasn't rich enough or something. And indeed I don't know whether he had not been a pauper all his life. He had given me some reason to infer that it was his impatience of comparative poverty that drove him out there.

"'. . . Who was not his friend who had heard him speak once?' she was saying. 'He drew men towards him by what was best in them.' She looked at me with intensity. 'It is the gift of the great,' she went on, and the sound of her low voice seemed to have the accompaniment of all the other sounds, full of mystery, desolation, and sorrow, I had ever heard — the ripple of the river, the soughing of the trees swayed by the wind, the murmurs of the crowds, the faint ring of incomprehensible words cried from afar, the whisper of a voice speaking from beyond the threshold of an eternal darkness. 'But you have heard him! You know!' she cried.

"'Yes, I know,' I said with something like despair in my heart, but bowing my head before the faith that was in her, before that great and saving illusion that shone with an unearthly glow in the darkness, in the triumphant darkness from which I could not have defended her — from which I could not even defend myself.

"'What a loss to me — to us!' — she corrected herself with beautiful generosity; then added in a murmur, 'To the world.' By the last gleams of twilight I could see the glitter of her eyes, full of tears — of tears that would not fall.

"'I have been very happy — very fortunate — very proud,' she went on. 'Too fortunate. Too happy for a little while. And now I am unhappy for — for life.'

"She stood up; her fair hair seemed to catch all the remaining light in a glimmer of gold. I rose too.

"'And of all this,' she went on mournfully, 'of all his promise, and of all his greatness, of his generous mind, of his noble heart, nothing remains — nothing but a memory. You and I ——'

"'We shall always remember him,' I said hastily.

"'No!' she cried. 'It is impossible that all this should be lost — that such a life should be sacrificed to leave nothing — but sorrow. You know what vast plans he had. I knew of them too — I could not perhaps understand — but others knew of them. Something must remain. His words, at least, have not died.'

"'His words will remain,' I said.

"'And his example,' she whispered to herself. 'Men looked up to him — his goodness shone in every act. His example ——'

"'True,' I said; 'his example too. Yes, his example. I forgot that.'

"'But I do not. I cannot — I cannot believe — not yet. I cannot believe that I shall never see him again, that nobody will see him again, never, never, never.'

"She put out her arms as if after a retreating figure, stretching them back and with clasped pale hands across the fading and narrow sheen of the window. Never see him! I saw him clearly enough then. I shall see this eloquent phantom as long as I live, and I shall see her too, a tragic and familiar Shade, resembling in this gesture another one, tragic also, and bedecked with powerless charms, stretching bare brown arms over the glitter of the infernal stream, the stream of darkness. She said suddenly very low, 'He died as he lived.'

"'His end,' said I, with dull anger stirring in me, 'was in every way worthy of his life.'

"'And I was not with him,' she murmured. My anger subsided before a feeling of infinite pity.

"'Everything that could be done —— ' I mumbled.

"'Ah, but I believed in him more than any one on earth — more than his own mother, more than — himself. He needed me! Me! I would have treasured every sigh, every word, every sign, every glance.'

"I felt like a chill grip on my chest. 'Don't,' I said, in a muffled voice.

"'Forgive me. I — I — have mourned so long in silence — in silence. . . . You were with him — to the last? I think of his loneliness. Nobody near to understand him as I would have understood. Perhaps no one to hear . . . '

"'To the very end,' I said shakily. 'I heard his very last words. . . .' I stopped in a fright.

"'Repeat them,' she murmured in a heartbroken tone. 'I want — I want — something — something — to — to live with.'

"I was on the point of crying at her, 'Don't you hear them?' The dusk was repeating them in a persistent whisper all around us, in a whisper that seemed to swell menacingly like the first whisper of a rising wind. 'The horror! The horror!'

"'His last word — to live with,' she insisted. 'Don't you understand I loved him — I loved him — I loved him!'

"I pulled myself together and spoke slowly.

"'The last word he pronounced was — your name.'

"I heard a light sigh and then my heart stood still, stopped dead short by an exulting and terrible cry, by the cry of inconceivable triumph and of unspeakable pain. 'I knew it — I was sure!' . . . She knew. She was sure. I heard her weeping; she had hidden her face in her hands. It seemed to me that the house would collapse before I could escape, that the heavens would fall upon my head. But nothing happened. The heavens do not fall for such a trifle. Would they have fallen, I wonder, if I had rendered Kurtz that justice which was his due? Hadn't he said he wanted only justice? But I couldn't. I could not tell her. It would have been too dark — too dark altogether. . . ."

Marlow ceased, and sat apart, indistinct and silent, in the pose of a meditating Buddha. Nobody moved for a time. "We have lost the first of the ebb," said the Director suddenly. I raised my head. The offing was barred by a black bank of clouds, and the tranquil waterway leading to the uttermost ends of the earth flowed sombre under an overcast sky — seemed to lead into the heart of an immense darkness.

PART TWO

Heart of Darkness:
A Case Study in
Contemporary Criticism

A Critical History of
Heart of Darkness

Heart of Darkness was published serially in *Blackwood's Magazine* in 1899. But it was not seriously reviewed until 1902, when it was reprinted in a hard-cover volume entitled *Youth*. Even then, the other two works published in the collection, *Youth* and *The End of the Tether*, were received more favorably. In an unsigned 1902 review Edward Garnett both explained and deplored the fact that *Heart of Darkness* was the least popular of the three tales. Calling it "too strong" a piece of "meat for the ordinary reader," he insisted that it was nonetheless "the high water mark" of Conrad's "talent," a "psychological masterpiece" relating "the sub-conscious life within us . . . to our conscious actions, feelings, and outlook." As such, Garnett concluded, it offers an "analysis of the deterioration of the white man's *morale*, when he is let loose from European restraint, and planted down in the tropics as an emissary of light armed to the teeth, to make trade profits out of the subject races" (Sherry 132–33). Responding to Garnett's review in a personal letter, Conrad wrote: "My dearest fellow you quite overcome me. And your brave attempt to grapple with the foggishness of *Heart of Darkness*, to explain what I myself tried to shape blindfold, as it were, touched me profoundly" (Karl and Davies 2:467–68).

The tone of Conrad's response is treacherously difficult to determine. But of this we can be sure: Garnett was right in declaring the novel to be about the immorality of whites in Africa. The idea behind *Heart of Darkness*, Conrad had written to William Blackwood one month before the first installment of the novel had appeared in *Blackwood's Magazine*, is "the criminality of inefficiency and pure selfishness when tackling the civilizing work in Africa." This much, too, we can feel certain of: Conrad knew that the theme of his book was not obvious, and that serious readers like Garnett *would* have to reflect before being rewarded by the discovery of meaning. "The idea is so wrapped up in secondary notions," he had admitted in an 1899 letter to R. B. Cunninghame Graham, "that You — even You! may miss it" (Karl and Davies 2:139–40, 157).

Conrad, of course, may be trying to sound humble in these letters, suggesting that his idea is obscured by "secondary notions" in a novel that is, consequently, "foggish." On the other hand, he may be asserting that meaning *should* lie beyond the details that enshroud it in a work of novelistic art, that the idea of a work should only emerge as the *product* of a reader's experience of more immediate, if secondary, details. "You must remember," Conrad goes on to say in the letter to Graham, "that I don't start with an abstract notion. I start with definite images and as their rendering is true some little effect is produced" (Karl and Davies 2:157–58).

Some early readers of Conrad, however, failed to find Conrad's images any more definite than his ideas. E. M. Forster, best known for his novel *A Passage to India* (1924), once wrote that "sentence after sentence" in Conrad "discharges its smoke screen into our abashed eyes," and he went on to accuse the author of being "misty" at "the edges" as well as "in the middle" (138). Forster was not the only artist-critic who found Conrad a little *too* fuzzy. The poet John Masefield (later to become poet laureate) declared that there is "too much cobweb" in *Heart of Darkness*, that Conrad's style, in general, is neither "vigorous, direct, effective, like that of Mr. [Rudyard] Kipling," nor "clear and fresh like that of [Robert Louis] Stevenson" (Sherry 142).

Not all the reviewers who commented on style, though, found the novel notable for its lack of directness, precision, or clarity. The reviewer for the *Athenaeum* commented on Conrad's atmosphere but did so in order to praise, not fault, it: "He presents the atmosphere in which his characters move and act with singular fidelity, by means of watchful and careful building in which the craftsman's methods are never obtrusive, and after turning to the last page of one of his books, we rise saturated by the very air they breathed" (Sherry 198). And an anonymous reviewer writing in the *Manchester Guardian* found in *Heart of Darkness* not atmosphere at all but, instead "a great expression of adventure and romance" (Sherry 134).

Was *Heart of Darkness* — is *Heart of Darkness* — a political novel, a psychological novel, or a simple adventure tale designed to give us a thrill? Is it primarily an atmospheric work and, if so, is the atmosphere so precisely evoked that we feel we breathe it, right alongside the characters? Or are Conrad's words like so much cobweb? The debate over these and other questions was intense during the decades that followed the publication of *Heart of Darkness*, and to a great extent, the various critical positions taken by reviewers in the first half of our century still guide us as we ask questions of the novel and arrive at interpretations of it. After all, no work is approached in a vacuum, and the interpretive history of a work is part of the context in which we read it. When we publish our views, even if we do so only in a comment to a few other readers of a particular work, we add to and alter slightly the language in which that work is and will be discussed. Those who follow are likely to locate their respective positions vis-à-vis our own.

Not surprisingly, then, when F. R. Leavis set out critically to assess *Heart of Darkness* fifty years after its serial publication, he praised strengths and attacked weaknesses in ways that had been prepared for him by previous critics. In his influential study of English fiction, *The Great Tradition*, Leavis begins by asserting that E. M. Forster was correct to fault Conrad for obscurity and a vaporous style. However, Leavis then insists that other critics were correct, too, in praising Conrad's ability to describe things and actions precisely, thereby creating an "overwhelming sinister and fantastic 'atmosphere'" (177). Leavis has it both ways by arguing that Conrad pictures places — such as the grove "greenish" with "gloom" in which Marlow stumbles upon diseased, starving Africans (p. 32)[1] — with description that can be terribly vivid. But the novelist becomes vague and foggy, according to Leavis, when he steps back to philosophize.

Part of the problem, Leavis concludes, is that Conrad tends to overburden philosophical passages with adjectives that obscure rather than describe. "There are places in *Heart of Darkness*," he points out, where Conrad has already "overworked" words like "'inscrutable,' 'inconceivable,' 'unspeakable.' . . . Yet still they recur." Quoting Conrad's sentence "It was the stillness of an implacable force brooding over an inscrutable intention" (p. 49), Leavis goes on to remark that

---

[1] Page references refer to the text of *Heart of Darkness* in this volume.

Conrad's vocabulary often backfires, particularly when it tries to express a sense of profundity or horror. Conrad repeatedly uses words such as "inexpressible" and "incomprehensible," Leavis hypothesizes, in order to "magnify" a "thrilled sense of the unspeakable potentialities of the human soul." But "the actual effect is not to magnify but rather to muffle" (Leavis 179).

Giving as an example the scene in which human heads are found mounted on posts surrounding Kurtz's house, Leavis praises the image, which he says tells us all we need to know, but faults Conrad for supplementing such images with what he calls the "adjectival and worse than supererogatory insistence on 'unspeakable rites,' 'unspeakable secrets,' 'monstrous passions.'" Conrad tries too hard, Leavis thinks, to "impose . . . a 'significance' that is merely an emotional insistence on the presence of what he can't produce. . . . He is intent on making a virtue out of not knowing what he means" (Leavis 180).

These are strong words coming from a critic who ranks Conrad as one of the four great novelists in a great tradition of British fiction. They are words, nonetheless, that express what other, earlier readers felt. More important, though, they are words that later critics have found useful. For what Leavis unwittingly gave to later critics was the language that, with revision, could be used to discuss not the flaws of *Heart of Darkness* but rather the special nature of the novel's greatness.

Albert J. Guerard, in his much-acclaimed 1958 study *Conrad the Novelist*, reaffirms but also drastically revises the views of *Heart of Darkness* afforded by Leavis. One way Guerard differs significantly from Leavis is in the attention he pays not to Kurtz but to Marlow. "F. R. Leavis," Guerard writes, "seems to regard him as a narrator only, providing a 'specific and concretely realized point of view'" (Guerard 38). Indeed, Marlow *was* to Leavis a mere agent, the character whose primary purpose in the narrative is to provide those "details and circumstances of the voyage" that make palpable the fantastic "atmosphere" Kurtz inhabits (Leavis 176). "But Marlow," Guerard asserts to the contrary, "is recounting a spiritual voyage of self-discovery," and it is that voyage and that discovery that should interest readers of *Heart of Darkness*. For Guerard the story is like a "powerful dream" in which Marlow meets up with his own, dark, passional nature. Marlow feels the excitement of what he calls the "wild and passionate uproar," finds himself fascinated by abominations, and, most important, meets a strange alter ego or double. The most important stage in Marlow's journey within, according to Guerard, is the one in which he comes to recognize his kinship with Kurtz, "a white man and sometimes idealist who had fully responded to the wilderness: a potential and fallen self. . . . At the climax Marlow follows Kurtz ashore, confounds the beat of the drum with the beating of his heart, . . . and brings [Kurtz] back to the ship. He returns to Europe a changed and more knowing man" (Guerard 39, 38).

By seeing the novel as a dream of self-discovery, Guerard not only expands upon what Edward Garnett said when he called *Heart of Darkness* a psychological masterpiece but also explains why the world has been so taken with this story that *is*, at least in some ways, fuzzy, smoky, misty, unclear. *Heart of Darkness* is ambiguous as a *dream* is ambiguous; it is powerful precisely to the extent that it is *not* precise. "If my summary [of the novel as a dream] has even a partial validity," Guerard concludes, "it should explain and to an extent justify some of the 'adjectival and worse than supererogatory insistence' to which F. R. Leavis . . . objects. I am willing to grant that the unspeakable rites and unspeakable secrets become wearisome, but the fact — at once literary and psychological — is that they must remain *unspoken*" (42). In other words, if *Heart of Darkness* were perfectly precise in its profoundest passages, it would not be dreamlike; more important, it could not seem like *our* dream. To say "murder" or "death" or "greed" or "lust," instead of using that more "misty" phrase, "The horror" (p. 86), would be to distance most readers from that horror. Thus Guerard makes use of Leavis even while seeming to reject him. He turns a vocabulary of critical objection into a language of critical analysis, a language that may be used to explain just why *Heart of Darkness* is so haunting.

Thomas Moser, who in 1957 published an important study entitled *Joseph Conrad: Achievement and Decline*, begins with two ideas: that Conrad "is as great as F. R. Leavis believe[s] him to be, and as serious and subtle as . . . Albert J. Guerard" has shown him to be. It is Guerard, though, who seems to have influenced Moser most directly. "*Heart of Darkness*, 'The Secret Sharer,' and *Lord Jim* are all principally concerned with the theme of self-knowledge," Moser asserts, sounding like Guerard. "We must recognize our potential weaknesses, our plague spots, in order to achieve a perceptive, moral life" (Moser 1, 24).

Moser, however, does more than repeat Guerard's reading of the novel; like Guerard and Leavis before him, he bends and adapts a strong predecessor's language in order to make it useful in a new way.

In stating that Conrad's early works show us that "we must recognize
our plague spots," Moser has already developed an idea only latent in
Guerard, namely, that Marlow in the jungle is like the reader in the
text, that somehow Marlow's quest for self-knowledge must be
doubled by our own. "It is difficult to discuss Conrad's technique
without referring to its effect upon the reader," Moser writes, "for
Conrad's masterly control of the reader's responses is one of the most
significant results of his unorthodox methods. By holding back information and moving forward and backward in time, Conrad catches up
and involves the reader in a moral situation, makes the reader's emotions follow a course analogous to that of the characters" (42).

In addition to expanding on Guerard's view of the novel as one of
self-discovery, Moser develops a still older view of the novel: that it is a
work critical of racist European imperialism. Unlike early reviewers,
however, Moser sees the theme of anti-imperialism as being inseparable from the novel's imagery, and he discusses the connection to
show that it was thematically useful to Conrad to create superficially
confusing imagery. In *Heart of Darkness*, Moser points out, the usual
pattern is reversed and "darkness means truth, whiteness means falsehood" (47). The reversal tells simultaneously a political truth about
races in the Congo, a psychological truth about Marlow and all of us
(the truth is within, therefore dark and obscure), and any number of
moral truths (the trade in ivory is dark and dirty). One pair of colors
can suggest all these different kinds of meanings, Moser adds, because
Heart of Darkness was written by "Conrad the artist," who happened
also to be "Conrad the moralist, . . . Conrad the psychologist," and
"Conrad the commentator on politics" (38).

Moser's reminder that Conrad was an *artist* was made time and
time again by the New Critics, who dominated Anglo-American academic criticism in the middle decades of the twentieth century. The
New Criticism — or formalism, as it is now usually called — was a reaction against the tendency to see poems and novels as products of the
author's personal and historical experience. Formalists such as William
K. Wimsatt warned against trying to discern an author's intention; our
time as readers is better spent, they suggested, in describing the way
the parts of the work interrelate to form beautiful artistic unities. Albert Guerard prepared the way for formalist readings of *Heart of
Darkness* by focusing attention on Marlow — a tale-teller — and his
narrative, rather than on its subjects: Africa, ivory, battle scenes, Kurtz.
Guerard also showed a formalist tendency in believing that Conrad's
dreamlike ambiguity may be part of the meaning, not just a fault of

Conrad's that gets in the way of some other meaning that Conrad surely intended us to see.

Numerous critics writing since 1960 have paid attention to the artistic form or unity of *Heart of Darkness*. Leo Gurko reminds us that "the novel . . . begins and ends on a yawl, on the deck of which Marlow is telling his story to four men." The unity provided by that opening and closing scene, moreover, is reinforced by descriptions of the scene. ("The sea-reach of the Thames stretched before us like the beginning of an interminable waterway"; "the sea and the sky were welded together without a joint" [p. 17].) Together, Gurko argues, Conrad's images lead us to view nature as a continuum, to see the story as a continuum like nature, and to conclude that the "theme of all experience being one experience . . . underlies the story, and appears in several variations" (Gurko 148). Marlow's lie to the Intended, for instance, is like Europe's imperialistic dealings in Africa. "The lie, like the imperialism, is an evil thing." But both are "redeemed," according to Gurko, "by a benevolent and idealistic motivation" (151).

In taking this rather tolerant view of imperialism, and in suggesting that Conrad took such a view, Gurko differs from most later critics who have written on the subject. For instance, in *Conrad's Politics*, published in 1967, Avrom Fleishman insists that "In Africa as well as in the Indies, the disruptive effects of imperialism on native society were clear to Conrad" (89). Whereas previous critics had emphasized the breakdown of the mores of white men sent to the tropics armed and in search of profits, Fleishman discusses the moral decay of Africans once Europeans have been loosed upon them. Several of Fleishman's predecessors had implied that *Heart of Darkness* tells how imperialism reduces white emissaries from a civilized to a primitive state, leaving them no better morally than the savages whom they exploit. Against this view, Fleishman responds correctively. The natives unspeakably treated by a degenerating Kurtz were not barbarians prone to committing unprovoked atrocities. Or, rather, they were not until Kurtz came among them and prompted them "to organized warfare in order to obtain ivory for export" (Fleishman 90).

Although he makes no mention of Fleishman's views, Bruce Johnson concurs with many of them in *Conrad's Models of Mind*, published four years after *Conrad's Politics*. Like Fleishman, Johnson disagrees with the notion that Conrad held tribal life in low esteem. And like Gurko, to whom he several times refers, Johnson finds in *Heart of Darkness* the view that nature is a unity, a continuum. Indeed, for Johnson, unity with nature is what the African natives have until "civilized" whites — who do not have this unity — disrupt and destroy it. Conrad, Johnson argues, held the Victorian view "that the savage is one with nature, while the civilized white man has fallen — for better or worse — from the primal unity" (Johnson 71). According to this view of Africans, the native "feels no sense of alienation" and, therefore, no "need to create his own contingent values and sanctions." Europeans, who *do* feel alienated from that "something great and invincible" we call nature, *do* create such values and sanctions. The combination, as Johnson sees it, can literally be deadly. The unalienated native tends "readily to accept what presents itself convincingly," as if it had "divine sanction" (Johnson 72). An alienated European like Kurtz, who shapes rather than accepts the world, exploits precisely this tendency. By presenting himself convincingly, Kurtz becomes a people's disruptive, destructive, even murderous god.

    In 1975, four years after the appearance of Johnson's important study, two very different essays were published that have had an enormous influence on the way in which *Heart of Darkness* has been read in the 1980s and 1990s. One of these, by Frederick Crews, was a book chapter entitled "Conrad's Uneasiness — and Ours." Rather than analyzing Conrad's "models of mind," as Johnson had done before him, Crews applies *to* Conrad's fiction psychoanalytic models developed by Sigmund Freud. In doing so, he finds *Heart of Darkness* to be an expression of the Oedipus complex, which involves the repressed childhood wish to displace the parent of the same sex and take his or her place in the affections of the parent of the opposite sex. Crews suggests that if the plot of *Heart of Darkness* "were recounted to a psychoanalyst as a dream," Kurtz, the "exposed sinner," would be "an image of the father, accused of sexual 'rites' with the mother." Marlow the "dreamer" would be an image of the son interrupting the "primal scene" by making his "journey" into the "maternal body" (56).
    The other, very different 1975 essay that has greatly influenced recent criticism was first given as a speech at the University of Massachusetts by the great Nigerian novelist Chinua Achebe. Achebe had complained about Conrad's "need . . . to set Africa up as the foil of Europe," to "project" an "image of Africa as . . . the antithesis of Europe and therefore of civilization" (119–20). "What actually worries Conrad," Achebe claims, "is the lurking hint of kinship, of common ancestry," between the people living on the banks of the Thames and those living on the banks of the Congo (120). Anticipating the objection that it is only Marlow who is troubled by the sense of kinship,

Achebe acknowledges that, through his "narrator behind a narrator" construction, Conrad has "set up layers of insulation between himself and the moral universe of his story." Achebe, however, believes that in the last analysis "Marlow seems to enjoy Conrad's complete confidence" (123). Why? Because "Conrad was a bloody racist" (124).

Achebe's "take" on Conrad, like that of Crews, is admittedly an extreme one. The notion that *Heart of Darkness* is a racist work, like the notion that we should view *Heart of Darkness* as a dream told by a patient named Charlie Marlow to his psychoanalyst, is one that many of you have already dismissed. And perhaps . . . *perhaps* with good reason. The paragraphs that follow summarize the views of critics who have written compellingly about *Heart of Darkness* in the 1980s and 1990s. What you will find, as you read them, is that the ideas of Crews and Achebe have led to some interesting debates — debates in which critics have given us new reasons to accept and reject, select and choose between, modify and develop the claim that *Heart of Darkness* reveals repressed passions or racist attitudes. Thanks to Crews and Achebe, in other words, we now have a spectrum of ideas about fiction, psychology, and racial attitudes somewhere along which your own positions and opinions probably fit.

Since Crews published his now-famous chapter, a number of critics have read Conrad in terms of the Oedipus complex. As Catharine Rising has noted in her book *Darkness at Heart: Fathers and Sons in Conrad* (1990), some of these interpreters view *Heart of Darkness* as Crews does, in terms of a sexual rivalry between Marlow (or Conrad) and his father. But others have viewed the story in terms of a more general, oedipal rivalry, one involving an illustrious, older man, a young man with mixed feelings about his elder, the death of the former, and the survival of the latter, who surpasses his father figure morally or artistically. (As psychoanalytic critic Joseph Dobrinsky has pointed out, Conrad's father, Apollo, was not only a political revolutionary but also a poet.)

A number of critics who have written on *Heart of Darkness* in the 1980s and 1990s have followed Crews's lead by applying psychological or psychoanalytic theory to *Heart of Darkness* but not by seeing Conrad's story as a manifestation of the Oedipus complex. Using Freud's notion that human beings are essentially double in nature — that all of us contain a rational, socialized self and a dark double, a repressed instinctual self — Donald M. Kartiganer viewed Kurtz as Marlow's "outlaw" alter ego in his 1985 article "Freud's Reading Process:

The Divided Protagonist Narrative and the Case of the Wolf-Man"
(8). Bettina Knapp subsequently viewed *Heart of Darkness* not as a tale
revealing Marlow's dark side but, rather, as one through which Conrad searched for *his* exiled "shadow" self, an identity consisting of "animal" traits he projects onto African blacks. Knapp's reading, rather
than being Freudian, is based on the writings of Carl Gustav Jung, a
psychoanalytic theorist who developed the theory that there is a collective human unconscious. According to Knapp's Jungian reading, Conrad's story of a journey to the heart of the African continent draws on
"archaic levels of the human psyche," levels inhabited by "archetypal"
images such as that of the waterway and those involving eating and
being eaten (50).

   One of the most interesting recent psychoanalytic readings, Barry
Stampfl's "Marlow's Rhetoric of (Self-) Deception in *Heart of Darkness*" (1991), focuses less on images and symbols than on syntax.
Using Freud's concept that repressed ideas sometimes are allowed to
surface so long as they are negated, Stampfl examines "Marlow's nega-
tives" (the oft-repeated word "impenetrable" would be an example)
and related "belief qualifiers." (Marlow says of dying slaves that it was
"as if" they were "overcome with a great weariness"; speaking of the
Company, he says that "It was just as though I had been let into a
conspiracy.") According to Stampfl, negative and highly qualified
terms often give us insight into what Marlow knows down deep to be
true (that the Congo has been penetrated — raped — by Europeans,
that the African slaves he sees *are* overcome by weariness). The knowledge that negations and belief qualifiers half cover up and half reveal is
not so much that of the id or the archaic unconscious as it is the
knowledge of political evil, the reality that Marlow's imperialistic culture would rather not acknowledge.

   Stampfl is not the only recent critic to take a modified psychoanalytic approach to the broader cultural issues raised in *Heart of Darkness*. In *Desire and Its Discontents* (1991), Eugene Goodheart similarly
takes the view that the "psychological aspect" and "political meanings" of Conrad's tale are intertwined, since "politics itself may be read
as enactment of desire" (23). (For Goodheart, civilized reason and repressed passions are not the opposites they seem to some Freudians;
they come together in the "'civilized' will to impose, to dominate, and
control" [24].) Other critics have used the vocabulary and insights of
psychoanalysis to examine not the global politics but the *gender* politics of *Heart of Darkness*. Claire Kahane does so in a discussion of the
scene in which Marlow lies to the Intended by telling the pure and

sheltered young girl that the last thing Kurtz said ("the horror!") was her name. Kahane finds in Marlow's lie a set of "Freudian switch-words"; a young woman's name substitutes for "the horror," which "echoes its homonym 'whore,'" which, in turn, reveals a deep-seated "fear of and rage at woman" (145).

The lie to the Intended has been a major focus of the few feminist readings of *Heart of Darkness* that have appeared, including the one by Johanna M. Smith that represents the feminist and gender approach in this volume. For Nina Pelikan Straus, the scene of Marlow's famous lie is but the most memorable of many that affect male and female readers differently, reminding the latter that this is a tale "concerned with a kind of mainstream male experience" that has been "deliberately hidden" from the women inside the text. Although not denying that "the sexism of Marlow and Kurtz" may be "part of the 'horror' that Conrad intends to disclose," Straus maintains that "the feminist reader's access" to Conrad's most famous work is "especially problematic," a fact she uses to explain "decades of nearly exclusive male commentary surrounding *Heart of Darkness*" (123–24). Putting the problem succinctly, Straus at one point comments that "For a woman reader" to "identify with Marlow" is to "court self-degradation" (130).

In "Reading Race and Gender in Conrad's Dark Continent" (1989), Bette London agrees with Straus that *Heart of Darkness* is an off-putting tale for female, not to mention feminist, readers. What makes London's article unique is her view that "gender and race" are "interlocking systems," not only in Conrad's novel but also in the patriarchal ideology in which it is grounded. Onto Africa is projected "the 'dark continent' of female sexuality," a sexuality and continent from which the novel's European women are excluded. But the same exclusion that renders the Intended something less than sexual renders her African counterpart something less than woman. (Referred to as a "wild and gorgeous apparition of a woman," Kurtz's "savage mistress" is little more than a symbol — of a sexuality that is dark and savage and of a dark savagery that is sexual.) London thus takes the following view: "Dependent upon unexamined assumptions, themselves culturally suspect, the novel, in its representations of sex and gender, supports dubious cultural claims; it participates in and promotes a racial as well as gender ideology that the narrative represents as transparent and 'self-evident'" (238).

In arguing that *Heart of Darkness* reproduces and reinforces racist and sexist attitudes, London demonstrates that she is substantially in agreement with Chinua Achebe and his now-famous 1975 assessment.

She complains, however, that in "detailing the distortions mapped by the novel's registers of race, [Achebe] reads gender univocally." He does so in spite of the fact that "the very features that inform Achebe's racial critique . . . mark the novel's representations of women as well. For these other 'rudimentary souls,' denied even the distinction of a name (the aunt, the Intended), also speak only to convict themselves. . . . Similarly, the narrative's projection of Africa as . . . 'the antithesis of Europe' coincides with its construction of the feminine as the foil to masculinity" (239).

London is hardly alone in agreeing with Achebe's basic claim. Susan Blake, for instance, has reinforced Achebe's viewpoint in her oft-cited 1990 article "Racism and the Classics: Teaching *Heart of Darkness.*" So has Benita Parry, who in *Conrad and Imperialism* (1983) argues that "although the resonances of white are rendered discordant [by *Heart of Darkness*], . . . black and dark do serve in the text as equivalences for the savage and unredeemed, the corrupt and degraded . . . the cruel and atrocious" (23). But the opposite position has also been taken, not only by European and North American critics like Mark Kinkead-Weeks but also by African and other critics speaking from the vantage point of the postcolonial world such as C. P. Sarvan, of the University of Zambia. (Both Sarvan and Kinkead-Weeks take strong issue with Achebe's statement that Marlow enjoys "Conrad's complete confidence.")

Speaking of Achebe, the celebrated South American novelist Wilson Harris wrote in 1990, "I am convinced his judgement or dismissal of *Heart of Darkness* is a profoundly mistaken one" (161). Harris takes the view that Conrad's work is a forward-looking "frontier novel," a text that "stands upon a threshold of capacity" that Conrad "pointed" toward but "never attained" (162). That view is shared by Peter Nazareth, a Ugandan who reminds his audience that "Jane Austen's characters in *Mansfield Park* could live a luxurious life while the patriarch left for the colonies; Conrad actually takes us to the colonies to show us what happened there when the patriarch or his agents arrived and how his wealth at home came from brutal colonial action. Conrad was therefore a mental liberator" (221).

One critic who has staked out a more-or-less middle ground between Achebe and his most outspoken opponents is Patrick Brantlinger, whose "*Heart of Darkness*: Anti-Imperialism, Racism, or Impressionism?" is reprinted in this volume. Another is Sandya Shetty, who in a 1989 article entitled "*Heart of Darkness*: Out of

Africa Some New Thing Never Comes" states that Achebe "is right on the mark" in suggesting that "Conrad's picture of Africa" is "an ideological construction rather than historical reality or pure artistic creation" (467). But she denies that Conrad paints as favorable a picture of Europe as Achebe suggests. In fact, she views Conrad as a critic of empire whose critique fails in ways that the theoretical writings of cultural critic Edward Said can help us understand. Shetty summarizes Said's argument this way: "The critic of empire who functions from within the dominant culture must find it well nigh impossible to venture far beyond the very ideological barriers which he purports to dissolve." Conrad fails to venture beyond or dissolve those barriers because, "rather than offering an alternative vocabulary for discussing racial and colonial politics," he relies heavily upon "the language of the dominant culture which he intends to criticize" (462). Given that fact, Shetty argues that "it cannot . . . be surprising that Conrad's colonial works participate in the very ideology which they attempt to expose and destroy" (463).

Other critics have sidestepped the question of Conrad's racism, preferring to focus on whether or not Conrad was supportive of imperialism, an institution that depended upon and reinforced racist attitudes. Hunt Hawkins, author of a series of articles on *Heart of Darkness* published between 1979 and 1992, has viewed the novel as a critique of Belgium's imperialist venture but its author as a man generally supportive of British imperialism and colonialism. (In *The Location of Culture* [1994], the postcolonial critic Homi K. Bhabha states that *Heart of Darkness* may be set in the Belgian Congo but "the power and presence of the English" permeates not only Marlow's discourse but also Conrad's [108].) In a 1991 article entitled "Exotic Nostalgia: Conrad and the New Imperialism," Chris Bongie suggests that Conrad's belief in and longing for community caused him to have ambivalent feelings about imperialism, which held out the (false) promise of worldwide community.

One of the more challenging treatments of this subject is to be found in Vincent P. Pecora's *Self and Form in Modern Narrative* (1989), which outlines the difficulties faced by a writer who wishes to critique an institution like imperialism from the outside. Imperialism contradicts itself in several ways (systematic oppression involving laissez-faire democracy, a grand scheme relying on small-scale entrepreneurs). As a further complication, any attempt to critique something as hegemonic — that is, generally accepted — as imperialism runs the risk of reinforcing the very ideology it intends to undermine, for the critique must rely on devices (such as irony) that can be overlooked and, therefore, that can and do backfire. Marlow's lie, according to Pecora, illustrates the difficulty Conrad faced, the double bind he was in: "an attempt to preserve" the "humanity his independence [from imperialism] requires," Marlow's "transgression" is also "a perfect preservation of imperialist rhetoric." That is to say, it does exactly what obfuscating imperialistic rhetoric does: it hides from the home folk what is being done in the colonies in the interests of empire and enlightenment (159).

It is impossible to mention everything influential that has been written on a novel like *Heart of Darkness*. A great deal of value has been published, and some of the most noteworthy contributions do not fit neatly in the novel's evolving interpretive history; rather than swimming in the main currents of Conrad criticism (or criticism in general), their authors branch far out on their own. To follow their arguments in a critical survey such as this one would require looping digressions. Had there been room for even two such digressions, I would have summed up *Reading for the Plot: Design and Intention in Narrative* (1984), in which Peter Brooks uses *Heart of Darkness* to deconstruct a commonly accepted distinction between plot and story, and I would have mentioned an essay that appeared in the first edition of this volume, Adena Rosmarin's "Darkening the Reader: Reader-Response Criticism and *Heart of Darkness*" (1989), which looks at Marlow's lie not from the vantage point of a feminist but, rather, from that of a critic interested in how readers make sense of what (lying) fictions leave out. Fortunately, the deconstructive position espoused by Brooks is powerfully present in the pages that follow, in J. Hillis Miller's "*Heart of Darkness* Revisited," and Peter J. Rabinowitz's brand-new reader-response approach to Conrad's novel deals with many of the same issues so admirably set forth by Rosmarin. Three other essays — Patrick Brantlinger's "*Heart of Darkness*: Anti-Imperialism, Racism, or Impressionism?," Johanna M. Smith's "'Too Beautiful Altogether': Ideologies of Gender and Empire in *Heart of Darkness*," and Brook Thomas's "Preserving and Keeping Order by Killing Time in *Heart of Darkness*" — round out this, the second Bedford Case Studies edition of *Heart of Darkness*. They respond to Achebe's charge that Conrad was a racist, London's claim that *Heart of Darkness* is sexist as well as racist, and the renewed insistence of almost everyone on reading Conrad with respect to history.

WORKS CITED

Achebe, Chinua. "An Image of Africa." *Massachusetts Review* 18 (1977): 782–94. Rpt. in *Joseph Conrad: Third World Perspectives*. Ed. Robert D. Hamner. Washington: Three Continents, 1990.

Bhabha, Homi K. *The Location of Culture*. London: Routledge, 1994.

Blake, Susan L. "Racism and the Classics: Teaching *Heart of Darkness*." *Joseph Conrad: Third World Perspectives*. Ed. Robert D. Hamner. Washington: Three Continents, 1990.

Bongie, Chris. "Exotic Nostalgia: Conrad and the New Imperialism." *Macropolitics of Nineteenth-Century Literature: Nationalism, Exoticism, Imperialism*. Ed. Jonathan Arac and Harriet Ritvo. Philadelphia: U of Pennsylvania P, 1991.

Brantlinger, Patrick. "*Heart of Darkness*: Anti-Imperialism, Racism, or Impressionism?" *Criticism* 27 (1985): 363–85. Rev. and rpt. as "Epilogue: Kurtz's 'Darkness' and Conrad's *Heart of Darkness*" in Brantlinger, *Rule of Darkness: British Literature and Imperialism, 1830–1914*. Ithaca: Cornell UP, 1988.

Brooks, Peter. *Reading for the Plot: Design and Intervention in Narrative*. New York: Knopf, 1984.

Crews, Frederick. *Out of My System: Psychoanalysis, Ideology, and Critical Methodology*. Oxford: Oxford UP, 1975.

Fleishman, Avrom. *Conrad's Politics*. Baltimore: Johns Hopkins UP, 1967.

Forster, E. M. *Abinger Harvest*. London: Edward Arnold, 1936.

Goodheart, Eugene. *Desire and Its Discontents*. New York: Columbia UP, 1991.

Guerard, Albert J. *Conrad the Novelist*. Cambridge: Harvard UP, 1958.

Gurko, Leo. *Joseph Conrad: Giant in Exile*. New York: Macmillan, 1962.

Harris, Wilson. "The Frontier on Which *Heart of Darkness* Stands." *Joseph Conrad: Third World Perspectives*. Ed. Robert D. Hamner. Washington: Three Continents, 1990.

Hawkins, Hunt. "Conrad and the Psychology of Colonialism." *Conrad Revisited: Essays for the Eighties*. Ed. Ross C Murfin. University: U of Alabama P, 1985.

———. "Conrad's Critique of Imperialism in *Heart of Darkness*." *PMLA* 94 (1979): 286–99.

———. "Conrad's *Heart of Darkness*: Politics and History." *Conradiana* 24 (1992): 207–17.

Johnson, Bruce. *Conrad's Models of Mind*. Minneapolis: U of Minnesota P, 1971.

Kahane, Claire. "Seduction and the Voice of the Text: *Heart of Darkness* and *The Good Soldier.*" *Seduction and Theory: Readings of Gender, Representation, and Rhetoric.* Ed. Dianne Hunter. Urbana: U of Illinois P, 1989.

Karl, Frederick R., and Laurence Davies, eds. *The Collected Letters of Joseph Conrad.* Cambridge: Cambridge UP, 1983.

Kartiganer, Donald M. *The Psychoanalytic Study of Literature.* Hillsdale: Analytic, 1985.

Knapp, Bettina. *Exile and the Writer: Exoteric and Esoteric Experiences: A Jungian Approach.* University Park: Pennsylvania State UP, 1991.

Leavis, F. R. *The Great Tradition.* New York: New York UP, 1963.

London, Bette. "Reading Race and Gender in Conrad's Dark Continent." *Criticism* 31 (1989): 235–52.

Moser, Thomas. *Joseph Conrad: Achievement and Decline.* Cambridge: Harvard UP, 1957.

Nazareth, Peter. "Out of Darkness: Conrad and Other Third World Writers." *Joseph Conrad: Third World Perspectives.* Ed. Robert D. Hamner. Washington: Three Continents, 1990.

Parry, Benita. *Conrad and Imperialism.* London: Macmillan, 1983.

Pecora, Vincent P. *Self and Form in Modern Narrative.* Baltimore: Johns Hopkins UP, 1989.

Rising, Catharine. *Darkness at Heart: Fathers and Sons in Conrad.* New York: Greenwood, 1990.

Rosmarin, Adena. "Darkening the Reader: Reader-Response Criticism and *Heart of Darkness.*" *Joseph Conrad, "Heart of Darkness."* Ed. Ross C Murfin. Case Studies in Contemporary Criticism. Boston: Bedford–St. Martin's, 1989.

Sherry, Norman, ed. *Conrad: The Critical Heritage.* London: Routledge, 1973.

Shetty, Sandya, "*Heart of Darkness:* Out of Africa Some New Thing Never Comes." *Journal of Modern Literature* 15 (1989): 461–74.

Stampfl, Barry. "Marlow's Rhetoric of (Self-) Deception in *Heart of Darkness.*" *Modern Fiction Studies* 37 (1991): 183–96.

Straus, Nina Pelikan. "The Exclusion of the Intended from Secret Sharing in Conrad's *Heart of Darkness.*" *Novel: A Forum on Fiction* 20 (1987): 123–37.

Reader-Response Criticism
and
Heart of Darkness

WHAT IS READER-RESPONSE CRITICISM?

Students are routinely asked in English courses for their reactions to the texts they are reading. Sometimes there are so many different reactions that we may wonder whether everyone has read the same text. And some students respond so idiosyncratically to what they read that we say their responses are "totally off the wall." This variety of response interests reader-response critics, who raise theoretical questions about whether our responses to a work are the same as its meanings, whether a work can have as many meanings as we have responses to it, and whether some responses are more valid than others. They ask what determines what is and what isn't "off the wall." What, in other words, is the wall, and what standards help us define it?

In addition to posing provocative questions, reader-response criticism provides us with models that aid our understanding of texts and the reading process. Adena Rosmarin has suggested that a literary text may be likened to an incomplete work of sculpture: to see it fully, we must complete it imaginatively, taking care to do so in a way that responsibly takes into account what exists. Other reader-response critics have suggested other models, for reader-response criticism is not a monolithic school of thought but, rather, an umbrella term covering a variety of approaches to literature.

Nonetheless, as Steven Mailloux has shown, reader-response critics *do* share not only questions but also goals and strategies. Two of the basic goals are to show that a work gives readers something to do and to describe what the reader does by way of response. To achieve those goals, the critic may make any of a number of what Mailloux calls "moves." For instance, a reader-response critic might typically (1) cite direct references to reading in the text being analyzed, in order to justify the focus on reading and show that the world of the text is continuous with the one in which the reader reads; (2) show how other non-reading situations in the text nonetheless mirror the situation the reader is in ("Fish shows how in *Paradise Lost* Michael's teaching of Adam in Book XI resembles Milton's teaching of the reader throughout the poem"); and (3) show, therefore, that the reader's response is, or is analogous to, the story's action or conflict. For instance, Stephen Booth calls *Hamlet* the tragic story of "an audience that cannot make up its mind" (Mailloux, "Learning" 103).

Although reader-response criticism is often said to have emerged in the United States in the 1970s, it is in one respect as old as the foundations of Western culture. The ancient Greeks and Romans tended to view literature as rhetoric, a means of making an audience react in a certain way. Although their focus was more on rhetorical strategies and devices than on the reader's (or listener's) response to those methods, the ancients by no means left the audience out of the literary equation. Aristotle thought, for instance, that the greatness of tragedy lay in its "cathartic" power to cleanse or purify the emotions of audience members. Plato, by contrast, worried about the effects of artistic productions, so much so that he advocated evicting poets from the Republic on the grounds that their words "feed and water" the passions!

In our own century, long before 1970, there were critics whose concerns and attitudes anticipated those of reader-response critics. One of these, I. A. Richards, is usually associated with formalism, a supposedly objective, text-centered approach to literature that reader-response critics of the 1970s roundly attacked. And yet in 1929 Richards managed to sound surprisingly *like* a 1970s-vintage reader-response critic, writing in *Practical Criticism* that "the personal situation of the reader inevitably (and within limits rightly) affects his reading, and many more are drawn to poetry in quest of some reflection of their latest emotional crisis than would admit it" (575). Rather than deploring this fact, as many of his formalist contemporaries would have done, Richards argued that the reader's feelings and experiences provide a kind of reality check, a way of testing the authenticity of emotions and events represented in literary works.

Approximately a decade after Richards wrote *Practical Criticism,* an American named Louise M. Rosenblatt published *Literature as Exploration* (1938). In that seminal book, now in its fourth edition (1983), Rosenblatt began developing a theory of reading that blurs the boundary between reader and text, subject and object. In a 1969 article entitled "Towards a Transactional Theory of Reading," she sums up her position by writing that "a poem is what the reader lives through under the guidance of the text and experiences as relevant to the text" (127). Rosenblatt knew her definition would be difficult for many to accept: "The idea that a *poem* presupposes a *reader* actively involved with a *text,*" she wrote, "is particularly shocking to those seeking to emphasize the objectivity of their interpretations" ("Transactional" 127).

Rosenblatt implicitly and generally refers to formalists (also called the "New Critics") when she speaks of supposedly objective interpreters shocked by the notion that a "poem" is something cooperatively produced by a "reader" and a "text." Formalists spoke of "the poem itself," the "concrete work of art," the "real poem." They had no interest in what a work of literature makes a reader "live through." In fact, in *The Verbal Icon* (1954), William K. Wimsatt and Monroe C. Beardsley defined as fallacious the very notion that a reader's response is relevant to the meaning of a literary work:

> The Affective Fallacy is a confusion between the poem and its *results* (what it *is* and what it *does*). . . . It begins by trying to derive the standards of criticism from the psychological effects of a poem and ends in impressionism and relativism. The outcome . . . is that the poem itself, as an object of specifically critical judgment, tends to disappear. (21)

Reader-response critics have taken issue with their formalist predecessors. Particularly influential has been Stanley Fish, whose early work is seen by some as marking the true beginning of contemporary reader-response criticism. In "Literature in the Reader: Affective Stylistics" (1970), Fish took on the formalist hegemony, the New Critical establishment, by arguing that any school of criticism that would see a work of literature as an object, claiming to describe what it *is* and never what it *does,* is guilty of misconstruing the very essence of literature and reading. Literature exists when it is read, Fish suggests, and its force is an affective force. Furthermore, reading is a temporal process. Formalists assume it is a spatial one as they step back and survey the literary work as if it were an object spread out before them. They may find elegant patterns in the texts they examine and reexamine, but they fail to take into account that the work is quite different to a reader who is turning the pages and being moved, or affected, by lines that appear and disappear as the reader reads.

In a discussion of the effect that a sentence penned by the seventeenth-century physician Thomas Browne has on a reader reading, Fish pauses to say this about his analysis and also, by extension, about his critical strategy: "Whatever is persuasive and illuminating about [it] is the result of my substituting for one question — what does this sentence mean? — another, more operational question — what does this sentence do?" He then quotes a line from John Milton's *Paradise Lost,* a line that refers to Satan and the other fallen angels: "Nor did they not perceive their evil plight." Whereas more traditional critics might say that the "meaning" of the line is "They did perceive their evil plight," Fish relates the uncertain movement of the reader's mind *to* that half-satisfying interpretation. Furthermore, he declares that "the reader's inability to tell whether or not 'they' do perceive and his involuntary question . . . are part of the line's *meaning,* even though they take place in the mind, not on the page" (*Text* 26).

The stress on what pages *do* to minds (and what minds do in response) pervades the writings of most, if not all, reader-response critics. Stephen Booth, whose book *An Essay on Shakespeare's Sonnets* (1969) greatly influenced Fish, sets out to describe the "reading experience that results" from a "multiplicity of organizations" in a sonnet by Shakespeare (*Essay* ix). Sometimes these organizations don't make complete sense, Booth points out, and sometimes they even seem curiously contradictory. But that is precisely what interests reader-response critics, who, unlike formalists, are at least as interested in fragmentary, inconclusive, and even unfinished texts as in polished, unified works. For it is the reader's struggle to *make sense* of a challenging work that reader-response critics seek to describe.

The German critic Wolfgang Iser has described that sense-making struggle in his books *The Implied Reader* (1972) and *The Act of Reading: A Theory of Aesthetic Response* (1976). Iser argues that texts are full of "gaps" (or "blanks," as he sometimes calls them). These gaps powerfully affect the reader, who is forced to explain them, to connect what they separate, to create in his or her mind aspects of a poem or novel or play that aren't *in* the text but that the text incites. As Iser puts it in *The Implied Reader*, the "unwritten aspects" of a story "draw the reader into the action" and "lead him to shade in the many outlines suggested by the given situations, so that these take on a reality of their own." These "outlines" that "the reader's imagination animates" in turn "influence" the way in which "the written part of the text" is subsequently read (276).

In *Self-Consuming Artifacts: The Experience of Seventeenth-Century Literature* (1972), Fish reveals his preference for literature that makes readers work at making meaning. He contrasts two kinds of literary presentation. By the phrase "rhetorical presentation," he describes literature that reflects and reinforces opinions that readers already hold; by "dialectical presentation," he refers to works that prod and provoke. A dialectical text, rather than presenting an opinion as if it were truth, challenges readers to discover truths on their own. Such a text may not even have the kind of symmetry that formalist critics seek. Instead of offering a "single, sustained argument," a dialectical text, or self-consuming artifact, may be "so arranged that to enter into the spirit and assumptions of any one of [its] . . . units is implicitly to reject the spirit and assumptions of the unit immediately preceding" (*Artifacts* 9). Whereas a critic of another school might try to force an explanation as to why the units are fundamentally coherent, the reader-response critic proceeds by describing how the reader deals with the sudden twists and turns that characterize the dialectical text, returning to earlier passages and seeing them in an entirely new light.

"The value of such a procedure," Fish has written, "is predicated on the idea of meaning as *an event*," not as something "located (presumed to be embedded) *in* the utterance" or "verbal object as a thing in itself" (*Text* 28). By redefining meaning as an event rather than as something inherent in the text, the reader-response critic once again locates meaning in time: the reader's time. A text exists and signifies while it is being read, and what it signifies or means will depend, to no small extent, on *when* it is read. (*Paradise Lost* had some meanings for a seventeenth-century Puritan that it would not have for a twentieth-century atheist.)

With the redefinition of literature as something that exists meaningfully only in the mind of the reader, with the redefinition of the literary work as a catalyst of mental events, comes a concurrent redefinition of the reader. No longer is the reader the passive recipient of those ideas that an author has planted in a text. "The reader is *active*," Rosenblatt insists ("Transactional" 123). Fish begins "Literature in the Reader" with a similar observation: "If at this moment someone were to ask, 'what are you doing,' you might reply, 'I am reading,' and thereby acknowledge that reading is . . . something *you do*" (*Text* 22). Iser, in focusing critical interest on the gaps in texts, on what is not expressed, similarly redefines the reader as an active maker.

Amid all this talk of "the reader," it is tempting and natural to ask, "Just who *is* the reader?" (Or, to place the emphasis differently, "Just who is *the* reader?") Are reader-response critics simply sharing their own idiosyncratic responses when they describe what a line from *Paradise Lost* does in and to the reader's mind? "What about my responses?" you may want to ask. "What if they're different? Would reader-response critics be willing to say that my responses are equally valid?"

Fish defines "the reader" in this way: "*the* reader is the *informed* reader." The informed reader (whom Fish sometimes calls "the *intended* reader") is someone who is "sufficiently experienced as a reader to have internalized the properties of literary discourses, including everything from the most local of devices (figures of speech, etc.) to whole genres." And, of course, the informed reader is in full possession of the "semantic knowledge" (knowledge of idioms, for instance) assumed by the text (*Artifacts* 406).

Other reader-response critics define "*the* reader" differently. Wayne C. Booth, in *A Rhetoric of Irony* (1974), uses the phrase "the implied reader" to mean the reader "created by the work." (Only "by agreeing to play the role of this created audience," Susan Suleiman explains, "can an actual reader correctly understand and appreciate the work" [8].) Gerard Genette and Gerald Prince prefer to speak of "the narratee, . . . the necessary counterpart of a given narrator, that is, the person or figure who receives a narrative" (Suleiman 13). Like Booth, Iser employs the term "the implied reader," but he also uses "the educated reader" when he refers to what Fish called the "informed reader."

Jonathan Culler, who in 1981 criticized Fish for his sketchy definition of the informed reader, set out in *Structuralist Poetics* (1975) to describe the educated or "competent" reader's education by elaborating those reading conventions that make possible the understanding of poems and novels. In retrospect, however, Culler's definitions seem sketchy as well. By "competent reader," Culler meant competent reader of "literature." By "literature," he meant what schools and colleges mean when they speak of literature as being part of the curriculum. Culler, like his contemporaries, was not concerned with the fact that curricular content is politically and economically motivated. And "he did not," in Mailloux's words, "emphasize how the literary competence he described was embedded within larger formations and traversed by political ideologies extending beyond the academy" ("Turns" 49). It remained for a later generation of reader-oriented critics to do those things.

The fact that Fish, following Rosenblatt's lead, defined reader-response criticism in terms of its difference from and opposition to the New Criticism or formalism should not obscure the fact that the formalism of the 1950s and early 1960s had a great deal in common with the reader-response criticism of the late 1960s and early 1970s. This has become increasingly obvious with the rise of subsequent critical approaches whose practitioners have proved less interested in the close reading of texts than in the way literature represents, reproduces, and/or resists prevailing ideologies concerning gender, class, and race. In a retrospective essay entitled "The Turns of Reader-Response Criticism" (1990), Mailloux has suggested that, from the perspective of hindsight, the "close reading" of formalists and "Fish's early 'affective stylistics'" seem surprisingly similar. Indeed, Mailloux argues, the early "reader talk of . . . Iser and Fish enabled the continuation of the formalist practice of close reading. Through a vocabulary focused on a text's manipulation of readers, Fish was especially effective in extending and diversifying the formalist practices that continued business as usual within literary criticism" (48).

Since the mid-1970s, however, reader-response criticism (once commonly referred to as the "School of Fish") has diversified and taken on a variety of new forms, some of which truly *are* incommensurate with formalism, with its considerable respect for the integrity and power of the text. For instance, "subjectivists" like David Bleich, Norman Holland, and Robert Crosman have assumed what Mailloux calls the "absolute priority of individual selves as creators of texts" (*Conventions* 31). In other words, these critics do not see the reader's response as one "guided" by the text but rather as one motivated by deep-seated, personal, psychological needs. What they find in texts is, in Holland's phrase, their own "identity theme." Holland has argued that as readers we use "the literary work to symbolize and finally to replicate ourselves. We work out through the text our own characteristic patterns of desire" ("UNITY" 816). Subjective critics, as you may already have guessed, often find themselves confronted with the following question: If all interpretation is a function of private, psychological identity, then why have so many readers interpreted, say,

Shakespeare's *Hamlet* in the same way? Different subjective critics have answered the question differently. Holland simply has said that common identity themes exist, such as that involving an oedipal fantasy. Meanwhile, Fish, who in the late 1970s moved away from reader-response criticism as he had initially helped define it, came up with a different answer to the question of why different readers tend to read the same works the same way. His answer, rather than involving common individual identity themes, involved common *cultural* identity. In "Interpreting the *Variorum*" (1976), he argues that the "stability of interpretation among readers" is a function of shared "interpretive strategies." These strategies, which "exist prior to the act of reading and therefore determine the shape of what is read," are held in common by "interpretive communities" such as the one constituted by American college students reading a novel as a class assignment (*Text* 167, 171). In developing the model of interpretive communities, Fish truly has made the break with formalist or New Critical predecessors, becoming in the process something of a social, structuralist, reader-response critic. Recently, he has been engaged in studying reading communities and their interpretive conventions in order to understand the conditions that give rise to a work's intelligibility.

Fish's shift in focus is in many ways typical of changes that have taken place within the field of reader-response criticism — a field that, because of those changes, is increasingly being referred to as "reader-*oriented*" criticism. Less and less common are critical analyses examining the transactional interface between the text and its individual reader. Increasingly, reader-oriented critics are investigating reading communities, as the reader-oriented cultural critic Janice A. Radway has done in her study of female readers of romance paperbacks (*Reading the Romance*, 1984). They are also studying the changing reception of literary works across time; see, for example, Mailloux in his "pragmatic readings" of American literature in *Interpretive Conventions* (1982) and *Rhetorical Power* (1989).

An important catalyst of this gradual change was the work of Hans Robert Jauss, a colleague of Iser's whose historically oriented reception theory (unlike Iser's theory of the implied reader) was not available in English book form until the early 1980s. Rather than focusing on the implied, informed, or intended reader, Jauss examined actual past readers. In *Toward an Aesthetic of Reception* (1982), he argued that the reception of a work or author tends to depend upon the reading public's "horizons of expectations." He noted that, in the morally conservative climate of mid-nineteenth-century France, *Madame Bo-*

vary was literally put on trial, its author Flaubert accused of glorifying adultery in passages representing the protagonist's fevered delirium via free indirect discourse, a mode of narration in which a third-person narrator tells us in an unfiltered way what a character is thinking and feeling.

As readers have become more sophisticated and tolerant, the popularity and reputation of *Madame Bovary* have soared. Sometimes, of course, changes in a reading public's horizons of expectations cause a work to be *less* well received over time. As American reception theorists influenced by Jauss have shown, Mark Twain's *Adventures of Huckleberry Finn* has elicited an increasingly ambivalent reaction from a reading public increasingly sensitive to demeaning racial stereotypes and racist language. The rise of feminism has prompted a downward revaluation of everything from Andrew Marvell's "To His Coy Mistress" to D. H. Lawrence's *Women in Love*.

Some reader-oriented feminists, such as Judith Fetterley, Patrocinio Schweickart, and Monique Wittig, have challenged the reader to become what Fetterley calls "the resisting reader." Arguing that literature written by men tends, in Schweickart's terms, to "immasculate" women, they have advocated strategies of reading that involve substituting masculine for feminine pronouns and male for female characters in order to expose the sexism inscribed in patriarchal texts. Other feminists, such as Nancy K. Miller in *Subject to Change* (1988), have suggested that there may be essential differences between the way women and men read and write.

That suggestion, however, has prompted considerable disagreement. A number of gender critics whose work is oriented toward readers and reading have admitted that there is such a thing as "reading like a woman" (or man), but they have also tended to agree with Peggy Kamuf that such forms of reading, like gender itself, are cultural rather than natural constructs. Gay and lesbian critics, arguing that sexualities have been similarly constructed within and by social discourse, have argued that there is a homosexual way of reading; Wayne Koestenbaum has defined "the (male twentieth-century first world) gay reader" as one who "reads resistantly for inscriptions of his condition, for texts that will confirm a social and private identity founded on a desire for other men. . . . Reading becomes a hunt for histories that deliberately foreknow or unwittingly trace a desire felt not by author but by reader, who is most acute when searching for signs of himself" (in Boone and Cadden, 176–77).

Given this kind of renewed interest in the reader and reading, some students of contemporary critical practice have been tempted to conclude that reader-oriented theory has been taken over by feminist, gender, gay, and lesbian theory. Others, like Elizabeth Freund, have suggested that it is deconstruction with which the reader-oriented approach has mixed and merged. Certainly, all of these approaches have informed and been informed by reader-response or reader-oriented theory. The case can be made, however, that there is in fact still a distinct reader-oriented approach to literature, one whose points of tangency are neither with deconstruction nor with feminist, gender, and so-called queer theory but, rather, with the new historicism and cultural criticism.

This relatively distinct form of reader theory is practiced by a number of critics, but is perhaps best exemplified by the work of scholars like Mailloux and Peter J. Rabinowitz. In *Before Reading: Narrative Conventions and the Politics of Interpretation* (1987), Rabinowitz sets forth four conventions or rules of reading, which he calls the rules of "notice," "signification," "configuration," and "coherence" — rules telling us which parts of a narrative are important, which details have a reliable secondary or special meaning, which fit into which familiar patterns, and how stories fit together as a whole. He then proceeds to analyze the misreadings and misjudgments of critics and to show that politics governs the way in which those rules are applied and broken. ("The strategies employed by critics when they read [Raymond Chandler's] *The Big Sleep*," Rabinowitz writes, "can teach us something about the structure of misogyny, not the misogyny of the novel itself, but the misogyny of the world outside it" [195].) In subsequent critical essays, Rabinowitz proceeds similarly, showing how a society's ideological assumptions about gender, race, and class determine the way in which artistic works are perceived and evaluated.

Mailloux, who calls his approach "rhetorical reception theory" or "rhetorical hermeneutics," takes a similar tack, insofar as he describes the political contexts of (mis)interpretation. In a recent essay on "Misreading as a Historical Act" (1993), he shows that a mid-nineteenth-century review of Frederick Douglass's slave *Narrative* by proto-feminist Margaret Fuller seems to be a misreading until we situate it "within the cultural conversation of the 'Bible politics' of 1845" (Machor 9). Woven through Mailloux's essay on Douglas and Fuller are philosophical pauses in which we are reminded, in various subtle ways, that all reading (including Mailloux's and our own) is culturally situated and likely to seem like *mis*reading someday. One such reflective pause, however, accomplishes more; in it, Mailloux reads the map of where reader-oriented criticism is today, affords a rationale for its being there, and plots its likely future direction. "However we have arrived at our present juncture," Mailloux writes,

> the current talk about historical acts of reading provides a welcome opportunity for more explicit consideration of how reading is historically contingent, politically situated, institutionally embedded, and materially conditioned; of how reading any text, literary or nonliterary, relates to a larger cultural politics that goes well beyond some hypothetical private interaction between an autonomous reader and an independent text; and of how our particular views of reading relate to the liberatory potential of literacy and the transformative power of education. (5)

In the essay that follows, Peter J. Rabinowitz begins by reminding us that, in 1975, the African novelist Chinua Achebe charged that Conrad was a racist and that *Heart of Darkness* is a racist novel. Rabinowitz summarizes the work of subsequent critics who have contested, concurred with, or modified Achebe's charge; more important, he proposes "a related question, one that is more dangerous because it touches more directly on our immediate lives. In what ways might *we*, Conrad's modern readers, be implicated in politically questionable activities as we interpret the text?" Rabinowitz wants "to think less about what Conrad did when he wrote than about what we do when we read." Rather than analyzing "the politics encoded" in a given text, Rabinowitz proposes to examine "the politics of interpretation," the "politics embedded in our [reading] practices."

When Rabinowitz uses the pronouns "our" and "we," he is seldom referring to us as individuals. Rather than focusing, as subjectivist reader-response critics have done, on personal or even idiosyncratic ways of reading, he emphasizes that "we" all belong to reading communities governed by certain "interpretive conventions," conventions that enforce a considerable degree of similarity between "our" readings. Instead of being interested in the ways in which our interpretations differ, Rabinowitz is interested in "the ways in which [they] overlap" — and the shared assumptions that underlie our interpretive strategies.

Rabinowitz proceeds by defining four kinds of rules that govern "our" way of reading works like *Heart of Darkness:* rules of "notice," "signification," "configuration," and "coherence." Although he admits that "different readers . . . are apt to apply different rules to the same text," he argues that, "regardless of the text, regardless of the particular choices that a given reader makes as he or she processes it," the interpretive rules all have a "political edge."

To illustrate his assertion, Rabinowitz distinguishes between the once-prevalent view that *Heart of Darkness* is about the "Nature of Man" and the more recent, postmodern notion that it is primarily concerned with language and textuality: in other words, that it is a self-referential work in which the medium is the message. Rabinowitz argues that "while what we might call the 'content' of these readings may have varied, the procedure that generates them is more stable." Whether arguing that *Heart of Darkness* is about human nature or textuality, critics past and present have applied the two-step "Rule of Abstract Displacement," the first step of which is to assume that the "'real' subject" of a text is "something that's not immediately apparent from the surface" (thus, Shakespeare's play *Hamlet* is "not really 'about' political infighting in the Danish court"). The second step of this interpretive rule is to generalize even further, until the subject of the text is seen to be some universal proposition with value for all human beings.

This interpretive process is political, Rabinowitz argues, insofar as it produces interpretations that "all share a hierarchical value system." This system privileges not what the text shows us directly but, rather, what it may indirectly suggest; in other words, it privileges the abstract (often manifested through the metaphorical) over the concrete. Such an interpretive process is political, according to Rabinowitz, because it allows us to gloss over the literal content of scenes such as the one in *Heart of Darkness* in which starving slaves die in a greenish gloom. As a consequence, readers may reach conclusions similar to Jacques Berthoud's: "What finally damns Kurtz is not the horror of the shrunken heads . . . nor even the ferocity of his raiding excursions, but *what these things indicate.*"

To further summarize Rabinowitz's essay would be to spoil the pleasure of reading it. Suffice it to say that interspersed between readings of *Heart of Darkness* — and readings of *readings* of *Heart of Darkness* — are references to Mrs. E. B. Duffey's "Etiquette for General Occasions," to James Ellroy's novel *The Big Nowhere,* and to the movies *Cat People, Kiss of the Spider Woman, Black Widow,* and *Blue Steel.* These references, made in an unusually casual, humorous, even friendly style, are hardly accidental — certainly not dispensable asides thrown into an otherwise serious argument about the deeply suspect politics of our reading practices. Rather, these references are part of Rabinowitz's reader-response strategy, for they make it virtually impossible for us not to engage actively in the unfolding argument, virtually impossible for us not to see that, as readers, we share common attitudes and experiences. In doing so, these references cause us to wonder whether in reading *Heart of Darkness* we, too, have been too quick to gloss over "precisely those aspects of the novel that might prompt a reader to think seriously about the problem of racism."

READER-RESPONSE CRITICISM: A SELECTED BIBLIOGRAPHY

Some Introductions to Reader-Response Criticism

Beach, Richard. *A Teacher's Introduction to Reader-Response Theories.* Urbana: NCTE, 1993.

Fish, Stanley E. "Literature in the Reader: Affective Stylistics." *New Literary History* 2 (1970): 123–61. Rpt. in Fish, *Text* 21–67, and in Primeau 154–79.

Freund, Elizabeth. *The Return of the Reader: Reader-Response Criticism.* London: Methuen, 1987.

Holub, Robert C. *Reception Theory: A Critical Introduction.* New York: Methuen, 1984.

Leitch, Vincent B. *American Literary Criticism from the Thirties to the Fighties.* New York. Columbia UP, 1988.

Mailloux, Steven. "Learning to Read: Interpretation and Reader-Response Criticism." *Studies in the Literary Imagination* 12 (1979): 93–108.

———. "Reader-Response Criticism?" *Genre* 10 (1977): 413–31.

———. "The Turns of Reader-Response Criticism." *Conversations: Contemporary Critical Theory and the Teaching of Literature.* Ed. Charles Moran and Elizabeth F. Penfield. Urbana: NCTE, 1990. 38–54.

Rabinowitz, Peter J. "Whirl Without End: Audience-Oriented Criticism." *Contemporary Literary Theory.* Ed. G. Douglas Atkins and Laura Morrow. Amherst: U of Massachusetts P, 1989. 81–100.

Rosenblatt, Louise M. "Towards a Transactional Theory of Reading." *Journal of Reading Behavior* 1 (1969): 31–47. Rpt. in Primeau 121–46.

Suleiman, Susan R. "Introduction: Varieties of Audience-Oriented Criticism." Suleiman and Crosman 3–45.

Tompkins, Jane P. "An Introduction to Reader-Response Criticism." Tompkins ix–xxiv.

Reader-Response Criticism in Anthologies and Collections

Flynn, Elizabeth A., and Patrocinio P. Schweickart, eds. *Gender and Reading: Essays on Readers, Texts, and Contexts.* Baltimore: Johns Hopkins UP, 1986.

Garvin, Harry R., ed. *Theories of Reading, Looking, and Listening.* Lewisburg: Bucknell UP, 1981. Essays by Cain and Rosenblatt.

Machor, James L., ed. *Readers in History: Nineteenth-Century American Literature and the Contexts of Response.* Baltimore: Johns Hopkins UP, 1993. Contains Mailloux essay "Misreading as a Historical Act: Cultural Rhetoric, Bible Politics, and Fuller's 1845 Review of Douglass's *Narrative.*"

Primeau, Ronald, ed. *Influx: Essays on Literary Influence.* Port Washington: Kennikat, 1977. Essays by Fish, Holland, and Rosenblatt.

Suleiman, Susan R., and Inge Crosman, eds. *The Reader in the Text: Essays on Audience and Interpretation.* Princeton: Princeton UP, 1980. See especially the essays by Culler, Iser, and Todorov.

Tompkins, Jane P., ed. *Reader-Response Criticism: From Formalism to Post-Structuralism.* Baltimore: Johns Hopkins UP, 1980. See especially the essays by Bleich, Fish, Holland, Prince, and Tompkins.

Reader-Response Criticism: Some Major Works

Bleich, David. *Subjective Criticism.* Baltimore: Johns Hopkins UP, 1978.

Booth, Stephen. *An Essay on Shakespeare's Sonnets.* New Haven: Yale UP, 1969.

Booth, Wayne C. *A Rhetoric of Irony.* Chicago: U of Chicago P, 1974.

Eco, Umberto. *The Role of the Reader: Explorations in the Semiotics of Texts.* Bloomington: Indiana UP, 1979.

Fish, Stanley Eugene. *Doing What Comes Naturally: Change, Rhetoric, and the Practice of Theory in Literary and Legal Studies.* Durham: Duke UP, 1989.

———. *Is There a Text in This Class? The Authority of Interpretive Communities.* Cambridge: Harvard UP, 1980. This volume contains most of Fish's most influential essays, including "Literature in the Reader: Affective Stylistics," "What It's Like to Read *L'Allegro* and *Il Penseroso*," "Interpreting the *Variorum*," "Is There a Text in This Class?" "How to Recognize a Poem When You See One," and "What Makes an Interpretation Acceptable?"

————. *Self-Consuming Artifacts: The Experience of Seventeenth-Century Literature*. Berkeley: U of California P, 1972.

————. *Surprised by Sin: The Reader in "Paradise Lost."* 2nd ed. Berkeley: U of California P, 1971.

Holland, Norman N. *5 Readers Reading*. New Haven: Yale UP, 1975.

————. "UNITY IDENTITY TEXT SELF." *PMLA* 90 (1975): 813–22.

Iser, Wolfgang. *The Act of Reading: A Theory of Aesthetic Response*. Baltimore: Johns Hopkins UP, 1978.

————. *The Implied Reader: Patterns of Communication in Prose Fiction from Bunyan to Beckett*. Baltimore: Johns Hopkins UP, 1974.

Jauss, Hans Robert. *Toward an Aesthetic of Reception*. Trans. Timothy Bahti. Intro. Paul de Man. Brighton, Eng.: Harvester, 1982.

Mailloux, Steven. *Interpretive Conventions: The Reader in the Study of American Fiction*. Ithaca: Cornell UP, 1982.

————. *Rhetorical Power*. Ithaca: Cornell UP, 1989.

Messent, Peter. *New Readings of the American Novel: Narrative Theory and Its Application*. New York: Macmillan, 1991.

Prince, Gerald. *Narratology*. New York: Mouton, 1982.

Rabinowitz, Peter J. *Before Reading: Narrative Conventions and the Politics of Interpretation*. Ithaca: Cornell UP, 1987.

Radway, Janice A. *Reading the Romance: Women, Patriarchy, and Popular Literature*. Chapel Hill: U of North Carolina P, 1984.

Rosenblatt, Louise M. *Literature as Exploration*. 4th ed. New York: MLA, 1983.

————. *The Reader, the Text, the Poem: The Transactional Theory of the Literary Work*. Carbondale: Southern Illinois UP, 1978.

Slatoff, Walter J. *With Respect to Readers: Dimensions of Literary Response*. Ithaca: Cornell UP, 1970.

Steig, Michael. *Stories of Reading: Subjectivity and Literary Understanding*. Baltimore: Johns Hopkins UP, 1989.

Exemplary Short Readings of Major Texts

Anderson, Howard. "*Tristram Shandy* and the Reader's Imagination." *PMLA* 86 (1971): 966–73.

Berger, Carole. "The Rake and the Reader in Jane Austen's Novels." *Studies in English Literature, 1500–1900* 15 (1975): 531–44.

Booth, Stephen. "On the Value of *Hamlet*." *Reinterpretations of*

English Drama: Selected Papers from the English Institute. Ed.
Norman Rabkin. New York: Columbia UP, 1969. 137–76.

Easson, Robert R. "William Blake and His Reader in *Jerusalem.*"
Blake's Sublime Allegory. Ed. Stuart Curran and Joseph A.
Wittreich. Madison: U of Wisconsin P, 1973. 309–28.

Kirk, Carey H. "*Moby-Dick:* The Challenge of Response." *Papers on
Language and Literature* 13 (1977): 383–90.

Leverenz, David. "Mrs. Hawthorne's Headache: Reading *The Scarlet
Letter.*" *Nathaniel Hawthorne, "The Scarlet Letter."* Ed. Ross C
Murfin. Case Studies in Contemporary Criticism. Boston:
Bedford–St. Martin's, 1991. 263–74.

Lowe-Evans, Mary. "Reading with a 'Nicer Eye': Responding to
Frankenstein." *Mary Shelley, "Frankenstein."* Ed. Johanna M.
Smith. Case Studies in Contemporary Criticism. Boston:
Bedford–St. Martin's, 1992. 215–29.

Rabinowitz, Peter J. "'A Symbol of Something': Interpretive Vertigo
in 'The Dead.'" *James Joyce, "The Dead."* Ed. Daniel R. Schwarz.
Case Studies in Contemporary Criticism. Boston: Bedford–St.
Martin's, 1994. 137–49.

Treichler, Paula. "The Construction of Ambiguity in *The
Awakening.*" *Kate Chopin, "The Awakening."* Ed. Nancy A.
Walker. Case Studies in Contemporary Criticism. Boston:
Bedford–St. Martin's, 1993. 308–28.

Other Works Referred to in
"What Is Reader-Response Criticism?"

Booth, Wayne C. *A Rhetoric of Irony.* Chicago: U of Chicago P,
1974.

Culler, Jonathan. *Structural Poetics: Structuralism, Linguistics, and the
Study of Literature.* Ithaca: Cornell UP, 1975.

Koestenbaum, Wayne. "Wilde's Hard Labor and the Birth of Gay
Reading." *Engendering Men: The Question of Male Feminist Criticism.* Ed. Joseph A. Boone and Michael Cadden. New York: Routledge, 1990.

Richards, I. A. *Practical Criticism.* New York: Harcourt, 1929. Rpt.
in *Criticism: The Major Texts.* Ed. Walter Jackson Bate. Rev. ed.
New York: Harcourt, 1970. 575.

Wimsatt, William K., and Monroe C. Beardsley. *The Verbal Icon.* Lex-
ington: U of Kentucky P, 1954. See especially the discussion of
"The Affective Fallacy," with which reader-response critics have so
sharply disagreed.

Reader-Oriented Approaches to
Heart of Darkness

Lenta, Margaret. "Narrators and Readers: 1902 and 1975." *Ariel: A Review of International English Literature* 20 (1989): 19–36.

Rosmarin, Adena. "Darkening the Reader: Reader-Response Criticism and *Heart of Darkness*." *Joseph Conrad, "Heart of Darkness."* Ed. Ross C Murfin. Case Studies in Contemporary Criticism. Boston: Bedford–St. Martin's, 1989.

Straus, Nina Pelikan. "The Exclusion of the Intended from Secret Sharing in Conrad's *Heart of Darkness*." *Novel: A Forum on Fiction* 20 (1987): 123–37.

A READER-RESPONSE PERSPECTIVE

PETER J. RABINOWITZ

Reader Response, Reader Responsibility:
Heart of Darkness and the
Politics of Displacement

Even before Chinua Achebe proclaimed in 1975 that "Joseph Conrad was a bloody racist" (9),[1] many critics had scrutinized the racial politics of Conrad's *Heart of Darkness*. But Achebe's stature as one of Africa's foremost novelists gave new urgency to the concerns about Conrad's ideology; and since then, it has been increasingly difficult to talk about the novel without coming to terms, either explicitly or implicitly, with Achebe's condemnation. Some critics have defended Conrad's political credentials. Brian W. Shaffer, for example, argues that Conrad's African fictions are "'rejoinders'" to philosopher Herbert Spencer's "typology of civilization" (46), which made a hierarchical distinction between militant societies ("simple, repressive,"

One of the most pleasant reader responsibilities is acknowledging friends and colleagues who have helped frame and refine arguments. In particular, I would like to thank Jamie Barlowe, Florence Martin, Maureen Miller, Nancy Rabinowitz, Mary Ann Smart, Michael Smith, Priscilla Walton, and the students of Mary Beth Shaddy's 1993–94 AP English classes in Dimond High School, Anchorage, Alaska.
[1]The essay was reprinted several times; and when Achebe revised it for inclusion in *Hopes and Impediments,* he changed the word "bloody" to the less inflammatory "thoroughgoing." This retrospective act of moderation, however, was ineffectual, since critics universally cite the earlier version.

and evolutionarily backward) and industrial societies ("complex, democratic," and more advanced) (47). Thus, although Conrad organizes his novel around Spencer's categories, he doesn't defend the norms of imperialism; rather, according to Shaffer, he "invokes, only to destroy, such norms, values, and myths" (55). Other critics, in contrast, have sifted through Conrad's text for further traces of his racism. Susan Blake, for instance, accepts Achebe's accusation and adds further charges of her own. Still others have staked out a more ambiguous ground. Patrick Brantlinger, among the most sophisticated, argues in an essay reprinted in this volume that *Heart of Darkness* "offers a powerful critique of at least some manifestations of imperialism and racism, as it simultaneously presents that critique in ways that can be characterized only as imperialist and racist. . . . The novel itself . . . cancels out its own best intentions" (279, 295).

The inquiry into Conrad's participation in the racism and imperialism of the nineteenth century is both important and illuminating. But it is also safe, since it directs the most severe indictments against someone who is conveniently dead. In this essay, then, I will propose a related question, one that is more dangerous because it touches more directly on our immediate lives. In what ways might *we*, Conrad's modern readers, be implicated in politically questionable activities as we interpret the text? In other words, I want to think less about what Conrad did when he wrote than about what we do when we read — I want to turn away from the qualities of the text (for instance, the "point of view itself" that Blake sees as "the real basis of what emerges as racism in literature" [400]) and focus instead on the actions of the reader. My concern here will thus be less with the politics of literature (that is, the politics encoded within particular texts that are already written and for which we as readers have no direct accountability) than with the politics of interpretation (that is, the politics embedded in our own practices and for which we are in fact responsible).

My argument stems from my interest in the strategies that readers employ as they try to make sense out of works of art.[2] In general, I refer to all such procedures as acts of interpretation — using a broad definition of "interpretation" as any act that facilitates our experience or our understanding of a work of art by providing a grid within which to receive it, a framework that guides (and hence limits) our responses.

---

[2]Although this essay centers on the interpretation of literature, similar issues arise in the other arts as well. For a study of parallel issues in music, see, for instance, my "Whiting the Wrongs of History."

It is easy, of course, to recognize the interpretive component in acts of explication that overtly distill a "meaning" from a text. For instance, when Ian Watt claims that "Conrad's writing and his mind in general aim to advance, not political programs, but moral understanding" (12), or when Robert F. Bergstrom sees the book as "the profound and resigned look into the face of human evil" (747), there is little doubt that interpretation is taking place. But it is no less an interpretive act when a reader engages with the characters, making judgments about the choices they make or the conditions under which they live — for instance, when a reader sympathizes with the sufferings of the "black shadows of disease and starvation," the enslaved workers who, "lost in uncongenial surroundings, fed on unfamiliar food," had sickened and crawled off to die in "the greenish gloom" of the "Inferno" of the ravine:

> Black shapes crouched, lay, sat between the trees, leaning against the trunks, clinging to the earth, half coming out, half effaced within the dim light, in all the attitudes of pain, abandonment, and despair. (p. 31)

Critical acts that aim at characterizing a text in more "objective" and "neutral" terms are interpretive as well, for in "describing" the work or placing it in a particular context, they too tell us how to take it, how to organize our perceptions and judgments of it. For instance, when Garrett Stewart describes the plot of *Heart of Darkness* as the story of "a level-headed seaman named Marlow [who] journeys to the Congo as steamer captain for a European trading company" (319), he may appear at first to be simply reporting what is indisputably there on the surface. But to call Marlow "level-headed" is already to take a position, to propose a way of thinking about the text. More significant (because it is more hidden), even referring to the unnamed river as "the Congo" is an interpretive act. For by placing the novel in a specific cultural context, Stewart suggests a particular vantage point from which to consider it, and hence encourages readers to ascribe a particular meaning to it.

Indeed, the interpretive significance of placing something in context is explicitly discussed at several points in the novel. Marlow points out, for instance, that the "tremor of far-off drums" he hears during his two-hundred-mile tramp to the Central Station might well sound "weird, appealing, suggestive, and wild" to European ears; but he recognizes that it might perhaps have a meaning "as profound . . . as the sound of bells in a Christian country" to someone who listens in the context of the African culture that produces the sound (p. 35). Similarly, the scribbling in the margins of the copy of *An Inquiry into some Points of Seamanship* that he finds in the hut below the Inner Station appears at first to be in cipher and hence an "extravagant mystery" (p. 54). But it suddenly changes meaning when the context changes, when he discovers that it is written not in a private code, but in Russian.

Even metacritical acts are usually profoundly interpretive. When, for instance, Bernhard Reitz discusses the various interpretations of "the symbolically depicted moral conflict" (41), he may at first be appearing to discuss the interpretive practice of others without making any interpretive commitment of his own. But he makes an interpretive move as soon as he asserts that the conflict is, in fact, "symbolic" — for this, too, provides a framework within which to make sense of the text.

Interpretive processes can be highly idiosyncratic, and as a consequence many reader critics have focused on the differences between readers. Indeed, David Bleich has argued that "the role of personality in response is the most fundamental fact of criticism" (4). Still, it is no less revealing to study the ways in which interpretations overlap than to study the ways in which they diverge.[3] After all, given the complexity of a literary text, especially one as intricate as *Heart of Darkness,* we would normally *expect* different people to read differently. It's the degree to which people read in similar ways that's surprising, and therefore arguably in even greater need of explanation.

Thus, for the purposes of this argument, I am not going to be concerned with the interpretive consequences of a reader's individuality (for instance, the consequences of the individual "identity theme" that Norman Holland, in *5 Readers Reading,* sees as providing the basic framework to which the reader *"assimilates"* a text [128; empha-

---

[3]Given the diversity of reader critics — broader than that within many other theoretical camps — it is perhaps appropriate to define my position with respect to that of some of my colleagues. Since my attention is directed toward interpretive procedures, especially those in place before the act of reading begins, I differ from those critics (for instance, the early Stanley Fish represented by "Affective Stylistics") whose main pursuit is reading as a temporal process, as well as from those (like David Bleich toward the end of *Readings and Feelings*) who are primarily concerned with how already completed interpretations are mediated within a particular community. Unlike Janice A. Radway in *Reading the Romance* or Norman N. Holland in *5 Readers Reading,* I am concerned here with hypothetical, rather than flesh-and-blood, readers — although I do, of course, take my evidence from the writings of actual (professional) readers. Finally, unlike many subjectivists, my focus here is on the experiences that readers share, rather than on their disagreements.

sis in original]). Rather, I am going to explore interpretation as the application of interpretive procedures that are conventional, in the specific sense that they are cultural products that are both taught and more-or-less communally agreed upon.

To be sure, conventions operate with different degrees of stringency, and in this regard interpretive conventions are less like traffic laws than like rules of etiquette. Interpretive conventions are not always formulated explicitly or with precision, although there is always a brisk business in guidebooks ready to fill you in on what you "need" to know. They are not always taught with rigor, although public acts of shaming (whether in a classroom or during a dinner conversation) can easily bend our behavior. They are historically variable, although there's always some continuity in the practices of a given culture. And different sorts of occasions allow both different sets of practices and different degrees of latitude: as Mrs. E. B. Duffey, for instance, pointed out in a once-famous guide to proper behavior, "it is not required of a gentleman in a railway car to relinquish his seat in favor of a lady," but the situation is "different" in streetcars (91–92). More important, like rules of behavior — note the gendered underpinnings of Mrs. Duffey's rules of behavior — rules of reading carry with them certain effects that can be broadly described as "political," in the sense that they reflect and influence the often-invisible systems of power relationships among various cultural and social groups.

So many rules govern social behavior that most people who have written about them have found it advisable to sort them according to what are assumed to be useful and appropriate categories. Mrs. Duffey, for instance, found it useful to break down "Etiquette for General Occasions" into rules for visits, rules for dinner parties and balls, and rules for courtship, among others. There are a similarly vast number of interpretive rules, and I have similarly found it helpful to keep them under control by sorting them into rough categories: rules of notice, signification, configuration, and coherence.[4] Let me take each in turn.

First, rules of notice. Certain critics insist that it is possible to account for everything that happens in a novel. Florence Ridley, for instance, braces up her interpretation of Conrad with the claim that, unlike the readings of other critics, hers "take[s] into consideration all of its parts" (44). In fact, however — as should be especially clear to anyone who has just tried to whack through the linguistic underbrush of *Heart of Darkness* — there is always more in any text of substance than

---

[4]For a fuller discussion, see my *Before Reading*.

any one reader can possibly deal with. As a result, in order to read, we have to decide when to skim, and when to pay special attention. And to do this, we rely on rules that allow us to determine what moments count as the narrative high points. One rule applied to most narratives in our culture, for instance, gives priority to the ending, so it's not surprising that so many essays have mulled over the lie that Marlow tells to Kurtz's Intended.

Second, once the rules of notice have underscored specific details in the text, readers use what I call rules of signification to extract particular meanings out of them. Rules of signification tell us, for example, when it is appropriate to assume that a literary snake has symbolic overtones (as when Conrad compares the river to "an immense snake uncoiled" [p. 22]) and when, in fact, a snake is just a reptile (say, the swamp adder that Sherlock Holmes encounters in Sir Arthur Conan Doyle's "The Adventure of the Speckled Band"). Likewise, rules of signification would have to be deployed, explicitly or implicitly, for Claire Kahane to defend her interpretive claim that in *Heart of Darkness*, the word "'horror' echoes its homonym 'whore'" (145).

Third, by applying rules of configuration, we can fit the details and their significances uncovered by the first two sets of rules into some more or less traditional preexisting design, thus allowing us to predict the course of the story to come. Rules of configuration lie at the heart of our literary expectations. For instance, one rule that operates in many texts of intense binary psychological conflict is a rule that I call the Rule of Magnetic Opposition. This rule urges us to expect that the line between protagonist and villain will turn out to be porous and that the protagonist will be tempted when drawn into the orbit of a sophisticated representative of evil who offers an invitation to explore the "dark side" of the psyche. This rule certainly generates expectations in *Heart of Darkness*, just as it generates expectations in such psychological thrillers as the film *Black Widow* or James Ellroy's novel *The Big Nowhere*. But rules of configuration are always double-edged. They certainly generate the satisfaction that results when expectations are fulfilled, for instance in Marlow's famous admission of complicity: "I did not betray Mr. Kurtz — it was ordered I should never betray him — it was written I should be loyal to the nightmare of my choice" (p. 81). But at the same time, they fuel the surprise that results when expectations are frustrated. Thus, we are apt to be taken aback when Megan Turner (Jamie Lee Curtis) flatly turns down Eugene Hunt (Ron Silver) when he tries to seduce her into his demented world of violence in Kathryn Bigelow's film *Blue Steel*; but that shock of reversal relies just as heavily on a prior rule of configuration as does the satisfaction of expectation in *Heart of Darkness*.

Finally, and most central to my essay here, there are rules of coherence, which allow us to fit the text together as a whole. As Norman N. Holland put it, "I have found it helpful to think of literary meaning spatially — as an idea that all the particular details of a work are 'about'" (*Dynamics* 5). Particularly important are rules that allow us to wrap up a work in the mantle of some larger thematic abstraction, as when Jerry Wasserman argues that "style is the theme" of *Heart of Darkness* (103), or when Conrad himself suggests that the "idea" of the book is "the criminality of inefficiency and pure selfishness when tackling the civilizing work in Africa" (*Letters* 139–40).

Any given reader is liable to apply different sets of rules to different kinds of texts. Indeed, I have argued elsewhere that genre is best understood not as a group of texts that share textual features but, rather, as a collection of texts that appear to invite similar interpretive strategies. And different readers, of course, are apt to apply different rules to the same text (this is what makes for interpretive difference). But — and this is a key point of my argument here — regardless of the text, regardless of the particular choices that a given reader makes as he or she processes it, those interpretive procedures always bring with them some kind of political edge.

To illustrate this claim, I would like to look at one of the specific rules of coherence that readers have widely (although not universally) used when trying to make sense of *Heart of Darkness*. At first, this might seem a quixotic project, for the interpretive procedures applied to the novel, even over the last forty years or so, appear nearly random. Indeed, there seems an almost bewildering variety of readings whose general outlines seem to shift with historical context, and whose details seem to vary from critic to critic even when the general outlines seem more or less stable. Especially before the New Criticism lost its respectability in college and university literature departments, for instance, critics often tried to make the novel cohere in terms of general claims about the nature of "Man." Florence Ridley, for instance, sums up this perspective when she argues that "Conrad is concerned with the process of acquiring understanding of self" (45). But even within this general rubric, there was little apparent agreement. Albert Guerard's famous exploration of the novel maps it out as an instance of "the journey within" (ch. 1) — specifically, Marlow's "journey toward and through certain facets or potentialities of self," his "spiritual voyage of self-discovery" (38). Lionel Trilling, looking at the novel from a different vantage point, sees Kurtz as "a hero of the spirit" — not an ordinary man, but someone who exemplifies "the essence of the modern belief about the nature of the artist, the man who goes down into that hell which is the historical beginning of the human soul" (18). Larry Sams offers yet a different spin: the novel "projects an existential choice: man may venture, like Kurtz, into the wilderness of his inner world, and from his own weakness . . . topple into madness and immoral behavior; or man may gaze, like Marlow, at the bestiality, . . . and manage enough control over the turbulence to live a moral life" (133).

"Nature of Man" interpretations are still common, I suspect, in many high school classes. But in university settings, readers are nowadays more apt to anchor themselves on more postmodern claims. For under the pressures of a growing disaffection with Enlightenment humanism in American universities, many academic readers steer away from universal "moral themes" (especially androcentric themes), making the novel cohere around issues of, say, language and textuality instead. Thus Charles Reeves, for instance, argues that "narratability" is the "obsessive theme" of both *Heart of Darkness* and *Lord Jim* (291). More specifically, he argues that because of the way Conrad sees language, his position approximates Friedrich Nietzsche's: "Indeed, its Nietzschean truth is that there is no truth-in-itself. . . . The narrative can disclose no perspective from which darkness and light may be finally differentiated" (303). Claire Kahane reads the novel in terms of linguistically and psychoanalytically inflected concerns. Arguing that modernist fictions tend to "substitute voice for plot, seducing the reader through a projection of the voice of the other rather than through the suspenseful turns of plot" (136), she concludes that the novel "evokes a seductive scene of hearing that echoes the ur-scenes of psychoanalysis" (137): that is, the so-called primal scene in which the infant witnesses or overhears the sexual activity of its parents. Indeed, she falls back on seduction and the primal scene not only to describe the technique of the novel but also to describe its "subject": "the primal oral/aural desire" (Kahane 142). Peter Brooks sees Marlow's story as a cover-up. That is, "the resonance" of Marlow's "ethical pronouncements," far from revealing the truth of his journey, in fact hide "a starker and possibly contradictory truth" (248). But this analysis leads, ultimately, not to moral and political insights but to linguistic insights: for Brooks, the rhetorical structure of the cover-up turns out to be more important than what is covered up, and the novel therefore finally makes sense as a self-reflexive meditation on language and narrative. The "tale . . . is ultimately most of all about transmission" (261); thus, "One finally needs to read *Heart of Darkness* as act of narration even more than as narrative or as story" (261).

In some modern readings, in fact, the novel threatens to disappear into self-referentiality. Thus, while Donald M. Kartiganer concedes the novel's engagement with imperialism, he ends up erasing imperialism's political significance through a double interpretive reorientation. First, he affiliates the novel with a larger genre that he calls "the divided narrative form" (155), a genre in which "the central protagonist is divided in half, into an observer and an actor, each fully characterized yet incomplete without the other" (151). Second, he takes that generic equivalence as a sign of a common thematics — specifically, a thematics focusing on the act of interpretation itself. By equating "the action of the narrative" with "what Gadamer has described as the hermeneutic task" (Kartiganer 152), "the act of interpretation" becomes "an explicit focus for whatever happens in the narrative." In the end, there's really no voyage to Africa at all. Rather, the text is transformed into "a formulation of criteria" for its own reading (Kartiganer 167).

Marlow as existential hero, Kurtz as artist-hero; the novel's subject as primal desires or as narratability: whatever else one can say, *Heart of Darkness* does not seem to encourage interpretive agreement. And yet, while what we might call the "content" of these readings may have varied, the procedure that generates them is far more stable. For all of the critics I have cited here in fact apply the same two-step rule of coherence, a rule that I call the Rule of Abstract Displacement. The first step involves an act of substitution: according to this rule, *good literature is always treated as if it were about something else.*[5] That is, whatever a work appears to be about on the surface, you always discover — especially if you are discussing it in a literature class — that its "real" subject lies in something that's not immediately apparent from the surface. *Animal Farm* is not really "about" agriculture; *Hamlet* is not really "about" political infighting in the Danish court. This substitution is linked, however, to a second step, an act of generalization.[6] As

---

[5]Although this rule is rarely expressed so baldly, one does find critics who assert it without apology. Wolfgang Iser, for instance, claims that "Whatever realities are transposed into the text, they turn into signs for something else" (3).

[6]True, with a limited group of texts (such as *romans à clef*), the reader substitutes something existing on more or less the same level of specificity as the original text. But more often than not, that "something else" is more abstract than what the text seems to mean on the surface.

Holland puts it, traditional interpretive practice assumes that "literary meaning is a statement of what in the literary work is of sufficient generality to be 'worth something to everybody'" — often in the form of a "universal proposition" (*Dynamics* 5).[7] Thus, to give one concrete example of the Rule of Abstract Displacement in action: J. Hillis Miller, in the essay in this volume, suggests that *Heart of Darkness* is a "parabolic" text in that it is "a realistic story" used "to express another reality or truth not otherwise expressible" (206). I would put it differently. It's not that certain texts "are" parables, but that under certain circumstances — for instance, when reading a densely written canonical modernist novel in an academic setting — we are accustomed to reading texts as if they were.

The drive to apply the Rule of Abstract Displacement is often manifested in the drive to read metaphorically. That drive is, in fact, so strong in our culture that it sometimes seems as if we had misheard the famous *Star Wars* injunction as "Metaphors be with you!" As a consequence, it is hard to resist the metaphorical potential of a text even when confronted by an explicit textual warning against it. Indeed, academic reading often exhibits what I call the *Cat People* phenomenon. I take the term from Jacques Tourneur's 1942 film with a screenplay by DeWitt Bodeen — a film famous in its own day and recanonized by its incorporation into Manuel Puig's novel *Kiss of the Spider Woman*.[8] In *Cat People*, Oliver Reed (played by Kent Smith) falls in love with Irena (Simone Simon), who tells him that she can't reciprocate because of a curse placed on the Serbian village in which she grew up: at the moment of sexual union, she will turn into a leopard and destroy her lover. Oliver, who overestimates his own patience in such matters, convinces her to marry him nonetheless. But as the marital consummation is continually deferred (and, consequently, de-furred), he finally persuades her to see a psychiatrist.

The session between Irena and her psychiatrist turns quickly into a dispute about the proper interpretive rules for Irena's narrative. Should the connection between woman and feline be read as an instance of literal transformation, or is it a metaphor for something else? Irena insists on interpreting the curse concretely and specifically: she

---

[7]In this influential book, of course, Holland separates his own practice from that of the New Critics — although his own procedure, to seek a "central fantasy or daydream . . . particular manifestations of which occur all through the text" (*Dynamics* 7) is not as far from New Critical practice as he believes.

[8]There was also a later film with the title *Cat People*, although a substantially different plot, starring Nastassia Kinski.

will *in fact* turn into a literal cat. Her psychiatrist, in contrast, believes that it should be understood as a representation by similarity: the cat is but a metaphorical projection of her psychosexual anxieties. The film's conclusion is a strong warning against rampant metaphorization: when the psychiatrist tries to prove his point by forcing himself on Irena, she turns into a leopard and, in a scene cast entirely in shadows, claws him to death.

What's more curious about this movie is the way in which viewers tend to "read" that scene. Certainly, on the level of what I've elsewhere called the narrative audience (the audience that views the events as "real"), Irena's is the "correct" reading of the situation. Nonetheless, as actual viewers trying to join the authorial audience (trying to understand the film as a work of art),[9] we are apt to continue to interpret as the psychiatrist does, and to treat the cat nonetheless as a metaphor. That is, at least for those accustomed to reading in academic terms, the story seems more evocative, and certainly more discussable "as literature," when read as a parable about the dangers of female desire than when read as a matter-of-fact narrative of a woman who turns into a killer cat.[10] That the film explicitly raises the possibility of that interpretation and then controverts it does not seem to have much impact on the way it is understood. And if the drive to read abstractly is so strong that even a firm admonition about the dangers of metaphoric reading is apt to be read metaphorically, what is likely to happen to a book, like *Heart of Darkness,* that doesn't have such warnings? It's no surprise, then, that the Rule of Abstract Displacement has almost completely colonized writings about Conrad's novel.

Thus, while the *content* of the thematization has shifted from claims about the "journey within" to claims about the act of interpretation, the same basic interpretive gesture has served as a common foundation. That is — to abstract from these readers in the same way that they abstract from the text — there is a continuity to these superficially varying interpretations, not in terms of what they see as the true "meaning" of the text but in terms of how they *get to it.* They all move by displacement from the specific to the abstract.

[9]For further explanation, see *Before Reading,* pages 93–104. For another distinction that can provide similar kinds of insights, see James Phelan's differentiations among three components of literary characters: the synthetic (a character as an artistic "construct"), the mimetic (characters as "images of possible people"), and the thematic (a character as support for larger thematic concern) (2–3).

[10]It may be for similar reasons that psychological readings of Henry James's *Turn of the Screw,* in which the governess is mad, continue to be more popular in academic settings than literal readings in which the ghosts she sees are real.

I have argued that this interpretive process is political. In what way? Simply this: these interpretations all share a hierarchical value system that privileges the second stage, the abstract. To give a particularly clear example: Jacques Berthoud takes on those critics who have faulted Conrad for being "insufficiently specific" about Kurtz's "inconceivable ceremonies and nameless lusts." He does so by maintaining that the specific facts do not really matter, since "what finally damns Kurtz is not the horror of the shrunken heads . . . nor even the ferocity of his raiding excursions, but *what these things indicate*" (54; emphasis added). For my purposes here, what Berthoud sees as the end result (or the content) of Kurtz's fall (the fact that by "tak[ing] upon himself the role of God . . . he has entered into a state of final self-deception" [54]) is less significant than the route he follows: Berthoud acts on the assumption that the specifics of the text, the surface details, "indicate" something both more general *and more important*.

It is in this notion of hierarchical "indicating" that we can see the political drift of this critical continuity. That is, while all of these critics point us "toward" different things which are designated as primary, they all point us *away* from the same thing which is deemed to be secondary: Conrad's specific descriptions of the horrors of an imperialist venture, precisely those aspects of the novel that might prompt a reader to think seriously about the problems of racism. Thus, among other things, they turn us away from the concrete images of the starvation brought by the Europeans. Think, for instance, of Marlow's harrowing description of the members of the chain gang: "I could see every rib, the joints of their limbs were like knots in a rope" (p. 30). Or think of the workers on the boat, paid "every week" with "three pieces of brass wire," forced to live on "a few lumps of some stuff like half-cooked dough, of a dirty lavender colour, they kept wrapped in leaves, and now and then swallowed a piece of, but so small that it seemed done more for the look of the thing than for any serious purpose of sustenance" (p. 57). What moral actions are we, as readers, engaged in when we take such images as indications of something more important?

Of course, as I suggested at the beginning of this essay, not all critics rely on abstract displacement: there are many, especially now in the wake of Achebe, who employ different rules of coherence — rules that in fact elevate the issues of race and imperialism as the primary materials of the novel. Granted, too, not all applications of the Rule of Abstract Displacement are political in the same way: it is an interpretive paradigm that underlies many feminist and anti-imperialist arguments, too. But I think it is fair to say that with regard to *this particular text,* the applications of the rule by many of the critics I have cited do have political consequences in common, consequences for the way they encourage readers to act. These critics are, furthermore, representative of a large body of influential Conrad criticism. As a result, in many classrooms, built into the very strategies students are trained to enlist as they interpret the text, are procedures that minimize the importance of such issues as race and imperialism by treating them, generally implicitly, as "less important" than such issues as the journey within and primal desires.

Thus, for instance, for Gloria Young, who extends the ground first cleared by Freud and Holland, Conrad is using the issues of colonialism to illustrate more important issues of psychology, specifically "Kurtz's regression into the unconscious primary processes, what Freud would call the id" (Young 255), exemplifying "what can result when the ego loses control of the unconscious processes of both the id and the superego" (Young 256). Even Bette London, whose aim is to trace out the political elements in the novel, nonetheless finds herself entangled in abstract displacement, as if infected by the critical climate in which she finds herself: "Constructing himself in Kurtz's image," she argues, "Marlow fulfills the colonial imperative Kurtz both travesties and enacts. He participates in what Henry Staten has called . . . Kurtz's 'sadistic project of mastery,' the epitome of the colonial design: 'the desire to force by violence a response from an unmoved and indifferent nature which is imaged as female.' Badgering his audience, as he does periodically, Marlow assaults their indifference, subjecting them to violent verbal harangues" (246). The moves here are significant: what begins with a clear recognition of the sadism of colonialism ends with the displacement of that physical brutality by equating it with Marlow's verbal style.

Some critics, such as Gary Adelman, have criticized this kind of displacement, but have placed the blame on Conrad himself, arguing that his novel is structured in such a way as to demand such reading strategies. There is certainly some validity to that observation. *Heart of Darkness* contains none of *Cat People's* warnings against metaphorizations, and plenty of apparent invitations to think symbolically. Indeed, Conrad himself noted in a letter that in "the last pages" of the book "the interview of the man and the girl . . . makes of that story something quite on another plane than an anecdote of a man who went mad in the Centre of Africa" (*Letters* 417). One thinks, too, of Marlow's description of the need to pay attention to hidden banks, sunken stones, and other potential dangers during his travel on the river:

> I had to keep guessing at the channel; I had to discern, mostly by inspiration, the signs of hidden banks; I watched for sunken stones; I was learning to clap my teeth smartly before my heart flew out, when I shaved by a fluke some infernal sly old snag that would have ripped the life out of the tin-pot steamboat and drowned all the pilgrims; I had to keep a look-out for the signs of dead wood we could cut up in the night for the next day's steaming. When you have to attend to things of that sort, to the mere incidents of the surface, the reality — the reality, I tell you — fades. The inner truth is hidden — luckily, luckily. (p. 49–50)

One rule of signification commonly applied to novels of this density urges us to treat such descriptions as metaphors for the act of reading the text: Doesn't that mean that Conrad wanted us to abstract from the concrete details?

Perhaps. Still, there is reason to believe that Conrad didn't intend the level of abstraction we find in contemporary critics of his novel. He himself insisted, in fact, that he had started with "definite images" rather than "an abstract notion" (*Letters* 158, 157) and admitted "the fault of having made Kurtz too symbolic or rather symbolic at all" (*Letters* 460). And even if Conrad *did* intend a certain measure of abstraction, are readers therefore absolved of responsibility for uncritically repeating that gesture? The key word here is "uncritically." My point is not that we should resist creating coherence in the texts we read, or even that we should resist the urge to seek that coherence in thematic abstractions. Nor am I suggesting that those readers who have found *Heart of Darkness* to be a source of insight into the human condition or the nature of narrative are somehow "wrong" in their interpretive conclusions. Rather, I hope to suggest that these interpretations, like all interpretations, have a political dimension — and that by participating in such readings without, at the same time, engaging in some self-reflection about what we are doing, we run the risk of habituating ourselves to problematic patterns of thought, blindly accepting — like the European crowds "electrified" by Kurtz's speeches (p. 89) or the Africans who "adored" him (p. 72) — what we ought to be holding up for discussion and debate.

WORKS CITED

Achebe, Chinua. "An Image of Africa: Racism in Conrad's *Heart of Darkness.*" *Hopes and Impediments: Selected Essays.* New York: Doubleday, 1989. 1–20. Rpt. of "An Image of Africa." *Research in African Literatures* 9.1 (1978): 1–15.

Adelman, Gary. *Heart of Darkness: Search for the Unconscious.* Boston: Twayne, 1987.

Bergstrom, Robert F. "Discovery of Meaning: Development of Formal Thought in the Teaching of Literature." *College English* 45.8 (1983): 745–55.

Berthoud, Jacques. *Joseph Conrad: The Major Phase.* Cambridge: Cambridge UP, 1978.

Blake, Susan L. "Racism and the Classics: Teaching *Heart of Darkness.*" *College Language Association Journal* 25.4 (1982): 396–404.

Bleich, David. *Readings and Feelings: An Introduction to Subjective Criticism.* Urbana: NCTE, 1975.

Brantlinger, Patrick. *Rule of Darkness: British Literature and Imperialism, 1830–1914.* Ithaca: Cornell UP, 1988.

Brooks, Peter. *Reading for the Plot: Design and Intention in Narrative.* New York: Knopf, 1984.

Conrad, Joseph. *The Collected Letters of Joseph Conrad, Volume 2: 1898–1902.* Ed. Frederick R. Karl and Laurence Davies. Cambridge: Cambridge UP, 1986.

Duffey, Mrs. E. B. *The Ladies' and Gentlemen's Etiquette: A Complete Manual of the Manners and Dress of American Society. Containing Forms of Letters, Invitations, Acceptances and Regrets. With a Copious Index.* New rev. ed. Philadelphia: David McKay, 1911.

Fish, Stanley. "Affective Stylistics." *Is There a Text in This Class?: The Authority of Interpretive Communities.* Cambridge: Harvard UP, 1980.

Guerard, Albert J. *Conrad the Novelist.* Cambridge: Harvard UP, 1958.

Holland, Norman N. *The Dynamics of Literary Response.* 1968. New York: Norton, 1975.

———. *5 Readers Reading.* New Haven: Yale UP, 1975.

Iser, Wolfgang. *The Fictive and the Imaginary: Charting Literary Anthropology.* Baltimore: Johns Hopkins UP, 1993.

Kahane, Claire. "Seduction and the Voice of the Text: *Heart of Darkness* and *The Good Soldier.*" *Seduction and Theory: Readings of*

Gender, Representation and Rhetoric. Ed. Dianne Hunter. Urbana: U of Illinois P, 1989. 135–53.

Kartiganer, Donald M. "The Divided Protagonist: Reading as Repetition and Discovery." *Texas Studies in Literature and Language* 30.2 (1988): 151–78.

London, Bette. "Reading Race and Gender in Conrad's Dark Continent." *Criticism: A Quarterly for Literature and the Arts* 31:3 (Summer 1989): 235–52.

Miller, J. Hillis. *"Heart of Darkness* Revisited." *Joseph Conrad, "Heart of Darkness."* Ed. Ross C Murfin. 2nd ed. Case Studies in Contemporary Criticism. Boston: Bedford–St. Martin's, 1996. 206–20.

Phelan, James. *Reading People, Reading Plots: Character, Progression, and the Interpretation of Narrative.* Chicago: U of Chicago P, 1989.

Rabinowitz, Peter J. *Before Reading: Narrative Conventions and the Politics of Interpretation.* Ithaca: Cornell UP, 1987.

———. "Whiting the Wrongs of History: The Resurrection of Scott Joplin." *Black Music Research Journal* 11.2 (1991): 157–76.

Radway, Janice A. *Reading the Romance: Women, Patriarchy, and Popular Literature.* Chapel Hill: U of North Carolina P, 1984.

Reeves, Charles Eric. "A Voice of Unrest: Conrad's Rhetoric of the Unspeakable." *Texas Studies in Literature and Language* 27.3 (1985): 284–310.

Reitz, Bernhard. "The Meaning of the Buddha-Comparisons in Joseph Conrad's *Heart of Darkness.*" *Fu Jen Studies* 13 (1980): 41–53.

Ridley, Florence H. "The Ultimate Meaning of 'Heart of Darkness.'" *Nineteenth-Century Fiction* 18 (1963): 43–53.

Sams, Larry Marshall. "Heart of Darkness: The Meaning Around the Nutshell." *International Fiction Review* 5.2 (1978): 129–33.

Shaffer, Brian W. "'Rebarbarizing Civilization': Conrad's African Fiction and Spencerian Sociology." *PMLA* 108.1 (1993): 45–58.

Stewart, Garrett. "Lying as Dying in *Heart of Darkness.*" *PMLA* 95.3 (1980): 319–31.

Trilling, Lionel. *Beyond Culture: Essays on Literature and Learning.* New York: Harcourt, 1965.

Wasserman, Jerry. "Narrative Presence: The Illusion of Language in *Heart of Darkness.*" *Critical Essays on Joseph Conrad.* Ed. Ted Billy. Boston: G. K. Hall, 1987. 102–13.

Watt, Ian. "Conrad's *Heart of Darkness* and the Critics." *North Dakota Quarterly* 57.3 (1989): 5–15.

Young, Gloria. "Kurtz as Narcissistic Megalomaniac in Joseph Conrad's *Heart of Darkness.*" *Working Papers in Linguistics and Literature.* Ed. A. Kakouriotis and R. Parkin-Gounelas. Thessaloniki: Aristotle U, 1989. 255–63.

Feminist and Gender
Criticism and
Heart of Darkness

WHAT ARE FEMINIST
AND GENDER CRITICISM?

Among the most exciting and influential developments in the field of literary studies, feminist and gender criticism participate in a broad philosophical discourse that extends far beyond literature, far beyond the arts in general. The critical *practices* of those who explore the representation of women and men in works by male or female, lesbian or gay writers inevitably grow out of and contribute to a larger and more generally applicable *theoretical* discussion of how gender and sexuality are constantly shaped by and shaping institutional structures and attitudes, artifacts and behaviors.

Feminist criticism was accorded academic legitimacy in American universities "around 1981," Jane Gallop claims in her book *Around 1981: Academic Feminist Literary Theory* (1992). With Gallop's title and approximation in mind, Naomi Schor has since estimated that "around 1985, feminism began to give way to what has come to be called gender studies" (275). Some would argue that feminist criticism became academically legitimate well before 1981. Others would take issue with the notion that feminist criticism and women's studies have been giving way to gender criticism and gender studies, and with the either/or distinction that such a claim implies. Taken together, however, Gallop and Schor provide us with a useful fact — that of feminist criticism's historical precedence — and a chronological focus on the early to mid-1980s, a period during which the feminist approach was unquestionably influential and during which new interests emerged, not all of which were woman centered.

During the early 1980s, three discrete strains of feminist theory and practice — commonly categorized as French, North American, and British — seemed to be developing. French feminists tended to focus their attention on language. Drawing on the ideas of the psychoanalytic philosopher Jacques Lacan, they argued that language as we commonly think of it — as public discourse — is decidedly phallocentric, privileging what is valued by the patriarchal culture. They also spoke of the possibility of an alternative, feminine language and of *l'écriture féminine:* women's writing. Julia Kristeva, who is generally seen as a pioneer of French feminist thought even though she dislikes the feminist label, suggested that feminine language is associated with the maternal and derived from the pre-oedipal fusion between mother and child. Like Kristeva, Hélène Cixous and Luce Irigaray associated feminine writing with the female body. Both drew an analogy between women's writing and women's sexual pleasure, Irigaray arguing that just as a woman's *"jouissance"* is more diffuse and complex than a man's unitary phallic pleasure ("woman has sex organs just about everywhere"), so "feminine" language is more diffuse and less obviously coherent than its "masculine" counterpart (*This Sex* 101–03).

Kristeva, who helped develop the concept of *l'écriture féminine,* nonetheless urged caution in its use and advocacy. Feminine or feminist writing that resists or refuses participation in "masculine" discourse, she warned, risks political marginalization, relegation to the outskirts (pun intended) of what is considered socially and politically significant. Kristeva's concerns were not unfounded: the concept of *l'écriture féminine* did prove controversial, eliciting different kinds of criticism from different kinds of feminist and gender critics. To some, the concept appears to give writing a biological basis, thereby suggesting that there is an *essential* femininity, and/or that women are *essentially* different from men. To others, it seems to suggest that men can write as women, so long as they abdicate authority, sense, and logic in favor of diffusiveness, playfulness, even nonsense.

While French feminists of the 1970s and early 1980s focused on language and writing from a psychoanalytic perspective, North American critics generally practiced a different sort of criticism.

Characterized by close textual reading and historical scholarship, it generally took one of two forms. Critics like Kate Millett, Carolyn Heilbrun, and Judith Fetterley developed what Elaine Showalter called the "feminist critique" of "male constructed literary history" by closely examining canonical works by male writers, exposing the patriarchal ideology implicit in such works and arguing that traditions of systematic masculine dominance are indelibly inscribed in our literary tradition. Fetterley urged women to become "resisting readers" — to notice how biased most of the classic texts by male authors are in their language, subjects, and attitudes and to actively reject that bias as they read, thereby making reading a different, less "immasculating" experience. Meanwhile, another group of North American feminists, including Showalter, Sandra Gilbert, Susan Gubar, and Patricia Meyer Spacks, developed a different feminist critical model — one that Showalter referred to as "gynocriticism." These critics analyzed great books by women from a feminist perspective, discovered neglected or forgotten women writers, and attempted to recover women's culture and history, especially the history of women's communities that nurtured female creativity.

The North American endeavor to recover women's history — for example, by emphasizing that women developed their own strategies to gain power within their sphere — was seen by British feminists like Judith Newton and Deborah Rosenfelt as an endeavor that "mystifies" male oppression, disguising it as something that has created a special world of opportunities for women. More important from the British standpoint, the universalizing and "essentializing" tendencies of French theory and a great deal of North American practice disguised women's oppression by highlighting sexual difference, thereby seeming to suggest that the dominant system may be impervious to change. As for the North American critique of male stereotypes that denigrate women, British feminists maintained that it led to counterstereotypes of female virtue that ignore real differences of race, class, and culture among women.

By now, the French, North American, and British approaches have so thoroughly critiqued, influenced, and assimilated one another that the work of most Western practitioners is no longer easily identifiable along national boundary lines. Instead, it tends to be characterized according to whether the category of *woman* is the major focus in the exploration of gender and gender oppression or, alternatively, whether the interest in sexual difference encompasses an interest in other differences that also define identity. The latter paradigm encompasses the work of feminists of color, Third World (preferably called postcolonial) feminists, and lesbian feminists, many of whom have asked whether the universal category of woman constructed by certain French and North American predecessors is appropriate to describe women in minority groups or non-Western cultures.

These feminists stress that, while all women are female, they are something else as well (such as African American, lesbian, Muslim Pakistani). This "something else" is precisely what makes them — including their problems and their goals — different from other women. As Armit Wilson has pointed out, Asian women living in Great Britain are expected by their families and communities to preserve Asian cultural traditions; thus, the expression of personal identity through clothing involves a much more serious infraction of cultural rules than it does for a Western woman. Gloria Anzaldúa has spoken personally and eloquently about the experience of many women on the margins of Eurocentric North American culture. "I am a border woman," she writes in *Borderlands: La Frontera = The New Mestiza* (1987). "I grew up between two cultures, the Mexican (with a heavy Indian influence) and the Anglo. . . . Living on the borders and in margins, keeping intact one's shifting and multiple identity and integrity is like trying to swim in a new element, an 'alien' element" (i).

Instead of being divisive and isolating, this evolution of feminism into femin*isms* has fostered a more inclusive, global perspective. The era of recovering women's texts, especially texts by white Western women, has been succeeded by a new era in which the goal is to recover entire cultures of women. Two important figures of this new era are Trinh T. Minh-ha and Gayatri Spivak. Spivak, in works such as *In Other Worlds: Essays in Cultural Politics* (1987) and *Outside in the Teaching Machine* (1993), has shown how political independence (generally looked upon by metropolitan Westerners as a simple and beneficial historical and political reversal) has complex implications for "subaltern" or subproletarian women.

The understanding of woman not as a single, deterministic category but rather as the nexus of diverse experiences has led some white, Western, "majority" feminists like Jane Tompkins and Nancy K. Miller to advocate and practice "personal" or "autobiographical" criticism. Once reluctant to reveal themselves in their analyses for fear of being labeled idiosyncratic, impressionistic, and subjective by men, some feminists are now openly skeptical of the claims to reason, logic, and objectivity that male critics have made in the past. With the advent of more personal feminist critical styles has come a powerful new interest in women's autobiographical writings, manifested in essays such as "Authorizing the Autobiographical" by Shari Benstock, which first appeared in her influential collection *The Private Self: Theory and Practice of Women's Autobiographical Writings* (1988).

Traditional autobiography, some feminists have argued, is a gendered, "masculinist" genre; its established conventions call for a life-plot that turns on action, triumph through conflict, intellectual self-discovery, and often public renown. The body, reproduction, children, and intimate interpersonal relationships are generally well in the background and often absent. Arguing that the lived experiences of women and men differ — women's lives, for instance, are often characterized by interruption and deferral — Leigh Gilmore has developed a theory of women's self-representation in her book *Autobiographics: A Feminist Theory of Self-Representation.*

Autobiographics was published in 1994, well after the chronological divide that, according to Schor, separates the heyday of feminist criticism and the rise of gender studies. Does that mean that Gilmore's book is a feminist throwback? Is she practicing gender criticism instead, the use of the word "feminist" in her book's subtitle notwithstanding? Or are both of these questions overly reductive? As implied earlier, many knowledgeable commentators on the contemporary critical scene are skeptical of the feminst/gender distinction, arguing that feminist criticism is by definition gender criticism and pointing out that one critic whose work *everyone* associates with feminism (Julia Kristeva) has problems with the feminist label while another critic whose name is continually linked with the gender approach (Teresa de Lauretis) continues to refer to herself and her work as feminist.

Certainly, feminist and gender criticism are not polar opposites but, rather, exist along a continuum of attitudes toward sex and sexism, sexuality and gender, language and the literary canon. There are, however, a few distinctions to be made between those critics whose writings are inevitably identified as being toward one end of the continuum or the other.

One distinction is based on focus: as the word implies, "feminists" have concentrated their efforts on the study of women and women's issues. Gender criticism, by contrast, has not been woman centered. It has tended to view the male and female sexes — and the masculine and feminine genders — in terms of a complicated continuum, much as we are viewing feminist and gender criticism. Critics like Diane K.

Lewis have raised the possibility that black women may be more like white men in terms of familial and economic roles, like black men in terms of their relationships with whites, and like white women in terms of their relationships with men. Lesbian gender critics have asked whether lesbian women are really more like straight women than they are like gay (or for that matter straight) men. That we refer to gay and lesbian studies as gender studies has led some to suggest that gender studies is a misnomer; after all, homosexuality is not a gender. This objection may easily be answered once we realize that one purpose of gender criticism is to criticize gender as we commonly conceive of it, to expose its insufficiency and inadequacy as a category.

Another distinction between feminist and gender criticism is based on the terms "gender" and "sex." As de Lauretis suggests in *Technologies of Gender* (1987), feminists of the 1970s tended to equate gender with sex, gender difference with sexual difference. But that equation doesn't help us explain "the differences among women, . . . the differences *within women*." After positing that "we need a notion of gender that is not so bound up with sexual difference," de Lauretis provides just such a notion by arguing that "gender is not a property of bodies or something originally existent in human beings"; rather, it is "the product of various social technologies, such as cinema" (2). Gender is, in other words, a construct, an effect of language, culture, and its institutions. It is gender, not sex, that causes a weak old man to open a door for an athletic young woman. And it is gender, not sex, that may cause one young woman to expect old men to behave in this way, another to view this kind of behavior as chauvinistic and insulting, and still another to have mixed feelings (hence de Lauretis's phrase "differences *within women*") about "gentlemanly gallantry."

Still another related distinction between feminist and gender criticism is based on the *essentialist* views of many feminist critics and the *constructionist* views of many gender critics (both those who would call themselves feminists and those who would not). Stated simply and perhaps too reductively, the term "essentialist" refers to the view that women are essentially different from men. "Constructionist," by contrast, refers to the view that most of those differences are characteristics not of the male and female sex (nature) but, rather, of the masculine and feminine genders (nurture). Because of its essentialist tendencies, "radical feminism," according to the influential gender critic Eve Kosofsky Sedgwick, "tends to deny that the meaning of gender or sexuality has ever significantly changed; and more damagingly, it can make future change appear impossible" (*Between Men* 13).

Most obviously essentialist would be those feminists who emphasize the female body, its difference, and the manifold implications of
that difference. The equation made by some avant-garde French feminists between the female body and the *maternal* body has proved
especially troubling to some gender critics, who worry that it may
paradoxically play into the hands of extreme conservatives and funda-
mentalists seeking to reestablish patriarchal family values. In her book
The Reproduction of Mothering (1978), Nancy Chodorow, a sociolo-
gist of gender, admits that what we call "mothering" — not having or
nursing babies but mothering more broadly conceived — is commonly
associated not just with the feminine gender but also with the female
sex, often considered nurturing by nature. But she critically interro-
gates the common assumption that it is in women's nature or biological destiny to "mother" in this broader sense, arguing that the separation of home and workplace brought about by the development of
capitalism and the ensuing industrial revolution made mothering *appear* to be essentially a woman's job in modern Western society.

If sex turns out to be gender where mothering is concerned, what
differences *are* grounded in sex — that is, nature? *Are* there *essential*
differences between men and women — other than those that are
purely anatomical and anatomically determined (for example, a man
can exclusively take on the job of feeding an infant milk, but he may
not do so from his own breast)? A growing number of gender critics
would answer the question in the negative. Sometimes referred to as
"extreme constructionists" and "postfeminists," these critics have
adopted the viewpoint of philosopher Judith Butler, who in her book
Gender Trouble (1990) predicts that "sex, by definition, will be shown
to have been gender all along" (8). As Naomi Schor explains their position, "there is nothing outside or before culture, no nature that is
not always and already enculturated" (278).

Whereas a number of feminists celebrate women's difference, postfeminist gender critics would agree with Chodorow's statement that
men have an "investment in difference that women do not have"
(Eisenstein and Jardine 14). They see difference as a symptom of oppression, not a cause for celebration, and would abolish it by dismantling gender categories and, ultimately, destroying gender itself. Since
gender categories and distinctions are embedded in and perpetuated
through language, gender critics like Monique Wittig have called for
the wholesale transformation of language into a nonsexist, and non-
heterosexist, medium.

Language has proved the site of important debates between feminist and gender critics, essentialists and constructionists. Gender critics have taken issue with those French feminists who have spoken of a feminine language and writing and who have grounded differences in language and writing in the female body.[1] For much the same reason, they have disagreed with those French-influenced Anglo-American critics who, like Toril Moi and Nancy K. Miller, have posited an essential relationship between sexuality and textuality. (In an essentialist sense, such critics have suggested that when women write, they tend to break the rules of plausibility and verisimilitude that men have created to evaluate fiction.) Gender critics like Peggy Kamuf posit a relationship only between *gender* and textuality, between what most men and women *become* after they are born and the way in which they write. They are therefore less interested in the author's sexual "signature" — in whether the author was a woman writing — than in whether the author was (to borrow from Kamuf) "Writing like a Woman."

Feminists like Miller have suggested that no man could write the "female anger, desire, and selfhood" that Emily Brontë, for instance, inscribed in her poetry and in *Wuthering Heights* (*Subject* 72). In the view of gender critics, it is and has been possible for a man to write like a woman, a woman to write like a man. Shari Benstock, a noted feminist critic whose investigations into psychoanalytic and poststructuralist theory have led her increasingly to adopt the gender approach, poses the following question to herself in *Textualizing the Feminine* (1991): "Isn't it precisely 'the feminine' in Joyce's writings and Derrida's that carries me along?" (45). In an essay entitled "Unsexing Language: Pronominal Protest in Emily Dickinson's 'Lay this Laurel,'" Anna Shannon Elfenbein has argued that "like Walt Whitman, Emily Dickinson crossed the gender barrier in some remarkable poems," such as "We learned to like the Fire / By playing Glaciers — when a Boy — " (Berg 215).

It is also possible, in the view of most gender critics, for women to read as men, men as women. The view that women can, and indeed have been forced to, read as men has been fairly noncontroversial.

---

[1]Because feminist/gender studies, not unlike sex/gender, should be thought of as existing along a continuum of attitudes and not in terms of simple opposition, attempts to highlight the difference between feminist and gender criticism are inevitably prone to reductive overgeneralization and occasional distortion. Here, for instance, French feminism is made out to be more monolithic than it actually is. Hélène Cixous has said that a few men (such as Jean Genet) have produced "feminine writing," although she suggests that these are exceptional men who have acknowledged their own bisexuality.

Everyone agrees that the literary canon is largely "androcentric" and that writings by men have tended to "immasculate" women, forcing them to see the world from a masculine viewpoint. But the question of whether men can read as women has proved to be yet another issue dividing feminist and gender critics. Some feminists suggest that men and women have some essentially different reading strategies and outcomes, while gender critics maintain that such differences arise entirely out of social training and cultural norms. One interesting outcome of recent attention to gender and reading is Elizabeth A. Flynn's argument that women in fact make the best interpreters of imaginative literature. Based on a study of how male and female students read works of fiction, she concludes that women come up with more imaginative, open-ended readings of stories. Quite possibly the imputed hedging and tentativeness of women's speech, often seen by men as disadvantages, are transformed into useful interpretive strategies — receptivity combined with critical assessment of the text — in the act of reading (Flynn and Schweickart 286).

In singling out a catalyst of the gender approach, many historians of criticism have pointed to Michel Foucault. In his *History of Sexuality* (1976, tr. 1978), Foucault distinguished sexuality (that is, sexual behavior or practice) from sex, calling the former a "technology of sex." De Lauretis, who has deliberately developed her theory of gender "along the lines of . . . Foucault's theory of sexuality," explains his use of "technology" this way: "Sexuality, commonly thought to be a natural as well as a private matter, is in fact completely constructed in culture according to the political aims of the society's dominant class" (*Technologies* 2, 12). Foucault suggests that homosexuality as we now think of it was to a great extent an invention of the nineteenth century. In earlier periods there had been "acts of sodomy" and individuals who committed them, but the "sodomite" was, according to Foucault, "a temporary aberration," not the "species" he became with the advent of the modern concept of homosexuality (42–43). By historicizing sexuality, Foucault made it possible for his successors to consider the possibility that all of the categories and assumptions that currently come to mind when we think about sex, sexual difference, gender, and sexuality are social artifacts, the products of cultural discourses.

In explaining her reason for saying that feminism began to give way to gender studies "around 1985," Schor says that she chose that date "in part because it marks the publication of *Between Men*," a seminal book in which Eve Kosofsky Sedgwick "articulates the insights of feminist criticism onto those of gay-male studies, which had up to then pursued often parallel but separate courses (affirming the existence of a homosexual or female imagination, recovering lost traditions, decoding the cryptic discourse of works already in the canon by homosexual or feminist authors)" (276). Today, gay and lesbian criticism is so much a part of gender criticism that some people equate it with the gender approach, while others have begun to prefer the phrase "sexualities criticism" to "gender criticism."

Following Foucault's lead, some gay and lesbian gender critics have argued that the heterosexual/homosexual distinction is as much a cultural construct as is the masculine/feminine dichotomy. Arguing that sexuality is a continuum, not a fixed and static set of binary oppositions, a number of gay and lesbian critics have critiqued heterosexuality as a norm, arguing that it has been an enforced corollary and consequence of what Gayle Rubin has referred to as the "sex/gender system." (Those subscribing to this system assume that persons of the male sex should be masculine, that masculine men are attracted to women, and therefore that it is natural for masculine men to be attracted to women and unnatural for them to be attracted to men.) Lesbian gender critics have also taken issue with their feminist counterparts on the grounds that they proceed from fundamentally heterosexual and even heterosexist assumptions. Particularly offensive to lesbians like the poet-critic Adrienne Rich have been those feminists who, following Doris Lessing, have implied that to make the lesbian choice is to make a statement, to act out feminist hostility against men. Rich has called heterosexuality "a beachhead of male dominance" that, "like motherhood, needs to be recognized and studied as a political institution" ("Compulsory Heterosexuality" 143, 145).

If there is such a thing as reading like a woman and such a thing as reading like a man, how then do lesbians read? Are there gay and lesbian ways of reading? Many would say that there are. Rich, by reading Emily Dickinson's poetry as a lesbian — by not assuming that "heterosexual romance is the key to a woman's life and work" — has introduced us to a poet somewhat different from the one heterosexual critics have made familiar (*Lies* 158). As for gay reading, Wayne Koestenbaum has defined "the (male twentieth-century first world) gay reader" as one who "reads resistantly for inscriptions of his condition, for texts that will confirm a social and private identity founded on a desire for other men. . . . Reading becomes a hunt for histories that deliberately foreknow or unwittingly trace a desire felt not by author but by reader, who is most acute when searching for signs of himself" (Boone and Cadden 176–77).

Lesbian critics have produced a number of compelling reinterpretations, or in-scriptions, of works by authors as diverse as Emily Dickinson, Virginia Woolf, and Toni Morrison. As a result of these provocative readings, significant disagreements have arisen between straight and lesbian critics and among lesbian critics as well. Perhaps the most famous and interesting example of this kind of interpretive controversy involves the claim by Barbara Smith and Adrienne Rich that Morrison's novel *Sula* can be read as a lesbian text — and author Toni Morrison's counterclaim that it cannot.

Gay male critics have produced a body of readings no less revisionist and controversial, focusing on writers as staidly classic as Henry James and Wallace Stevens. In Melville's *Billy Budd* and *Moby-Dick*, Robert K. Martin suggests, a triangle of homosexual desire exists. In the latter novel, the hero must choose between a captain who represents "the imposition of the male on the female" and a "Dark Stranger" (Queequeg) who "offers the possibility of an alternate sexuality, one that is less dependent upon performance and conquest" (5).

Masculinity as a complex construct producing and reproducing a constellation of behaviors and goals, many of them destructive (like performance and conquest) and most of them injurious to women, has become the object of an unprecedented number of gender studies. A 1983 issue of *Feminist Review* contained an essay entitled "Anti-Porn: Soft Issue, Hard World," in which B. Ruby Rich suggested that the "legions of feminist men" who examine and deplore the effects of pornography on women might better "undertake the analysis that can tell us why men like porn (not, piously, why this or that exceptional man does *not*)" (Berg 185). The advent of gender criticism makes precisely that kind of analysis possible. Stephen H. Clark, who alludes to Ruby Rich's challenge, reads T. S. Eliot "as a man." Responding to "Eliot's implicit appeal to a specifically masculine audience — '"You! hypocrite lecteur! — mon semblable, — mon *frère!*'" — Clark concludes that poems like "Sweeney Among the Nightingales" and "Gerontion," rather than offering what they are usually said to offer — "a social critique into which a misogynistic language accidentally seeps" — instead articulate a masculine "psychology of sexual fear and desired retaliation" (Berg 173).

Some gender critics focusing on masculinity have analyzed "the anthropology of boyhood," a phrase coined by Mark Seltzer in an article in which he comparatively reads, among other things, Stephen

Crane's *Red Badge of Courage*, Jack London's *White Fang*, and the first *Boy Scouts of America* handbook (Boone and Cadden 150). Others have examined the fear men have that artistry is unmasculine, a guilty worry that surfaces perhaps most obviously in "The Custom-House," Hawthorne's lengthy preface to *The Scarlet Letter*. Still others have studied the representation in literature of subtly erotic disciple-patron relationships, relationships like the ones between Nick Carraway and Jay Gatsby, Charlie Marlow and Lord Jim, Doctor Watson and Sherlock Holmes, and any number of characters in Henry James's stories. Not all of these studies have focused on literary texts. Because the movies have played a primary role in gender construction during our lifetimes, gender critics have analyzed the dynamics of masculinity (vis-à-vis femininity and androgyny) in films from *Rebel Without a Cause* to *Tootsie* to last year's Best Picture. One of the "social technologies" most influential in (re)constructing gender, film is one of the media in which today's sexual politics is most evident.

Necessary as it is, in an introduction such as this one, to define the difference between feminist and gender criticism, it is equally necessary to conclude by unmaking the distinction, at least partially. The two topics just discussed (film theory and so-called "queer theory") give us grounds for undertaking that necessary deconstruction. The alliance I have been creating between gay and lesbian criticism on one hand and gender criticism on the other is complicated greatly by the fact that not all gay and lesbian critics are constructionists. Indeed, a number of them (Robert K. Martin included) share with many feminists the *essentialist* point of view; that is to say, they believe homosexuals and heterosexuals to be essentially different, different by nature, just as a number of feminists believe men and women to be different.

In film theory and criticism, feminist and gender critics have so influenced one another that their differences would be difficult to define based on any available criteria, including the ones outlined above. Cinema has been of special interest to contemporary feminists like Minh-ha (herself a filmmaker) and Spivak (whose critical eye has focused on movies including *My Beautiful Laundrette* and *Sammie and Rosie Get Laid*). Teresa de Lauretis, whose *Technologies of Gender* (1987) has proved influential in the area of gender studies, continues to publish film criticism consistent with earlier, unambiguously feminist works in which she argued that "the representation of woman as spectacle — body to be looked at, place of sexuality, and object of desire — so pervasive in our culture, finds in narrative cinema its most complex expression and widest circulation" (*Alice* 4).

Feminist film theory has developed alongside a feminist performance theory grounded in Joan Riviere's recently rediscovered essay "Womanliness as a Masquerade" (1929), in which the author argues that there is no femininity that is *not* masquerade. Marjorie Garber, a contemporary cultural critic with an interest in gender, has analyzed the constructed nature of femininity by focusing on men who have apparently achieved it — through the transvestism, transsexualism, and other forms of "cross-dressing" evident in cultural productions from Shakespeare to Elvis, from "Little Red Riding Hood" to *La Cage aux Folles*. The future of feminist and gender criticism, it would seem, is not one of further bifurcation but one involving a refocusing on femininity, masculinity, and related sexualities, not only as represented in poems, novels, and films but also as manifested and developed in video, on television, and along the almost infinite number of waystations rapidly being developed on the information highways running through an exponentially expanding cyberspace.

In the epigraph to Johanna M. Smith's essay "Too Beautiful Altogether," Hélène Cixous argues that, through history, men have seen women as a "'dark continent' to penetrate and to 'pacify.'" Smith accepts Cixous's metaphorical characterization of patriarchal subjugation as geographical conquest, but she also significantly develops Cixous's insight by suggesting that there is an actual (not just metaphorical) *link* between the subjugation of women in Western society and the historical colonization of non-Western women *and* men by European powers. The imperialist and patriarchal ideologies that have colluded to silence and subjugate are of course reflected in a novel like Conrad's *Heart of Darkness,* since works of literature inevitably reflect the dominant ideologies of the age in which they were written. But when seen from a fresh critical perspective, an imaginative work by a visionary writer may also be seen to reveal *contradictions* within ideologies, particularly ideologies that are beginning to break down. (Both the imperialistic ideology of civilizing through conquest and the patriarchal ideology of "separate spheres" were "under pressure in the late nineteenth century," Smith points out.) We can see through the contradictions within ideologies of gender and of empire, Smith suggests, when we see *Heart of Darkness* through the lens of "feminist 'revision.'"

Approaching Marlow's narrative as the product of a moment both in the history of imperialism and in the history of patriarchy, Smith shows how patriarchal and imperialist ideologies guide the creation of the novel's (minor) women characters, either causing them to remain silent (for if they spoke, they would surely condemn their oppressors, calling them what they are) or causing them to speak the myths men would have them speak.

Smith's essay affords an excellent example of the feminist approach because, at one point or another, it reflects the interests and practices of each of the now-traditional forms of feminist criticism. By beginning her essay with the admission that a man's novel about manly adventure may not seem important to the feminist enterprise, Smith reminds us of the priorities of American gynocritics, which were to recover and analyze literary works written by women. In her subsequent attention to the subject of silent women and women who speak but speak as men — as well as in her suggestion that feminist readers may hear Conrad's women speaking their mind through the "gaps" in Marlow's discourse — Smith shows an awareness of French feminist issues. Smith's analysis even more obviously exemplifies the feminist critique of a literary work by a man, in the way that it points out how Conrad, through Marlow, repeats a belief system that domesticates women, thereby subjugating them to a separate, secondary sphere.

But Smith's essay is far more than a reprise of traditional feminist approaches. It reflects the insights of contemporary, postcolonial feminism(s) in its sensitivity to matters of race, class, and nationality. (Smith shows that the gender construct defining the femininity of the story's dark-skinned native women is very different from the one defining the identity of Marlow's aunt or Kurtz's Intended.) "Too Beautiful Altogether" also reflects the thinking of most feminist gender critics insofar as it views the feminine not as an essential quality of *woman* but rather as a cultural construct, the several versions of which prescribe the identity of women, groups of women. In its final pages, Smith's essay even addresses the construct of masculinity, thereby reflecting the concerns of nonfeminist as well as feminist gender critics. "The ideology of separate spheres enables masculine imperialism," Smith argues. "By creating an alternative women's sphere 'lest ours get worse,' men can continue to confront their 'own true stuff' in their world. And the violence with which Marlow's lie sacrifices the Intended to this masculine world," Smith concludes, "indicates the strength of its homosocial bonds."

FEMINIST AND GENDER CRITICISM: A SELECTED BIBLIOGRAPHY

French Feminist Theory

Cixous, Hélène. "The Laugh of the Medusa." Trans. Keith Cohen and Paula Cohen. *Signs* 1 (1976): 875–93.

Cixous, Hélène, and Catherine Clément. *The Newly Born Woman.* Trans. Betsy Wing. Minneapolis: U of Minnesota P, 1986.

Irigaray, Luce. *An Ethics of Sexual Difference.* Trans. Carolyn Burke and Gillian C. Gill. Ithaca: Cornell UP, 1993.

————. *This Sex Which Is Not One.* Trans. Catherine Porter. Ithaca: Cornell UP, 1985.

Jones, Ann Rosalind. "Inscribing Femininity: French Theories of the Feminine." *Making a Difference: Feminist Literary Criticism.* Ed. Gayle Green and Coppélia Kahn. London: Methuen, 1985. 80–112.

————. "Writing the Body: Toward an Understanding of *L'Écriture féminine.*" Showalter, *The New Feminist Criticism* 361–77.

Kristeva, Julia. *Desire in Language: A Semiotic Approach to Literature and Art.* Ed. Leon S. Roudiez. Trans. Thomas Gora, Alice Jardine, and Roudiez. New York: Columbia UP, 1980.

Marks, Elaine, and Isabelle de Courtivron, eds. *New French Feminisms: An Anthology.* Amherst: U of Massachusetts P, 1980.

Moi, Toril, ed. *French Feminist Thought: A Reader.* Oxford: Basil Blackwell, 1987.

Feminist Theory: Classic Texts, General Approaches, Collections

Abel, Elizabeth, and Emily K. Abel, eds. *The "Signs" Reader: Women, Gender, and Scholarship.* Chicago: U of Chicago P, 1983.

Barrett, Michèle, and Anne Phillips. *Destabilizing Theory: Contemporary Feminist Debates.* Stanford: Stanford UP, 1992.

Beauvoir, Simone de. *The Second Sex.* 1953. Trans. and ed. H. M. Parshley. New York: Bantam, 1961.

Benstock, Shari. *Textualizing the Feminine: On the Limits of Genre.* Norman: U of Oklahoma P, 1991.

Butler, Judith. *Gender Trouble: Feminism and the Subversion of Identity.* New York: Routledge, 1990.

de Lauretis, Teresa, ed. *Feminist Studies/Critical Studies.* Bloomington: Indiana UP, 1986.

Felman, Shoshana. "Women and Madness: The Critical Phallacy." *Diacritics* 5 (1975): 2–10.

Fetterley, Judith. *The Resisting Reader: A Feminist Approach to American Fiction.* Bloomington: Indiana UP, 1978.

Fuss, Diana. *Essentially Speaking: Feminist, Nature and Difference.* New York: Routledge, 1989.

Gallop, Jane. *Around 1981: Academic Feminist Literary Theory.* New York: Routledge, 1992.

———. *The Daughter's Seduction: Feminism and Psychoanalysis.* Ithaca: Cornell UP, 1982.

hooks, bell. *Feminist Theory: From Margin to Center.* Boston: South End, 1984.

Kolodny, Annette. "Dancing Through the Minefield: Some Observations on the Theory, Practice, and Politics of a Feminist Literary Criticism." Showalter, *The New Feminist Criticism* 144–67.

———. "Some Notes on Defining a 'Feminist Literary Criticism.'" *Critical Inquiry* 2 (1975): 78.

Lovell, Terry, ed. *British Feminist Thought: A Reader.* Oxford: Basil Blackwell, 1990.

Meese, Elizabeth, and Alice Parker, eds. *The Difference Within: Feminism and Critical Theory.* Philadelphia: John Benjamins, 1989.

Miller, Nancy K., ed. *The Poetics of Gender.* New York: Columbia UP, 1986.

Millett, Kate. *Sexual Politics.* Garden City: Doubleday, 1970.

Rich, Adrienne. *On Lies, Secrets, and Silence: Selected Prose, 1966–1979.* New York: Norton, 1979.

Showalter, Elaine. "Toward a Feminist Poetics." Showalter, *The New Feminist Criticism* 125–43.

———, ed. *The New Feminist Criticism: Essays on Women, Literature, and Theory.* New York: Pantheon, 1985.

Stimpson, Catherine R. "Feminist Criticism." *Redrawing the Boundaries: The Transformation of English and American Literary Studies.* Ed. Stephen Greenblatt and Giles Gunn. New York: MLA, 1992. 251–70.

Warhol, Robyn, and Diane Price Herndl, eds. *Feminisms: An Anthology of Literary Theory and Criticism.* New Brunswick, NJ: Rutgers UP, 1991.

Weed, Elizabeth, ed. *Coming to Terms: Feminism, Theory, Politics.* New York: Routledge, 1989.

Woolf, Virginia. *A Room of One's Own.* New York: Harcourt, 1929.

Women's Writing and Creativity

Abel, Elizabeth, ed. *Writing and Sexual Difference*. Chicago: U of Chicago P, 1982.

Berg, Temma F., ed. *Engendering the Word: Feminist Essays in Psychosexual Poetics*. Co-ed. Anna Shannon Elfenbein, Jeanne Larsen, and Elisa Kay Sparks. Urbana: U of Illinois P, 1989.

DuPlessis, Rachel Blau. *The Pink Guitar: Writing as Feminist Practice*. New York: Routledge, 1990.

Finke, Laurie. *Feminist Theory, Women's Writing*. Ithaca: Cornell UP, 1992.

Gilbert, Sandra M., and Susan Gubar. *The Madwoman in the Attic: The Woman Writer and the Nineteenth-Century Literary Imagination*. New Haven: Yale UP, 1979.

Homans, Margaret. *Bearing the Word: Language and Female Experience in Nineteenth-Century Women's Writing*. Chicago: U of Chicago P, 1986.

Jacobus, Mary, ed. *Women Writing and Writing about Women*. New York: Barnes, 1979.

Miller, Nancy K. *Subject to Change: Reading Feminist Writing*. New York: Columbia UP, 1988.

Newton, Judith Lowder. *Women, Power and Subversion: Social Strategies in British Fiction, 1778–1860*. Athens: U of Georgia P, 1981.

Poovey, Mary. *The Proper Lady and the Woman Writer: Ideology as Style in the Works of Mary Wollstonecraft, Mary Shelley, and Jane Austen*. Chicago: U of Chicago P, 1984.

Showalter, Elaine. *A Literature of Their Own: British Women Novelists from Brontë to Lessing*. Princeton: Princeton UP, 1977.

Spacks, Patricia Meyer. *The Female Imagination*. New York: Knopf, 1975.

Feminism, Race, Class, and Nationality

Anzaldúa, Gloria. *Borderlands: La Frontera = The New Mestiza*. San Francisco: Spinsters/Aunt Lute, 1987.

Christian, Barbara. *Black Feminist Criticism: Perspectives on Black Women Writers*. New York: Pergamon, 1985.

hooks, bell. *Ain't I a Woman?: Black Women and Feminism*. Boston: South End, 1981.

———. *Black Looks: Race and Representation*. Boston: South End, 1992.

Kaplan, Cora. *Sea Changes: Essays on Culture and Feminism.* London: Verso, 1986.

Moraga, Cherrie, and Gloria Anzaldúa. *This Bridge Called My Back: Writings by Radical Women of Color.* New York: Kitchen Table, 1981.

Newton, Judith, and Deborah Rosenfelt, eds. *Feminist Criticism and Social Change: Sex, Class, and Race in Literature and Culture.* New York: Methuen, 1985.

Pryse, Marjorie, and Hortense Spillers, eds. *Conjuring: Black Women, Fiction, and Literary Tradition.* Bloomington: Indiana UP, 1985.

Robinson, Lillian S. *Sex, Class, and Culture.* 1978. New York: Methuen, 1986.

Smith, Barbara. "Towards a Black Feminist Criticism." Showalter, *The New Feminist Criticism* 168–85.

Feminism and Postcoloniality

Emberley, Julia. *Thresholds of Difference: Feminist Critique, Native Women's Writings, Postcolonial Theory.* Toronto: U of Toronto P, 1993.

Mohanty, Chandra Talpade, Ann Russo, and Lourdes Torres, eds. *Third World Women and the Politics of Feminism.* Bloomington: Indiana UP, 1991.

Schipper, Mineke, ed. *Unheard Words: Women and Literature in Africa, the Arab World, Asia, the Caribbean, and Latin America.* London: Allison, 1985.

Spivak, Gayatri Chakravorty. *In Other Worlds: Essays in Cultural Politics.* New York: Methuen, 1987.

———. *Outside in the Teaching Machine.* New York: Routledge, 1993.

Trinh T. Minh-ha. *Woman, Native, Other: Writing Postcoloniality and Feminism.* Bloomington: Indiana UP, 1989.

Wilson, Armit. *Finding a Voice: Asian Women in Britain.* 1979. London: Virago, 1980.

Women's Self-Representation and Personal Criticism

Benstock, Shari, ed. *The Private Self: Theory and Practice of Women's Autobiographical Writings.* Chapel Hill: U of North Carolina P, 1988.

Gilmore, Leigh. *Autobiographics: A Feminist Theory of Self-Representation.* Ithaca: Cornell UP, 1994.

Martin, Biddy, and Chandra Talpade Mohanty. "Feminist Politics: What's Home Got to Do with It?" *Life/Lines: Theorizing Women's Autobiography.* Ed. Bella Brodski and Celeste Schenck. Ithaca: Cornell UP, 1988.

Miller, Nancy K. *Getting Personal: Feminist Occasions and Other Autobiographical Acts.* New York: Routledge, 1991.

Smith, Sidonie. *A Poetics of Women's Autobiography: Marginality and the Fictions of Self-Representation.* Bloomington: Indiana UP, 1988.

Feminist Film Theory

de Lauretis, Teresa. *Alice Doesn't: Feminism, Semiotics, Cinema.* Bloomington: Indiana UP, 1986.

Doane, Mary Ann. *Re-vision: Essays in Feminist Film Criticism.* Frederick: U Publications of America, 1984.

Modleski, Tania. *Feminism without Women: Culture and Criticism in a "Postfeminist" Age.* New York: Routledge, 1991.

Mulvey, Laura. *Visual and Other Pleasures.* Bloomington: Indiana UP, 1989.

Penley, Constance, ed. *Feminism and Film Theory.* New York: Routledge, 1988.

Studies of Gender and Sexuality

Boone, Joseph A., and Michael Cadden, eds. *Engendering Men: The Question of Male Feminist Criticism.* New York: Routledge, 1990.

Butler, Judith. *Gender Trouble: Feminism and the Subversion of Identity.* New York: Routledge, 1990.

Chodorow, Nancy. *The Reproduction of Mothering: Psychoanalysis and the Sociology of Gender.* Berkeley: U of California P, 1978.

Claridge, Laura, and Elizabeth Langland, eds. *Out of Bounds: Male Writing and Gender(ed) Criticism.* Amherst: U of Massachusetts P, 1990.

de Lauretis, Teresa. *Technologies of Gender: Essays on Theory, Film, and Fiction.* Bloomington: Indiana UP, 1987.

Doane, Mary Ann. "Masquerade Reconsidered: Further Thoughts on the Female Spectator." *Discourse* 11 (1988–89): 42–54.

Eisenstein, Hester, and Alice Jardine, eds. *The Future of Difference.* Boston: G. K. Hall, 1980.

Flynn, Elizabeth A., and Patrocinio P. Schweickart, eds. *Gender and*

Reading: Essays on Readers, Texts, and Contexts. Baltimore: Johns Hopkins UP, 1986.

Foucault, Michel. *The History of Sexuality: Volume I: An Introduction.* Trans. Robert Hurley. New York: Random, 1978.

Kamuf, Peggy. "Writing Like a Woman." *Women and Language in Literature and Society.* New York: Praeger, 1980. 284–99.

Laqueur, Thomas. *Making Sex: Body and Gender from the Greeks to Freud.* Cambridge: Harvard UP, 1990.

Riviere, Joan. "Womanliness as a Masquerade." 1929. Rpt. in *Formations of Fantasy.* Ed. Victor Burgin, James Donald, and Cora Kaplan. London: Methuen, 1986. 35–44.

Rubin, Gayle. "Thinking Sex: Notes for a Radical Theory of the Politics of Sexuality." Abelove et al., *The Lesbian and Gay Reader* 3–44.

———. "The Traffic in Women: Notes on the 'Political Economy' of Sex." *Toward an Anthropology of Women.* Ed. Rayna R. Reiter. New York: Monthly Review, 1975. 157–210.

Schor, Naomi. "Feminist and Gender Studies." *Introduction to Scholarship in Modern Languages and Literatures.* Ed. Joseph Gibaldi. New York: MLA, 1992. 262–87.

Sedgwick, Eve Kosofsky. *Between Men: English Literature and Male Homosocial Desire.* New York: Columbia UP, 1988.

———. "Gender Criticism." *Redrawing the Boundaries. The Transformation of English and American Literary Studies.* Ed. Stephen Greenblatt and Giles Gunn. New York: MLA, 1992. 271–302.

Lesbian and Gay Criticism

Abelove, Henry, Michèle Aina Barale, and David Halperin, eds. *The Lesbian and Gay Studies Reader.* New York: Routledge, 1993.

Butters, Ronald, John M. Clum, and Michael Moon, eds. *Displacing Homophobia: Gay Male Perspectives in Literature and Culture.* Durham: Duke UP, 1989.

Craft, Christopher. *Another Kind of Love: Male Homosexual Desire in English Discourse, 1850–1920.* Berkeley: U of California P, 1994.

de Lauretis, Teresa. *The Practice of Love: Lesbian Sexuality and Perverse Desire.* Bloomington: Indiana UP, 1994.

Dollimore, Jonathan. *Sexual Dissidence: Augustine to Wilde, Freud to Foucault.* Oxford: Clarendon, 1991.

Fuss, Diana, ed. *Inside/Out: Lesbian Theories, Gay Theories.* New York: Routledge, 1991.

Garber, Marjorie. *Vested Interests: Cross-Dressing and Cultural Anxiety*. New York: Routledge, 1992.

Halperin, David M. *One Hundred Years of Homosexuality and Other Essays on Greek Love*. New York: Routledge, 1990.

The Lesbian Issue. Special issue, *Signs* 9 (1984).

Martin, Robert K. *Hero, Captain, and Stranger: Male Friendship, Social Critique, and Literary Form in the Sea Novels of Herman Melville*. Chapel Hill: U of North Carolina P, 1986.

Munt, Sally, ed. *New Lesbian Criticism: Literary and Cultural Readings*. New York: Harvester Wheatsheaf, 1992.

Rich, Adrienne. "Compulsory Heterosexuality and Lesbian Existence." Elizabeth Abel and Emily K. Abel, *The "Signs" Reader*, 139–68.

Stimpson, Catherine R. "Zero Degree Deviancy: The Lesbian Novel in English." *Critical Inquiry* 8 (1981): 363–79.

Weeks, Jeffrey. *Sexuality and Its Discontents: Meanings, Myths, and Modern Sexualities*. London: Routledge, 1985.

Wittig, Monique. "The Mark of Gender." Miller, *The Poetics of Gender*, 63–73.

———. "One Is Not Born a Woman." *Feminist Issues* 1.2 (1981): 47–54.

———. *The Straight Mind and Other Essays*. Boston: Beacon, 1992.

Queer Theory

Butler, Judith. *Bodies That Matter: On the Discursive Limits of "Sex."* New York: Routledge, 1993.

Cohen, Ed. *Talk on the Wilde Side: Towards a Genealogy of Discourse on Male Sexualities*. New York: Routledge, 1993.

de Lauretis, Teresa, ed. Issue on Queer Theory, *differences* 3.2 (1991).

Sedgwick, Eve Kosofsky. *Epistemology of the Closet*. Berkeley: U of California P, 1991.

———. *Tendencies*. Durham: Duke UP, 1993.

Sinfield, Alan. *Cultural Politics — Queer Reading*. Philadelphia: U of Pennsylvania P, 1994.

———. *The Wilde Century: Effeminacy, Oscar Wilde, and the Queer Moment*. New York: Columbia UP, 1994.

Warner, Michael, ed. *Fear of a Queer Planet: Queer Politics and Social Theory*. Minneapolis: U of Minnesota P, 1993.

Feminist and Gender Approaches to
Heart of Darkness

Bode, Rita. "'They . . . Should Be Out of It': The Women of *Heart of Darkness.*" *Conradiana* 26 (1994): 20–34.

Hyland, Peter. "The Little Woman in *Heart of Darkness.*" *Conradiana* 20 (1988): 3–11.

London, Bette. "Reading Race and Gender in Conrad's Dark Continent." *Criticism* 31 (1989): 235–52. Rpt. in London, *The Appropriated Voice: Narrative Authority in Conrad, Forster, and Woolf.* Ann Arbor: U of Michigan P, 1990.

Straus, Nina Pelikan. "The Exclusion of the Intended from Secret Sharing in Conrad's *Heart of Darkness.*" *Novel: A Forum on Fiction* 20 (1987): 123–37.

Sullivan, Zoreh T. "Enclosure, Darkness, and the Body: Conrad's Landscape." *Centennial Review* 25 (1981): 59–79.

A FEMINIST AND GENDER PERSPECTIVE

JOHANNA M. SMITH

"Too Beautiful Altogether":
Ideologies of Gender and Empire in
Heart of Darkness

. . . what [men] have said so far, for the most part, stems from the opposition activity/passivity, from the power relation between a fantasized obligatory virility meant to invade, to colonize, and the consequential phantasm of woman as a "dark continent" to penetrate and to "pacify."

–HÉLÈNE CIXOUS, "The Laugh of the Medusa"

A story about manly adventure narrated and written by men, *Heart of Darkness* might seem an unpropitious subject for feminist criticism. As my epigraph suggests, however, two colonizing ideologies operate in Conrad's story, and a feminist reading can interrogate these interrelated ideologies of gender and empire. To do such a reading is to engage in a feminist critique of ideology, for "feminist thinking is really *re* thinking, an examination of the way certain assumptions about women and the female character enter into the fundamental

assumptions that organize all our thinking" (Jehlen 189). Such re-
thinking about *Heart of Darkness* reveals collusive imperatives of empire and gender: Marlow's narrative aims to "colonize" and "pacify"
both savage[1] darkness and women. By silencing the native laundress
and symbolizing the equally silent savage woman and the Company
women, Marlow reconstructs his experience of the darkness they stand
for. The story's two speaking European women, Marlow's aunt and
Kurtz's Intended, perform a similar function. By restricting unsatisfactory feminine versions of imperialist ideology to them, Marlow is able
to create his own masculine version to keep the darkness at bay.

In what follows I use "ideology" in two senses, to mean not only a
conscious system of meaning, either imposed or willingly adopted, but
also the unconscious grounding of individual experience. In the first
sense, ideology refers to the processes whereby "meaning is produced,
challenged, reproduced, transformed" (Barrett 73). An ideology works
to construct a unified and consensual meaning for contradictory experiences and perceptions, by mystifying or disguising such contradictions. Ideologies often achieve this mystification by disguising custom-
ary social systems as natural relations; cultural systems in which one
nation or gender is dominant over another, for instance, are represented as the natural order. It is through this guise of "the natural"
that the second sense of ideology operates. Because we take for
granted what is "natural," an ideology becomes the unexamined
ground of experience, "the very condition of our experience of the
world" (Belsey 5). Thus internalized, ideology becomes cultural practice, the way we live. Because it *is* practice, however, it does not remain static. As our experiences and formulations of what is "natural"
shift, ideology must continually be "renewed, recreated, defended, and
modified" (Williams 112). And in the course of such modifications, an
ideology's contradictions may become visible.

To specify how ideological contradictions become visible in a literary text, the concept of discourse is helpful. A discourse is "a domain
of language-use" (Belsey 5), a specific mode of speaking, writing, and
thinking that includes certain shared assumptions. But a discourse is
not simply a system of signs with a fixed content and modes of representation; rather it is a set of practices that "*construct* the objects of
which they speak" (Humphries 108; emphasis added). In this sense,

---

[1]The terms "savage" and "native" belong in quotation marks, to indicate their ideological valence. I have decided against this typographical awkwardness, but I ask the
reader to remember the imperialist presuppositions behind these words.

an ideology may be "*inscribed in* discourse" (Belsey 5); an ideology of gender or empire, for instance, is written into a term like "feminine" or "savage." Now, a literary text creates its own discourse, but this discourse is not independent of others, for "the language of ideology" (Belsey 107) is the literary text's "raw material." And like ideologies, discourses are "not natural and inevitable" (During 35) but "historical, provisional and open to change." Hence a literary text can "indicate the bounds within which particular meanings are constructed and negotiated in a given social formation" (Barrett 81). And if that social formation and its ideologies are in the process of modification, a text's literary and ideological discourses may contradict themselves and each other. Such contradictions may open gaps in the literary text that show ideology to be not "natural" but constructed, not fixed but shifting, not seamless but split.

To illustrate such gaps in *Heart of Darkness*'s ideology of empire, I turn to the clash of discourses first in a text by Kurtz and then in Marlow's response to it. Kurtz's report to the International Society for the Suppression of Savage Customs opens with a discourse of empire that mystifies conquest as humanitarianism: "'By the simple exercise of our will we can exert a power for good practically unbounded'" (p. 66). If conquest of the other is thus represented ideologically as "a power for good," then "the simple exercise of our will" in the suppression of savage customs is legitimated. As I have noted, however, dominant ideologies are not as monolithic or stable as Kurtz's sentence would like to imply. Under stress, an ideology may be brought out of the realm of the "natural" or unexamined; thus demystified, its contradictions become visible. The "New Imperialism" of the late nineteenth century, what Conrad calls "the new gang — the gang of virtue" (p. 41), was under precisely this kind of stress, a pressure to justify itself as "the transformation of an enlightened despotism into an even more luminous paternalism" (Bongie 275). That pressure splits Kurtz's text, so that a gap appears between his early advocacy of the "new gang" and the end of his report, "scrawled evidently much later": "'Exterminate all the brutes!'" (p. 66). This clash of discourses reveals the contradiction between the brutality of conquest and the mystifying "power for good" of imperialist ideology.

Marlow's response to Kurtz's report dramatizes additional contradictions. He admits to "tingl[ing] with enthusiasm" (p. 66) for the "unbounded power of eloquence" in Kurtz's "moving appeal to every altruistic sentiment" (p. 66), but he vacillates about the report's conclusion: at one moment it is "terrifying," at another it is "that valuable postscriptum." The irony of the latter phrase functions here, as irony does throughout his narrative, as "evasion" (Klein 114); it enables him to tell, as if he were detached from its purpose, a story that affirms the ideologies on which his culture operates. Thus Marlow embodies "the uneasy position of the intellectual, unable to support fully, or challenge directly, the interests of the dominant class" (Glenn 253). Specifically, Marlow's ironic detachment intends to evade what is hinted by the gap between his two responses to the conclusion of Kurtz's report: his investment in the Company's imperialist project, his seduction by Kurtz's eloquence. If we approach such gaps in Marlow's discourse with feminist "re-vision" (Rich 35) — the act of "entering an old text from a new critical direction" — we can see the contradictions that his ideological discourses of empire and gender work to mystify. I begin with his representations of the native laundress, the savage woman, and the Company women.

The early episode involving the Company's chief accountant and his native laundress clarifies both the Company's imperialist-masculinist brutality and Marlow's collusion in it. Just prior to meeting the accountant, Marlow encounters a chain gang and its black overseer whose glance of complicity "seemed to take me into partnership" (p. 31) in "the great cause." This form of the "cause" momentarily undermines Marlow's masculinity; unlike the "strong, lusty, red-eyed devils" of conquest that "drove men — men, I tell you," this form is "flabby, pretending, weak-eyed." The accountant whom Marlow then meets is similarly feminized; sporting an "elegance of get-up" (p. 32) that makes him look like "a hairdresser's dummy," he is an effeminate professional rather than a "strong, lusty" conqueror. Yet Marlow respects the "apple-pie order" of the accountant's books, especially in contrast with the surrounding "muddle" of "dusty niggers" and such. And his reaction to the man's "get-up" is ironic yet appreciative; the accountant had "verily accomplished something" by keeping up his appearance, and his clean shirts are "achievements of character" that demonstrate his "backbone." Irony here enables Marlow to displace an appalling "flabby" imperialism with the accountant's comic "backbone."

That irony also mystifies Marlow's complicity in such "achievements of character" by occluding the laundress who provides the backbone's starch. The accountant tells Marlow that he has been "teaching one of the native women" to launder his shirts (p. 33); but, he adds, "'It was difficult. She had a distaste for the work.'" This representation of his "teaching" overcoming her "distaste" mystifies the Company man's oppression of an African woman, and here Marlow shows his collusion in the accountant's masculinism. Ideologies of empire and gender both operate in his account of this episode, but only the first is mocked; hence a gap opens in the text between the imperial oppression visible to Marlow when it sends native *men* to the grove of death, and the masculine oppression that remains invisible to him because it seems "natural" that a native woman should do a white man's laundry. In this gap the laundress becomes vividly present by virtue of her absence; here she, rather than Marlow or the accountant, might speak of her "distaste for the work."

That the laundress is silenced indicates Marlow's power, as the masculine narrator of *his* story, to conceal not only her story but those of the other silent women in *Heart of Darkness*. If we turn to his representation of the savage woman, we can see the purposes this silencing serves. Like Kurtz's eloquence in support of imperialism, Marlow's narrative is a mystification of power relations that shows that "[men] want to keep woman in the place of mystery, consign her to mystery, as they say 'keep her in her place, keep her at a distance'" (Cixous 49). As Marlow uses the savage woman to symbolize the enigma of the jungle, his ideological project is to distance and control both mysteries.

The savage woman who appears as Kurtz is being carried onto Marlow's ship is "the nexus where the discourses of imperialism and patriarchy coincide" (Mongia 146–47). As Marlow constructs her, she is the dark continent of both the African jungle and female sexuality. "A wild and gorgeous apparition of a woman" (p. 77), she is "savage and superb, wild-eyed and magnificent," "ominous and stately." When she appears,

the immense wilderness, the colossal body of the fecund and mysterious life seemed to look at her, pensive, as though it had been looking at the image of its own tenebrous and passionate soul.

In this symbology Marlow distances the woman's body by conflating her with the jungle: as the jungle takes on a body, the woman becomes the "image" of the jungle's "soul."[2] By symbolizing the

---

[2]In criticism as well as literature, such symbolizing is "particularly sinister" for women (Robinson 7); Jungian "pronouncements about The Masculine and The Feminine," for example, tend to perpetuate "specious generalizations" about both men's and women's psyches. Although Sullivan's reading of the story is Jungian, she points to the ideological uses of such generalizations when she notes that the savage woman, like the Intended, is "recognized, suppressed and rejected" in the service of masculinist and imperialist aims (79).

woman and personifying the jungle, Marlow works to contain and control both; thus stylized and immobilized, a complex of potentially dangerous forces becomes "pensive" and nonthreatening.

Once the woman moves toward the ship, however, those forces again become threatening, and Marlow again works to contain them. As she approaches the ship, "looking at us . . . like the wilderness itself" (p. 77) and "brooding over an inscrutable purpose," she represents for Marlow a menacing jungle sexuality. He has already described the jungle's absorption of Kurtz as sexual cannibalism: "it had taken him, loved him, embraced him, got into his veins, consumed his flesh" (p. 64). As that earlier moment had "feminize[d] the relation between the adventurer and topography" (Mongia 139), so too does the savage woman's "brooding" approach to the ship. She throws up her arms "as though in an uncontrollable desire to touch the sky" (p. 78), and at this moment shadows of the jungle "gather the steamer into a shadowy embrace." In this gesture of appropriation by the woman/jungle, "the boundaries of masculinity — knowledge, restraint, and order — are under siege" (Mongia 141). Even if the content of her gesture is not sexuality but the "wild sorrow" and "dumb pain" Marlow sees in her face, this too threatens the boundaries of masculine restraint, for Marlow has already (over)responded to a similar loss of Kurtz. In his earlier fear that Kurtz was dead, the "startling extravagance" of his sorrow was "even such as I had noticed in the howling sorrow of these savages" (p. 63). And his backpedaling from grief in that scene indicated his masculine view that "unrestrained grief should be left to the natives and the women" (Staten 723). Faced in the savage woman with not only the threat of sexuality but the allure of grief, Marlow contains both with his stylized representation of a woman reaching for the sky, the unattainable.

As Marlow turns the savage woman's body into a symbol of the jungle, this process serves both masculinist and imperialist ends. It is an effort to defuse and control the power and sexuality both of the woman who "tread[s] the earth proudly" (p. 77) and of that "fecund" earth itself. As an ideology of gender works to distance and conquer the savage woman's body, so an ideology of empire works to distance and conquer the mysterious life of the jungle. And Marlow successfully silences the savage woman; like the native laundress, she does not speak in his narrative. Like the laundress's silence, however, this one creates a gap in the text, a sign of ideological stress that makes visible the fragility of such containment. Such a gap thus reveals "the truth which ideology represses, its own existence as ideology itself" (Belsey 63).

Further instances of ideology *as* ideology appear when we re-vision Marlow's representation of the savage woman's adornments. After detailing the "barbarous ornaments" she wears (p. 77), he concludes that "[s]he must have had the value of several elephant tusks on her." The woman's body is here commodified, to become merely the thing on which "value" is displayed. Although Marlow notes that her hair is shaped like a helmet and that she wears leggings and gauntlets, he dismisses these martial signs as "charms" that have meaning only as proto-ivory. And although he relays the Russian's report that the woman "'talk[s] like a fury'" (p. 78), he does not record her speech. If we reverse Marlow's emphasis and concentrate on the woman's military ornaments and vehement talk, they suggest that she might not be the conventionally feminine (sexually and emotionally dependent on Kurtz) or conventionally native (economically dependent on the ivory trade) figure constructed by Marlow's ideological narrative. She might be a woman warrior whose gestures and speech, remaining unreadable, give her the power that her "*formidable* silence" indicates (emphasis added). If such an interpretation demystifies Marlow's, however, it also runs the risk of forgetting that the savage woman is finally "an inaccessible blankness circumscribed by an interpretable text" (Spivak 264). In other words, to presume to speak for an Other is to follow Marlow's strategy, to produce a representation as ideologically grounded as his

I have already noted the utility of men's efforts to keep women a mystery, to "'keep her in her place, keep her at a distance'" (Cixous 49). Marlow's third such effort to mask his collusion in imperialism appears in his distancing representation of the two women he encounters at the Company's Brussels office. The mystery of these two women is overdetermined by Marlow's relentless symbolizing. His insistence on their knitting links them with the three Fates of Greek and Roman mythology, who weave the thread of life and thus control human destiny. Furthermore, when Marlow describes the elder knitter "pilot[ing]" (p. 25) young men into the Company, the verb connects her with Charon, the pilot who ferries the dead across the Styx into Hades. These representations are part of the narrative retrospection intended to protect Marlow from the realization his narrative revives, that in this office he had contracted himself to the Company and to its imperialist "conspiracy." Hence he displaces the responsibility for his decision onto the younger woman "introducing, introducing continuously [young men] to the unknown," and onto the elder woman, "uncanny and fateful" in her "unconcerned wisdom." Marlow crossed the boundary between the self and the other, between individual adventure and Company conspiracy, once he stepped through the office door; hence he attempts to distance the troubling aspects of his decision behind the apparently solid boundary of gender difference.

Yet this maneuver is only momentarily successful, for the elder woman returns into Marlow's narrative. As he begins his journey into the jungle to retrieve Kurtz, this woman "obtruded herself upon my memory" (p. 81), breached the boundary established by his displacement. Her reappearance serves as a double signal that Marlow's effort to distance the Other — the women of the Company and the troubling imperialism he transferred to them — was bound to fail. When the elder Company woman intrudes in the shape of "the knitting old woman with the cat," the uneasiness Marlow displaced now returns with greater strength for its repression. This silent figure of civilized domesticity only *seems* incongruous in the jungle; her reappearance dramatizes the futility of Marlow's attempt to separate the realm of domesticity from that of colonial adventure, the feminine sphere from the masculine.

Like the ideology of imperialism, the ideology of separate, gendered spheres was under pressure in the late nineteenth century. Single and financially independent, the New Woman was becoming visible in the stores, offices, and streets of Europe and even in the dark continent; Mary Kingsley was one of several women travelers in Africa. Yet *Heart of Darkness* clings to the older ideology of separate spheres, in an effort to resolve the contradictions of Marlow's position vis-à-vis Kurtz. Marlow's experience of Kurtz places him in a "feminine predicament," a situation of perceived physical and/or social powerlessness (Klein 102–06). On the one hand, Marlow is seduced by the "unbounded power of eloquence" in Kurtz's imperialist ideology; on the other hand, he is also drawn to Kurtz's final summation, "'The horror! The horror!'" (p. 86), because it too is "the expression of some sort of belief" (p. 87). Marlow attempts to escape this feminine predicament by his representations of his aunt and the Intended. Through them he constructs a feminine world of "idea"-belief to stand alongside the masculine world of Kurtz's "horror"-belief; located in separate spheres, these contradictory ideologies can coexist. And so that Marlow can stabilize his masculinity by confronting feminine ideologies of empire, the two European women are not silenced. By mocking the lack of imperial experience that their words convey, he can represent his own experience as a manly encounter with truth; through their echoes of the case Kurtz made for imperialism, he can reverse the powerlessness evinced in his response to Kurtz's eloquence. Marlow's construction of these women dramatizes the point of his story, its manful effort to shore up an ideology of imperialism with an ideology of separate spheres.

The belief that will later bc grounded in the aunt and the Intended first emerges in Marlow's preface to his narrative.

> The conquest of the earth, which mostly means the taking it away from those who have a different complexion or slightly flatter noses than ourselves, is not a pretty thing when you look into it too much. What redeems it is the idea only . . . not a sentimental pretence but an idea, and an unselfish belief in the idea — something you can set up, and bow down before, and offer a sacrifice to. . . . (p. 21)

Although this credo precedes the story Marlow tells his hearers, it is important to remember that he has already "looked into" such a "conquest of the earth." Recuperating that experience requires an ideology whereby an ugly exercise of power ("Exterminate all the brutes!") is redeemed by an idea. Like his irony, Marlow's belief in the "idea" behind imperialism is a retrospective attempt to mask his complicity in the Company's imperialism. But Marlow's statement displays all the contradictions he intends it to suppress: between the reality and the idea of conquest, between an idea and a "sentimental pretence" (how would one tell the difference?), between an "unselfish belief" and a self-serving hypocrisy. After these framing sentences, Marlow "broke off" before beginning his tale; this gap reveals the contradiction between his need for an imperialist "idea" and his experience of the horror, a contradiction he attempts to resolve by constructing the feminine sphere of his aunt and the Intended.

Marlow's representations of his aunt perform several functions in his narrative. He first mentions her in connection with his difficulties in getting hired by the Company. After his own efforts and those of his male relatives fail, his aunt, who believes in "the glorious idea" behind the Company (p. 23), successfully intercedes for him. His condescending construction of her, as "a dear enthusiastic soul" who was "determined to make no end of fuss," intends to disguise the failure of his own "fuss." Marlow's next comment on this transaction displays a "class-based ambivalence" (Glenn 248) toward "bourgeois women collaborating in and acting as apologists for" ventures like the

Company. When he admits that "would you believe it? — I tried the women. I, Charlie Marlow, set the women to work — to get a job. Heavens!" (p. 23), his jocularity implies that no woman could have influence in such masculine matters, and thus that the world of experience is and should be a man's world.

During Marlow's farewell visit to his aunt, he uses her feminine lack of experience and debased imperialist rhetoric to construct the "sentimental pretence" that can be distinguished from "an idea" and then rejected. Like her room, which "most soothingly looked just as you would expect a lady's drawing-room to look" (p. 27), her "emissary of light" school of imperialism is represented as bourgeois and feminine. She quotes Scripture "brightly" (in other words, she is uncritically devout); she is "carried off her feet" by "rot" and "humbug" (unlike Marlow, who knows a sentimental pretence when he sees one). And her "glorious idea" of his work — "'weaning those ignorant millions from their horrid ways'" — is womanly idealism, whereas his response — "the Company was run for profit" — is manly realism.

But his aunt's belief in "weaning those ignorant millions" is not unambiguously feminine: it is a variant of the masculine imperialism in Kurtz's "exert[ing] a power for good practically unbounded." Why, then, do these words from Kurtz have "the unbounded power of eloquence" for Marlow, at least initially, whereas he dismisses his aunt's similar vision out of hand? To answer this question, we must examine a central passage in which Marlow equates truth with the masculine recognition of "fact." Commenting on one of his aunt's "bright" remarks, Marlow says:

> It's queer how out of touch with truth women are. They live in a world of their own, and there had never been anything like it, and never can be. It is too beautiful altogether, and if they were to set it up it would go to pieces before the first sunset. Some confounded fact we men have been living contentedly with ever since the day of creation would start up and knock the whole thing over. (p. 27)

Here it is assumed ("It's queer" — that is, strange but true) that all women (extrapolating from one woman) are out of touch with "truth," which is identified with masculine "fact." It follows that the nonfactual "world of their own" that women inhabit is "too beautiful" to exist; in the man's world "there had never been anything like it, and never can be." It also follows that "truth" can be experienced only in the masculine sphere. This is the burden of Marlow's description of native rites and his response to them. These rites display "truth stripped of its cloak" (p. 52); if they "were man enough," Marlow tells his male hearers, they would admit their response to such truth, as he did; in fact, to "meet that truth with his own true stuff" one must be "as much of a man" as the natives.

To this exclusively masculine sphere of experience and truth, Marlow then adds the capacity for belief. He first defines a man's "true stuff" as "inborn strength" (p. 52); he then distinguishes this inborn strength from "principles," which are mere "acquisitions, clothes, pretty rags"; and he concludes that true manly stuff is finally "a deliberate belief." By equating "a man's true stuff" with both his "inborn strength" and his "deliberate belief," Marlow constructs stuff/ strength/belief as "inborn" in men, natural to them. Even though a man's belief is acquired ("deliberate"), it is made to seem different in kind from principles, that "acquisition" with a whiff of the feminine ("pretty rags"). Belief, then, becomes a fully masculine activity: it inheres naturally in men and surfaces through manly experience. While his aunt is not "man enough" to experience savagery so as to come to "truth" and "deliberate belief," both Kurtz and Marlow are. The aunt's feminine version of imperialism is thus a "sentimental pretence" because, unlike Kurtz's "idea," it is not — and by definition cannot be — validated by experience. Through this process of mystification, Marlow has produced an ideological defense of masculine belief. Filtered through his manly experience of truth, belief in the imperialist "idea" can now be used to redeem a reality that is "not pretty."

To fully recuperate Kurtzian imperialism from the taint of a "too beautiful" feminine ideology, however, Marlow must cope with a "confounded fact": that Kurtz's own final recognition of "the horror" belies the "idea" that redeems conquest. As Marlow puts this difficulty, "No eloquence could have been so withering to one's belief in mankind as his final burst of sincerity" (p. 83). Here the contradiction between the eloquence of imperialism and the brutality of its exercise, which Marlow had earlier read in Kurtz's report, directly enters his experience. Kurtz's initial "eloquence" now stands in stark contrast to his final "sincerity," and this sincerity threatens to wither the "belief in mankind" that legitimates imperialism for Marlow. If this new voice were to drown out Kurtz's earlier eloquence, then belief in the "idea" would become impossible and Marlow's experience would become what he fears it to be: "one immense jabber . . . without any kind of sense" (p. 64). And even as Marlow attempts to belittle Kurtz as "very little more than a voice" (p. 64), he remains troubled by "voices, voices — even the girl herself — now — ."

The placing of this first mention of Kurtz's Intended indicates the uses Marlow will make of her. The reference marks a "long" silence (p. 64) in Marlow's narrative, a gap after he reveals his fear of "jabber" and before he states the "deliberate belief" he has now invested in the Intended.

> Oh, she is out of it — completely. They — the women I mean — are out of it — should be out of it. We must help them to stay in that beautiful world of their own, lest ours gets worse. Oh, she had to be out of it.

That an ideology of separate spheres enables masculine imperialism could hardly be more clearly stated. Where Marlow had earlier dismissed this woman's world as "too beautiful altogether," its ideality is now essential: carefully kept "out of it," separated from "our" world of experience, the feminine sphere of "idea" will prevent the masculine sphere of "fact" from deteriorating. Marlow's speech thus suggests how "the masculine production of feminine identity works in the interests of the dominant ideology" (London 238). Specifically, it suggests his need to construct a "beautiful world" around the Intended. There he can order the cacophony of "voices, voices" — Kurtz's "eloquence," his "sincerity," and the Intended's "echo of his magnificent eloquence" (p. 88) — by setting her speech off against the others. And there he can contain Kurtzian imperialism, by embodying in the Intended an "unselfish belief" in the now purified "idea."

Like all the women in this story, then, the Intended is Marlow's construct. As he had earlier commodified the savage woman's body, he now reduces the Intended to a "pure brow" (p. 91) "illumined by the unextinguishable light of belief and love" (p. 92). He locates in her a "beautiful generosity" (p. 93) and "a mature capacity for fidelity, for belief, for suffering" (p. 91) — in short, the "unselfish belief" he requires. Most important, her faith in the power of Kurtzian eloquence enables Marlow to contain and transform that eloquence. "Bowing [his] head before the faith that was in her, before that great and saving illusion" (p. 93), Marlow removes the threat of eloquence from the sphere of his own experience and translates it into her "out of it" world. A faith in Kurtz's eloquence would have been a delusion in the man's sphere where it was contradicted by Kurtz's belief in the horror. In the Intended's feminine sphere, however, it becomes the "great and saving illusion" with which Marlow orders the "jabber" that would otherwise destroy his belief in the "idea." As Marlow bows before her faith, then, he fulfills his ideological project of creating the redeeming idea — "something you can set up, and bow down before, and offer a sacrifice to" (p. 21). While he appears to be bowing to *her*, he is in fact idolizing his own "idea" — the "something" he has "set up" in her.

To complete his posture of belief, however, Marlow must "offer a sacrifice," and who better than the Intended with her "capacity for suffering"? Hence his lie, telling her that Kurtz's last words were her name. It is true that Marlow feels he has sacrificed *himself*: even though he "hate[s], detest[s], and can't bear a lie" (p. 42), he tells this one out of his "infinite pity" for her suffering (p. 94). But if Marlow conceives himself as a "heroic deliverer" (Straus 129) rescuing the Intended from grief, with his "chivalric" lie he is in fact "underscoring an ideology that defines a protective lie as a moral act" when performed by a man. And surely the particular lie Marlow chooses is meant to satisfy his "dull anger" (p. 94) with the Intended's naïveté and her insistence that he give her something "to live with." He and his audience — and the reader — know that by substituting the Intended's name for "the horror" he equates the two; her ignorance of this equation becomes a punishing humiliation. Further intimations of assault are the setting — a "place of cruel and absurd mysteries" (p. 92) — and her responding to the lie with "an exulting and terrible cry" (p. 94) of "unspeakable pain" and "inconceivable triumph." With these four obfuscatory adjectives, Marlow suggests that he has sacrificed the Intended to her own "saving illusion," a suggestion that justifies his act: the pain he intended to inflict is validated (like the rape victim, she asked for it) by the accompanying triumph (and she liked it).[3]

Marlow's lie also functions to stabilize both the feminine sphere of "saving illusion" and the masculine sphere of "confounded fact." The lie protects the "beautiful world" of women that now enshrines his "deliberate belief"; because Marlow *knows* it is a lie, however, the world in which men experience the truth of horror continues to stand. Thus "Marlow brings truth to men by . . . bringing falsehood to women" (Straus 130). When he states that telling the Intended the

---

[3]Staten (736–39) argues that Marlow functions as Kurtz's emissary, thereby fulfilling the latter's sadistic project of forcing the Intended into the total mourning that will confirm his existence. While Staten gives full value to the Intended's cry, his reading nonetheless shares in Marlow's commodification of her: Staten's tendency to reduce her to a cry is not unlike Marlow's tendency to reduce her to a function of himself.

truth would have been "too dark altogether" (p. 94), the echo of "too beautiful altogether" reverberates with this defensive rationale for cordoning off the woman's world. By creating an alternative women's sphere "lest ours gets worse," men can continue to confront their "own true stuff" in their world. And the violence with which Marlow's lie sacrifices the Intended to this masculine world indicates the strength of its homosocial bonds. As he successfully competes with the Intended for "the status of Kurtz's most enduring conquest" (London 245), the pain he inflicts on her dramatizes how women are used "to deny, distort, and censor men's passionate love for one another" (Straus 134). And not only women: Marlow's description of his helmsman's death becomes "a supreme moment of male bonding" with his hearers (London 248), and his similar reductions of native men to conduits of narrative "delineate the common ground Marlow and his audience occupy" as white men (London 249). Thus, although Marlow consistently browbeats and insults his audience — and, by extension, Conrad's — finally the white bourgeois male reader is included in Marlow's "voice of cultural authority." With all these techniques of "artistic force" (Fogel 20) — the lie to the Intended, Marlow's offhand uses of the word "nigger," Conrad's "insistent, domineering" style (Fogel 21) — *Heart of Darkness* demonstrates the brutality in discourses of empire and gender.

I conclude with the issues raised by Conrad's style, for they are useful entries into recent critical re-visions of *Heart of Darkness*'s ideological discourses. In 1978, the Nigerian novelist Chinua Achebe termed Conrad "a bloody racist" (9), in part because of the stylistic "trickery" (4) with which he purported to describe Africa and Africans but in fact dehumanized them. Like Patrick Brantlinger's essay in this volume, essays by Benita Parry, Sandya Shetty, and Reynold Humphries analyze the extent to which Conrad's imperialist discourse "functions to hide the expansionism" of the Western bourgeoisie (Humphries 114) and to "naturalize its presence in the Third World." For André Brink, Conrad's stylistic obfuscations suggest that a "readymade, conventional, eurocentric, male language" (4) is inadequate to "give literary substance to Africa"; as this language breaks down into jabber, "Woman" (5) becomes "the ground of meaning" in *Heart of Darkness*. Brink here replicates Conrad's gender ideology; in contrast, one feminist reading attributes the novel's "density and inaccessibility" not to the breakdown of its masculine language but to its "extremely masculine historical referentiality" (Straus 124), and another analyzes

how the text enacts "the construction of the white male speaking subject as narrative authority" (London 239). Where John McClure and
Patrick Parrinder analyze Conrad's dependence on conventions of the
popular fiction that glorified imperial adventure, Padmini Mongia focuses on how such conventions construct African and European
women as sites where anxieties of gender as well as empire are played
out. In my feminist reading of *Heart of Darkness*, I too have tried to
show the utility for imperialist ideology of a gender ideology that constructs a feminine sphere as "too beautiful altogether."

WORKS CITED

Achebe, Chinua. "An Image of Africa." *Research in African Litera-
ture* 9.1 (Spring 1978): 1–15.
Barrett, Michèle. "Ideology and the Cultural Production of Gender."
*Feminist Criticism and Social Change: Sex, Class and Race in Lit-
erature and Culture*. Ed. Judith Newton and Deborah Rosenfelt.
New York: Methuen, 1985. 65–85.
Belsey, Catherine. *Critical Practice*. London: Methuen, 1980.
Bongie, Chris. "Exotic Nostalgia: Conrad and the New Imperialism."
*Macropolitics of Nineteenth-Century Literature: Nationalism, Ex-
oticism, Imperialism*. Ed. Jonathan Arac and Harriet Ritvo.
Philadelphia: U of Pennsylvania P, 1991. 268–85.
Brink, André. "Woman and Language in Darkest Africa: The Quest
for Articulation in Two Postcolonial Novels." *Literator* 13.1 (Apr.
1992): 1–14.
Cixous, Hélène. "Castration or Decapitation?" Trans. Annette Kuhn.
Signs 7 (1981): 41–55.
During, Simon. "Postmodernism or Post-Colonialism Today." *Tex-
tual Practice* 1.1 (Spring 1987): 32–47.
Fogel, Aaron. *Coercion to Speak: Conrad's Poetics of Dialogue*. Cam-
bridge: Harvard UP, 1985.
Glenn, Ian. "Conrad's *Heart of Darkness:* A Sociological Reading."
Literature and History 13.2 (Autumn 1987): 238–56.
Humphries, Reynold. "The Discourse of Colonialism: Its Meaning
and Relevance for Conrad's Fiction." *Conradiana* 21.2 (Summer
1989): 107–33.
Jehlen, Myra. "Archimedes and the Paradox of Feminist Criticism."
Feminist Theory: A Critique of Ideology. Ed. Nannerl O. Keohane
et al. Chicago: U of Chicago P, 1972. 189–215.
Klein, Karen. "The Feminine Predicament in Conrad's *Nostromo*."

Brandeis Essays in Literature. Ed. John Hazel Smith. Waltham: Brandeis University English and American Literature Department, 1983. 101–16.

London, Bette. "Reading Race and Gender in Conrad's Dark Continent." *Criticism* 31.3 (Summer 1989): 235–52.

McClure, John A. "Late Imperial Romance." *Raritan* 10.4 (Spring 1991): 111–30.

Mongia, Padmini. "Empire, Narrative, and the Feminine in *Lord Jim* and *Heart of Darkness.*" *Contexts for Conrad.* Ed. Keith Carabine et al. Boulder: East European Monographs, 1993. 135–50.

Parrinder, Patrick. "*Heart of Darkness:* Geography as Apocalypse." *Fin de Siècle/Fin du Globe: Fears and Fantasies of the Late Nineteenth Century.* Ed. John Stokes. Houndmills, Eng.: Macmillan, 1992. 85–102.

Parry, Benita. *Conrad and Imperialism: Ideological Boundaries and Visionary Frontiers.* London: Macmillan, 1983.

Rich, Adrienne "When We Dead Awaken: Writing as Re-Vision." *On Lies, Secrets and Silence: Selected Prose, 1966–1978.* New York: Norton, 1979. 33–49.

Robinson, Lillian S. *Sex, Class, and Culture.* New York: Methuen, 1978.

Shetty, Sandya. "*Heart of Darkness:* Out of Africa Some New Thing Rarely Comes." *Journal of Modern Literature* 15.4 (Spring 1989): 461–74.

Spivak, Gayatri Chakravorty. "Three Women's Texts and a Critique of Imperialism." *"Race," Writing, and Difference.* Ed. Henry Louis Gates, Jr. Chicago: U of Chicago P, 1985. 262–80.

Staten, Henry. "Conrad's Mortal Word." *Critical Inquiry* 12.4 (1986): 720–40.

Straus, Nina Pelikan. "The Exclusion of the Intended from Secret Sharing in Conrad's *Heart of Darkness.*" *Novel: A Forum on Fiction* 20 (1987): 123–37.

Sullivan, Zohreh T. "Enclosure, Darkness, and the Body: Conrad's Landscape." *Centennial Review* 25 (1981): 59–79.

Williams, Raymond. *Marxism and Literature.* Oxford: Oxford UP, 1978.

Deconstruction
and
Heart of Darkness

WHAT IS DECONSTRUCTION?

Deconstruction has a reputation for being the most complex and forbidding of contemporary critical approaches to literature, but in fact almost all of us have, at one time, either deconstructed a text or badly wanted to deconstruct one. Sometimes when we hear a lecturer effectively marshal evidence to show that a book means primarily one thing, we long to interrupt and ask what he or she would make of other, conveniently overlooked passages that seem to contradict the lecturer's thesis. Sometimes, after reading a provocative critical article that *almost* convinces us that a familiar work means the opposite of what we assumed it meant, we may wish to make an equally convincing case for our former reading of the text. We may not think that the poem or novel in question better supports our interpretation, but we may recognize that the text can be used to support *both* readings. And sometimes we simply want to make that point: texts can be used to support seemingly irreconcilable positions.

To reach this conclusion is to feel the deconstructive itch. J. Hillis Miller, the preeminent American deconstructor, puts it this way: "Deconstruction is not a dismantling of the structure of a text, but a demonstration that it has already dismantled itself. Its apparently solid ground is no rock but thin air" ("Stevens' Rock" 341). To deconstruct a text isn't to show that all the high old themes aren't there to be found in it. Rather, it is to show that a text — not unlike DNA with its double helix — can have intertwined, opposite "discourses" — strands of narrative, threads of meaning.

Ultimately, of course, deconstruction refers to a larger and more complex enterprise than the practice of demonstrating that a text can have contradictory meanings. The term refers to a way of reading texts practiced by critics who have been influenced by the writings of the French philosopher Jacques Derrida. It is important to gain some understanding of Derrida's project and of the historical backgrounds of his work before reading the deconstruction that follows, let alone attempting to deconstruct a text.

Derrida, a philosopher of language who coined the term *deconstruction,* argues that we tend to think and express our thoughts in terms of opposites. Something is black but not white, masculine and therefore not feminine, a cause rather than an effect, and so forth. These mutually exclusive pairs or dichotomies are too numerous to list but would include beginning/end, conscious/unconscious, presence/absence, and speech/writing. If we think hard about these dichotomies, Derrida suggests, we will realize that they are not simply oppositions; they are also hierarchies in miniature. In other words, they contain one term that our culture views as being superior and one term viewed as negative or inferior. Sometimes the superior term seems only subtly superior (*speech, cause*), but at other times we know immediately which term is culturally preferable (*presence, beginning,* and *consciousness* are easy choices). But the hierarchy always exists.

Of particular interest to Derrida, perhaps because it involves the language in which all the other dichotomies are expressed, is the hierarchical opposition "speech/writing." Derrida argues that the "privileging" of speech, that is, the tendency to regard speech in positive terms and writing in negative terms, cannot be disentangled from the privileging of presence. (Postcards are written by absent friends; we read Plato because he cannot speak from beyond the grave.) Furthermore, according to Derrida, the tendency to privilege both speech and presence is part of the Western tradition of *logocentrism,* the belief that in some ideal beginning were creative *spoken* words, such as "Let there be light," spoken by an ideal, *present* God.[1] According to logocentric

---

[1]Derrida sometimes uses the word *phallogocentrism* to indicate that there is "a certain indissociability" between logocentrism and the "phallocentrism" (Derrida, *Acts* 57) of a culture whose God created light, the world, and man before creating woman — from Adam's rib. "Phallocentrism" is another name for patriarchy. The role that deconstruction has played in feminist analysis will be discussed later.

tradition, these words can now be represented only in unoriginal speech or writing (such as the written phrase in quotation marks above). Derrida doesn't seek to reverse the hierarchized opposition between speech and writing, or presence and absence, or early and late, for to do so would be to fall into a trap of perpetuating the same forms of thought and expression that he seeks to deconstruct. Rather, his goal is to erase the boundary between oppositions such as speech and writing, and to do so in such a way as to throw the order and values implied by the opposition into question.

Returning to the theories of Ferdinand de Saussure, who invented the modern science of linguistics, Derrida reminds us that the association of speech with present, obvious, and ideal meaning — and writing with absent, merely pictured, and therefore less reliable meaning — is suspect, to say the least. As Saussure demonstrated, words are *not* the things they name and, indeed, they are only arbitrarily associated with those things. A word, like any sign, is what Derrida has called a "deferred presence"; that is to say, "the signified concept is never present in itself," and "every concept is necessarily . . . inscribed in a chain or system, within which it refers to another and to other concepts" ("Différance" 138, 140). Neither spoken nor written words have present, positive, identifiable attributes themselves. They have meaning only by virtue of their difference from other words (*red, read, reed*) and, at the same time, their contextual relationship to those words. Take *read* as an example. To know whether it is the present or past tense of the verb — whether it rhymes with *red* or *reed* — we need to see it in relation to some other words (for example, *yesterday*).

Because the meanings of words lie in the differences between them and in the differences between them and the things they name, Derrida suggests that all language is constituted by *différance*, a word he has coined that puns on two French words meaning "to differ" and "to defer": words are the deferred presences of the things they "mean," and their meaning is grounded in difference. Derrida, by the way, changes the *e* in the French word *différence* to an *a* in his neologism *différance;* the change, which can be seen in writing but cannot be heard in spoken French, is itself a playful, witty challenge to the notion that writing is inferior or "fallen" speech.

In *Dissemination* (1972) and *De la grammatologie* [*Of Grammatology*] (1967), Derrida begins to redefine writing by deconstructing some old definitions. In *Dissemination,* he traces logocentrism back to Plato, who in the *Phaedrus* has Socrates condemn writing and who, in all the great dialogues, powerfully postulates that metaphysical longing for origins and ideals that permeates Western thought. "What Derrida does in his reading of Plato," Barbara Johnson points out in her translator's introduction to *Dissemination*, "is to unfold dimensions of Plato's *text* that work against the grain of (Plato's own) Platonism" (xxiv). Remember: that is what deconstruction does, according to Miller; it shows a text dismantling itself.

In *Of Grammatology*, Derrida turns to the *Confessions* of Jean-Jacques Rousseau and exposes a grain running against the grain. Rousseau — who has often been seen as another great Western idealist and believer in innocent, noble origins — on one hand condemned writing as mere representation, a corruption of the more natural, childlike, direct, and therefore undevious speech. On the other hand, Rousseau acknowledged his own tendency to lose self-presence and blurt out exactly the wrong thing in public. He confesses that, by writing at a distance from his audience, he often expressed himself better: "If I were present, one would never know what I was worth," Rousseau admitted (Derrida, *Of Grammatology* 142). Thus, Derrida shows that one strand of Rousseau's discourse made writing seem a secondary, even treacherous supplement, while another made it seem necessary to communication.

Have Derrida's deconstructions of *Confessions* and the *Phaedrus* explained these texts, interpreted them, opened them up and shown us what they mean? Not in any traditional sense. Derrida would say that anyone attempting to find a single, homogeneous or universal meaning in a text is simply imprisoned by the structure of thought that would oppose two readings and declare one to be right and not wrong, correct rather than incorrect. In fact, any work of literature that we interpret defies the laws of Western logic, the laws of opposition and noncontradiction. From deconstruction's point of view, texts don't say "A and not B." They say "A and not-A." "Instead of a simple 'either/or' structure," Johnson explains, "deconstruction attempts to elaborate a discourse that says *neither* 'either/or' *nor* 'both/and' nor even 'neither/nor,' while at the same time not totally abandoning these logics either. The word deconstruction is meant to undermine the either/or logic of the opposition 'construction/destruction.' Deconstruction is both, it is neither, and it reveals the way in which both construction and destruction are themselves not what they appear to be" (Johnson, *World* 12–13).

Although its ultimate aim may be to criticize Western idealism and logic, deconstruction began as a response to structuralism and to for-

malism, another structure-oriented theory of reading. Using Saussure's theory as Derrida was to do later, European structuralists attempted to create a *semiology*, or science of signs, that would give humankind at once a scientific and a holistic way of studying the world
and its human inhabitants. Roland Barthes, a structuralist who later
shifted toward poststructuralism, hoped to recover literary language
from the isolation in which it had been studied and to show that the
laws that govern it govern all signs, from road signs to articles of clothing. Claude Lévi-Strauss, a structural anthropologist who studied
everything from village structure to the structure of myths, found in
myths what he called *mythemes*, or building blocks, such as basic plot
elements. Recognizing that the same mythemes occur in similar myths
from different cultures, he suggested that all myths may be elements of
one great myth being written by the collective human mind.

Derrida did not believe that structuralists had the concepts that
would someday explain the laws governing human signification and
thus provide the key to understanding the form and meaning of everything from an African village to Greek myth to Rousseau's *Confessions*.
In his view, the scientific search by structural anthropologists for what
unifies humankind amounts to a new version of the old search for the
lost ideal, whether that ideal be Plato's bright realm of the Idea or the
Paradise of Genesis or Rousseau's unspoiled Nature. As for the structuralist belief that texts have "centers" of meaning, in Derrida's view
that derives from the logocentric belief that there is a reading of the
text that accords with "the book as seen by God." Jonathan Culler,
who thus translates a difficult phrase from Derrida's *L'Écriture et la
différence* [*Writing and Difference*] (1967) in his book *Structuralist
Poetics* (1975), goes on to explain what Derrida objects to in structuralist literary criticism:

> [When] one speaks of the structure of a literary work, one does so
> from a certain vantage point: one starts with notions of the mean-
> ing or effects of a poem and tries to identify the structures respon-
> sible for those effects. Possible configurations or patterns that make
> no contribution are rejected as irrelevant. That is to say, an intu-
> itive understanding of the poem functions as the "centre". . . . :
> it is both a starting point and a limiting principle. (244)

Deconstruction calls into question assumptions made about literature by formalist, as well as by structuralist, critics. Formalism, or the
New Criticism as it was once commonly called, assumes a work of literature to be a freestanding, self-contained object, its meanings found

in the complex network of relations that constitute its parts (images, sounds, rhythms, allusions, and so on). To be sure, deconstruction is somewhat like formalism in several ways. Both formalism and deconstruction are text-oriented approaches whose practitioners pay a great deal of attention to rhetorical *tropes* (forms of figurative language including allegory, symbol, metaphor, and metonymy). And formalists, long before deconstructors, discovered counterpatterns of meaning in the same text. Formalists find ambiguity: deconstructors find undecidability. On close inspection, however, the formalist understanding of rhetorical tropes or figures is quite different from that of deconstruction, and undecidability turns out to be different from the ambiguity formalists find in texts.

Formalists, who associated literary with figurative language, made qualitative distinctions between types of figures of speech; for instance, they valued symbols and metaphors over metonyms. (A metonym is a term standing for something with which it is commonly associated or contiguous; we use metonymy when we say we had "the cold plate" for lunch.) From the formalist perspective, metaphors and symbols are less arbitrary figures than metonyms and thus rank more highly in the hierarchy of tropes: a metaphor ("I'm feeling blue") supposedly involves a special, intrinsic, nonarbitrary relationship between its two terms (the feeling of melancholy and the color blue); a symbol ("the river of life") allegedly involves a unique fusion of image and idea.

From the perspective of deconstruction, however, these distinctions are suspect. In "The Rhetoric of Temporality" Paul de Man deconstructs the distinction between symbol and allegory; elsewhere, he, Derrida, and Miller have similarly questioned the metaphor/metonymy distinction, arguing that all figuration is a process of linguistic substitution. In the case of a metaphor (or symbol), they claim, we have forgotten what juxtaposition or contiguity gave rise to the association that now seems mysteriously special. Derrida, in "White Mythology," and de Man, in "Metaphor (*Second Discourse*)," have also challenged the priority of literal over figurative language, and Miller has gone so far as to deny the validity of the literal/figurative distinction, arguing that all words are figures because all language involves *catachresis,* "the violent, forced, or abusive importation of a term from another realm to name something which has no proper name" (Miller, *Ariadne* 21).

The difference between the formalist concept of literary ambiguity and the deconstructive concept of undecidability is as significant as the gap between formalist and deconstructive understandings of figurative language. Undecidability, as de Man came to define it, is a complex notion easily misunderstood. There is a tendency to assume it refers to readers who, when forced to decide between two or more equally plausible and conflicting readings, throw up their hands and decide that the choice can't be made. But undecidability in fact debunks this whole notion of reading as a decision-making process carried out on texts by readers. To say we are forced to choose or decide, or that we are unable to do so, is to locate the problem of undecidability falsely within ourselves, rather than recognizing that it is an intrinsic feature of the text.

Undecidability is thus different from ambiguity, as understood by formalists. Formalists believed that a complete understanding of a literary work is possible, an understanding in which ambiguities will be resolved objectively by the reader, even if only in the sense that they will be shown to have definite, meaningful functions. Deconstructors do not share that belief. They do not accept the formalist view that a work of literary art is demonstrably unified from beginning to end, in one certain way, or that it is organized around a single center that ultimately can be identified and defined. Neither do they accept the concept of irony as simply saying one thing and meaning another thing that will be understood with certainty by the reader. As a result, deconstructors tend to see texts as more radically heterogeneous than do formalists. The formalist critic ultimately makes sense of ambiguity; undecidability, by contrast, is never reduced, let alone mastered by deconstructive reading, although the incompatible possibilities between which it is impossible to decide can be identified with certainty.

For critics practicing deconstruction, a literary text is neither a sphere with a center nor an unbroken line with a definite beginning and end. In fact, many assumptions about the nature of texts have been put in question by deconstruction, which in Derrida's words "dislocates the borders, the framing of texts, everything which should preserve their immanence and make possible an internal reading or merely reading in the classical sense of the term" ("Some Statements" 86). A text consists of words inscribed in and inextricable from the myriad discourses that inform it; from the point of view of deconstruction, the boundaries between any given text and that larger text we call language are always shifting.

It was that larger text that Derrida was referring to when he made his famous statement "*there is nothing outside the text*" (*Grammatology* 158). To understand what Derrida meant by that statement, consider the following: we know the world through language, and the acts and

practices that constitute that "real world" (the Oklahoma City bomb-
ing, the decision to marry) are inseparable from the discourses out of
which they arise and as open to interpretation as any work of literature. Derrida is not alone in deconstructing the world/text opposition. De Man viewed language as something that has great power in
individual, social, and political life. Geoffrey Hartman, who was closely
associated with deconstruction during the 1970s, wrote that "nothing
can lift us out of language" (xii).

Once we understand deconstruction's view of the literary text —
as words that are part of and that resonate with an immense linguistic
structure in which we live and move and have our being — we are in a
better position to understand why deconstructors reach points in their
readings at which they reveal, but cannot decide between, incompatible interpretive possibilities. A text is not a unique, hermetically
sealed space. Perpetually open to being seen in the light of new contexts, any given text has the potential to be different each time it is
read. Furthermore, as Miller has shown in *Ariadne's Thread: Story
Lines* (1992), the various "terms" and "famil[ies] of terms" we use in
performing our readings invariably affect the results. Whether we
choose to focus on a novel's characters or its realism, for instance,
leads us to different views of the same text. "No one thread," Miller
asserts, "can be followed to a central point where it provides a means
of overseeing, controlling, and understanding the whole" (21).

Complicating matters still further is the fact that the individual
words making up narratives — the words out of which we make our
mental picture of a character or place — usually have several (and
often have conflicting) meanings due to the complex histories of their
usage. (If your professor tells the class that you have written a "fulsome report" and you look up the word *fulsome* in a contemporary
dictionary, you will learn that it can mean either "elaborate" or "offensive"; if, for some reason, you don't know what *offensive* means, you
will find out that it can equally well describe your favorite quarterback
and a racist joke.) "Each word," as Miller puts it, "inheres in a
labyrinth of branching interverbal relationships"; often there are "forks
in the etymological line leading to bifurcated or trifurcated roots."
Deconstructors often turn to etymology, not to help them decide
whether a statement means this or that, but rather as a way of revealing the coincidence of several meanings in the same text. "The effect
of etymological retracing," Miller writes, "is not to ground the work
solidly but to render it unstable, equivocal, wavering, groundless"
(*Ariadne* 19).

Deconstruction is not really interpretation, the act of choosing between or among possible meanings. Derrida has glossed de Man's statement that "there is no need to deconstruct Rousseau" by saying that "this was another way of saying: there is always already deconstruction, at work *in* works, especially *literary* works. It cannot be applied, after the fact and from outside, as a technical instrument. Texts deconstruct *themselves* by themselves" (Derrida, *Memoires* 123). If deconstruction is not interpretation, then what is it? Deconstruction may be defined as reading, as long as reading is defined as de Man defined it — as a process involving moments of what he called *aporia* or terminal uncertainty, and as an act performed with full knowledge of the fact that all texts are ultimately unreadable (if reading means reducing a text to a single, homogeneous meaning). Miller explains unreadability by saying that although there are moments of great lucidity in reading, each "lucidity will in principle contain its own blind spot requiring a further elucidation and exposure of error, and so on, ad infinitum. . . . One should not underestimate, however, the productive illumination produced as one moves through these various stages of reading" (*Ethics* 42, 44).

Miller's point is important because, in a sense, it deconstructs or erases the boundary between the readings of deconstructors and the interpretations of more traditional critics. It suggests that all kinds of critics have had their moments of lucidity; It also suggests that critics practicing deconstruction know that their *own* insights — even their insights into what is or isn't contradictory, undecidable, or unreadable in a text — are hardly the last word. As Art Berman writes, "In *Blindness and Insight* de Man demonstrates that the apparently well-reasoned arguments of literary critics contain contradiction at their core; yet there is no alternative path to insight. . . . The readers of criticism recognize the blindness of their predecessors, reorganize it, and thereby gain both the insight of the critics and a knowledge of the contradiction that brings forth insight. Each reader, of course, has his own blindness; and the criticism of criticism is not a matter of rectifying someone else's mistakes" (Berman 239–40).

When de Man spoke of the resistance to theory he referred generally to the antitheoretical bias in literary studies. But he might as well have been speaking specifically of the resistance to deconstruction, as expressed not only in academic books and journals but also in popular magazines such as *Newsweek*. Attacks on deconstruction became more common and more personal some four years after de Man's death in

1983. That was the year that a Belgian scholar working on a doctoral thesis discovered ninety-two articles that de Man had written during World War II for the Brussels newspaper *Le Soir*, a widely read French-language daily that had fallen under Nazi control during the German occupation of Belgium. Ultimately, one hundred and seventy articles by de Man were found in *Le Soir*; another ten were discovered in *Het Vlaamsche Land*, a collaborationist newspaper published in Flemish. These writings, which date from 1941 (when de Man was twenty-one years old), ceased to appear before 1943, by which time it had become clear to most Belgians that Jews were being shipped to death camps such as Auschwitz.

De Man's wartime journalism consists mainly, but not entirely, of inoffensive literary pieces. In one article de Man takes Germany's triumph in World War II as a given, places the German people at the center of Western civilization, and foresees a mystical era involving suffering but also faith, exaltation, and rapture. In another article, entitled *"Les Juifs dans la littérature actuelle"* ["Jews in Present-day Literature"], de Man scoffs at the notion that Jewish writers have significantly influenced the literature of his day and, worse, considers the merits of creating a separate Jewish colony that would be isolated from Europe.

No one who had known de Man since his immigration to the United States in 1948 had found him to be illiberal or anti-Semitic. Furthermore, de Man had spent his career in the United States demystifying or, as he would have said, "debunking" the kind of ideological assumptions (about the relationship between aesthetics and national cultures) that lie behind his most offensive Belgian newspaper writings. The critic who in *The Resistance to Theory* (1986) argued that literature must not become "a substitute for theology, ethics, etc." (de Man 24) had either changed radically since writing of the magical integrity and wholeness of the German nation and its culture or had not deeply believed what he had written as a young journalist.

These points have been made in various ways by de Man's former friends and colleagues. Geoffrey Hartman has said that de Man's later work, the work we associate with deconstruction, "looks like a belated, but still powerful, act of conscience" (26–31). Derrida, who like Hartman is a Jew, has read carefully de Man's wartime discourse, showing it to be "split, disjointed, engaged in incessant conflicts" (Hamacher, Hertz, and Keenan 135). "On the one hand," Derrida finds *"unpardonable"* de Man's suggestion that a separate Jewish colony be set up; "on the other hand," he notes that of the four writers de Man praises in the same article (André Gide, Franz Kafka, D. H. Lawrence, and Ernest Hemingway), not one was German, one (Kafka) *was* Jewish, and all four "represent everything that Nazism . . . would have liked to extirpate from history and the great tradition" (Hamacher, Hertz, and Keenan 145).

While friends asserted that some of de Man's statements were unpardonable, deconstruction's severest critics tried to use a young man's sometimes deplorable statements as evidence that a whole critical movement was somehow morally as well as intellectually flawed. As Andrej Warminski summed it up, "the 'discovery' of the 1941–42 writings is being used to perpetuate the old myths about so-called 'deconstruction'" (Hamacher, Hertz, and Keenan 389). Knowing what some of those myths are — and why, in fact, they *are* myths — aids our understanding in an indirect, contrapuntal way that is in keeping with the spirit of deconstruction.

In his book *The Ethics of Reading* (1987), Miller refutes two notions commonly repeated by deconstruction's detractors. One is the idea that deconstructors believe a text means nothing in the sense that it means whatever the playful reader *wants* it to mean. The other is the idea that deconstruction is "immoral" insofar as it refuses to view literature in the way it has traditionally been viewed, namely, "as the foundation and embodiment, the means of preserving and transmitting, the basic humanistic values of our culture" (9). Responding to the first notion, Miller points out that neither Derrida nor de Man "has ever asserted the freedom of the reader to make the text mean anything he or she wants it to mean. Each has in fact asserted the reverse" (10). As for the second notion — that deconstructors are guilty of shirking an ethical responsibility because their purpose is not to (re)discover and (re)assert the transcendent and timeless values contained in great books — Miller argues that "this line of thought" rests "on a basic misunderstanding of the way the ethical moment enters into the act of reading" (9). That "ethical moment," Miller goes on to argue, "is not a matter of response to a thematic content asserting this or that idea about morality. It is a much more fundamental 'I must' responding to the language of literature in itself. . . . Deconstruction is nothing more or less than good reading as such" (9–10). Reading itself, in other words, is an act that leads to further ethical acts, decisions, and behaviors in a real world involving relations to other people and to society at large. For these, the reader must take responsibility, as for any other ethical act.

A third commonly voiced objection to deconstruction is to its playfulness, to the evident pleasure its practitioners take in teasing out all the contradictory interpretive possibilities generated by the words in a text, their complex etymologies and contexts, and their potential to be read figuratively or even ironically. Certainly, playfulness and pleasure are aspects of deconstruction. In his book *The Post Card* (1987), Derrida specifically associates deconstruction with pleasure; in an interview published in a collection of his essays entitled *Acts of Literature* (1992), he speculates that "it is perhaps this *jouissance* which most irritates the all-out adversaries of deconstruction" (56). But such adversaries misread deconstruction's "jouissance," its pleasurable playfulness. Whereas they see it as evidence that deconstructors view texts as tightly enclosed fields on which they can play delightfully useless little word games, Derrida has said that the "subtle and intense pleasure" of deconstruction arises from the "dismantl[ing]" of repressive assumptions, representations, and ideas — in short, from the "lifting of repression" (*Acts* 56–57). As Gregory S. Jay explains in his book *America the Scrivener: Deconstruction and the Subject of Literary History* (1990), "Deconstruction has been not only a matter of reversing binary oppositions but also a matter of disabling the hierarchy of values they enable and of speculating on alternative modes of knowing and of acting" (xii).

Far from viewing literature as a word-playground, Derrida, in Derek Attridge's words, "emphasizes . . . literature as an institution," one "not given in nature or the brain but brought into being by processes that are social, legal, and political, and that can be mapped historically and geographically" (*Acts* 23). By thus characterizing Derrida's emphasis, Attridge counters the commonest of the charges that have been leveled at deconstructors, namely, that they divorce literary texts from historical, political, and legal institutions.

In *Memoires for Paul de Man* (1986), Derrida argues that, where history is concerned, "deconstructive discourses" have pointedly and effectively questioned "the classical assurances of history, the genealogical narrative, and periodizations of all sorts" (15) — in other words, the tendency of historians to view the past as the source of (lost) truth and value, to look for explanations in origins, and to view as unified epochs (for example, the Victorian period, 1837–1901) what are in fact complex and heterogenous times in history. As for politics, Derrida points out that de Man invariably "says something about institutional structures and the political stakes of hermeneutic conflicts," which is to say that de Man's commentaries acknowledge that conflicting interpretations reflect and are reflected in the politics of institutions (such as the North American university).

In addition to history and politics, the law has been a subject on which deconstruction has had much to say of late. In an essay on Franz Kafka's story "Before the Law," Derrida has shown that for Kafka the law as such exists but can never be confronted by those who would do so and fulfill its commands. Miller has pointed out that the law "may only be confronted in its delegates or representatives or by its effects on us or others" (*Ethics* 20). What or where, then, is the law itself? The law's presence, Miller suggests, is continually deferred by narrative, that is, writing about or on the law which constantly reinterprets the law in the attempt to reveal what it really is and means. This very act of (re)interpretation, however, serves to "defer" or distance the law even further from the case at hand, since the (re)interpretation takes precedence (and assumes prominence) over the law itself. (As Miller defines it, narrative would include everything from a Victorian novel that promises to reveal moral law to the opinion of a Supreme Court justice regarding the constitutionality of a given action, however different these two documents are in the conventions they follow and the uses to which they are put.) Miller likens the law to a promise, "the validity of [which] does not lie in itself but in its future fulfillment," and to a story "divided against itself" that in the end "leaves its readers . still in expectation" (*Ethics* 33).

Because the facts about deconstruction are very different from the myth of its playful irreverence and irrelevance, a number of contemporary thinkers have found it useful to adapt and apply deconstruction in their work. For instance, a deconstructive theology has been developed. Architects have designed and built buildings grounded, as it were, in deconstructive architectural theory. In the area of law, the Critical Legal Studies movement has, in Christopher Norris's words, effectively used "deconstructive thinking" of the kind de Man used in analyzing Rousseau's *Social Contract* "to point up the blind spots, conflicts, and antinomies that plague the discourse of received legal wisdom." Critical legal theorists have debunked "the formalist view of law," that is, the "view which holds law to be a system of neutral precepts and principles," showing instead how the law "gives rise to various disabling contradictions," such as "the problematic distinction between 'private' and 'public' domains." They have turned deconstruction into "a sophisticated means of making the point that all legal discourse is performative in character, i.e., designed to secure assent through its rhetorical power to convince or persuade" (Norris,

Deconstruction and the Interests 17). Courtroom persuasion, Gerald Lopez has argued in a 1989 article in the *Michigan Law Review*, consists of storytelling as much as argument (Clayton 13).

In the field of literary studies, the influence of deconstruction may be seen in the work of critics ostensibly taking some other, more political approach. Barbara Johnson has put deconstruction to work for the feminist cause. She and Shoshana Felman have argued that chief among those binary oppositions "based on repression of differences with entities" is the opposition man/woman (Johnson, *Critical* x). In a reading of the "undecidability" of "femininity" in Balzac's story "The Girl with the Golden Eyes," Felman puts it this way: "the rhetorical hierarchization of the . . . opposition between the sexes is . . . such that woman's *difference* is suppressed, being totally subsumed by the reference of the feminine to masculine identity" ("Rereading" 25).

Elsewhere, Johnson, Felman, and Gayatri Spivak have combined Derrida's theories with the psychoanalytic theory of Jacques Lacan to analyze the way in which gender and sexuality are ultimately textual, grounded in language and rhetoric. In an essay on Edmund Wilson's reading of Henry James's story *The Turn of the Screw*, Felman has treated sexuality as a form of rhetoric that can be deconstructed, shown to contain contradictions and ambiguities that more traditional readings of sexuality have masked. Gay and lesbian critics have seen the positive implications of this kind of analysis, hence Eve Kosofsky Sedgwick's admission in the early pages of her book *Epistemology of the Closet* (1990): "One main strand of argument in this book is deconstructive, in a fairly specific sense. The analytic move it makes is to demonstrate that categories presented in a culture as symmetrical binary oppositions . . . actually subsist in a more unsettled and dynamic tacit relation" (9–10).

In telling "The Story of Deconstruction" in his book on contemporary American literature and theory, Jay Clayton assesses the current status of this unique approach. Although he notes how frequently deconstructive critics have been cited for their lack of political engagement, he concludes that deconstruction, "a movement accused of formalism and arid intellectualism, participates in the political turn of contemporary culture" (34). He suggests that what began as theory in the late 1960s and 1970s has, over time, developed into a method employed by critics taking a wide range of approaches to literature — ethnic, feminist, new historicist, Marxist — in addition to critics outside of literary studies per se who are involved in such areas as Critical

Legal Studies and Critical Race Theory, which seeks to "sustain a complementary relationship between the deconstructive energies of Critical Legal Studies and the constructive energies of civil rights activism" (58).

Clayton cites the work of Edward Said as a case in point. Through 1975, the year that his *Beginnings: Intention and Method* was published, Said was employing a form of deconstructive criticism that, in Clayton's words, emphasized the "power" of texts "to initiate projects in the real world" (45–46). Said became identified with cultural and postcolonial criticism, however, beginning in 1978 with the publication of his book *Orientalism*, in which he deconstructs the East/West, Orient/Occident opposition. Said argues that Eastern and Middle Eastern peoples have for centuries been stereotyped by the Western discourses of "orientalism," a textuality that in no way reflects the diversity and differences that exist among the peoples it claims to represent. According to Said, that stereotyping not only facilitated the colonization of vast areas of the globe by the so-called West but also still governs, to a great extent, relations with the Arab and the so-called Eastern world. The expansion of Said's field of vision to include not just literary texts but international relations is powerfully indicative of the expanding role that deconstruction currently plays in developing contemporary understandings of politics and culture, as well as in active attempts to intervene in these fields.

The purpose of deconstruction, Miller has written, is to show "the existence in literature of structures of language which contradict the law of non-contradiction." Why find the grain that runs against the grain? To restore what Miller has called "the strangeness of literature," to reveal the "capacity of each work to surprise the reader," to demonstrate that "literature continually exceeds any formula or theory with which the critic is prepared to encompass it" (*Fiction* 5).

In the essay that follows, Miller does all these things, including admitting that his own reading is "exceeded" by *Heart of Darkness*. In the last paragraph of his essay, he confesses his own complicity as a demystifying commentator: "I have attempted," he writes, "to perform an act of generic classification, with all the covert violence and unreason of that act, since no work is wholly commensurate with the boundaries of any genre."

The generic classification Miller refers to is his attempt to classify *Heart of Darkness* as an apocalypse and the apocalypse as an extended parable. (Whereas a parable is a little allegorical story designed to reveal some moral truth, an apocalypse is a highly figurative book of revelation or prophecy.) Of course, as a poststructuralist writing in opposition to the tradition of Western metaphysics, Miller classifies parables and apocalypses as genres that only *seem* to reveal spectral truths, be they the Bright Ideal or the Heart of Darkness. Miller deconstructs Jesus' parable of the sower to show how it is against itself; what its words reveal, Miller contends, is that if you need them then you cannot understand them. Miller also deconstructs Conrad's parable about the two kinds of stories, the parable of the "nut and the moonlit haze." (You will recall the contrast made between the "yarns of seamen . . . , the whole meaning of which" lies inside like a nut in a shell, and Marlow's stories, the meaning of which is said to lie "outside, enveloping the tale," which brings "it out only as a glow brings out a haze" [p. 20].) The narrator's distinction begins to unravel, the more Miller discusses it — and the more he discusses the story Marlow actually tells.

What Miller is really unraveling, of course, is a set of hierarchized, binary oppositions between kinds of texts. By questioning the privileged status of apocalypses, parables, and Marlow's stories, he is erasing numerous boundaries: between the Bible and literature, high forms of narrative and low, and, ultimately, between literature and criticism. (He sets himself and us in the same line of "guilty witnesses" that includes the narrator, whose witness of Marlow perpetuates what Marlow witnessed, and Marlow himself.) And, of course, Miller is deconstructing the metaphor/metonymy opposition. Parables, apocalypses, and allegories are shown to be like metaphors; in strange ways, they can supposedly highlight invisible things with which they are, supposedly, fundamentally and inevitably involved. They supposedly allow us to experience, in the present, such things as Timeless Truth, the End, or the Beginning. In fact, Miller's reading contends, parables and apocalypses cannot reveal metaphysical secrets because, like all signs, they are metonyms, no more intrinsically involved with ultimate truths than the cold plate we order is with the plate, than the mist around the moon is with the sun's reflected light.

Conrad's distinctions, Miller shows, are "made in terms of figures," and even these figures, by an "unavoidable necessity," have to have other, different, supplemental figures to explain them. (Marlow's tales bring out meaning *as* a glow brings out a haze, *in the likeness* of one of these misty halos. . . .) To highlight the figurative nature of language, as Miller does throughout his reading of *Heart of Darkness,* is a typical poststructuralist move. Equally typical, though, is Miller's wondering whether all these figures of figures, supplements to supplements, necessarily carry us further away from Marlow's experience and its meaning. Like the fellows on the *Nellie,* who are said by Marlow to "see more than I could," for "you see me," figures "see" — and show — us more than a sailor like Marlow could possibly have experienced (p. 43).

Implicit in all of Miller's critical procedures, of course, is the poststructuralist assumption that *Heart of Darkness* defies the logic of noncontradiction. Like anything written — and the "apocalypse is after all a written not an oral genre" — *Heart of Darkness* says both "A" and "not-A." Its figures both illuminate their own workings and undermine them; it promises to reveal something and then shows us that that something (pure darkness) is what cannot be seen or shown, except as an absence. An ironic text, it is founded, Miller says, on unreason and is "indeterminate or undecidable in meaning."

The unfolding of indeterminacies requires an unusual style, one that Miller deploys adeptly in *"Heart of Darkness* Revisited." "I begin with three questions," Miller begins. (Are there three? Are they answered or even answerable?) "I shall approach an answer . . . by [a] . . . roundabout way." To write is to defer, just as to read the book of Revelation is to know what has not yet entered human experience. Miller's argument defers many central questions while drawing us close, in the process, to the workings of Conrad's text.

DECONSTRUCTION:
A SELECTED BIBLIOGRAPHY

Writings on Deconstruction

Arac, Jonathan, Wlad Godzich, and Wallace Martin, eds. *The Yale Critics: Deconstruction in America.* Minneapolis: U of Minnesota P, 1983. See especially the essays by Bové, Godzich, Pease, and Corngold.

Berman, Art. *From the New Criticism to Deconstruction: The Reception of Structuralism and Post-Structuralism.* Urbana: U of Illinois P, 1988.

Butler, Christopher. *Interpretation, Deconstruction, and Ideology: An Introduction to Some Current Issues in Literary Theory.* Oxford: Oxford UP, 1984.

Clayton, Jay. *The Pleasure of Babel: Contemporary American Literature and Theory.* New York: Oxford UP, 1993.

Culler, Jonathan. *On Deconstruction: Theory and Criticism After Structuralism*. Ithaca: Cornell UP, 1982.

———. *Structuralist Poetics: Structuralism, Linguistics, and the Study of Literature*. Ithaca: Cornell UP, 1975. See especially ch. 10.

Esch, Deborah. "Deconstruction." *Redrawing the Boundaries: The Transformation of English and American Literary Studies*. Ed. Stephen Greenblatt and Giles Gunn. New York: MLA, 1992. 374–91.

Feminist Studies 14 (1988). Special issue on deconstruction and feminism.

Hamacher, Werner, Neil Hertz, and Thomas Keenan. *Responses: On Paul de Man's Wartime Journalism*. Lincoln: U of Nebraska P, 1989.

Hartman, Geoffrey. "Blindness and Insight." *The New Republic*, 7 Mar. 1988.

Jay, Gregory S. *America the Scrivener: Deconstruction and the Subject of Literary History*. Ithaca: Cornell UP, 1990.

Leitch, Vincent B. *American Literary Criticism from the Thirties to the Eighties*. New York: Columbia UP, 1988. See especially ch. 10, "Deconstructive Criticism."

———. *Cultural Criticism, Literary Theory, Poststructuralism*. New York: Columbia UP, 1992.

Loesberg, Jonathan. *Aestheticism and Deconstruction: Pater, Derrida, and de Man*. Princeton: Princeton UP, 1991.

Melville, Stephen W. *Philosophy Beside Itself: On Deconstruction and Modernism*. Theory and History of Lit. 27. Minneapolis: U of Minnesota P, 1986.

Norris, Christopher. *Deconstruction and the Interests of Theory*. Oklahoma Project for Discourse and Theory 4. Norman: U of Oklahoma P, 1989.

———. *Deconstruction: Theory and Practice*. London: Methuen, 1982. Rev. ed. London: Routledge, 1991.

———. *Paul de Man, Deconstruction and the Critique of Aesthetic Ideology*. New York: Routledge, 1988.

Weber, Samuel. *Institution and Interpretation*. Minneapolis: U of Minnesota P, 1987.

Works by de Man, Derrida, and Miller

de Man, Paul. *Allegories of Reading*. New Haven: Yale UP, 1979. See especially ch. 1, "Semiology and Rhetoric," and ch. 7, "Metaphor (*Second Discourse*)."

————. *Blindness and Insight*. New York: Oxford UP, 1971. Minneapolis: U of Minnesota P, 1983. The 1983 edition contains important essays not included in the original edition.

————. "Phenomenality and Materiality in Kant." *Hermeneutics: Questions and Prospects*. Ed. Gary Shapiro and Alan Sica. Amherst: U of Massachusetts P, 1984. 121–44.

————. *The Resistance to Theory*. Minneapolis: U of Minnesota P, 1986.

————. *Romanticism and Contemporary Culture*. Ed. E. S. Burt, Kevin Newmarkj, and Andrzej Warminski. Baltimore: Johns Hopkins UP, 1993.

————. *Wartime Journalism, 1939–1943*. Lincoln: U of Nebraska P, 1989.

Derrida, Jacques. *Acts of Literature*. Ed. Derek Attridge. New York: Routledge, 1992.

————. "Différance." *Speech and Phenomena*. Trans. David B. Alison. Evanston: Northwestern UP, 1973.

————. *Dissemination*. 1972. Trans. Barbara Johnson. Chicago: U of Chicago P, 1981. See especially the concise, incisive "Translator's Introduction," which provides a useful point of entry into this work and others by Derrida.

————. "Force of Law: The 'Mystical Foundation of Authority.' " Trans. Mary Quaintance. *Deconstruction and the Possibility of Justice*. Ed. Drucilla Cornell, Michel Rosenteld, and David Gray Carlson. New York: Routledge, 1992. 3–67.

————. *Given Time. 1, Counterfeit Money*. Trans. Peggy Kamuf. Chicago: U of Chicago P, 1992.

————. *Margins of Philosophy*. Trans. Alan Bass. Chicago: U of Chicago P, 1982. Contains the essay "White Mythology: Metaphor in the Text of Philosophy."

————. *Memoires for Paul de Man*. Wellek Library Lectures. Trans. Cecile Lindsay, Jonathan Culler, and Eduardo Cadava. New York: Columbia UP, 1986.

————. *Of Grammatology*. 1967. Trans. Gayatri C. Spivak. Baltimore: Johns Hopkins UP, 1976.

————. "Passions." *Derrida: A Critical Reader*. Ed. David Wood. Cambridge: Basil Blackwell, 1992.

————. *The Post Card: From Socrates to Freud and Beyond*. Trans. with intro. Alan Bass. Chicago: U of Chicago P, 1987.

————. "Some Statements and Truisms about Neo-logisms, Newisms, Postisms, and Other Small Seisisms." *The States of "Theory."* New York: Columbia UP, 1990. 63–94.

————. *Specters of Marx.* Trans. Peggy Kamuf. New York: Routledge, 1994.

————. *Writing and Difference.* 1967. Trans. Alan Bass. Chicago: U of Chicago P, 1978.

Miller, J. Hillis. *Ariadne's Thread: Story Lines.* New Haven: Yale UP, 1992.

————. *The Ethics of Reading: Kant, de Man, Eliot, Trollope, James, and Benjamin.* New York: Columbia UP, 1987.

————. *Fiction and Repetition: Seven English Novels.* Cambridge: Harvard UP, 1982.

————. *Hawthorne and History: Defacing It.* Cambridge: Basil Blackwell, 1991. Contains a bibliography of Miller's work from 1955 to 1990.

————. *Illustrations.* Cambridge: Harvard UP, 1992.

————. "Stevens' Rock and Criticism as Cure." *Georgia Review* 30 (1976): 3–31, 330–48.

————. *Typographies.* Stanford: Stanford UP, 1994.

————. *Versions of Pygmalion.* Cambridge: Harvard UP, 1990.

Essays on Deconstruction and Poststructuralism

Barthes, Roland. *S/Z.* Trans. Richard Miller. New York: Hill, 1974. In this influential work, Barthes turns from a structuralist to a poststructuralist approach.

Benstock, Shari. *Textualizing the Feminine: On the Limits of Genre.* Norman: U of Oklahoma P, 1991.

Bloom, Harold, et al., eds. *Deconstruction and Criticism.* New York: Seabury, 1979. Includes essays by Bloom, de Man, Derrida, Miller, and Hartman.

Chase, Cynthia. *Decomposing Figures.* Baltimore: Johns Hopkins UP, 1986.

Cohen, Tom. *Anti-Mimesis: From Plato to Hitchcock.* Cambridge: Cambridge UP, 1994.

Elam, Diane. *Feminism and Deconstruction: Ms. en Abyme.* New York: Routledge, 1994.

Felman, Shoshana. "Rereading Femininity." Special Issue on "Feminist Readings: French Texts/American Contexts," *Yale French Studies* 62 (1981).

————. "Turning the Screw of Interpretation." *Literature and Psychoanalysis: The Question of Reading: Otherwise.* Special issue, *Yale*

French Studies 55–56 (1978): 3–508. Baltimore: Johns Hopkins UP, 1982.

Harari, Josué, ed. *Textual Strategies: Perspectives in Post-Structuralist Criticism.* Ithaca: Cornell UP, 1979.

Johnson, Barbara. *The Critical Difference: Essays in the Contemporary Rhetoric of Reading.* Baltimore: Johns Hopkins UP, 1980.

———. *A World of Difference.* Baltimore: Johns Hopkins UP, 1987.

Krupnick, Mark, ed. *Displacement: Derrida and After.* Bloomington: Indiana UP, 1987.

Meese, Elizabeth, and Alice Parker, eds. *The Difference Within: Feminism and Critical Theory.* Philadelphia: John Benjamins, 1989.

Sedgwick, Eve Kosofsky. *Epistemology of the Closet.* Berkeley: U of California P, 1990.

Ulmer, Gregory L. *Applied Grammatology.* Baltimore: Johns Hopkins UP, 1985.

———. *Teletheory: Grammatology in the Age of Video.* New York: Routledge, 1989.

Deconstructive and Poststructuralist Approaches to Conrad and *Heart of Darkness*

Bonney, William. *Thorns and Arabesques: Contexts for Conrad's Fiction.* Baltimore: Johns Hopkins UP, 1980.

Brooks, Peter. "An Unreadable Report: Conrad's *Heart of Darkness.*" *Reading for the Plot: Design and Intention in Narrative.* New York: Knopf, 1984.

Mansell, Darrell. "Trying to Bring Literature Back Alive: The Ivory in Joseph Conrad's *Heart of Darkness.*" *Criticism* 33 (1991): 205–15.

Pecora, Vincent. "The Sounding Empire: Conrad's *Heart of Darkness.*" *Self and Form in Modern Narrative.* Baltimore: Johns Hopkins UP, 1989.

A DECONSTRUCTIVE PERSPECTIVE

J. HILLIS MILLER

Heart of Darkness Revisited

I begin with three questions: Is it a senseless accident, a result of the crude misinterpretation or gross transformation of the mass media that the cinematic version of *Heart of Darkness* is called *Apocalypse Now*, or is there already something apocalyptic about Conrad's novel in itself? What are the distinctive features of an apocalyptic text? How would we know when we had one in hand?

I shall approach an answer to these questions by the somewhat roundabout way of an assertion that if *Heart of Darkness* is perhaps only problematically apocalyptic, there can be no doubt that it is parabolic. The distinctive feature of a parable, whether sacred or secular, is the use of a realistic story, a story in one way or another based firmly on what Marx calls man's "real conditions of life, and his relations with his kind," to express another reality or truth not otherwise expressible (Marx 476). When the disciples ask Jesus why he speaks to the multitudes in parables, he answers, "Therefore speak I to them in parables: because they seeing see not; and hearing they hear not, neither do they understand" (Matthew 13:13). A little later Matthew tells the reader that "without a parable spake he not unto them: That it might be fulfilled which was spoken by the prophet, saying, I will open my mouth in parables; I will utter things which have been kept secret from the foundation of the world" (Matthew 13:34–35). Those things which have been kept secret from the foundation of the world will not be revealed until they have been spoken in parable, that is, in terms which the multitude who lack spiritual seeing and hearing nevertheless see and hear, namely, the everyday details of their lives of fishing, farming, and domestic economy.

Conrad's story is a parable, in part, because it is grounded firmly in the details of real experience. Biographers such as Ian Watt, Frederick Karl, and Norman Sherry tell us all that is likely to be learned of Conrad's actual experience in the Congo, as well as of the historical originals of Kurtz, the particolored harlequin-garbed Russian, and other characters in the novel. If parables are characteristically grounded in representations of realistic or historical truth, *Heart of Darkness* admirably fulfills this requirement of parable. But it fills another requirement, too. Conrad's novel is a parable because, although it is based on what Marx called "real conditions," its narrator attempts through his tale to reveal some as-yet-unseen reality.

Unlike allegory, which tries to shed light on the past or even on our origins, parable tends to be oriented toward the future, toward last things, toward the mysteries of the kingdom of heaven and how to get there. Parable tends to express what Paul at the end of Romans, in echo of Matthew, calls "the revelation of the mystery, which was kept secret since the world began, but now is made manifest" (Romans 16:25–26). Parable, as we can now see, has at least one thing in common with apocalypse: it too is an act of unveiling that which has never been seen or known before. Apocalypse *means* unveiling; an apocalypse is a narrative unveiling or revelation. The last book of the Bible is the paradigmatic example of apocalypse in our tradition, though it is by no means the only example. The book of Revelation seeks to unveil a mystery of the future, namely, what will happen at time's ending.

My contention, then, is that *Heart of Darkness* fits, in its own way, the definitions of both parable and apocalypse, and that much illumination is shed on it by interpreting it in the light of these generic classifications. As Marlow says of his experience in the heart of darkness: "It was somber enough too — . , . not very clear either. No, not very clear, And yet it seemed to throw a kind of light" (p. 22). A narrative that sheds light, that penetrates darkness, that clarifies and illuminates — this is one definition of that mode of discourse called parabolic or apocalyptic, but it might also serve to define the work of criticism or interpretation. All criticism claims to be enlightenment or *Aufklärung*.

How, though, does a story enlighten or clarify: in what ways may narratives illuminate or unveil? Conrad's narrator distinguishes between two different ways in which a narrative may be related to its meaning:

> The yarns of seamen have a direct simplicity, the whole meaning of which lies within the shell of a cracked nut. But Marlow was not typical (if his propensity to spin yarns be excepted), and to him the meaning of an episode was not inside like a kernel but outside [Ms: outside in the unseen], enveloping the tale which brought it out only as a glow brings out a haze, in the likeness of one of these misty halos that sometimes are made visible by the spectral illumination of moonshine. (pp. 19–20)

The narrator here employs two figures to describe two kinds of stories: simple tales and parables. Through the two figures, moreover, Conrad attempts to present the different ways in which these two kinds of narration relate to their meanings.

The meanings of the stories of most seamen, says the narrator, are inside the narration like the kernel of a cracked nut. I take it the narrator means the meanings of such stories are easily expressed, detachable from the stories and open to paraphrase in other terms, as when one draws an obvious moral: "Crime doesn't pay," or "Honesty is the best policy," or "The truth will out," or "Love conquers all." The figure of the cracked nut suggests that the story itself, its characters and narrative details, are the inedible shell which must be removed and discarded so the meaning of the story may be assimilated. This relation of the story to its meaning is a particular version of the relation of container to thing contained. The substitution of contained for container, in this case meaning for story, is one version of that figure called in classical rhetoric *synecdoche*, but this is a metonymic rather than a metaphorical synecdoche.[1] The meaning is adjacent to the story, contained within it as nut within shell, but the meaning has no intrinsic similarity or kinship to the story. Its relation to the story that contains it is purely contingent. The one happens to touch the other, as shell surrounds nut, as bottle its liquid contents, or as shrine-case its iconic image.

It is far otherwise with Marlow's stories. Their meaning — like the meaning of a parable — is outside, not in. It envelops the tale rather than being enveloped by it. The relation of container and thing contained is reversed. The meaning now contains the tale. Moreover, perhaps because of that enveloping containment, or perhaps for more obscure reasons, the relation of the tale to its meaning is no longer that of dissimilarity and contingency. The tale is the necessary agency of the bringing into the open or revelation of that particular meaning. It is not so much that the meaning is like the tale. It is not. But the tale is in preordained correspondence to or in resonance with the meaning. The tale magically brings the "unseen" meaning out and makes it visible.

Conrad has the narrator express this subtle concept of parabolic narration according to the parabolic "likeness" of a certain atmos-

---

[1] In metaphorical synecdoche a part of something is used to signify the whole: "I see a sail" means "I see a ship." A metonymic synecdoche is one in which the signifying part is really only something contiguous with the thing signified, not intrinsic to it; "the bottle" is a metonymic synecdoche for liquor, since glass cannot really be part of liquor in the way a sail is part of a ship.

pheric phenomenon. "Likeness" is a homonym of the German *Gleich-nis*, which is itself a term for parable. The meaning of a parable appears in the "spectral" likeness of the story that reveals it, or rather, it appears in the likeness of an exterior light surrounding the story, just as the narrator's theory of parable appears not as such but in the "likeness" of the figure he proposes. Thus, the figure does double duty, both as a figure for the way Marlow's stories express their meaning and as a figure for itself, so to speak; that is, as a figure for its own mode of working. This is according to a mind-twisting torsion of the figure back on itself that is a regular feature of such figuration, parables of parable, or stories about storytelling. The figure both illuminates its own workings and at the same time obscures or undermines it, since a figure of a figure is an absurdity, or, as Wallace Stevens puts it, there is no such thing as a metaphor of a metaphor. What was the figurative vehicle of the first metaphor automatically becomes the literal tenor of the second metaphor.[2]

Let us look more closely at the exact terms of the metaphor Conrad's narrator proposes. To Marlow, the narrator says, "the meaning of an episode was not inside like a kernel but outside, enveloping the tale which brought it out only as a glow brings out a haze, in the likeness of one of these spectral illuminations of moonshine." The first simile here ("as a glow") is doubled by a second, similitude of a similitude ("in the likeness of . . ."). The "haze" is there all around on a dark night, but, like the meaning of one of Marlow's tales, it is invisible, inaudible, intangible in itself, like the darkness, or like that "something great and invincible" Marlow is aware of in the African wilderness, something "like evil or truth, waiting patiently for the passing away of this fantastic invasion" (p. 38). The haze, too, is like the climactic name for that truth, the enveloping meaning of the tale: "the horror," those last words of Kurtz that seem all around in the gathering darkness when Marlow makes his visit to Kurtz's Intended and tells his lie. "The dusk," Marlow says, "was repeating them in a persistent whisper all around us, in a whisper that seemed to swell menacingly like the first whisper of a rising wind. 'The horror! The horror!'" (p. 94).

[2]The "vehicle" of a figurative expression is the term used to refer to something else; the "tenor" is the person, thing, or concept referred to by the vehicle. In the metaphorical synecdoche used as an example in footnote 1 on p. 208, "sail" is the vehicle, "ship" the tenor; in the metonymic synecdoche, "bottle" is the vehicle, "liquor" the tenor. If you say you feel blue to mean you feel sad, "blue" is the vehicle, "sadness" the tenor.

The working of Conrad's figure is much more complex than perhaps it at first appears, both in itself and in the context of the fine grain
of the texture of language in *Heart of Darkness* as a whole, as well as in
the context of the traditional complex of figures, narrative motifs, and
concepts to which it somewhat obscurely alludes. The atmospheric
phenomenon that Conrad uses as the vehicle of his parabolic metaphor
is a perfectly real one, universally experienced. It is as referential and as
widely known as the facts of farming Jesus uses in the parable of the
sower. If you sow your seed on stony ground it will not be likely to
sprout. An otherwise invisible mist or haze at night will show up as a
halo around the moon. As in the case of Jesus' parable of the sower,
Conrad uses his realistic and almost universally known facts as the
means of expressing indirectly another truth less visible and less widely
known, just as the narrative of *Heart of Darkness* as a whole is based on
the facts of history and on the facts of Conrad's life but uses these to
express something transhistorical and transpersonal, the evasive and
elusive "truth" underlying both historical and personal experience.

Both Jesus' parable of the sower and Conrad's parable of the
moonshine in the mist, curiously enough, have to do with their own
efficacy — that is, with the efficacy of parable. Both are posited on
their own necessary failure. Jesus' parable of the sower will give more
only to those who already have and will take away from those who
have not even what they have. If you can understand the parable you
do not need it. If you need it you cannot possibly understand it. You
are stony ground on which the seed of the word falls unavailing. Your
eyes and ears are closed, even though the function of parables is to
open the eyes and ears of the multitude to the mysteries of the kingdom of heaven. In the same way, Conrad, in a famous passage in the
preface to *The Nigger of the "Narcissus,"* tells his readers, "My task
which I am trying to achieve is, by the power of the written word, to
make you hear, to make you feel — it is, before all, to make you *see*."
No reader of Conrad can doubt that he means to make the reader see
not only the vivid facts of the story he tells but the evasive truth behind them, of which they are the obscure revelation, what Conrad
calls, a bit beyond the famous phrase from the preface just quoted,
"that glimpse of truth for which you have forgotten to ask." To see
the facts, out there in the sunlight, is also to see the dark truth that lies
behind them. All Conrad's work turns on this double paradox: first the
paradox of the two senses of seeing, seeing as physical vision and seeing as seeing through, as penetrating to or unveiling the hidden invisible truth, and second the paradox of seeing the darkness in terms of

the light. Nor can the careful reader of Conrad doubt that in Conrad's case too, as in the case of the Jesus of the parable of the sower, the goal of tearing the veil of familiarity from the world and making us *see* cannot be accomplished. If we see the darkness already, we do not need *Heart of Darkness*. If we do not see it, reading *Heart of Darkness* or even hearing Marlow tell it will not help us. We shall remain among those who "seeing see not; and hearing they hear not, neither do they understand." Marlow makes this clear in an extraordinary passage in *Heart of Darkness*, one of those places in which the reader is returned to the primary scene of narration on board the *Nellie*. Marlow is explaining the first lie he told for Kurtz, his prevarication misleading the bricklayer at the Central Station into believing he (Marlow) has great power back home:

> "I became in an instant as much of a pretence as the rest of the be-witched pilgrims. This simply because I had a notion it somehow would be of help to that Kurtz whom at the time I did not see — you understand. He was just a word for me. I did not see the man in the name any more than you do. Do you see him? Do you see the story? Do you see anything? It seems to me I am trying to tell you a dream — making a vain attempt, because no relation of a dream can convey the dream-sensation, that commingling of ab-surdity, surprise, and bewilderment in a tremor of struggling re-volt, that notion of being captured by the incredible which is of the very essence of dreams. . . ."
>
> He was silent for a while.
> ". . . No, it is impossible; it is impossible to convey the life-sensation of any given epoch of one's existence — that which makes its truth, its meaning — its subtle and penetrating essence. It is impossible. We live, as we dream — alone. . . ."
>
> He paused again as if reflecting, then added:
> "Of course in this you fellows see more than I could then. You see me, whom you know. . . ."
>
> It had become so pitch dark that we listeners could hardly see one another. For a long time already he, sitting apart, had been no more to us than a voice. There was not a word from anybody. The others might have been asleep, but I was awake. I listened, I listened on the watch for the sentence, for the word, that would give me the clue to the faint uneasiness inspired by this narrative that seemed to shape itself without human lips in the heavy night-air of the river. (pp. 42–43)

The denial of the possibility of making the reader see by means of literature is made here through a series of moves, each one ironically going beyond and undermining the one before. When this passage is set against the one about the moonshine, the two together bring out into the open, like a halo in the mist, the way *Heart of Darkness* is posited on the impossibility of achieving its goal of revelation, or, to put this another way, the way it is a revelation of the impossibility of revelation.

In Conrad's parable of the moonshine, the moon shines already with reflected and secondary light. Its light is reflected from the primary light of that sun which is almost never mentioned as such in *Heart of Darkness*. The sun is only present in the glitter of its reflection from this or that object, for example, the surface of that river which, like the white place of the unexplored Congo on the map, fascinates Marlow like a snake. In one passage it is moonlight, already reflected light, which is reflected again from the river: "The moon had spread over everything a thin layer of silver — over the rank grass, over the mud, upon the wall of matted vegetation standing higher than the wall of a temple, over the great river I could see through a sombre gap glittering, glittering, as it flowed broadly by without a murmur" (p. 42). In the case of the parable of the moonshine too that halo brought out in the mist is twice-reflected light. The story, according to Conrad's analogy, the facts that may be named and seen, is the moonlight, while the halo brought out around the moon by the reflection of the moonlight from the diffused, otherwise invisible droplets of the mist, is the meaning of the tale, or rather, the meaning of the tale is the darkness that is made visible by that halo of twice-reflected light. But of course the halo does nothing of the sort. It only makes visible more light. What can be seen is only what can be seen. In the end this is always only more light, direct or reflected. The darkness is in principle invisible and remains invisible. All that can be said is that the halo gives the spectator indirect knowledge that the darkness is there. The glow brings out the haze, the story brings out its meaning, by magically generating knowledge that something is there, the haze in one case, the meaning of the story, inarticulate and impossible to be articulated, in any direct way at least, in the other. The expression of the meaning of the story is never the plain statement of that meaning but is always no more than a parabolic "likeness" of the meaning, as the haze is brought out "in the likeness of one of those misty halos that sometimes are made visible by the spectral illumination of moonshine."

In the passage in which Marlow makes explicit his sense of the impossibility of his enterprise, he says to his auditors on the *Nellie* first that he did not see Kurtz in his name any more than they do. The auditors of any story are forced to see everything of the story "in its name," since a story is made of nothing but names and their adjacent words. There is nothing to see literally in any story except the words on the page, the movement of the lips of the teller. Unlike Marlow, his listeners never have a chance to see or experience directly the man behind the name. The reader, if he or she happens at this moment to think of it (and the passage is clearly an invitation to such thinking, an invocation of it), is in exactly the same situation as that of Marlow's auditors, only worse. When Marlow appeals to his auditors, Conrad is by a kind of ventriloquism appealing to his readers: "Do you see him? Do you see the story? Do you see anything? It seems to me I am trying to tell you a dream — making a vain attempt." Conrad speaks through Marlow to us. The reader too can reach the truth behind the story only through names, never through any direct perception or experience. In the reader's case it is not even names proffered by a living man before him, only names coldly and impersonally printed on the pages of the book he holds in his hand. Even if the reader goes behind the fiction to the historical reality on which it is based, as Ian Watt and others have done, he or she will only confront more words on more pages — Conrad's letters or the historical records of the conquest and exploitation of the Congo. The situation of the auditors, even of a living speaker, Marlow says, is scarcely better, since what a story must convey through names and other words is not the fact but the "life-sensation" behind the fact "which makes its truth, its meaning — its subtle and penetrating essence." This is once more the halo around the moon, the meaning enveloping the tale. This meaning is as impossible to convey by way of the life-facts that may be named as the "dream-sensation" is able to be conveyed through a relation of the bare facts of the dream. Anyone knows this who has ever tried to tell another person his dream and has found how lame and flat, or how laughable, it sounds, since "no relation of a dream can convey the dream-sensation." According to Marlow's metaphor or proportional analogy: as the facts of a dream are to the dream-sensation, so the facts of a life are to the life-sensation. Conrad makes an absolute distinction between experience and the interpretation of written or spoken signs. The sensation may only be experienced directly and may by no means, oral or written, be communicated to another: "We live, as we dream, alone."

Nevertheless, Marlow tells his auditors, they have one direct or experimental access to the truth enveloping the story: "You fellows see more than I could then. You see me, whom you know." There is a double irony in this. To see the man who has had the experience is to have an avenue to the experience for which the man speaks, to which he bears witness. Marlow's auditors see more than he could then — that is, before his actual encounter with Kurtz. Ironically, the witness cannot bear witness for himself. He cannot see himself or cannot see through himself or by means of himself, in spite of, or in contradiction of, Conrad's (or Marlow's) assertion a few paragraphs later that work is "the chance to find yourself. Your own reality — for yourself, not for others — what no other man can ever know. They can only see the mere show, and never can tell what it really means" (p. 44). Though each man can only experience his own reality, his own truth, the paradox involved here seems to run, he can only experience it through another or by means of another as witness to a truth deeper in, behind the other. Marlow's auditors can only learn indirectly, through Marlow, whom they see. They therefore know more than he did. Marlow could only learn through Kurtz, when he finally encountered him face to face. The reader of *Heart of Darkness* learns through the relation of the primary narrator, who learned through Marlow, who learned through Kurtz. This proliferating relay of witnesses, one behind another, each revealing another truth further in which turns out to be only another witness, corresponds to the narrative form of *Heart of Darkness.* The novel is a sequence of episodes, each structured according to the model of appearances, signs, which are also obstacles or veils. Each veil must be lifted to reveal a truth behind which always turns out to be another episode, another witness, another veil to be lifted in its turn. Each such episode is a "fact dazzling, to be seen, like the foam on the depths of the sea, like a ripple on an unfathomable enigma" (p. 58), the fact for example that though the cannibal Africans on Marlow's steamer were starving, they did not eat the white men. But behind each enigmatic fact is only another fact. The relay of witness behind witness behind witness, voice behind voice behind voice, each speaking in ventriloquism through the one next farther out, is a characteristic of the genre of the apocalypse. In the book of Revelation, God speaks through Jesus, who speaks through a messenger angel, who speaks through John of Patmos, who speaks to us.

There is another reason beyond the necessities of revelation for this structure. The truth behind the last witness, behind Kurtz for example in *Heart of Darkness,* is, no one can doubt it, death, "the horror"; or, to put this another way, "death" is another name for what

Kurtz names "the horror." No man can confront that truth face to face and survive. Death or the horror can only be experienced indirectly, by way of the face and voice of another. The relay of witnesses both reveals death and, luckily, hides it. As Marlow says, "the inner truth is hidden — luckily, luckily" (p. 50). This is another regular feature of the genre of the apocalypse. The word "apocalypse" means "unveiling," "revelation," but what the apocalypse unveils is not the truth of the end of the world it announces, but the act of unveiling. The unveiling unveils unveiling. It leaves it readers, auditors, witnesses, as far as ever from the always "not quite yet" of the imminent revelation — luckily. Marlow says it was not his own near-death on the way home down the river, "not my own extremity I remember best," but Kurtz's "extremity that I seem to have lived through." Then he adds, "True, he had made that last stride, he had stepped over the edge, while I had been permitted to draw back my hesitating foot. And perhaps in this is the whole difference; perhaps all the wisdom, and all truth, and all sincerity, are just compressed into that inappreciable moment of time in which we step over the threshold of the invisible. Perhaps!" (pp. 87–88). Marlow, like Orpheus returning without Eurydice from the land of the dead, comes back to civilization with nothing, nothing to bear witness to, nothing to reveal by the process of unveiling that makes up the whole of the narration of *Heart of Darkness* Marlow did not go far enough into the darkness, but if he had, like Kurtz he could not have come back. All the reader gets is Marlow's report of Kurtz's last words, that and a description of the look on Kurtz's face: "It was as though a veil had been rent. I saw on that ivory face the expression of sombre pride, of ruthless power, of craven terror — of an intense and hopeless despair" (p. 86).

I have suggested that there are two ironies in what Marlow says when he breaks his narration to address his auditors directly. The first irony is the fact that the auditors see more than Marlow did because they see Marlow, whom they know; the second is that we readers of the novel see no living witness. (By Marlow's own account that is not enough. Seeing only happens by direct experience, and no act of reading is direct experience. The book's claim to give the reader access to the dark truth behind appearance is withdrawn by the terms in which it is proffered.) But there is, in fact, a third irony in this relay of ironies behind ironies in that Marlow's auditors of course do not see Marlow either. It is too dark. They hear only his disembodied voice. "It had become so pitch dark," says the narrator, "that we listeners could hardly see one another. For a long time already he, sitting apart, had been no more to us than a voice." Marlow's narrative does not seem to be spoken by a living incarnate witness, there before his auditors in the flesh. It is a "narrative that seemed to shape itself without human lips in the heavy night-air of the river." This voice can be linked to no individual speaker or writer as the ultimate source of its messages, not to Marlow, nor to Kurtz, nor to the first narrator, nor even to Conrad himself. The voice is spoken by no one to no one. It always comes from another, from the other of any identifiable speaker or writer. It traverses all these voices as what speaks through them. It gives them authority and at the same time dispossesses them, deprives them of authority, since they only speak with the delegated authority of another. As Marlow says of the voice of Kurtz and of all the other voices, they are what remain as a dying unanimous and anonymous drone or clang that exceeds any single identifiable voice and in the end is spoken by no one: "A voice. He was very little more than a voice. And I heard — him — it — this voice — other voices — all of them were so little more than voices — and the memory of that time itself lingers around me, impalpable, like a dying vibration of one immense jabber, silly, atrocious, sordid, savage, or simply mean, without any kind of sense. Voices, voices — . . ." (p. 64).

For the reader, too, *Heart of Darkness* lingers in the mind or memory chiefly as a cacophony of dissonant voices. It is as though the story were spoken or written not by an identifiable narrator but directly by the darkness itself, just as Kurtz's last words seem whispered by the circumambient dusky air when Marlow makes his visit to Kurtz's Intended, and just as Kurtz himself presents himself to Marlow as a voice, a voice which exceeds Kurtz and seems to speak from beyond him: "Kurtz discoursed. A voice! a voice! It rang deep to the very last. It survived his strength to hide in the magnificent folds of eloquence the barren darkness of his heart" (p. 85). Kurtz has "the gift of expression, the bewildering, the illuminating, the most exalted and the most contemptible, the pulsating stream of light, or the deceitful flow from the heart of an impenetrable darkness" (p. 63). Kurtz has intended to use his eloquence as a means of "wringing the heart of the wilderness," but "the wilderness had found him out early, and had taken on him a terrible vengeance for the fantastic invasion" (p. 74). The direction of the flow of language reverses. It flows from the darkness instead of toward it. Kurtz is "hollow at the core" (p. 74), and so the wilderness can speak through him, use him so to speak as a ventriloquist's dummy through which its terrible messages may be broadcast to the world: "Exterminate all the brutes!" "The horror!" (pp. 66, 86).

The speaker to is spoken through. Kurtz's disembodied voice, or the voice behind voice behind voice of the narrators, or that "roaring chorus of articulated, rapid, breathless utterance" (p. 84) shouted by the natives on the bank, when Kurtz is taken on board the steamer — these are in the end no more direct a testimony of the truth than the words on the page as Conrad wrote them. The absence of a visible speaker of Marlow's words and the emphasis on the way Kurtz is a disembodied voice function as indirect expressions of the fact that *Heart of Darkness* itself is words without person, words which cannot be traced back to any single personality. This is once more confirmation of my claim that *Heart of Darkness* belongs to the genre of the parabolic apocalypse. The apocalypse is after all a written not an oral genre, and, as Jacques Derrida has pointed out, one characteristic of an apocalypse is that it turns on the invitation or "Come" spoken or written always by someone other than the one who seems to utter or write it.[3]

A full exploration of the way *Heart of Darkness* is an apocalypse would need to be put under the multiple aegis of the converging figures of irony, antithesis, catachresis, synecdoche, aletheia, and personification. Irony is a name for the pervasive tone of Marlow's narration, which undercuts as it affirms. Antithesis identifies the division of what is presented in the story in terms of seemingly firm oppositions that always ultimately break down. Catachresis is the proper name for a parabolic revelation of the darkness by means of visible figures that do not substitute for any possible literal expression of that darkness. Synecdoche is the name for the questionable relation of similarity between the visible sign, the skin of the surface, the foam on the sea, and what lies behind it, the pulsating heart of darkness, the black depths of the sea. Unveiling or *aletheia* labels that endless process of apocalyptic revelation that never quite comes off. The revelation is always future. Personification, finally, is a name for the consistent presentation of the darkness as some kind of living creature with a heart, ultimately as a woman who unmans all those male questors who try to dominate her. This pervasive personification is most dramatically embodied in the native woman, Kurtz's mistress: "the immense wilderness, the colossal body of the fecund and mysterious life seemed to look at her, pensive, as though it had been looking at the image of its own tenebrous and passionate soul" (p. 77).

---

[3]See Jacques Derrida, "D'un ton apocalyptique adopté naguère en philosophie," in *Les Fins de l'homme,* ed. Phillippe Lacoue-Labarthe and Jean-Luc Nancy (Paris: Flammarion, 1981), pp. 445–79, especially p. 468ff. The essay has been translated by John P. Learey, Jr., and published in the 1982 number of *Seineia* (pp. 62–97).

Heart of Darkness is perhaps most explicitly apocalyptic in announcing the end, the end of Western civilization, or of Western imperialism, the reversal of idealism into savagery. As is always the case
with apocalypses, the end is announced as something always imminent, never quite yet. Apocalypse is never now. The novel sets
women, who are out of it, against men, who can live with the facts
and have a belief to protect them against the darkness. Men can
breathe dead hippo and not be contaminated. Male practicality and
idealism reverse, however. They turn into their opposites because
they are hollow at the core. They are vulnerable to the horror. They
are the horror. The idealistic suppression of savage customs becomes,
"Exterminate all the brutes!" Male idealism is the same thing as the
extermination of the brutes. The suppression of savage customs is
the extermination of the brutes. This is not just word play but actual
fact, as the history of the white man's conquest of the world has
abundantly demonstrated. This conquest means the end of the
brutes, but it means also, in Conrad's view of history, the end of
Western civilization, with its ideals of progress, enlightenment, and
reason, its goal of carrying the torch of civilization into the
wilderness and wringing the heart of the darkness. Or it is the
imminence of that end which has never quite come as long as there
is someone to speak or write of it.

I claim to have demonstrated that *Heart of Darkness* is not only
parabolic but also apocalyptic. It fits that strange genre of the apocalyptic text, the sort of text that promises an ultimate revelation without
giving it, and says always "Come" and "Wait." But there is an extra
twist given to the paradigmatic form of the apocalypse in *Heart of
Darkness*. The *Aufklärung* or enlightenment in this case is of the fact
that the darkness can never be enlightened. The darkness enters into
every gesture of enlightenment to enfeeble it, to hollow it out, to corrupt it and thereby to turn its reason into unreason, its pretense of
shedding light into more darkness. Marlow as narrator is in complicity
with this reversal in the act of identifying it in others. He too claims,
like the characteristic writer of an apocalypse, to know something no
one else knows and to be qualified on that basis to judge and enlighten them. "I found myself back in the sepulchral city," says Marlow of his return from the Congo,

> resenting the sight of people hurrying through the streets to filch
> a little money from each other, to devour their infamous cookery,
> to gulp their unwholesome beer, to dream their insignificant and
> silly dreams. They trespassed upon my thoughts. They were in-

truders whose knowledge of life was to me an irritating pretence, because I felt so sure they could not possibly know the things I knew. (p. 88)

The consistent tone of Marlow's narration is ironical. Irony is truth-telling or a means of truth-telling, of unveiling. At the same time it is a defense against the truth. This doubleness makes it, though it seems so coolly reasonable, another mode of unreason, the unreason of a fundamental undecidability. If irony is a defense, it is also inadvertently a means of participation. Though Marlow says, "I have a voice too, and for good or evil mine is the speech that cannot be silenced" (p. 52), as though his speaking were a cloak against the darkness, he too, in speaking ironically, becomes, like Kurtz, one of those speaking tubes or relay stations through whom the darkness speaks. As theorists of irony from Friedrich Schlegel and Soren Kierkegaard to Paul de Man have argued, irony is the one trope that cannot be mastered or used as an instrument of mastery. An ironic statement is essentially indeterminate or undecidable in meaning. The man who attempts to say one thing while clearly meaning another ends up by saying the first thing too, in spite of himself. One irony leads to another. The ironies proliferate into a great crowd of little conflicting ironies. It is impossible to know in just what tone of voice one should read one of Marlow's sardonic ironies. Each is uttered simultaneously in innumerable conflicting tones going all the way from the lightest and most comical to the darkest, most somber and tragic. It is impossible to decide exactly which quality of voice should be allowed to predominate over the others. Try reading aloud the passage cited above and you will see this. Marlow's tone and meaning are indeterminate; his description of the clamor of native voices on the shore or of the murmur of all those voices he remembers from that time in his life also functions as an appropriate displaced description of his own discourse. Marlow's irony makes his speech in its own way another version of that multiple cacophonous and deceitful voice flowing from the heart of darkness, "a complaining clamour, modulated in savage discords," or a "tumultuous and mournful uproar," another version of that "one immense jabber, silly, atrocious, sordid, savage, or simply mean, without any kind of sense," not a voice, but voices (pp. 55, 64). In this inextricable tangle of voices and voices speaking within voices, Marlow's narration fulfills, no doubt without deliberate intent on Conrad's part, one of the primary laws of the genre of the apocalypse.

The final fold in this folding in of complicities in these ambiguous acts of unveiling is my own complicity as demystifying commentator. Behind or before Marlow is Conrad, and before or behind him stands the reader or critic. My commentary unveils a lack of decisive unveiling in *Heart of Darkness*. I have attempted to perform an act of generic classification, with all the covert violence and unreason of that act, since no work is wholly commensurate with the boundaries of any genre. By unveiling the lack of unveiling in *Heart of Darkness*, I have become another witness in my turn, as much guilty as any other in the line of witnesses of covering over while claiming to illuminate. My *Aufklärung* too has been of the continuing impenetrability of Conrad's *Heart of Darkness*.

WORK CITED

Marx, Karl. "Manifesto of the Communist Party." *The Marx-Engels Reader*. Ed. Robert C. Tucker. New York: Norton, 1978.

The New Historicism
and
Heart of Darkness

WHAT IS THE NEW HISTORICISM?

The title of Brook Thomas's *The New Historicism and Other Old Fashioned Topics* (1991) is telling. Whenever an emergent theory, movement, method, approach, or group gets labeled with the adjective "new," trouble is bound to ensue, for what is new today is either established, old, or forgotten tomorrow. Few of you will have heard of the band called "The New Kids on the Block." New Age book shops and jewelry may seem "old hat" by the time this introduction is published. The New Criticism, or formalism, is just about the oldest approach to literature and literary study currently being practiced. The new historicism, by contrast, is *not* as old-fashioned as formalism, but it is hardly new, either. The term "new" eventually and inevitably requires some explanation. In the case of the new historicism, the best explanation is historical.

Although a number of influential critics working between 1920 and 1950 wrote about literature from a psychoanalytic perspective, the majority took what might generally be referred to as the historical approach. With the advent of the New Criticism, however, historically oriented critics almost seemed to disappear from the face of the earth. The dominant New Critics, or formalists, tended to treat literary works as if they were self-contained, self-referential objects. Rather than basing their interpretations on parallels between the text and historical contexts (such as the author's life or stated intentions in writing the work), these critics concentrated on the relationships *within* the text that give it its form and meaning. During the heyday of the New Criticism, concern about the interplay between literature and history virtually disappeared from literary discourse. In its place was a concern about intratextual repetition, particularly of images or symbols but also of rhythms and sound effect.

About 1970 the New Criticism came under attack by reader-response critics (who believe that the meaning of a work is not inherent in its internal form but rather is cooperatively produced by the reader and the text) and poststructuralists (who, following the philosophy of Jacques Derrida, argue that texts are inevitably self-contradictory and that we can find form in them only by ignoring or suppressing conflicting details or elements). In retrospect it is clear that, their outspoken opposition to the New Criticism notwithstanding, the reader-response critics and poststructuralists of the 1970s were very much *like* their formalist predecessors in two important respects: for the most part, they ignored the world beyond the text and its reader, and, for the most part, they ignored the historical contexts within which literary works are written and read.

Jerome McGann first articulated this retrospective insight in 1985, writing that "a text-only approach has been so vigorously promoted during the last thirty-five years that most historical critics have been driven from the field, and have raised the flag of their surrender by yielding the title 'critic,' and accepting the title 'scholar' for themselves" (*Inflections* 17). Most, but not all. The American Marxist Fredric Jameson had begun his 1981 book *The Political Unconscious* with the following two-word challenge: "Always historicize!" (9). Beginning about 1980, a form of historical criticism practiced by Louis Montrose and Stephen Greenblatt had transformed the field of Renaissance studies and begun to influence the study of American and English Romantic literature as well. And by the mid-1980s, Brook Thomas was working on an essay in which he suggests that classroom discussions of Keats's "Ode on a Grecian Urn" might begin with questions such as the following: Where would Keats have seen such an urn? How did a Grecian urn end up in a museum in England? Some very important historical and political realities, Thomas suggests, lie behind and inform Keats's definitions of art, truth, beauty, the past, and timelessness.

When McGann lamented the surrender of "most historical critics," he no doubt realized what is now clear to everyone involved in the study of literature. Those who had *not* yet surrendered — had not yet "yield[ed] the title 'critic'" to the formalist, reader-response, and post-structuralist "victors" — were armed with powerful new arguments and intent on winning back long-lost ground. Indeed, at about the same time that McGann was deploring the near-complete dominance of critics advocating the text-only approach, Herbert Lindenberger was sounding a more hopeful note: "It comes as something of a surprise," he wrote in 1984, "to find that history is making a powerful comeback" ("New History" 16).

We now know that history was indeed making a powerful comeback in the 1980s, although the word is misleading if it causes us to imagine that the historical criticism being practiced in the 1980s by Greenblatt and Montrose, McGann and Thomas, was the same as the historical criticism that had been practiced in the 1930s and 1940s. Indeed, if the word "new" still serves any useful purpose in defining the historical criticism of today, it is in distinguishing it from the old historicism. The new historicism is informed by the poststructuralist and reader-response theory of the 1970s, plus the thinking of feminist, cultural, and Marxist critics whose work was also "new" in the 1980s. New historicist critics are less fact- and event-oriented than historical critics used to be, perhaps because they have come to wonder whether the truth about what really happened can ever be purely and objectively known. They are less likely to see history as linear and progressive, as something developing toward the present or the future ("teleological"), and they are also less likely to think of it in terms of specific eras, each with a definite, persistent, and consistent *Zeitgeist* ("spirit of the times"). Consequently, they are unlikely to suggest that a literary text has a single or easily identifiable historical context.

New historicist critics also tend to define the discipline of history more broadly than it was defined before the advent of formalism. They view history as a social science and the social sciences as being properly historical. In *Historical Studies and Literary Criticism* (1985), McGann speaks of the need to make "sociohistorical" subjects and methods central to literary studies; in *The Beauty of Inflections: Literary Investigations in Historical Method and Theory* (1985), he links sociology and the future of historical criticism. "A sociological poetics," he writes, "must be recognized not only as relevant to the analysis of poetry, but in fact as central to the analysis" (62). Lindenberger cites anthropology as particularly useful in the new historical analysis of literature, especially anthropology as practiced by Victor Turner and Clifford Geertz.

Geertz, who has related theatrical traditions in nineteenth-century Bali to forms of political organization that developed during the same period, has influenced some of the most important critics writing the new kind of historical criticism. Due in large part to Geertz's anthropological influence, new historicists such as Greenblatt have asserted that literature is not a sphere apart or distinct from the history that is relevant to it. That is what the old criticism tended to do: present the background information you needed to know before you could fully appreciate the separate world of art. The new historicists have used what Geertz would call "thick description" to blur distinctions, not only between history and the other social sciences but also between background and foreground, historical and literary materials, political and poetical events. They have erased the old boundary line dividing historical and literary materials, showing that the production of one of Shakespeare's historical plays was a political act and historical event, while at the same time showing that the coronation of Elizabeth I was carried out with the same care for staging and symbol lavished on works of dramatic art.

In addition to breaking down barriers that separate literature and history, history and the social sciences, new historicists have reminded us that it is treacherously difficult to reconstruct the past as it really was, rather than as we have been conditioned by our own place and time to believe that it was. And they know that the job is utterly impossible for those who are unaware of that difficulty and insensitive to the bent or bias of their own historical vantage point. Historical criticism must be "conscious of its status as interpretation," Greenblatt has written (*Renaissance* 4). McGann obviously concurs, writing that "historical criticism can no longer make any part of [its] sweeping picture unselfconsciously, or treat any of its details in an untheorized way" (*Studies* 11).

Unselfconsciously and *untheorized* are the key words in McGann's statement. When new historicist critics of literature describe a historical change, they are highly conscious of, and even likely to discuss, the *theory* of historical change that informs their account. They know that the changes they happen to see and describe are the ones that their theory of change allows or helps them to see and describe. And they know, too, that their theory of change is historically determined. They seek to minimize the distortion inherent in their perceptions and representations by admitting that they see through preconceived notions; in other words, they learn to reveal the color of the lenses in the glasses that they wear.

Nearly everyone who wrote on the new historicism during the 1980s cited the importance of the late Michel Foucault. A French philosophical historian who liked to think of himself as an archaeologist of human knowledge, Foucault brought together incidents and phenomena from areas of inquiry and orders of life that we normally regard as being unconnected. As much as anyone, he encouraged the new historicist critic of literature to redefine the boundaries of historical inquiry.

Foucault's views of history were influenced by the philosopher Friedrich Nietzsche's concept of a *wirkliche* ("real" or "true") history that is neither melioristic (that is, "getting better all the time") nor metaphysical. Like Nietzsche, Foucault didn't see history in terms of a continuous development toward the present. Neither did he view it as an abstraction, idea, or ideal, as something that began "In the beginning" and that will come to THE END, a moment of definite closure, a Day of Judgment. In his own words, Foucault "abandoned [the old history's] attempts to understand events in terms of . . . some great evolutionary process" (*Discipline and Punish* 129). He warned a new generation of historians to be aware of the fact that investigators are themselves "situated." It is difficult, he reminded them, to see present cultural practices critically from within them, and because of the same cultural practices, it is extremely difficult to enter bygone ages. In *Discipline and Punish: The Birth of the Prison* (1975), Foucault admitted that his own interest in the past was fueled by a passion to write the history of the present.

Like Marx, Foucault saw history in terms of power, but his view of power probably owed more to Nietzsche than to Marx. Foucault seldom viewed power as a repressive force. He certainly did not view it as a tool of conspiracy used by one specific individual or institution against another. Rather, power represents a whole web or complex of forces; it is that which produces what happens. Not even a tyrannical aristocrat simply wields power, for the aristocrat is himself formed and empowered by a network of discourses and practices that constitute power. Viewed by Foucault, power is "positive and productive," not "repressive" and "prohibitive" (Smart 63). Furthermore, no historical event, according to Foucault, has a single cause; rather, it is intricately connected with a vast web of economic, social, and political factors.

A brief sketch of one of Foucault's major works may help clarify some of his ideas. *Discipline and Punish* begins with a shocking but accurate description of the public drawing and quartering of a Frenchman who had botched his attempt to assassinate King Louis XV in 1757. Foucault proceeds by describing rules governing the daily life of modern Parisian felons. What happened to torture, to punishment as public spectacle? he asks. What complex network of forces made it disappear? In working toward a picture of this "power," Foucault turns up many interesting puzzle pieces, such as the fact that in the early years of the nineteenth century, crowds would sometimes identify with the prisoner and treat the executioner as if *he* were the guilty party. But Foucault sets forth a related reason for keeping prisoners alive, moving punishment indoors, and changing discipline from physical torture into mental rehabilitation: colonization. In this historical period, people were needed to establish colonies and trade, and prisoners could be used for that purpose. Also, because these were politically unsettled times, governments needed infiltrators and informers. Who better to fill those roles than prisoners pardoned or released early for showing a willingness to be rehabilitated? As for rehabilitation itself, Foucault compares it to the old form of punishment, which began with a torturer extracting a confession. In more modern, "reasonable" times, psychologists probe the minds of prisoners with a scientific rigor that Foucault sees as a different kind of torture, a kind that our modern perspective does not allow us to see as such.

Thus, a change took place, but perhaps not as great a change as we generally assume. It may have been for the better or for the worse; the point is that agents of power didn't make the change because mankind is evolving and, therefore, more prone to perform good-hearted deeds. Rather, different objectives arose, including those of a new class of doctors and scientists bent on studying aberrant examples of the human mind. And where do we stand vis-à-vis the history Foucault tells? We are implicated by it, for the evolution of discipline as punishment into the study of the human mind includes the evolution of the "disciplines" as we now understand that word, including the discipline of history, the discipline of literary study, and now a discipline that is neither and both, a form of historical criticism that from the vantage point of the 1980s looked "new."

Foucault's type of analysis has been practiced by a number of literary critics at the vanguard of the back-to-history movement. One of them is Greenblatt, who along with Montrose was to a great extent responsible for transforming Renaissance studies in the early 1980s and revitalizing historical criticism in the process. Greenblatt follows Foucault's lead in interpreting literary devices as if they were continuous with all other representational devices in a culture; he therefore turns to scholars in other fields in order to better understand the workings of literature. "We wall off literary symbolism from the symbolic structures operative elsewhere," he writes, "as if art alone were a human creation, as if humans themselves were not, in Clifford Geertz's phrase, cultural artifacts" (*Renaissance* 4).

Greenblatt's name, more than anyone else's, is synonymous with the new historicism; his essay entitled "Invisible Bullets" (1981) has been said by Patrick Brantlinger to be "perhaps the most frequently cited example of New Historicist work" ("Cultural Studies" 45). An English professor at the University of California, Berkeley — the early academic home of the new historicism — Greenblatt was a founding editor of *Representations*, a journal published by the University of California Press that is still considered today to be *the* mouthpiece of the new historicism.

In *Learning to Curse* (1990), Greenblatt cites as central to his own intellectual development his decision to interrupt his literary education at Yale University by accepting a Fulbright fellowship to study in England at Cambridge University. There he came under the influence of the great Marxist cultural critic Raymond Williams, who made Greenblatt realize how much — and what — was missing from his Yale education. "In Williams' lectures," Greenblatt writes, "all that had been carefully excluded from the literary criticism in which I had been trained — who controlled access to the printing press, who owned the land and the factories, whose voices were being repressed as well as represented in literary texts, what social strategies were being served by the aesthetic values we constructed — came pressing back in upon the act of interpretation" (2).

Greenblatt returned to the United States determined not to exclude such matters from his own literary investigations. Blending what he had learned from Williams with poststructuralist thought about the indeterminacy or "undecidability" of meaning, he eventually developed a critical method that he now calls "cultural poetics." More tentative and less overtly political than cultural criticism, it involves what Thomas calls "the technique of montage. Starting with the analysis of a particular historical event, it cuts to the analysis of a particular literary text. The point is not to show that the literary text reflects the historical event but to create a field of energy between the two so that we come to see the event as a social text and the literary text as a social event" ("New Literary Historicism" 490). Alluding to deconstructor Jacques Derrida's assertion that "there is nothing outside the text," Montrose explains that the goal of this new historicist criticism is to show the "historicity of texts and the textuality of history" (Veeser 20).

The relationship between the cultural poetics practiced by a number of new historicists and the cultural criticism associated with Marxism is important, not only because of the proximity of the two approaches but also because one must recognize the difference between the two to understand the new historicism. Still very much a part of the contemporary critical scene, cultural criticism (sometimes called "cultural studies" or "cultural critique") nonetheless involves several tendencies more compatible with the old historicism than with the thinking of new historicists such as Greenblatt. These include the tendency to believe that history is driven by economics; that it is determinable even as it determines the lives of individuals; and that it is progressive, its dialectic one that will bring about justice and equality.

Greenblatt does not privilege economics in his analyses and views individuals as agents possessing considerable productive power. (He says that "the work of art is the product of a negotiation between a creator or class of creators . . . and the institutions and practices of a society" [*Learning* 158]: he also acknowledges that artistic productions are "intensely marked by the private obsessions of individuals," however much they may result from "collective negotiation and exchange" [*Negotiations* vii].) His optimism about the individual, however, should not be confused with optimism about either history's direction or any historian's capacity to foretell it. Like a work of art, a work of history is the negotiated product of a private creator and the public practices of a given society.

This does not mean that Greenblatt does not discern historical change, or that he is uninterested in describing it. Indeed, in works from *Renaissance Self-Fashioning* (1980) to *Shakespearean Negotiations* (1988), he has written about Renaissance changes in the development of both literary characters and real people. But his view of change — like his view of the individual — is more Foucauldian than Marxist. That is to say, it is not melioristic or teleological. And, like Foucault, Greenblatt is careful to point out that any one change is connected with a host of others, no one of which may simply be identified as cause or effect, progressive or regressive, repressive or enabling.

Not all of the critics trying to lead students of literature back to history are as Foucauldian as Greenblatt. Some even owe more to Marx than to Foucault. Others, like Thomas, have clearly been more influenced by Walter Benjamin, best known for essays such as "Theses on the Philosophy of History" and "The Work of Art in the Age of Mechanical Reproduction." Still others — McGann, for example — have followed the lead of Soviet critic M. M. Bakhtin, who viewed literary works in terms of discourses and dialogues between the official, legitimate voices of a society and other, more challenging or critical voices echoing popular or traditional culture. In the "polyphonic" writings of Rabelais, for instance, Bakhtin found that the profane language of Carnival and other popular festivals offsets and parodies the "legitimate" discourses representing the outlook of the king, church, and socially powerful intellectuals of the day.

Moreover, there are other reasons not to consider Foucault the single or even central influence on the new historicism. First, he critiqued the old-style historicism to such an extent that he ended up being antihistorical, or at least ahistorical, in the view of a number of new historicists. Second, his commitment to a radical remapping of the relations of power and influence, cause and effect, may have led him to adopt too cavalier an attitude toward chronology and facts. Finally, the very act of identifying and labeling *any* primary influence goes against the grain of the new historicism. Its practitioners have sought to "decenter" the study of literature, not only by overlapping it with historical studies (broadly defined to include anthropology and sociology) but also by struggling to see history from a decentered perspective. That struggle has involved recognizing (1) that the historian's cultural and historical position may not afford the best purview of a given set of events and (2) that events seldom have any single or central cause. In keeping with these principles, it may be appropriate to acknowledge Foucault as just one of several powerful, interactive intellectual forces rather than to declare him the single, master influence.

Throughout the 1980s it seemed to many that the ongoing debates about the sources of the new historicist movement, the importance of Marx or Foucault, Walter Benjamin or Mikhail Bakhtin, and the exact locations of all the complex boundaries between the new historicism and other "isms" (Marxism and poststructuralism, to name only two) were historically contingent functions of the new historicism *newness*. In the initial stages of their development, new intellectual movements are difficult to outline clearly because, like partially developed photographic images, they are themselves fuzzy and lacking in definition. They respond to disparate influences and include thinkers who represent a wide range of backgrounds; like movements that are disintegrating, they inevitably include a broad spectrum of opinions and positions.

From the vantage point of the 1990s, however, it seems that the inchoate quality of the new historicism is characteristic rather than a function of newness. The boundaries around the new historicism remain fuzzy, not because it hasn't reached its full maturity but because, if it is to live up to its name, it must always be subject to revision and redefinition as historical circumstances change. The fact that so many critics we label new historicist are working right at the border of Marxist, poststructuralist, cultural, postcolonial, feminist, and now even a new form of reader-response (or at least reader-oriented) criticism is evidence of the new historicism's multiple interests and motivations, rather than of its embryonic state.

New historicists themselves advocate and even stress the need to perpetually redefine categories and boundaries — whether they be disciplinary, generic, national, or racial — not because definitions are unimportant but because they are historically constructed and thus subject to revision. If new historicists like Thomas and reader-oriented critics like Steven Mailloux and Peter Rabinowitz seem to spend most of their time talking over the low wall separating their respective fields, then maybe the wall is in the wrong place. As Catherine Gallagher has suggested, the boundary between new historicists and feminists studying "people and phenomena that once seemed insignificant, indeed outside of history: women, criminals, the insane" often turns out to be shifting or even nonexistent (Veeser 43).

If the fact that new historicists all seem to be working on the border of another school should not be viewed as a symptom of the new historicism's newness (or disintegration), neither should it be viewed as evidence that new historicists are intellectual loners or divisive outriders who enjoy talking over walls to people in other fields but who share no common views among themselves. Greenblatt, McGann, and Thomas all started with the assumption that works of literature are simultaneously influenced by and influencing reality, broadly defined. Whatever their disagreements, they share a belief in referentiality — a belief that literature refers to and is referred to by things outside itself — stronger than that found in the works of formalist, poststructuralist, and even reader-response critics. They believe with Greenblatt that the "central concerns" of criticism "should prevent it from permanently sealing off one type of discourse from another or decisively separating works of art from the minds and lives of their creators and their audiences" (*Renaissance* 5).

McGann, in his introduction to *Historical Studies and Literary Criticism*, turns referentiality into a rallying cry:

> What will not be found in these essays . . . is the assumption, so common in text-centered studies of every type, that literary works are self-enclosed verbal constructs, or looped intertextual fields of autonomous signifiers and signifieds. In these essays, the question of referentiality is once again brought to the fore. (3)

In "Keats and the Historical Method in Literary Criticism," he suggests a set of basic, scholarly procedures to be followed by those who have rallied to the cry. These procedures, which he claims are "practical derivatives of the Bakhtin school," assume that historicist critics will study a literary work's "point of origin" by studying biography and bibliography. The critic must then consider the expressed intentions of the author, because, if printed, these intentions have also modified the developing history of the work. Next, the new historicist must learn the history of the work's reception, as that body of opinion has become part of the platform on which we are situated when we study the work at our own particular "point of reception." Finally, McGann urges the new historicist critic to point toward the future, toward his or her *own* audience, defining for its members the aims and limits of the critical project and injecting the analysis with a degree of self-consciousness that alone can give it credibility (*Inflections* 62).

In his introduction to a collection of new historical writings on *The New Historicism* (1989), H. Aram Veeser stresses the unity among new historicists, not by focusing on common critical procedures but, rather, by outlining five "key assumptions" that "continually reappear and bind together the avowed practitioners and even some of their critics":

1. that every expressive act is embedded in a network of material practices;
2. that every act of unmasking, critique, and opposition uses the tools it condemns and risks falling prey to the practice it exposes;
3. that literary and non-literary texts circulate inseparably;
4. that no discourse, imaginative or archival, gives access to unchanging truths nor expresses inalterable human nature;
5. finally, . . . that a critical method and a language adequate to describe culture under capitalism participate in the economy they describe. (xi)

These same assumptions are shared by a group of historians practicing what is now commonly referred to as "the new cultural history." Influenced by *Annales*-school historians in France, post-Althusserian Marxists, and Foucault, these historians share with their new historicist counterparts not only many of the same influences and assumptions but also the following: an interest in anthropological and sociological subjects and methods; a creative way of weaving stories and anecdotes about the past into revealing thick descriptions; a tendency to focus on nontraditional, noncanonical subjects and relations (historian Thomas Laqueur is best known for *Making Sex: Body and Gender from the Greeks to Freud* [1990]); and some of the same journals and projects.

Thus, in addition to being significantly unified by their own interests, assumptions, and procedures, new historicist literary critics have participated in a broader, interdisciplinary movement toward unification virtually unprecedented within and across academic disciplines. Their tendency to work along disciplinary borderlines, far from being evidence of their factious or fractious tendencies, has been precisely what has allowed them to engage historians in a conversation certain to revolutionize the way in which we understand the past, present, and future.

In the essay that follows, Brook Thomas begins by claiming that if we are to catch a glimpse of the hazy truths that *Heart of Darkness* has to offer, we are going to have to approach Conrad's work with a renewed willingness to read historically. After all, the epigraph to his essay shows Conrad thought of fiction as history. Thomas begins his approach by providing a kind of history *of* history, by reminding us that, during the nineteenth century, history tended to be seen as an organic development toward the present. Consequently, the discontinuities of history were overlooked or, at least, glossed over by historians who all the while believed that they were describing the past as it really was.

Thomas critiques the old history not only to avoid its pitfalls but also because he sees Conrad as a kind of prototype of the new historicist, as a writer who, though in some ways biased in the ways of his culture, was nonetheless effective at debunking the melioristic historicism of his own age. Thomas uses "counter-memory," a phrase of Foucault's, to describe Conrad's picture of Kurtz, a man who gives the lie to meliorism by showing how the most "civilized" of Europeans can also be subhuman in savagery. In Thomas's view, Conrad anticipated the new historicism, too, by not choosing to try to tell how it was in the Congo via an objective-sounding, third-person, omniscient narrative. Even though Conrad had himself been there, he chose to tell his story indirectly, through an idiosyncratic, first-person narrator, Marlow, whose narrative is in turn relayed by another narrator who presumably has not even been to Africa. This elaborate structure makes us aware of structure *as* structure; thus, the novel doesn't pretend to offer us a perfectly clear, uncluttered, unbiased, perfectly natural view of the facts of the past.

Thomas, of course, is a newer historicist than Conrad; we can see this by the characteristics of his own text. The text praises Nietzsche, who helped decenter Western historical narrative, which had tended to assume that Western, idealist values were central and definitive and to judge the past of other cultures accordingly. Thomas also makes use of biographical and bibliographical information and, especially, of Conrad's own writings about his works. Those nonfiction writings, because they have shaped the critical reception of the fiction, must be attended to by the new historicist, in whose view the history of a work includes the work's point of origin, its point of reception, and even its future relationship with its audience. Finally, Thomas is not only familiar with but also adept at using the insights of avant-garde schools of criticism that have flourished since the demise of the old history. And yet, even as he uses them, he distances himself from them by situating them historically.

But Thomas can ill afford to historically situate and critically account for everyone and everything — from Conrad to reader-response criticism to the deconstructive readings of J. Hillis Miller — except himself. Were he to do so he would fall into the old trap in which the historical critic fails because he fails to admit his own historical limitations and consequent capacity for failure. Thomas implicitly does the former and explicitly admits the latter. "There is no guarantee that we will penetrate to the . . . heart of *Heart of Darkness*," Thomas writes. There is, in its place, only the conviction that the heart of Conrad's novel can only be approached by the critic who practices sociohistorical criticism.

THE NEW HISTORICISM: A SELECTED BIBLIOGRAPHY

The New Historicism: Further Reading

Brantlinger, Patrick. "Cultural Studies vs. the New Historicism." *English Studies/Cultural Studies: Institutionalizing Dissent.* Ed. Isaiah Smithson and Nancy Ruff. Urbana: U of Illinois P, 1994. 43–58.

Cox, Jeffrey N., and Larry J. Reynolds, eds. *New Historical Literary Study*. Princeton: Princeton UP, 1993.

Dimock, Wai-Chee. "Feminism, New Historicism, and the Reader." *American Literature* 63 (1991): 601–22.

Howard, Jean. "The New Historicism in Renaissance Studies." *English Literary Renaissance* 16 (1986): 13–43.

Lindenberger, Herbert. *The History in Literature: On Value, Genre, Institutions*. New York: Columbia UP, 1990.

———. "Toward a New History in Literary Study." *Profession: Selected Articles from the Bulletins of the Association of Departments of English and the Association of the Departments of Foreign Languages*. New York: MLA, 1984. 16–23.

Liu, Alan. "The Power of Formalism: The New Historicism." *English Literary History* 56 (1989): 721–71.

McGann, Jerome. *The Beauty of Inflections: Literary Investigations in Historical Method and Theory*. Oxford: Clarendon–Oxford UP, 1985.

———. *Historical Studies and Literary Criticism*. Madison: U of Wisconsin P, 1985. See especially the introduction and the essays in the following sections: "Historical Methods and Literary Interpretations" and "Biographical Contexts and the Critical Object."

Montrose, Louis Adrian. "Renaissance Literary Studies and the Subject of History." *English Literary Renaissance* 16 (1986): 5–12.

Morris, Wesley. *Toward a New Historicism*. Princeton: Princeton UP, 1972.

New Literary History 21 (1990). "History and . . ." (special issue). See especially the essays by Carolyn Porter, Rena Fraden, Clifford Geertz, and Renato Rosaldo.

Representations. This quarterly journal, printed by the University of California Press, regularly publishes new historicist studies and cultural criticism.

Thomas, Brook. "The Historical Necessity for — and Difficulties with — New Historical Analysis in Introductory Courses." *College English* 49 (1987): 509–22.

———. *The New Historicism and Other Old-Fashioned Topics*. Princeton: Princeton UP, 1991.

———. "The New Literary Historicism." *A Companion to American Thought*. Ed. Richard Wightman Fox and James T. Klappenberg. New York: Basil Blackwell, 1995.

———. "Walter Benn Michaels and the New Historicism: Where's the Difference?" *Boundary 2* 18 (1991): 118–59.

Veeser, H. Aram, ed. *The New Historicism*. New York: Routledge,

1989. See especially Vceser's introduction, Louis Montrose's "Professing the Renaissance," Catherine Gallagher's "Marxism and the New Historicism," and Frank Lentricchia's "Foucault's Legacy: A New Historicism?"

Wayne, Don E. "Power, Politics and the Shakespearean Text: Recent Criticism in England and the United States." *Shakespeare Reproduced: The Text in History and Ideology*. Ed. Jean Howard and Marion O'Connor. New York: Methuen, 1987. 47–67.

Winn, James A. "An Old Historian Looks at the New Historicism." *Comparative Studies in Society and History* 35 (1993): 859–70.

The New Historicism: Influential Examples

The new historicism has taken its present form less through the elaboration of basic theoretical postulates and more through certain influential examples. The works listed represent some of the most important contributions guiding research in this area.

Bercovitch, Sacvan. *The Rites of Assent: Transformations in the Symbolic Construction of America*. New York: Routledge, 1993.

Brown, Gillian. *Domestic Individualism: Imagining Self in Nineteenth-Century America*. Berkeley: U of California P, 1990.

Dollimore, Jonathan. *Radical Tragedy: Religion, Ideology and Power in the Drama of Shakespeare and His Contemporaries*. Brighton, Eng.. Harvester, 1984.

Dollimore, Jonathan, and Alan Sinfield, eds. *Political Shakespeare: New Essays in Cultural Materialism*. Manchester, Eng.: Manchester UP, 1985. This volume occupies the borderline between new historicist and cultural criticism. See especially the essays by Dollimore, Greenblatt, and Tennenhouse.

Gallagher, Catherine. *The Industrial Reformation of English Fiction*. Chicago: U of Chicago P, 1985.

Goldberg, Jonathan. *James I and the Politics of Literature*. Baltimore: Johns Hopkins UP, 1983.

Greenblatt, Stephen J. *Learning to Curse: Essays in Early Modern Culture*. New York: Routledge, 1990.

———. *Marvelous Possessions: The Wonder of the New World*. Chicago: U of Chicago P, 1991.

———. *Renaissance Self-Fashioning from More to Shakespeare*. Chicago: U of Chicago P, 1980. See chapter 1 and the chapter on *Othello* titled "The Improvisation of Power."

———. *Shakespearean Negotiations: The Circulation of Social Energy in Renaissance England*. Berkeley: U of California P, 1988. See especially "The Circulation of Social Energy" and "Invisible Bullets."

Liu, Alan. *Wordsworth, the Sense of History*. Stanford: Stanford UP, 1989.

Marcus, Leah. *Puzzling Shakespeare: Local Reading and Its Discontents*. Berkeley: U of California P, 1988.

McGann, Jerome. *The Romantic Ideology*. Chicago: U of Chicago P, 1983.

Michaels, Walter Benn. *The Gold Standard and the Logic of Naturalism: American Literature at the Turn of the Century*. Berkeley: U of California P, 1987.

Montrose, Louis Adrian. "'Shaping Fantasies': Figurations of Gender and Power in Elizabethan Culture." *Representations* 2 (1983): 61–94. One of the most influential early new historicist essays.

Mullaney, Steven. *The Place of the Stage: License, Play, and Power in Renaissance England*. Chicago: U of Chicago P, 1987.

Orgel, Stephen. *The Illusion of Power: Political Theater in the English Renaissance*. Berkeley: U of California P, 1975.

Sinfield, Alan. *Literature, Politics, and Culture in Postwar Britain*. Berkeley: U of California P, 1989.

Tennenhouse, Leonard. *Power on Display: The Politics of Shakespeare's Genres*. New York: Methuen, 1986.

Foucault and His Influence

As I point out in the introduction to the new historicism, some new historicists would question the "privileging" of Foucault implicit in this section heading ("Foucault and His Influence") and the following one ("Other Writers and Works"). They might cite the greater importance of one of those other writers or point out that to cite a central influence or a definitive cause runs against the very spirit of the movement.

Foucault, Michel. *The Archaeology of Knowledge*. Trans. A. M. Sheridan Smith. New York: Harper, 1972.

———. *Discipline and Punish: The Birth of the Prison*. 1975. Trans. Alan Sheridan. New York: Pantheon, 1978.

———. *The History of Sexuality*, Vol. 1. Trans. Robert Hurley. New York: Pantheon, 1978.

———. *Language, Counter-Memory, Practice*. Ed. Donald F.

Bouchard. Trans. Donald F. Bouchard and Sherry Simon. Ithaca: Cornell UP, 1977.

———. *The Order of Things: An Archaeology of the Human Sciences.* New York: Vintage, 1973.

———. *Politics, Philosophy, Culture.* Ed. Lawrence D. Kritzman. Trans. Alan Sheridan et al. New York: Routledge, 1988.

———. *Power/Knowledge.* Ed. Colin Gordon. Trans. Colin Gordon et al. New York: Pantheon, 1980.

———. *Technologies of the Self.* Ed. Luther H. Martin, Huck Gutman, and Patrick H. Hutton. Amherst: U of Massachusetts P, 1988.

Dreyfus, Hubert L., and Paul Rabinow. *Michel Foucault: Beyond Structuralism and Hermeneutics.* Chicago: U of Chicago P, 1983.

Sheridan, Alan. *Michel Foucault: The Will to Truth.* New York: Tavistock, 1980.

Smart, Barry. *Michel Foucault.* New York: Ellis Horwood and Tavistock, 1985.

Other Writers and Works of Interest to New Historicist Critics

Bakhtin, M. M. *The Dialogic Imagination: Four Essays.* Ed. Michael Holquist. Trans. Caryl Emerson. Austin: U of Texas P, 1981. Bakhtin wrote many influential studies on subjects as varied as Dostoyevsky, Rabelais, and formalist criticism. But this book, in part due to Holquist's helpful introduction, is probably the best place to begin reading Bakhtin.

Benjamin, Walter. "The Work of Art in the Age of Mechanical Reproduction." 1936. *Illuminations.* Ed. Hannah Arendt. Trans. Harry Zohn. New York: Harcourt, 1968.

Fried, Michael. *Absorption and Theatricality: Painting and Beholder in the Works of Diderot.* Berkeley: U of California P, 1980.

Geertz, Clifford. *The Interpretation of Cultures.* New York: Basic, 1973.

———. *Negara: The Theatre State in Nineteenth-Century Bali.* Princeton: Princeton UP, 1980.

Goffman, Erving. *Frame Analysis.* New York: Harper, 1974.

Jameson, Fredric. *The Political Unconscious.* Ithaca: Cornell UP, 1981.

Koselleck, Reinhart. *Futures Past.* Trans. Keith Tribe. Cambridge: MIT P, 1985.

Said, Edward. *Orientalism.* New York: Columbia UP, 1978.

Turner, Victor. *The Ritual Process: Structure and Anti-Structure.* Chicago: Aldine, 1969.

Young, Robert. *White Mythologies: Writing History and the West.* New York: Routledge, 1990.

New Historicist (and Recent Historical) Approaches to *Heart of Darkness*

Brantlinger, Patrick. "*Heart of Darkness:* Anti-Imperialism, Racism, or Impressionism?" *Criticism* 27 (1985): 363–85.

Glenn, Ian. "Conrad's *Heart of Darkness:* A Sociological Reading." *Literature and History* 13 (1987): 238–56.

Hawkins, Hunt. "Conrad and the Psychology of Colonialism." *Conrad Revisited: Essays for the Eighties.* University: U of Alabama P, 1985.

———. "Conrad's *Heart of Darkness:* Politics and History." *Conradiana* 24 (1992): 207–17.

———. "Joseph Conrad, Roger Casement, and the Congo Reform Movement." *Journal of Modern Literature* 9 (1981–82): 65–80.

Humphries, Reynold. "The Discourse of Colonialism: Its Meaning and Relevance for Conrad's Fiction." *Conradiana* 21 (1989): 107–33.

Parry, Benita. *Conrad and Imperialism.* London: Macmillan, 1983.

A NEW HISTORICIST PERSPECTIVE

BROOK THOMAS

Preserving and Keeping Order
by Killing Time in *Heart of Darkness*

Fiction is history, human history, or it is nothing. But it is also more than that; it stands on firmer ground, being based on the reality of forms and the observation of social phenomena, whereas history is based on documents, and the reading of print and handwriting — on second-hand impression. Thus fiction is nearer truth. But let that pass. A historian may be an artist too, and a novelist is a historian, the preserver, the keeper, the expounder, of human experience.

–JOSEPH CONRAD, *Notes on Life and Letters*

We can start, contrary to current critical practices, with some old-fashioned generalizations about the history of ideas. And, when we journey, as we must, to more specificity about Conrad's story there is no guarantee that we will penetrate to the essential Truth — or non-Truth — lying at the heart of *Heart of Darkness;* certainly not in a story informing us that for Marlow "the meaning of an episode was not inside like a kernel but outside, enveloping the tale which brought it out only as a glow brings out a haze, in the likeness of one of these misty halos that sometimes are made visible by the spectral illumination of moonshine" (p. 20). But we may be able to come closer to a truth that we can glimpse only if we read historically the narrative that Conrad weaves in his role as a historian of human experience.

1

The century that preceded the 1899 publication of *Heart of Darkness* was the great century of historiography; that is to say, the one in which history sought to become a science. The eighteenth century's emphasis on natural, universal laws that governed human society did not suddenly vanish, but it was superseded by an emphasis on the organic development of peoples and nations, developments that became the object of study for the new science of history. In medieval times events in history had been seen as *exempla:* as illustrations of moral laws or truths. Relying on the sense of time that allowed anticipations

of Christianity to be read into the ancient world and the Old Testa-
ment, historians in the Middle Ages had placed an event in the past on
the same temporal plane as the present. Past and present events were
interchangeable, capable of being interpreted to exhibit a moral truth
to guide behavior. With the advent of a self-consciously modern age in
the Renaissance, this sense of time began to alter.

Defining itself as a distinct epoch that had broken with that which
came before, the Renaissance produced thinkers who, increasingly,
considered events in the present to be different in kind from events in
the past. Events were unique to the epochs in which they occurred.
History no longer merely took place *in* time, it also took place
through time; that is, history became temporalized. As a result, the
passage of time gave each generation a novel perspective on the past.
Past events were no longer so easily interpreted to be timeless *exempla*. Instead, they needed to be continually reinterpreted from the
standpoint of a new present. To enter the Renaissance, Reinhart
Koselleck writes in *Futures Past* (1985), is to enter the *Neuzeit*, the
age of "new time."

By the eighteenth century this sense of history's temporality was
widely held. Goethe, for instance, felt that it was self-evident that each
generation had to rewrite world history. Nonetheless, eighteenth-
century histories still stressed the universality of history. This stress on
universal history continued to link history to moral philosophy, since
history was often used to illustrate natural laws and the natural rights
of man. The rise of the science of history was an attempt to break even
this connection with moral philosophy. As the great spokesman of
nineteenth-century historiography Leopold von Ranke wrote, his task
was not to judge the past or to instruct the present for the profit of future ages, but "to show only what actually happened (*wie es eigentlich
gewesen*)" (Bann 10). To accomplish this goal, Ranke emphasized the
difference between primary and secondary sources. A history that
wanted accurately to relate the past needed to rely on primary
sources — documents actually produced in the period — not secondary ones — documents recording another period's interpretation
of the past.

From our twentieth-century perspective Ranke's goal to tell only
what actually happened sometimes seems naive. For instance, the attempt to reconstruct the past on the basis of primary source material
seems to neglect the very real difficulties that arise in giving the past
representation. As we are continually reminded by literary critics
today, no history can possibly relate the past as it really was because

our histories will always be influenced by our present perspective. Furthermore, histories are written in language; the rhetoric the historian adopts shapes and determines his representation of the past. This critical commonplace of today is in turn indebted to the insights of people like Conrad who, in the passage I quote at the start of this essay, reminds us that the documents that Ranke called "primary" sources merely give the historian a "second-hand impression" of an age. One of the concerns of this essay is to understand historically why Conrad felt that "the reality of forms and observation of social phenomena" in his fiction produce more truthful histories than those of most historians.

At least part of the reason is the crisis in historicism that occurred in the late nineteenth and early twentieth centuries. If historicism rested on the belief that the historian could objectively reconstruct the past, the ultimate truth it delivered seemed to be the impossibility of discovering the truth. Feeling that their task was to relive an era as sympathetically as possible by blotting out everything they knew about the latter course of history, historians came to see that all beliefs were historically contingent, including the belief in scientific objectivity. If this awareness came dangerously close to what Friedrich Meinecke called "the bottomless pit of relativism," it was tolerated because historicism retained a faith in progress (Iggers 175). Nineteenth-century histories might demonstrate that beliefs were historically contingent, but many adopted a teleological narrative structure: in other words, one that assumed that history had a design or purpose and that whatever was becoming was right. Values changed, but they were always appropriate to their age, and they progressed and developed over time. Even this faith, however, was undermined by the way historicism linked its histories to the emergence of individual nations. As each nation's history emerged, it became clear that not all narratives of progress could be right. If academic dispute did not bring this point home, World War I did.

But even before the destruction of the war, many Europeans had lost faith in the values that gave coherence to the historicist project. Increasingly, the attempt to give an objective description of the past gave way to modern subjectivist philosophies. As J. Hillis Miller summarizes, "Historicism does not mean merely an awareness of the contradictory diversity of cultures and attitudes. The ancient world had that. The modern historical sense means rather the loss of faith in the possibility of ever discovering the right and true culture, the right and true philosophy or religion" (*Disappearance* 10).

2

Miller's passage is an excellent one to place Conrad's fiction in the context of the history of ideas. By having Kurtz, who embodies Europe's most noble ideals, recognize the horror at the heart of darkness, Conrad brings us face to face with the disillusionment that many twentieth-century thinkers continue to confront, although much of the culture operates by trying to forget it. Marlow embodies this double perspective. On the one hand, back in Europe Marlow tries to forget Kurtz, "to surrender personally all that remained of him with me to that oblivion which is the last word of our common fate" (p. 90). On the other, Marlow cannot will Kurtz's memory away. For him and the reader it serves as what the French historian Michel Foucault has called a "counter-memory," a memory that disrupts the narrative of enlightened progress that official European culture tried to tell about its history. Unable completely to repress this counter-memory when he visits Kurtz's Intended, whose forehead, as the room grows darker, "remained illumined by the unextinguishable light of belief and love" (p. 92), Marlow refuses to destroy her illusions and tells her that the last word Kurtz had uttered was her name, thus linking this woman and all she stands for with "the horror." Official memory of light and counter-memory of darkness are in Conrad's narrative inextricably connected, even though the official memory's ascendancy depends upon the lies that repress the counter-memory.

In a world in which the truth that Marlow tells about civilized Europe is expressed through a lie, it is no wonder that Conrad claimed that fiction is nearer to truth than history. The way Conrad's art approaches the truth is not by stating it but by reminding us of the lie that accompanies every effort to name the truth. Art is closer to truth only in so far as it carries within it the counter-memory that its efforts to express the truth repress, just as the ivory keys of the grand piano that Marlow sees as he waits to greet the Intended become an emblem for the exploitation that Europe's high culture tried to cover up. Embodying the structural relationship between what is said and what is left unsaid, Conrad's story proves to be truer than history, not in its explicit statements but in its forms.

For instance, Conrad does not offer an omniscient narrative perspective that knows and states how it really was. Instead, he constructs a story in which his perspective gives way to a narrator's, that gives way to Marlow's, that gives way to Kurtz's. If this perspective does not tell us the truth, there is a certain truth in the formal techniques that illustrate the impossibility of directly stating the truth. Similarly, the linear narrative of nineteenth-century historicism, in which we move progressively toward a fuller understanding, is replaced by a narrative that concludes with a lie. Even so, there is a certain truth in the way the story unfolds, moving forward and backward in time, its narrative flow interrupted by Marlow's addresses to his audience and his own psychological avoidance of the actual encounter with Kurtz, who is mentioned early in the story but is not met until pages later.

To enter the world of *Heart of Darkness* is, in other words, to enter the world of modern fiction, a world in which authors' technical innovations responded to the loss of faith described by Miller as the "modern historical sense." But if the crisis in historicism helps place *Heart of Darkness* in context, the story also places the context in context. For Conrad's narrative about a European's journey to the heart of Africa helps us see the extent to which the crisis in late-nineteenth-century European thought was related to Europe's contact with what some recent critics, following Jacques Lacan's revision of Hegel, have come to call "the Other." It is probably no accident that the most important British modernist novelists are situated in positions on the borders of mainstream British culture that force them to encounter "the Other." Perhaps no other writer in the twentieth century achieved a mastery over the English language to match James Joyce. But Joyce was in an important sense a colonial writer, an Irish Catholic who spent his life in self-imposed exile on the Continent and who considered English an acquired tongue. An exiled Pole, Conrad quite literally wrote in an acquired language. D. H. Lawrence meanwhile came from a working-class family in the Midlands, carrying an accent that marked his difference from those producing "proper" English arts and letters. Only Virginia Woolf and E. M. Forster could be considered insiders. And Woolf, as a woman, occupied her own border country, while Forster's greatest work, *A Passage to India*, is about the encounter between East and West. Indeed, Europe's encounter with the non-European, so poignantly portrayed by Conrad in *Heart of Darkness,* played a part in one of the most important aspects of modern thought: Europe's discovery of "the Other" within itself.

As early as the late eighteenth century, Europeans had been forced to alter their view of a universal history centered in Europe. Paradoxically, this alteration resulted from the very imperialistic, overseas expansion that drew its ideological justification from the belief that reason, progress, and enlightenment emanated from the West. Brought into contact with such various cultures, Europeans found it impossible to retain belief in one universal culture. Instead, there were many cultures, each with its own history. Recognition of non-European cultures did not mean the abandonment of a Eurocentric perspective. Quite the contrary. Nineteenth-century historicism was adept at absorbing all cultures into a Eurocentric history. Nonetheless, the very presence of "the Other" within those histories heightened the possibility that their narratives would be "decentered." The crisis in historicism can be linked to this decentering, a decentering made possible, ironically, by the success of the West's imperialism.

One of the most important expressions of the decentering of Western narratives of progress and rationality is found in the work of the German philosopher Friedrich Nietzsche, who died the year after Conrad's story appeared. Nietzsche has had a strong influence on recent poststructuralist thought. It is, I think, no accident that two essays cited as starting points for poststructuralism contain explicit critiques of Eurocentrism. One is Paul de Man's "Crisis in Criticism" (1967), which emphasizes the blindness of the philosopher Edmund Husserl to non-Western cultures. The other is Jacques Derrida's "Structure, Sign, and Play in the Discourse of the Human Sciences" (1966), which points out that even the noble efforts to understand non-European cultures by the structuralist anthropologist Claude Lévi-Strauss inevitably adopt a Western perspective. Offering a theory that assures us that the desire for the presence of the truth is inevitably an unfulfilled desire, poststructuralism can productively analyze the world Conrad presents in *Heart of Darkness*. It can also serve as a sort of new faith, albeit a negative one, for critics like Miller trying to cope with the loss of confidence in the Eurocentric view that is dramatized by Conrad's narrative. In turn, Conrad's narrative helps locate the historical situation that created the conditions for the formation of poststructuralist thought.

This reciprocal relation between *Heart of Darkness* and poststructuralism also holds for another approach that proves so fruitful in reading Conrad's story: psychoanalysis. Albert J. Guerard's use of Sigmund Freud to describe *Heart of Darkness* as "A Journey Within" remains one of the most important pieces of Conrad criticism. Certainly, a powerful aspect of Conrad's story is the economy by which his tale about a physical journey into the darkness of Africa becomes a story about a psychological journey into the darkness of the human unconscious. But it is not only the case that psychoanalysis can be used to illuminate Conrad's narrative. Freud's narrative about the human psyche is also illuminated *by* narratives like Conrad's about what happens

when a rational Westerner journeys into Africa. While it is commonplace to consider psychoanalysis a new scientific theory, one that provides a universal account of the structure of the human mind, an examination of Freud's metaphors suggests that we might consider
psychoanalysis a historical event as well, one partly enabled by Western
narratives about encounters with "the Other."

There are numerous similarities between Freud's narrative about
the unconscious and Conrad's narrative about the European encounter with the non-European. Trying to describe the "wild and gorgeous apparition" (p. 77) of the African woman trying to protect
Kurtz, Marlow tells his audience, "She stood looking at us without a
stir, and like the wilderness itself, with an air of brooding over an inscrutable purpose" (p. 77). Freud, in a famous passage, compares female sexuality to the dark continent of Africa. For both of these Western males the otherness of female sexuality is described in terms of the
otherness of the African continent. Just as in Freud's theory the unconscious eludes representation and rational understanding, so in
Conrad's narrative Africa eludes all attempts of the Western mind —
especially a male mind — to understand it. In this context we can better appreciate Marlow's description of himself as a young boy staring,
as did Conrad, at the "many blank spaces" on the map of the world.
Vowing some day to visit those unexplored regions, he finds, by the
time he sets out on his journey, that what had once been "a blank
space of delightful mystery — a white patch for a boy to dream gloriously over" — had become "a place of darkness" (p. 22). Finally recognized by the West, those unexplored, blank spots on the globe
known as Africa were represented as darkness, the same metaphor psychoanalysis uses to represent the unexplored areas of the mind.

The way *Heart of Darkness* helps us analyze some of the critical approaches we use to analyze it proves very satisfying for our classical
sense of balance. Having arrived at this symmetrical formulation, however, we should not rest too comfortably, because it raises a problem.
To merge critical approaches and text is to risk the disappearance of
the encounter with "the Other," which seemed of such historical significance. Just as in Conrad's story what seems to be an encounter
with another turns out to be an encounter with the self — so that
Marlow's encounter with Kurtz really becomes an encounter with
himself and readers' encounters with Marlow transform into encounters with themselves — so in some critical schools today even the otherness of the story we are reading is denied. Although we can hold a
material object in our hand with *Heart of Darkness* written on the title

page and the words Conrad wrote printed on the pages to follow, we are told that what we call the text is in fact the product of our interpretations.

Ironically, then, a project that seems intent on decentering a Eurocentric point of view turns out to be the most Eurocentric of all. For just as Conrad's story can be read, not as a story about Africa, but actually as a story about Europe, so the decentering set in motion by Europe's encounter with "the Other" can be read as a statement about European thought, not about that which is foreign to it. Thinking we are encountering something outside of ourselves or Western culture, we end up merely discovering "the Other" within ourselves, a discovery that could be described as the most imperialistic of all, since what was once thought to be truly different is now absorbed into a system that accounts for its own decentering. In the meantime, "the Other" seems to be of interest only in so far as it can help the West in its task of self-definition.

3

If Conrad's narrative is one of the most effective expressions of the encounter between self and "Other," between the European and non-European, our task is not to affirm the truth of his narrative but to interrogate it. And what needs interrogation is Conrad's representation of the non-European. Why, we need to ask, in this narrative about Europe's encounter with Africa are Africans reduced to the mere function of providing us a spectral illumination about Europe? To answer that question we can turn to a passage in which Marlow describes the Africans:

> The earth seemed unearthly. We are accustomed to look upon the shackled form of a conquered monster, but there — there you could look at a thing monstrous and free. It was unearthly, and the men were — No, they were not inhuman. Well, you know, that was the worst of it — this suspicion of their not being inhuman. It would come slowly to one. They howled and leaped, and spun, and made horrid faces; but what thrilled you was just the thought of their humanity — like yours — the thought of your remote kinship with this wild and passionate uproar. Ugly. Yes, it was ugly enough; but if you were man enough you would admit to yourself that there was in you just the faintest trace of a response to the terrible frankness of that noise, a dim suspicion of there being a meaning in it which you — you so remote from the night of first ages — could comprehend. And why not? The mind

of man is capable of anything — because everything is in it, all the past as well as all the future. What was there after all? Joy, fear, sorrow, devotion, valour, rage — who can tell? — but truth — truth stripped of its cloak of time. (pp. 51–52)

Starting the paragraph with the paradox that the earth seemed unearthly, Marlow sets up the expectation that the human beings inhabiting that unearthly earth will be inhuman, an expectation easy to arouse because it would confirm his listeners' racial prejudices. But Conrad's narrative disrupts such commonplace prejudices. The horror of the story is not that the Africans are a deviant form of humanity, but that the monster is also within the Europeans who consider themselves superior. Thus, the passage suggests a number of ironic reversals. On the one hand, the African continent is a shackled and conquered monster. On the other, it is the European conquerors who are conquered, as their ruthless and violent imperialism unleashes their latent savagery, making them more monstrous than those they profess to civilize. Whereas the West has a tradition of believing that to make the unknown known it has to be brought under control, Marlow suggests that what allows Westerners to understand Africans is loss of control. Released from the constraints of civilization, Europeans can feel a kinship with those people who on the surface seem so different. Understanding of the non-Western can occur, therefore, only when the West is conquered by the very people it feels it is conquering. True courage, a courage in Marlow's world reserved for men (". . . but if you were man enough . . ."), comes in admitting the possibility of being conquered by "the Other," an "Other" that exists all along within the European.

One of the most obvious reasons why Westerners do not immediately recognize "the African" within themselves is the physical difference between races. But for Marlow physical differences, such as skin color, are a surface deception. The real otherness is not physical but temporal. When Westerners travel to Africa, they make a temporal journey as well as a physical one. As Marlow tells his listeners, "Going up that river was like travelling back to the earliest beginnings of the world, when vegetation rioted on the earth and the big trees were kings" (p. 49). The incomprehensibility of the landscape and the people inhabiting it is caused because to travel to Africa is to travel to prehistoric times.

We were wanderers on a prehistoric earth, on an earth that wore the aspect of an unknown planet. We could have fancied ourselves the first of men taking possession of an accursed inheritance, to be subdued at the cost of profound anguish and of excessive toil. But suddenly, as we struggled round a bend, there would be a glimpse of rush walls, of peaked grass-roofs, a burst of yells, a whirl of black limbs, a mass of hands clapping, of feet stamping, of bodies swaying, of eyes rolling, under the droop of heavy and motionless foliage. The steamer toiled along slowly on the edge of a black and incomprehensible frenzy. The prehistoric man was cursing us, praying to us, welcoming us — who could tell? We were cut off from the comprehension of our surroundings; we glided past like phantoms, wondering and secretly appalled, as sane men would be before an enthusiastic outbreak in a madhouse. We could not understand because we were too far and could not remember, because we were travelling in the night of first ages, of those ages that are gone, leaving hardly a sign — and no memories. (p. 51)

But Marlow eventually does comprehend these people. He can because, as different as they seem from civilized human beings, they constitute the prehistory of the West. If the veneer of civilization has made Westerners forget the truth of their prehistory, the function of Conrad's art is to make them remember what they have forgotten. As he writes in the preface to *The Nigger of the "Narcissus,"* his task is, "by the power of the written word," to present "that glimpse of truth for which you have forgotten to ask." The way he stimulates his readers' memories, however, is at odds with the way nineteenth-century historians tried to do so. As we saw, for the historians time constituted reality. The truth of an event had to do with the time in which it took place. To discover a truth we had forgotten was to reconstruct it historically. But Conrad has a different notion of temporality. For him truth has to be discovered by stripping it of "its cloak of time." The passage of history does not lead to continually new truths. Instead, it places a barrier between us and the memory of our prehistory. Truth is not to be found by remembering history but by forgetting it.

The belief that truth is located in a realm of a prehistory that is still present but disguised by modern life is typical of modernist writers. T. S. Eliot, for instance, praised the work of Wyndham Lewis for "sinking to the most primitive and forgotten, returning to the origin and bringing something back, seeking the beginning and the end" (Matthiessen 466). Whereas for nineteenth-century historians the past and present existed on different temporal planes, for many modernists past and present occupied the same plane. Flattening history in *The Waste Land*, Eliot continually juxtaposes past and present, just as in *Heart of Darkness* Marlow links the past of England with the present of Africa by comparing the Thames to the Congo: "And this also . . . has been one of the dark places of the earth" (p. 19).

Europeans like Conrad, then, possessed not only a progressive, Eurocentric vision of world history but also the temporal sense of the synchronicity of the nonsynchronic. It seemed to them, in other words, that by studying other, primitive-seeming cultures existing simultaneously (or synchronically) with their own, they could study something chronologically disparate, namely, their own deep, prehistoric past. Each culture, it seemed, had its own temporal logic. Whereas the West followed a fairly steady line of progress (despite a backward slide in the "Dark Ages"), other cultures plotted different curves. Thus, at any moment, the world's cultures were at different stages of development. To employ a widely used metaphor, some countries were developed, others underdeveloped. Since the standard of development remained European, cultures different from Europe were, almost by definition, underdeveloped, and the most underdeveloped land of all was Africa, which still existed in a prehistoric state. Drawing on this notion of the synchronicity of the nonsynchronic, Conrad is able to turn a story about a present journey to Africa into a journey to Europe's past, as well as one into each human being's primitive psyche.

Conrad's reliance on the temporal notion that allowed the West to absorb non-Western cultures into its view of history indicates how complicated his portrayal of Western imperialism is. One effect of his inversion of the West's narrative about "the Other" is to undercut its self-righteous superiority. Africa does not embody a lesser truth because it exists in an earlier stage of history. Instead, it embodies a more profound, if unspeakable, truth because it has not traveled as far from its prehistoric origins. Thus, like Freud and Nietzsche, Conrad subverts prevailing European values, offering a "counter-memory" to the belief in rationality and progress.

He also challenges accounts that have abandoned a belief in progress while holding onto a belief in European superiority. *Heart of Darkness* is in part a response to conditions that produced Charles Pearson's *National Life and Character* (1893). Just as Marlow notes that at the time of his journey Africa "was not a blank space anymore" (p. 22), so Pearson proclaims that at the end of the century there are no new lands for Europeans to explore and conquer. The result, this proud Englishman predicts, will be the inevitable and gradual decline of influence by Europeans and especially Anglo-Saxons, whose exemplary individualistic character is compatible with life in the temperate zones but not in the tropics, where future economic growth will occur. By having the heart of Africa conquer its would-be European conquerors, Conrad in part confirms Pearson's view. But Conrad offers a different reason for the European defeat. If Pearson argues that Europeans are constitutionally unfit for tropical climates, Conrad suggests that the European character that Pearson values is nothing more than the cloak of civilization. It is in Africa that Marlow discovers his "remote kinship" (p. 51) with "savages" that other Europeans dismiss as inhuman. Pearson stresses people's differences; Conrad stresses their commonality.

Nonetheless, Conrad's stress on commonality risks making Africans of interest to him only for what they reveal about Europeans. Conrad may challenge prevailing European narratives about "the Other," but by simply inverting them he remains within a Eurocentric logic. Indeed, Conrad's subversion of prevailing values yields a conservative, not a radical, social vision.

The political message of Conrad's encounter with the non-European may well be anti-imperialistic, but not because Conrad espouses liberation of the people he associates with a dark truth about human nature. Instead, for Conrad, European control of non-European cultures is a symptom of its inability to control "the Other" within itself. Conrad's political theory, like that of Hobbes, remains one of control and restraint. There is, it seems, a counter-memory to this narrative that reveals the counter-memory of Western notions of progress, enlightenment, and even decline. We can try to evoke it by examining Conrad's fictional forms.

4

For Conrad narrative has a function similar to that of history. Inevitably taking place within time, narrative, like history, disguises a truth that he feels exists prior to time. Just as the nature of European humanity is to be discovered in an encounter with Africans who exist in a state prior to history, so the meaning of Conrad's tale seems to exist in a realm prior to narrative time. Nonetheless, just as we have to travel through history to encounter our prehistory, so we have to travel through narrative to encounter a meaning that lies deeper than the tale's narrative surface.

To recognize the impossibility of bringing an atemporal truth into narrative representation is to start to understand the importance of one of the most noticeable formal characteristics of Conrad's narrative:

its breaks and gaps. Disrupting the narrative flow, they suggest something that resists narrativization; that is, the glimpse of the truth we have forgotten to ask. For instance, the first interruption of Marlow's story occurs when Marlow cries out about his inability adequately to represent Kurtz in words.

> He was just a word for me. I did not see the man in the name any more than you do. Do you see him? Do you see the story? Do you see anything? It seems to me I am trying to tell you a dream — making a vain attempt, because no relation of a dream can convey the dream-sensation, that commingling of absurdity, surprise, and bewilderment in a tremor of struggling revolt, that notion of being captured by the incredible which is the very essence of dreams. . . . (p. 42)

Marlow's outcry is an obvious reminder to the reader of Conrad's own task as a novelist, for he must make his audience see not only Kurtz but also Marlow. And Conrad's task is even more difficult than Marlow's. Marlow's listeners have access to the voice of someone who has seen Kurtz. Conrad's audience confronts nothing but silent, black words on a white page. But Marlow's outcry does more than comment on the difficulty of representation in words.

To remain within narrative is to remain within the realm of consciousness that veils truth. By interrupting the flow of Marlow's narrative Conrad establishes contact with his readers, momentarily freeing them from the shackles of a linear narrative and throwing them back on their own imaginations. In their imaginations, which contain "all the past as well as the future," not in conscious attention to the story's surface, readers will be able to evoke the memory of their prehistory necessary to comprehend the story's meaning. It was, for instance, in a dreamlike state that Marlow was able to remember his kinship with prehistoric humanity. "There were moments when one's past came back to one, as it will sometimes when you have not a moment to spare to yourself; but it came in the shape of an unrestful and noisy dream, remembered with wonder amongst the overwhelming realities of this strange world of plants, and water, and silence" (p. 49). To relate a dream is to distort the dream-sensation. In *Heart of Darkness* Conrad's disruption of narrative forms works to recreate a dream-sensation in the reader.

But it is not quite so simple. If words seem to block us from a deeper truth accessible only through the imagination, it is words that provoke the imagination. It is, for instance, the mention of Kurtz's name that provokes Marlow's outcry over his inability to use words to make us see Kurtz. Since the very narrative that must be disrupted in order for us to have a glimpse of a forgotten truth is our only means to approach that truth, the gaps in Marlow's narrative can be said to serve a different function from the one we have examined. If, on the one hand, they suggest a truth that resists narrativization, on the other, they reveal Marlow's reluctance to continue his narrative journey toward the glimpse of truth he experienced at the heart of darkness. For Marlow to mention Kurtz is to recall all that Kurtz came to embody for him. Not yet capable of facing that horror, Marlow interrupts the story that inevitably leads to Kurtz. The very breaks and gaps that seem to be the only way to suggest the truth also indicate an avoidance of it.

If these two functions seem at odds, they ultimately converge, because for Conrad "the horror" is associated with the inability fully to represent the truth and what that inability implies about the human condition. So long as truth cannot fully be represented, lies become part of the truth of the world. Indeed, immediately preceding the first interruption of the story Marlow announces his hatred of lies. This hatred does not, however, stem from Marlow's love of truth over falsehood, for what he hates about lies is that they remind him of the inevitable truth of mortality. "There is a taint of death, a flavour of mortality in lies — which is exactly what I hate and detest in the world — what I want to forget" (p. 42). Marlow wants to forget the truth of human finitude that lies remind him of: the truth of our existence in a fallen state in which we cannot have full access to truth, a state making lies inevitable. The lie Marlow tells Kurtz's Intended at the end of the story signals Marlow's ability to overcome his hatred of lies and his acceptance of a world of finitude. At odds with the Enlightenment's faith in humankind's ability through time to liberate itself by expanding its sphere of influence in the world in order to gain a fuller access to truth, Marlow's vision has affinities with a medieval view that a fallen humankind will never have full knowledge of God's truth. For Conrad, as for many contemporary theorists, humanity's finitude is intricately related to humanity's existence within language. Language, our only access to truth, by its very nature offers only a trace of what it seeks to represent. To be within language is to be in a perpetual state of lost presence.

Politically for Conrad this necessitates the acceptance of a world in which lies and repression are inevitable, a political vision that is intricately linked to the seemingly contradictory functions of a narrative that, on the one hand, helps reveal the horror at the heart of darkness and, on the other, serves to cover it up and hold it at bay. Humanity, or the male part of it at least, must confront the horror Kurtz had the courage to face. Survival of the species, however, demands that unlike Kurtz it must not succumb to it, but instead, like Marlow, learn to cover it up. The work of civilization is a lie, but since the alternative is so terrifying it must go on.

In a world in which all other values seem to be relativized, restraint, therefore, becomes an important value for Conrad. In *Heart of Darkness* restraint is by no means the sole property of Westerners. For Marlow the Africans who accompany him on the journey up the river display more restraint than any European when they resist "the devilry of lingering starvation" (p. 57) by not killing and eating the whites. Marlow, however, cannot explain this restraint, which he finds a mystery greater than the inexplicable sounds of savagery emanating from the primeval forest. He cannot explain it, because for Marlow restraint is associated with work, the work of civilization that separates the West from the savage forest. How much Marlow values work is made clear in another break in his narrative.

Interrupted by a skeptical grunt from one of his listeners, Marlow responds.

You wonder I didn't go ashore for a howl and a dance? Well, no   I didn't. Fine sentiments, you say? Fine sentiments be hanged! I had no time. I had to mess about with white-lead and strips of woollen blanket helping to put bandages on those leaky steam-pipes — I tell you. I had to watch the steering, and circumvent those snags, and get the tin-pot along by hook or by crook. There was surface-truth enough in these things to save a wiser man. (p. 52)

The necessity to work, just to keep the ship moving, not some idealistic values, keeps Marlow from participating in "unspeakable rites" (p. 66). And, as the reference to "surface-truth" reminds us, Conrad self-consciously compares Marlow's journey up the river to the act of narrating that journey. As a comment directly before another break in Marlow's tale makes even clearer, Conrad's narrative also offers a surface truth that hides a profounder truth. "When you have to attend to things of that sort, to the mere incidents of the surface, the reality — the reality, I tell you — fades. The inner truth is hidden — luckily, luckily" (p. 50).

Within the logic set up by the implied analogy between Marlow's journey and his narrative, the leaky steam-pipes that threaten to sink the ship invite comparison with the gaps and breaks in Marlow's narrative. Just as covering the holes in the steam-pipes allows the ship to continue its journey on the surface of the river, so filling the gaps in Marlow's narrative allows the surface narrative to continue, thus protecting us from the groundless horror they suggest. Told by an agent at the station about "the necessity for every man to get on," Marlow responds, "Did I see it? I saw it. What more did I want? What I really wanted was rivets, by Heaven! Rivets. To get on with the work — to stop the hole. Rivets I wanted" (p. 43). But rivets, although in abundance at a station closer to shore, are not available. Thus, Marlow, like Conrad, must improvise techniques that will allow him to stop the holes so dangerously exposed and difficult to repair in this outpost of progress.

5

In the final two paragraphs of his preface to *The Nigger of the "Narcissus,"* Conrad explicitly compares his work as an artist to the work of civilization by referring to "the workman of art." But there is an important difference. Workers' hands are kept so busy that they never take a moment to glimpse "the truth." Thus, the hand of a writer must produce a work that arrests,

> for the space of a breath, the hands busy about the work of the
> earth, and compel men entranced by the sight of distant goals to
> glance for a moment at the surrounding vision of form and colour,
> of sunshine and shadows; to make them pause for a look, for a
> sigh, for a smile — such is the aim, difficult and evanescent, and
> reserved only for a very few to achieve. But sometimes, by the de-
> serving and the fortunate, even that task is accomplished. And
> when it is accomplished — behold! — all the truth of life is there:
> a moment of vision, a sigh, a smile — and the return to an eternal
> rest.

What interests me most about this passage is the effect that the work of art has, according to Conrad, on the workers of the earth. The initial image is one of labor — hands busy at toil. The final image is one of tranquility — an eternal rest. That final image is clearly an image of death, but, as J. Hillis Miller points out, it also suggests a return "to the forgetful sleep of everyday life" (*Poets* 39). The implication is, therefore, that after people have had a glimpse of the truth of life provided by the workman of art their lives of everyday labor can be considered ones of rest. Arrested for the space of a breath, the hands busy about the work of the earth are set in motion again, returning to the world of time that, because it protects them from the truth at the heart of darkness, is actually one of repose. Serving to protect humanity from the horror it discovers when truth is stripped from the cloak of time, work not only takes place within history but also produces history. It is work, then, that constructs the lie of civilization that hides humanity, necessarily, from the prehistoric truth about itself.

But what if Conrad's location of truth in an atemporal realm is itself a lie? What if the horror of human existence is not to be found in a realm of savagery that we discover by escaping history, but instead lies within history itself — not a Eurocentric construction of a universal History, but one that refuses to indulge in Conrad's mystification that turns Africa into the mere site of Europe's prehistory? If this is the case, work might serve a very different function from the one Conrad attributes to it.

Just as the narrative Conrad uses to hold the horror at bay produces gaps and breaks that bring us face to face with it, so the very work that is supposed to cover up the horror might also produce it. Rather than protecting humanity from an unnameable horror, work might be part of the unnamed horror of Conrad's story. Whereas Conrad sees work providing Europeans with the restraint and discipline necessary to control the horror of "the Other" within themselves, European history records the horror of the enforced labour of others — European and non-European — to maintain structures of domination. Work does indeed restrain. Perhaps, however, the reason why people with hands busy about the work of the earth are restrained from seeing a glimpse of the truth is not because they repress an unconscious world of the imagination that contains an ahistorical truth about the reality of forms, but because they are given no time to become conscious of the history of how the time of their lives has been wasted. Or to put this another way, the unconsciousness of narratives about the unconscious might turn out to be the history of human labor.

As we have seen, Conrad's tale easily lends itself to psychoanalytical and poststructuralist analyses at the same time that it helps us place in a historical context both psychoanalysis's narrative about the journey to the unconscious and poststructuralism's narrative about the decentering of the West's logocentrism. Conrad's representation of work indicates the need to introduce another form of narrative explanation in our attempt to analyze *Heart of Darkness:* Karl Marx's insistence that historians tell the history of work. Whereas the affinities of

Conrad's narrative with Freudian and Nietzschean narratives help explain how it serves as a counter-memory to prevailing Eurocentric narratives, its differences from the Marxist narrative help expose the counter-memory of such counter-narratives. To say this is not to argue that the Marxist narrative is the master narrative that explains all others. But so long as there are those who offer narratives of human history that neglect the role human labor has played in shaping history — or even more, who, like Conrad, offer a narrative in which human labor hides us from the "truth" of human experience — so long as such narratives influence our sense of history, Marx's narrative will serve as a reminder of acts of repression.

Like Conrad, Marx constructs a narrative in which human beings quite literally make history through their labor. But, unlike Conrad, Marx would consider any escape from that history to be an escape from the truth of human experience. People are prone to escape from the truth *within* human history because it is not a pleasant one. Human beings might make history, but they do not, Marx reminds us, make it under conditions of their own choosing. Humanity's lack of control over the conditions under which it labors makes history, as it is for Joyce's Stephen Dedalus, a nightmare from which we are trying to awake. The role the historian plays in helping us awaken from the nightmare of history is quite different for Conrad and Marx. In expounding human experience Conrad's novelist as historian becomes its "preserver" and "keeper." He does so by revealing a prehistorical, unchanging truth about humanity. In expounding human experience, Marx's philosopher as historian tries to help change it. He does so by providing explanations of the historical forces that keep humanity from laboring under conditions of its own choosing with the hope that consciousness of those conditions can help liberate humanity from them. Any new historical criticism worthy of its name will share in this goal of using historical analysis as a way to help those in the present work toward the construction of a new future, a future in which work is not only used as a means to control "the Other" within, but also directed toward liberating ourselves to help improve the lives of others truly different from us. In terms of Conrad's *Heart of Darkness* this means recognizing that, whereas Conrad's attempt to separate truth and history serves the important function of demystifying nineteenth-century notions of progress and European superiority, it generates a mystification of its own by absorbing the encounter with "the Other" into a narrative about European identity. Precisely because Conrad's narrative tells us more about Europe than the Africa it supposedly represents, it compels us, not to strip truth from the cloak of time, but to imagine a radically different form of temporal narrative that allows "the Other" to be represented.

WORKS CITED

Bann, Stephen. *The Clothing of Clio*. Cambridge: Cambridge UP, 1984.

Guerard, Albert J. *Conrad the Novelist*. Cambridge: Harvard UP, 1958. New York: Atheneum, 1967.

Iggers, George G. *The German Conception of History*. Middletown: Wesleyan UP, 1968.

Kosellek, Reinhart. *Futures Past*. Trans. Keith Tribe. Cambridge: MIT P, 1985.

Matthiessen, F. O. *American Renaissance*. New York: Oxford UP, 1941.

Miller, J. Hillis. *The Disappearance of God*. Cambridge: Harvard UP, 1963.

———. *Poets of Reality*. Cambridge: Harvard UP, 1965.

Pearson, Charles H. *National Life and Character: A Forecast*. London: Macmillan, 1893.

Cultural Criticism

and

Heart of Darkness

WHAT IS CULTURAL CRITICISM?

What do you think of when you think of culture? The opera or ballet? A performance of a Mozart symphony at Lincoln Center or a Rembrandt show at the De Young Museum in San Francisco? Does the phrase "cultural event" conjure up images of young people in jeans and T-shirts — or of people in their sixties dressed formally? Most people hear "culture" and think "high culture." Consequently, when they first hear of cultural criticism, most people assume it is more formal than, well, say, formalism. They suspect it is "highbrow," in both subject and style.

Nothing could be further from the truth. Cultural critics oppose the view that culture refers exclusively to high culture, Culture with a capital C. Cultural critics want to make the term refer to popular, folk, urban, and mass (mass-produced, -disseminated, -mediated, and -consumed) culture, as well as to that culture we associate with the so-called classics. Raymond Williams, an early British cultural critic whose ideas will later be described at greater length, suggested that "art and culture are ordinary"; he did so not to "pull art down" but rather to point out that there is "creativity in all our living. . . . We create our human world as we have thought of art being created" (*Revolution* 37).

Cultural critics have consequently placed a great deal of emphasis on what Michel de Certeau has called "the practice of everyday life." Rather than approaching literature in the elitist way that academic literary critics have traditionally approached it, cultural critics view it more as an anthropologist would. They ask how it emerges from and competes with other forms of discourse within a given culture (science, for instance, or television). They seek to understand the social contexts in which a given text was written, and under what conditions it was — and is — produced, disseminated, read, and used.

Contemporary cultural critics are as willing to write about *Star Trek* as they are to analyze James Joyce's *Ulysses*, a modern literary classic full of allusions to Homer's *Odyssey*. And when they write about *Ulysses*, they are likely to view it as a collage reflecting and representing cultural forms common to Joyce's Dublin, such as advertising, journalism, film, and pub life. Cultural critics typically show how the boundary we tend to envision between high and low forms of culture — forms thought of as important on one hand and relatively trivial on the other — is transgressed in all sorts of exciting ways within works on both sides of the putative cultural divide.

A cultural critic writing about a revered classic might contrast it with a movie, or even a comic-strip version produced during a later period. Alternatively, the literary classic might be seen in a variety of other ways: in light of some more common form of reading material (a novel by Jane Austen might be viewed in light of Gothic romances or ladies' conduct manuals); as the reflection of some common cultural myths or concerns (*Adventures of Huckleberry Finn* might be shown to reflect and shape American myths about race and concerns about juvenile delinquency); or as an example of how texts move back and forth across the alleged boundary between "low" and "high" culture. For instance, one group of cultural critics has pointed out that although Shakespeare's history plays probably started off as popular works enjoyed by working people, they were later considered "highbrow" plays that only the privileged and educated could appreciate. That view of them changed, however, due to later film productions geared toward a national audience. A film version of *Henry V* produced during World War II, for example, made a powerful, popular, patriotic statement about England's greatness during wartime (Humm, Stigant, and Widdowson 6–7). More recently, cultural critics have analyzed the "cultural work" accomplished cooperatively by Shakespeare and Kenneth Branagh in the latter's 1992 film production of *Henry V*.

In combating old definitions of what constitutes culture, of course, cultural critics sometimes end up contesting old definitions of what constitutes the literary canon, that is, the once-agreed-upon honor roll of Great Books. They tend to do so, however, neither by adding books (and movies and television sitcoms) *to* the old list of texts that every "culturally literate" person should supposedly know nor by substituting some kind of counterculture canon. Instead, they tend to critique the very *idea* of canon.

Cultural critics want to get us away from thinking about certain works as the "best" ones produced by a given culture. They seek to be more descriptive and less evaluative, more interested in relating than in rating cultural products and events. They also aim to discover the (often political) reasons *why* a certain kind of aesthetic or cultural product is more valued than others. This is particularly true when the product in question is one produced since 1945, for most cultural critics follow Jean Baudrillard (*Simulations,* 1981) and Andreas Huyssen (*The Great Divide,* 1986) in thinking that any distinctions that may once have existed between high, popular, and mass culture collapsed after the end of World War II. Their discoveries have led them beyond the literary canon, prompting them to interrogate many other value hierarchies. For instance, Pierre Bourdieu in *Distinction: A Social Critique of the Judgment of Taste* (1984 [1979]) and Dick Hebdige in *Hiding the Light: On Images and Things* (1988) have argued that definitions of "good taste" — which are instrumental in fostering and reinforcing cultural discrimination — tell us at least as much about prevailing social, economic, and political conditions as they do about artistic quality and value.

In an article entitled "The Need for Cultural Studies," four groundbreaking cultural critics have written that "Cultural Studies should . . . abandon the goal of giving students access to that which represents a culture." A literary work, they go on to suggest, should be seen in relation to other works, to economic conditions, or to broad social discourses (about childbirth, women's education, rural decay, and so on) within whose contexts it makes sense. Perhaps most important, critics practicing cultural studies should counter the prevalent notion of culture as some preformed whole. Rather than being static or monolithic, culture is really a set of interactive *cultures,* alive and changing, and cultural critics should be present- and even future-oriented. They should be "resisting intellectuals," and cultural studies should be "an emancipatory project" (Giroux et al. 478–80).

The paragraphs above are peppered with words like *oppose, counter, deny, resist, combat, abandon,* and *emancipatory.* What such words quite accurately suggest is that a number of cultural critics view themselves in political, even oppositional, terms. Not only are they likely to take on the literary canon, they are also likely to oppose the institution of the university, for that is where the old definitions of culture as high culture (and as something formed, finished, and canonized) have been most vigorously preserved, defended, and reinforced.

Cultural critics have been especially critical of the departmental structure of universities, which, perhaps more than anything else, has kept the study of the "arts" relatively distinct from the study of history, not to mention from the study of such things as television, film, advertising, journalism, popular photography, folklore, current affairs, shoptalk, and gossip. By maintaining artificial boundaries, universities have tended to reassert the high/low culture distinction, implying that all the latter subjects are best left to historians, sociologists, anthropologists, and communication theorists. Cultural critics have taken issue with this implication, arguing that the way of thinking reinforced by the departmentalized structure of universities keeps us from seeing the aesthetics of an advertisement as well as the propagandistic elements of a work of literature. Cultural critics have consequently mixed and matched the analytical procedures developed in a variety of disciplines. They have formed — and encouraged other scholars to form — networks and centers, often outside of those enforced departmentally.

Some initially loose interdisciplinary networks have, over time, solidified to become cultural studies programs and majors. As this has happened, a significant if subtle danger has arisen. Richard Johnson, who along with Hebdige, Stuart Hall, and Richard Hoggart was instrumental in developing the Center for Contemporary Cultural Studies at Birmingham University in England, has warned that cultural studies must not be allowed to turn into yet another traditional academic discipline — one in which students encounter a canon replete with soap operas and cartoons, one in which belief in the importance of such popular forms has become an "orthodoxy" (39). The only principles that critics doing cultural studies can doctrinally espouse, Johnson suggests, are the two that have thus far been introduced: the principle that "culture" has been an "inegalitarian" concept, a "tool" of "condescension," and the belief that a new, "interdisciplinary (and even antidisciplinary)" approach to *true* culture (that is, to the forms in which culture currently lives) is required now that history, art, and the communications media are so complex and interrelated (42).

The object of cultural study should not be a body of works assumed to comprise or reflect a given culture. Rather, it should be human consciousness, and the goal of that critical analysis should be to understand and show how that consciousness is itself forged and formed, to a great extent, by cultural forces. "Subjectivities," as Johnson has put it, are "produced, not given, and are . . . objects of inquiry" inevitably related to "social practices," whether those involve factory rules, supermarket behavior patterns, reading habits, advertisements, myths, or languages and other signs to which people are exposed (44–45).

Although the United States has probably contributed more than any other nation to the *media* through which culture is currently expressed, and although many if not most contemporary practitioners of cultural criticism are North American, the evolution of cultural criticism and, more broadly, cultural studies has to a great extent been influenced by theories developed in Great Britain and on the European continent.

Among the Continental thinkers whose work allowed for the development of cultural studies are those whose writings we associate with structuralism and poststructuralism. Using the linguistic theory of Ferdinand de Saussure, structuralists suggested that the structures of language lie behind all human organization. They attempted to create a *semiology* — a science of signs — that would give humankind at once a scientific and holistic way of studying the world and its human inhabitants. Roland Barthes, a structuralist who later shifted toward poststructuralism, attempted to recover literary language from the isolation in which it had been studied and to show that the laws that govern it govern all signs, from road signs to articles of clothing. Claude Lévi-Strauss, an anthropologist who studied the structures of everything from cuisine to villages to myths, looked for and found recurring, common elements that transcended the differences within and between cultures.

Of the structuralist and poststructuralist thinkers who have had an impact on the evolution of cultural studies, Jacques Lacan is one of three whose work has been particularly influential. A structuralist psychoanalytic theorist, Lacan posited that the human unconscious is structured like a language and treated dreams not as revealing symptoms of repression but, rather, as forms of discourse. Lacan also argued that the ego, subject, or self that we think of as being natural (our individual human nature) is in fact a product of the social order and its symbolic systems (especially, but not exclusively, language). Lacan's thought has served as the theoretical underpinning for cultural critics seeking to show the way in which subjectivities are produced by social discourses and practices.

Jacques Derrida, a French philosopher whose name has become synonymous with poststructuralism, has had an influence on cultural criticism at least as great as that of Lacan. The linguistic focus of structuralist thought has by no means been abandoned by poststructuralists, in spite of their opposition to structuralism's tendency to find universal patterns instead of textual and cultural contradictions. Indeed, Derrida has provocatively asserted that "*there is nothing outside the text*" (*Grammatology* 158), by which he means something like the following: we come to know the world through language, and even our most worldly actions and practices (the Gulf War, the wearing of condoms) are dependent upon discourses (even if they deliberately contravene those discourses). Derrida's "deconstruction" of the world/text distinction, like his deconstruction of so many of the hierarchical oppositions we habitually use to interpret and evaluate reality, has allowed cultural critics to erase the boundaries between high and low culture, classic and popular literary texts, and literature and other cultural discourses that, following Derrida, may be seen as manifestations of the same textuality.

Michel Foucault is the third Continental thinker associated with structuralism and/or poststructuralism who has had a particularly powerful impact on the evolution of cultural studies — and perhaps *the* strongest influence on American cultural criticism and the so-called new historicism, an interdisciplinary form of cultural criticism whose evolution has often paralleled that of cultural criticism. Although Foucault broke with Marxism after the French student uprisings of 1968, he was influenced enough by Marxist thought to study cultures in terms of power relationships. Unlike Marxists, however, Foucault refused to see power as something exercised by a dominant class over a subservient class. Indeed, he emphasized that power is not just repressive power, that is, a tool of conspiracy by one individual or institution against another. Power, rather, is a whole complex of forces; it is that which produces what happens.

Thus even a tyrannical aristocrat does not simply wield power but is empowered by "discourses" — accepted ways of thinking, writing, and speaking — and practices that embody, exercise, and amount to power. Foucault tried to view all things, from punishment to sexuality, in terms of the widest possible variety of discourses. As a result, he traced what he called the "genealogy" of topics he studied through texts that more traditional historians and literary critics would have overlooked, examining (in Lynn Hunt's words) "memoirs of deviants, diaries, political treatises, architectural blueprints, court records, doctors' reports — appl[ying] consistent principles of analysis in search of moments of reversal in discourse, in search of events as loci of the conflict where social practices were transformed" (Hunt 39). Foucault tended not only to build interdisciplinary bridges but also, in the process, to bring into the study of culture the "histories of women, homosexuals, and minorities" — groups seldom studied by those interested in Culture with a capital C (Hunt 45).

Of the British influences on cultural studies and criticism, two stand out prominently. One, the Marxist historian E. P. Thompson, revolutionized the study of the industrial revolution by writing about its impact on human attitudes, even consciousness. He showed how a shared cultural view, specifically that of what constitutes a fair or just price, influenced crowd behavior and caused such things as the "food riots" of the eighteenth and nineteenth centuries (during which the women of Nottingham repriced breads in the shops of local bakers, paid for the goods they needed, and carried them away). The other, even more important early British influence on contemporary cultural criticism and cultural studies was Raymond Williams, who coined the phrase "culture is ordinary." In works like *Culture and Society: 1780–1950* (1958) and *The Long Revolution* (1961) Williams demonstrated that culture is not fixed and finished but, rather, living and evolving. One of the changes he called for was the development of a common socialist culture.

Although Williams dissociated himself from Marxism during the period 1945–58, he always followed the Marxist practice of viewing culture in relation to ideologies, which he defined as the "residual," "dominant," or "emerging" ways of viewing the world held by classes or individuals holding power in a given social group. He avoided dwelling on class conflict and class oppression, however, tending instead to focus on people as people, on how they experience the conditions in which they find themselves and creatively respond to those conditions through their social practices. A believer in the resiliency of the individual, Williams produced a body of criticism notable for what Stuart Hall has called its "humanism" (63).

As is clearly suggested in several of the preceding paragraphs, Marxism is the background to the background of cultural criticism.

What isn't as clear is that some contemporary cultural critics consider themselves Marxist critics as well. It is important, therefore, to have some familiarity with certain Marxist concepts — those that would have been familiar to Foucault, Thompson, and Williams, plus those espoused by contemporary cultural critics who self-identify with Marxism. That familiarity can be gained from an introduction to the works of four important Marxist thinkers: Mikhail Bakhtin, Walter Benjamin, Antonio Gramsci, and Louis Althusser.

Bakhtin was a Russian, later a Soviet, critic so original in his thinking and wide ranging in his influence that some would say he was never a Marxist at all. He viewed literary works in terms of discourses and dialogues *between* discourses. The narrative of a novel written in a society in flux, for instance, may include an official, legitimate discourse, plus others that challenge its viewpoint and even its authority. In a 1929 book on Dostoyevsky and the 1940 study *Rabelais and His World,* Bakhtin examined what he calls "polyphonic" novels, each characterized by a multiplicity of voices or discourses. In Dostoyevsky the independent status of a given character is marked by the difference of his or her language from that of the narrator. (The narrator's language may itself involve a dialogue involving opposed points of view.) In works by Rabelais, Bakhtin finds that the (profane) languages of Carnival and of other popular festivities play against and parody the more official discourses of the magistrates and the church. Bakhtin's relevance to cultural criticism lies in his suggestion that the dialogue involving high and low culture takes place not only between classic and popular texts but also between the "dialogic" voices that exist within all great books.

Walter Benjamin was a German Marxist who, during roughly the same period, attacked fascism and questioned the superior value placed on certain traditional literary forms that he felt conveyed a stultifying "aura" of culture. He took this position in part because so many previous Marxist critics (and, in his own day, Georg Lukács) had seemed to prefer nineteenth-century realistic novels to the modernist works of their own time. Benjamin not only praised modernist movements, such as dadaism, but also saw as promising the development of new art forms utilizing mechanical production and reproduction. These forms, including photography, radio, and film, promised that the arts would become a more democratic, less exclusive, domain. Anticipating by decades the work of those cultural critics interested in mass-produced, mass-mediated, and mass-consumed culture, Benjamin analyzed the meanings and (defensive) motivations behind words like *unique* and *authentic* when used in conjunction with mechanically reproduced art.

Antonio Gramsci, an Italian Marxist best known for his *Prison Notebooks* (first published in 1947), critiqued the very concept of literature and, beyond that, of culture in the old sense, stressing the importance of culture more broadly defined and the need for nurturing and developing proletarian, or working-class, culture. He argued that all intellectual or cultural work is fundamentally political and expressed the need for what he called "radical organic" intellectuals. Today's cultural critics urging colleagues to "legitimate the notion of writing reviews and books for the general public," to "become involved in the political reading of popular culture," and more generally to "repoliticize" scholarship have viewed Gramsci as an early precursor (Giroux et al. 482).

Gramsci related literature to the ideologies — the prevailing ideas, beliefs, values, and prejudices — of the culture in which it was produced. He developed the concept of "hegemony," which refers at once to the process of consensus-formation and to the authority of the ideologies so formed, that is to say, their power to shape the way things look, what they would seem to mean, and, therefore, what reality *is* for the majority of people. But Gramsci did not see people, even poor people, as the helpless victims of hegemony, as ideology's pathetic robots. Rather, he believed that people have the freedom and power to struggle against and shape ideology, to alter hegemony, to break out of the weblike system of prevailing assumptions and to form a new consensus. As Patrick Brantlinger has suggested in *Crusoe's Footprints: Cultural Studies in Britain and America* (1990), Gramsci rejected the "intellectual arrogance that views the vast majority of people as deluded zombies, the victims or creatures of ideology" (100).

Of those Marxists who, after Gramsci, explored the complex relationship between literature and ideology, the French Marxist Louis Althusser had a significant impact on cultural criticism. Unlike Gramsci, Althusser tended to portray ideology as being in control of people, and not vice versa. He argued that the main function of ideology is to reproduce the society's existing relations of production, and that that function is even carried out in literary texts. In many ways, though, Althusser is as good an example of how Marxism and cultural criticism part company as he is of how cultural criticism is indebted to Marxists and their ideas. For although Althusser did argue that literature is relatively autonomous — more independent of ideology than, say, church, press, or state — he meant literature in the high cultural sense, certainly not the variety of works that present-day cultural critics routinely examine alongside those of Tolstoy and Joyce, Eliot and Brecht. Popular fictions, Althusser assumed, were mere packhorses designed (however unconsciously) to carry the baggage of a culture's ideology, or mere brood mares destined to reproduce it.

Thus, while a number of cultural critics would agree both with Althusser's notion that works of literature reflect certain ideological formations and with his notion that, at the same time, literary works may be relatively distant from or even resistant to ideology, they have rejected the narrow limits within which Althusser and some other Marxists (such as Georg Lukács) have defined literature. In "Marxism and Popular Fiction" (1986), Tony Bennett uses *Monty Python's Flying Circus* and another British television show, *Not the 9 o'clock News*, to argue that the Althusserian notion that all forms of culture belong "among [all those] many material forms which ideology takes . . . under capitalism" is "simply not true." The "entire field" of "popular fiction" — which Bennett takes to include films and television shows as well as books — is said to be "replete with instances" of works that do what Bennett calls the "work" of "distancing." That is, they have the effect of separating the audience from, not rebinding the audience to, prevailing ideologies (249).

Although Marxist cultural critics exist (Bennett himself is one, carrying on through his writings what may be described as a lovers' quarrel with Marxism), most cultural critics are not Marxists in any strict sense. Anne Beezer, in writing about such things as advertisements and women's magazines, contests the "Althusserian view of ideology as the construction of the subject" (qtd. in Punter 103). That is, she gives both the media she is concerned with and their audiences more credit than Althusserian Marxists presumably would. Whereas they might argue that such media make people what they are, she points out that the same magazines that, admittedly, tell women how to please their men may, at the same time, offer liberating advice to women about how to preserve their independence by not getting too serious romantically. And, she suggests, many advertisements advertise their status as ads, just as many people who view or read them see advertising as advertising and interpret it accordingly.

The complex sort of analysis that Beezer has brought to bear on women's magazines and advertisements has been focused on paperback romance novels by Tania Modleski and Janice A. Radway in *Loving with a Vengeance* (1982) and *Reading the Romance* (1984), respectively. Radway, a feminist cultural critic who uses but ultimately goes beyond Marxism, points out that many women who read romances do so in order to carve out a time and space that is wholly their own, not to be intruded upon by husbands or children. Although many such novels end in marriage, the marriage is usually between a feisty and independent heroine and a powerful man she has "tamed," that is, made sensitive and caring. And why do so many of these stories involve such heroines and end as they do? Because, as Radway demonstrates through painstaking research into publishing houses, bookstores, and reading communities, their consumers *want* them to. They don't buy — or, if they buy they don't recommend — romances in which, for example, a heroine is raped: thus, in time, fewer and fewer such plots find their way onto the racks by the supermarket checkout.

Radway's reading is typical of feminist cultural criticism in that it is *political*, but not exclusively about oppression. The subjectivities of women may be "produced" by romances — the thinking of romance readers may be governed by what is read — but the same women also govern, to a great extent, what gets written or produced, thus performing "cultural work" of their own. Rather than seeing all forms of popular culture as manifestations of ideology, soon to be remanifested in the minds of victimized audiences, cultural critics tend to see a sometimes disheartening but always dynamic synergy between cultural forms and the culture's consumers. Their observations have increasingly led to an analysis of consumerism, from a feminist but also from a more general point of view. This analysis owes a great deal to the work of de Certeau, Hall, and, especially, Hebdige, whose 1979 book *Subculture: The Meaning of Style* paved the way for critics like John Fiske (*Television Culture*, 1987), Greil Marcus (*Dead Elvis*, 1991), and Rachel Bowlby (*Shopping with Freud*, 1993). These later critics have analyzed everything from the resistance tactics employed by television audiences to the influence of consumers on rock music styles to the psychology of consumer choice.

The overlap between feminist and cultural criticism is hardly surprising, especially given the recent evolution of feminism into various femin*isms*, some of which remain focused on "majority" women of European descent, others of which have focused instead on the lives and writings of minority women in Western culture and of women living in Third World (now preferably called postcolonial) societies. The culturalist analysis of value hierarchies within and between cultures has inevitably focused on categories that include class, race, national origin, gender, and sexualities; the terms of its critique have proved useful to contemporary feminists, many of whom differ from their predecessors insofar as they see *woman* not as a universal category but, rather, as one of several that play a role in identity- or subject-formation. The influence of cultural criticism (and, in some cases, Marxist class analysis) can be seen in the work of contemporary feminist critics such as Gayatri Spivak, Trinh T. Minh-ha, and Gloria Anzaldúa, each of whom has stressed that while all women are female, they are something else as well (such as working-class, lesbian, Native American, Muslim Pakistani) and that that something else must be taken into account when their writings are read and studied.

The expansion of feminism and feminist literary criticism to include multicultural analysis, of course, parallels a transformation of education in general. On college campuses across North America, the field of African-American studies has grown and flourished. African-American critics have been influenced by and have contributed to the cultural approach by pointing out that the white cultural elite of North America has tended to view the oral-musical traditions of African Americans (traditions that include jazz, the blues, sermons, and folktales) as entertaining, but nonetheless inferior. Black writers, in order not to be similarly marginalized, have produced texts that, as Henry Louis Gates has pointed out, fuse the language and traditions of the white Western canon with a black vernacular and traditions derived from African and Caribbean cultures. The resulting "hybridity" (to use Homi K. Bhabha's word), although deplored by a handful of black separatist critics, has proved both rich and complex — fertile ground for many cultural critics practicing African-American criticism.

Interest in race and ethnicity at home has gone hand in hand with a new, interdisciplinary focus on colonial and postcolonial societies abroad, in which issues of race, class, and ethnicity also loom large. Edward Said's book *Orientalism* (1978) is generally said to have inaugurated postcolonial studies, which in Bhabha's words "bears witness to the unequal and uneven forces of cultural representation involved in the contest for political and social authority within the modern world order" ("Postcolonial Criticism" 437). *Orientalism* showed how Eastern and Middle Eastern peoples have for centuries been systematically stereotyped by the West, and how that stereotyping facilitated the colonization of vast areas of the East and Middle East by Westerners. Said's more recent books, along with postcolonial studies by Bhabha and Patrick Brantlinger, are among the most widely read and discussed works of literary scholarship. Brantlinger focuses on British literature of the Victorian period, examining representations of the colonies in

works written during an era of imperialist expansion. Bhabha comple-
ments Brantlinger by suggesting that modern Western culture is best
understood from the postcolonial perspective.

Thanks to the work of scholars like Brantlinger, Bhabha, Said,
Gates, Anzaldúa, and Spivak, education in general and literary study in
particular is becoming more democratic, decentered (less patriarchal
and Eurocentric), and multicultural. The future of literary criticism
will owe a great deal indeed to those early cultural critics who demonstrated that the boundaries between high and low culture are at once
repressive and permeable, that culture is common and therefore includes all forms of popular culture, that cultural definitions are inevitably political, and that the world we see is seen through society's
ideology. In a very real sense, the future of education *is* cultural studies.

In the essay that follows, Patrick Brantlinger begins by alluding to
a now-famous claim — made in 1975 by African novelist Chinua
Achebe — that Conrad was a racist and that *Heart of Darkness* is a
racist work. He then summarizes the dramatically opposed view of
Cedric Watts, one of the many critics who have rejected Achebe's assertion. Implicitly asking how the same text could strike different readers in such different ways, Brantlinger comes up with a compelling
answer, namely, that "*Heart of Darkness* . . . offers a powerful critique
of at least certain manifestations of imperialism and racism, at the
same time that it presents that critique in ways that can only be characterized as both imperialist and racist."

Brantlinger draws a parallel between the mixed signals given out
by *Heart of Darkness* and its author's lukewarm opposition to imperialism in real life. Conrad was sympathetic with the goals of the Congo
Reform Association, founded by his friend Roger Casement, but generally "backed away from involvement," contributing less to the association's work than writers such as Mark Twain and Sir Arthur Conan
Doyle. Furthermore, Brantlinger points out, "the worst feature of imperialism for Conrad may not have been its violence toward the 'miserable' and 'helpless,' but the lying propaganda used to cover its bloody
tracks." What bothered Conrad more than the thought of starving,
Congolese chain gangs was the realization that their exploitation was
being characterized in Europe as a noble act of philanthropy.

One of the most interesting aspects of Brantlinger's essay is his
claim that in writing *Heart of Darkness* Conrad drew as much upon
books and newspaper articles written after his return to Europe as
upon his own experiences in the Congo in 1890. While in Africa, for

instance, Conrad "probably saw little or no evidence of cannibalism, despite the stress upon it in his story"; he would have learned about the savage practices of cutting off heads or limbs from "exposé literature" chronicling the horrors of the 1891 war between Arab slave traders and King Leopold's forces, both of which employed Congolese slave-soldiers. What doesn't come through, either in the accounts Conrad read or the novel he subsequently wrote, is that many of the atrocities described were not so much the traditional practices of the Congolese natives as they were the exploitative, intimidating tactics of their Belgian and Arab oppressors.

That "Conrad portrays the moral bankruptcy of imperialism by showing European motives and actions to be no better than African fetishism and savagery" is a telling indication of the novel's at once anti-imperialist and racist tone, according to Brantlinger. He writes that Conrad "paints Kurtz and Africa with the same tarbrush. His version of evil — the form taken by Kurtz's Satanic behavior — is 'going native.' In short, evil *is* African in Conrad's story; if it is also European, that's because some number of white men in the heart of darkness behave like Africans."

Another important aspect of Brantlinger's essay is his use of Fredric Jameson's Marxist argument that another famous novel by Conrad, *Lord Jim*, is characterized by a split between a hollow, modernist "will to style" (which according to Jameson is the source of Conrad's "impressionism") and "the mass culture tendencies of romance conventions." Brantlinger deconstructs Jameson's opposition, arguing that "on some level, the 'impressionism' of Conrad's novels and their romance features are identical." Certainly, "romance conventions" and "heroic adventure themes" do as much to advance "imperialist propaganda" as the modernist (and/or impressionist) will to style does to blur the depiction — thereby obscuring the reader's awareness — of atrocities.

Brantlinger is typical of cultural critics in using Marxist thought while *fusing* it with the thinking of non-Marxist postcolonial critics such as Edward Said. Equally representative is his insistence upon seeing a Great Work of Art like *Heart of Darkness* not only in terms of literary modernism but also as a work informed by newspapers, exposé literature, and mass culture romances. Finally, though, Brantlinger's essay exemplifies cultural criticism in that it places the text in the context of postcolonial politics, seeing it in terms not only of the political reality it supposedly represents but also in terms of the politically motivated *representations* of that political reality.

CULTURAL CRITICISM:
A SELECTED BIBLIOGRAPHY

General Introductions to
Cultural Criticism, Cultural Studies

Bathrick, David. "Cultural Studies." *Introduction to Scholarship in Modern Languages and Literatures.* Ed. Joseph Gibaldi. New York: MLA, 1992.

Brantlinger, Patrick. *Crusoe's Footprints: Cultural Studies in Britain and America.* New York: Routledge, 1990.

——. "Cultural Studies vs. the New Historicism." *English Studies/ Cultural Studies: Institutionalizing Dissent.* Ed. Isaiah Smithson and Nancy Ruff. Urbana: U of Illinois P, 1994. 43–58.

Brantlinger, Patrick, and James Naremore, eds. *Modernity and Mass Culture.* Bloomington: Indiana UP, 1991.

Brummett, Barry. *Rhetoric in Popular Culture.* New York: St. Martin's, 1994.

Desan, Philippe, Priscilla Parkhurst Ferguson, and Wendy Griswold. "Editors' Introduction: Mirrors, Frames, and Demons: Reflections on the Sociology of Literature." *Literature and Social Practice.* Ed. Desan, Ferguson, and Griswold. Chicago: U of Chicago P, 1989. 1–10.

During, Simon, ed. *The Cultural Studies Reader.* New York: Routledge, 1993.

Eagleton, Terry. "Two Approaches in the Sociology of Literature." *Critical Inquiry* 14 (1988): 469–76.

Easthope, Antony. *Literary into Cultural Studies.* New York: Routledge, 1991.

Fisher, Philip. "American Literary and Cultural Studies since the Civil War." *Redrawing the Boundaries: The Transformation of English and American Literary Studies.* Ed. Stephen Greenblatt and Giles Gunn. New York: MLA, 1992. 232–50.

Giroux, Henry, David Shumway, Paul Smith, and James Sosnoski. "The Need for Cultural Studies: Resisting Intellectuals and Oppositional Public Spheres." *Dalhousie Review* 64.2 (1984): 472–86.

Graff, Gerald, and Bruce Robbins. "Cultural Criticism." *Redrawing the Boundaries: The Transformation of English and American Literary Studies.* Ed. Stephen Greenblatt and Giles Gunn. New York: MLA, 1992. 419–36.

Grossberg, Lawrence, Cary Nelson, and Paula A. Treichler, eds. *Cultural Studies*. New York: Routledge, 1992.

Gunn, Giles. *The Culture of Criticism and the Criticism of Culture*. New York: Oxford UP, 1987.

Hall, Stuart. "Cultural Studies: Two Paradigms." *Media, Culture and Society* 2 (1980): 57–72.

Humm, Peter, Paul Stigant, and Peter Widdowson, eds. *Popular Fictions: Essays in Literature and History*. New York: Methuen, 1986.

Hunt, Lynn, ed. *The New Cultural History: Essays*. Berkeley: U of California P, 1989.

Johnson, Richard. "What Is Cultural Studies Anyway?" *Social Text: Theory/Culture/Ideology* 16 (1986–87): 38–80.

Pfister, Joel. "The Americanization of Cultural Studies." *Yale Journal of Criticism* 4 (1991): 199–229.

Punter, David, ed. *Introduction to Contemporary Critical Studies*. New York: Longman, 1986. See especially Punter's "Introduction: Culture and Change" 1–18, Tony Dunn's "The Evolution of Cultural Studies" 71–91, and the essay "Methods for Cultural Studies Students" by Anne Beezer, Jean Grimshaw, and Martin Barker 95–118.

Storey, John. *An Introductory Guide to Cultural Theory and Popular Culture*. Athens: U of Georgia P, 1993.

Turner, Graeme. *British Cultural Studies: An Introduction*. Boston: Unwin Hyman, 1990.

Cultural Studies:
Some Early British Examples

Hoggart, Richard. *Speaking to Each Other*. 2 vols. London: Chatto, 1970.

———. *The Uses of Literacy: Changing Patterns in English Mass Culture*. Boston: Beacon, 1961.

Thompson, E. P. *The Making of the English Working Class*. New York: Harper, 1958.

———. *William Morris: Romantic to Revolutionary*. New York: Pantheon, 1977.

Williams, Raymond. *Culture and Society, 1780–1950*. 1958. New York: Harper, 1966.

———. *The Long Revolution*. New York: Columbia UP, 1961.

Cultural Studies:
Continental and Marxist Influences

Althusser, Louis. *For Marx*. Trans. Ben Brewster. New York: Pantheon, 1969.

———. "Ideology and Ideological State Apparatuses." *Lenin and Philosophy*. Trans. Ben Brewster. New York: Monthly Review P, 1971. 127–86.

Althusser, Louis, and Étienne Balibar. *Reading Capital*. Trans. Ben Brewster. New York: Pantheon, 1971.

Bakhtin, Mikhail. *The Dialogic Imagination: Four Essays*. Ed. Michael Holquist. Trans. Caryl Emerson. Austin: U of Texas P, 1981.

———. *Rabelais and His World*. Trans. Hélène Iswolsky. Cambridge: MIT P, 1968.

Baudrillard, Jean. *Simulations*. Trans. Paul Foss, Paul Patton, and Philip Beitchnan. 1981. New York: Semiotext(e), 1983.

Benjamin, Walter. *Illuminations*. Ed. with intro. Hannah Arendt. Trans. Harry H. Zohn. New York: Harcourt, 1968.

Bennett, Tony. "Marxism and Popular Fiction." Humm, Stigant, and Widdowson 237–65.

Bourdieu, Pierre. *Distinction: A Social Critique of the Judgment of Taste*. Trans. Richard Nice. Cambridge: Harvard UP, 1984.

de Certeau, Michel. *The Practice of Everyday Life*. Trans. Steven F. Rendall. Berkeley: U of California P, 1984.

Foucault, Michel. *Discipline and Punish: The Birth of the Prison*. Trans. Alan Sheridan. New York: Pantheon, 1978.

———. *The History of Sexuality*. Trans. Robert Hurley. Vol. 1. New York: Pantheon, 1978.

Gramsci, Antonio. *Selections from the Prison Notebooks*. Ed. Quintin Hoare and Geoffrey Nowell Smith. New York: International, 1971.

Modern Cultural Studies:
Selected British and American Examples

Bagdikian, Ben H. *The Media Monopoly*. Boston: Beacon, 1983.

Bowlby, Rachel. *Shopping with Freud*. New York: Routledge, 1993.

Chambers, Iain. *Popular Culture: The Metropolitan Experience*. New York: Methuen, 1986.

Colls, Robert, and Philip Dodd, eds. *Englishness: Politics and Culture, 1880–1920*. London: Croom Helm, 1986.

Denning, Michael. *Mechanic Accents: Dime Novels and Working-Class Culture in America.* New York: Verso, 1987.

Fiske, John. "British Cultural Studies and Television." *Channels of Discourse: Television and Contemporary Criticism.* Ed. Robert C. Allen. Chapel Hill: U of North Carolina P, 1987.

————. *Television Culture.* New York: Methuen, 1987.

Hebdige, Dick. *Hiding the Light: On Images and Things.* New York: Routledge, 1988.

————. *Subculture: The Meaning of Style.* London: Methuen, 1979.

Huyssen, Andreas. *After the Great Divide: Modernism, Mass Culture, Postmodernism.* Bloomington: Indiana UP, 1986.

Marcus, Greil. *Dead Elvis: A Chronicle of a Cultural Obsession.* New York: Doubleday, 1991.

————. *Lipstick Traces: A Secret History of the Twentieth Century.* Cambridge: Harvard UP, 1989.

Modleski, Tania. *Loving with a Vengeance: Mass-Produced Fantasies for Women.* Hamden: Archon, 1982.

Poovey, Mary. *Uneven Developments: The Ideological Work of Gender in Mid-Victorian England.* Chicago: U of Chicago P, 1988.

Radway, Janice A. *Reading the Romance: Women, Patriarchy, and Popular Literature.* Chapel Hill: U of North Carolina P, 1984.

Reed, T. V. *Fifteen Jugglers, Five Believers: Literary Politics and the Poetics of American Social Movements.* Berkeley: U of California P, 1992.

Ethnic and Minority Criticism, Postcolonial Studies

Anzaldúa, Gloria. *Borderlands: La Frontera = The New Mestiza.* San Francisco: Spinsters/Aunt Lute, 1987.

Baker, Houston. *Blues, Ideology, and Afro-American Literature: A Vernacular Theory.* Chicago: U of Chicago P, 1984.

————. *The Journey Back: Issues in Black Literature and Criticism.* Chicago: U of Chicago P, 1980.

Bhabha, Homi K. *The Location of Culture.* New York: Routledge, 1994.

————, ed. *Nation and Narration.* New York: Routledge, 1990.

————. "Postcolonial Criticism." *Redrawing the Boundaries: The Transformation of English and American Literary Studies.* Ed. Stephen Greenblatt and Giles Gunn. New York: MLA, 1992. 437–65.

Brantlinger, Patrick. *Rule of Darkness: British Literature and Imperialism, 1830–1914.* Ithaca: Cornell UP, 1988.

Gates, Henry Louis, Jr. *Black Literature and Literary Theory.* New York: Methuen, 1984.

———, ed. *"Race," Writing, and Difference.* Chicago: U of Chicago P, 1986.

Gayle, Addison. *The Black Aesthetic.* Garden City: Doubleday, 1971.

———. *The Way of the New World: The Black Novel in America.* Garden City: Doubleday, 1975.

JanMohamed, Abdul. *Manichean Aesthetics: The Politics of Literature in Colonial Africa.* Amherst: U of Massachusetts P, 1983.

JanMohamed, Abdul, and David Lloyd, eds. *The Nature and Context of Minority Discourse.* New York: Oxford UP, 1991.

Kaplan, Amy, and Donald E. Pease, eds. *Cultures of United States Imperialism.* Durham: Duke UP, 1983.

Neocolonialism. Special issue, *Oxford Literary Review* 13 (1991).

Said, Edward. *After the Last Sky: Palestinian Lives.* New York: Pantheon, 1986.

———. *Culture and Imperialism.* New York: Knopf, 1993.

———. *Orientalism.* New York: Pantheon, 1978.

———. *The World, the Text, and the Critic.* Cambridge: Harvard UP, 1983.

Spivak, Gayatri Chakravorty. *In Other Worlds: Essays in Cultural Politics.* New York: Methuen, 1987.

Stepto, Robert B. *From Behind the Veil: A Study of Afro-American Narrative.* Urbana: U of Illinois P, 1979.

Young, Robert. *White Mythologies: Writing, History, and the West.* London: Routledge, 1990.

Cultural Studies of *Heart of Darkness*

Bongie, Chris. "Exotic Nostalgia: Conrad and the New Imperialism." *Macropolitics of Nineteenth-Century Literature: Nationalism, Exoticism, Imperialism.* Ed. Jonathan Arac and Harriet Ritvo. Philadelphia: U of Pennsylvania P, 1991.

Greiff, Louis K. "Soldier, Sailor, Surfer, Chef: Conrad's Ethics and the Margins of *Apocalypse Now.*" *Literature/Film Quarterly* 20 (1992): 188–98.

Hamner, Robert D., ed. *Joseph Conrad: Third World Perspectives.* Washington: Three Continents, 1990.

McClure, John A. "Late Imperial Romance." *Raritan* 10 (1991): 111–30.

Ruppel, Richard. "*Heart of Darkness* and the Popular Exotic Stories of the 1890s." *Conradiana* 21 (1989): 3–14.

Shetty, Sandya. "*Heart of Darkness:* Out of Africa Some New Thing Never Comes." *Journal of Modern Literature* 15 (1989): 461–74.

A CULTURAL PERSPECTIVE

PATRICK BRANTLINGER

Heart of Darkness:
Anti-Imperialism, Racism, or Impressionism?

In a 1975 lecture at the University of Massachusetts, Nigerian novelist Chinua Achebe attacked *Heart of Darkness* as "racist." Conrad "projects the image of Africa as 'the other world,' the antithesis of Europe and therefore of civilization, a place where man's vaunted intelligence and refinement are finally mocked by triumphant bestiality" (Achebe 783). Supposedly the great demystifier, Conrad is instead a "purveyor of comforting myths" (Achebe 784) and even "a bloody racist" (788). Achebe adds: "That this simple truth is glossed over in criticisms of his work is due to the fact that white racism against Africa is such a normal way of thinking that its manifestations go completely undetected" (788). Achebe would therefore like to strike Conrad's novella from the curriculum, where it has been one of the most frequently taught works of modern fiction in English classes from Chicago to Bombay to Johannesburg.

Achebe's diatribe has provoked a number of vigorous defenses of *Heart of Darkness*, which predictably stress Conrad's critical stance toward imperialism and also the wide acceptance of racist language and categories in the late Victorian period. Cedric Watts, for example, argues that "really Conrad and Achebe are on the same side" (204). Achebe simply gets carried away by his understandable aversion to racial stereotyping. "Far from being a 'purveyor of comforting myths,'" Watts declares, "Conrad most deliberately and incisively debunks such myths" (197). Acknowledging that Conrad employed the stereotypic language common in his day, Watts contends that he nevertheless rose above racism:

Achebe notes with indignation that Conrad (in the "Author's Note" to *Victory*) speaks of an encounter with a "buck nigger" in Haiti which gave him an impression of mindless violence. Achebe might as well have noted the reference in *The Nigger of the "Narcissus"*. . . . to a "tormented and flattened face — a face pathetic and brutal: the tragic, the mysterious, the repulsive mask of a nigger's soul." He might have noted, also, that Conrad's letters are sprinkled with casual anti-Semitic references. It is the same in the letters of his friend [R. B. Cunninghame] Graham. Both Conrad and Graham were influenced by the climate of prejudice of their times. . . . What is interesting is that the best work of both men seems to transcend such prejudice. (208)

Their work "transcends prejudice," Watts believes, partly because they both attack imperialism. Watts is one of the many critics who interpret *Heart of Darkness* as an exposé of imperialist rapacity and violence. Kurtz's career in deviltry obviously undermines imperialist ideology, and the greed of the "faithless pilgrims" — the white sub-Kurtzes, so to speak — is perhaps worse. "The conquest of the earth," Marlow declares, "which mostly means the taking it away from those who have a different complexion or slightly flatter noses than ourselves, is not a pretty thing when you look into it too much" (p. 21). There is nothing equivocal about that remark; Conrad entertained no illusions about imperialist violence. But Marlow distinguishes between British imperialism and that of the other European powers: the red parts of the map are good to see, he says, "because one knows that some real work is done in there" (p. 24). *Heart of Darkness* is specifically about what Conrad saw in King Leopold's African empire in 1890; the extent to which his critique can be generalized to imperialism beyond the Congo is unclear.

The politics of Conrad's story are complicated by its ambiguous style. I will use "impressionism" as a highly inadequate term to refer to its language and narrative structure, in part because Fredric Jameson uses it in his diagnosis of the "schizophrenic" nature of *Lord Jim* (219). Conrad's "impressionism" is for some critics his most praiseworthy quality, while for others it appears instead to be a means of obfuscation, allowing him to mask his "nihilism," or to maintain contradictory values, or both. Interpretations of *Heart of Darkness* that read it as only racist (and therefore imperialist), or conversely as only anti-imperialist (and therefore antiracist), inevitably founder on its "impressionism." To point only to the most obvious difficulty, the narrative frame filters everything that is said not just through Marlow, but also through the anonymous primary narrator. At what point is it safe to assume that Conrad/Marlow express a single point of view? And even supposing that Marlow speaks directly for Conrad, does Conrad/ Marlow agree with the values expressed by the primary narrator? Whatever the answers, *Heart of Darkness*, I believe, offers a powerful critique of at least certain manifestations of imperialism and racism, at the same time that it presents that critique in ways that can only be characterized as both imperialist and racist. "Impressionism" is the fragile skein of discourse that expresses — or disguises — this "schizophrenic" contradiction as an apparently harmonious whole.

I

In *Conrad and Imperialism* (1983), Benita Parry argues that "by revealing the disjunctions between high-sounding rhetoric and sordid ambitions and indicating the purposes and goals of a civilisation dedicated to global . . . hegemony, Conrad's writings [are] more destructive of imperialism's ideological premises than [are] the polemics of his contemporary opponents of empire" (10). Perhaps. It is at least certain that Conrad was appalled by the "high-sounding rhetoric" that had been used to mask the "sordid ambitions" of King Leopold II of Belgium, Conrad's ultimate employer during his six months in the Congo in 1890. *Heart of Darkness* expresses not only what Conrad saw and partially recorded in his "Congo Diary," but also the revelations of atrocities that began appearing in the British press as early as 1888 and that reached a climax twenty years later, when in 1908 the mounting scandal forced the Belgian government to take control of Leopold's private domain. During that period the population of the Congo was reduced by perhaps one half; as many as 6,000,000 persons may have been uprooted, tortured, and murdered through the forced labor system used to extract ivory and what reformers called "red rubber."[1] Conrad was sympathetic to the Congo Reform Association, established in 1903 partly by his friend Roger Casement whom he had met in Africa, and Casement got him to write a propaganda letter in which Conrad says: "It is an extraordinary thing that the conscience of Europe which seventy years ago . . . put down the slave trade on humanitarian grounds tolerates the Congo state today" (Morel, *Rule* 351–52). There follows some patronizing language contrasting the

---

[1] For a history of British humanitarian protest against Leopold's policies, see S. J. Cookey, *Britain and the Congo Question, 1885–1913* (London: Longman, 1968).

brutalities visited upon the Congolese with the legal protections given to horses in Europe, but Conrad's intention is clear enough.

There is little to add to Hunt Hawkins's account of Conrad's relations with the Congo Reform Association. Its leader, Edmund Morel, who quoted Conrad's letter to Casement in *King Leopold's Rule in Africa* (1904), called *Heart of Darkness* the "most powerful thing ever written on the subject" (Hawkins 293). But as Hawkins notes, apart from writing the letter to Casement, Conrad backed away from involvement with the Association. Other prominent novelists who'd never been to the Congo contributed as much or more to its work. Mark Twain volunteered "King Leopold's Soliloquy," and Sir Arthur Conan Doyle wrote a book for the Association called *The Crime of the Congo*. Hawkins notes that Conrad "had little faith in agitation for political reform because words were meaningless, human nature unimprovable, and the universe dying" — hardly views that would encourage engagement in a cause like that of the Association (292–93).

All the same, in at least one other work of fiction Conrad registered his abhorrence of King Leopold's rape of the Congo. This is the minor but highly revealing fantasy that Conrad coauthored with Ford Madox Hueffer, *The Inheritors: An Extravagant Story* (1901). Conrad's role in its writing may have been slight, but was still substantial enough to make plain that he shared the views expressed in it. Briefly, the protagonist meets a beautiful young woman who claims to come from the "fourth dimension" and to be one of those who "shall inherit the earth."

> The Dimensionists were to come in swarms, to materialise, to devour like locusts. . . . They were to come like snow in the night: in the morning one would look out and find the world white. . . . As to methods, we should be treated as we ourselves treat the inferior races. (Conrad and Hueffer 16)

Far from being meek, the "inheritors" are obviously modern-day imperialists, satirically depicted as invaders from a "spiritualist" alternative world. But apart from the young woman and one other character, the invasion does not occur during the course of the novel, although the satire upon imperialism is maintained through the portrayal of the Duc de Mersch and his "System for the Regeneration of the Arctic Regions" (46). Like King Leopold, "the foreign financier — they called him the Duc de Mersch — was by way of being a philanthropist on megalomaniac lines." He proves ultimately to be no philanthropist at all, but just the sort of "gigantic and atrocious fraud" that Conrad believed Leopold to be. All one needs to do to read *The Inheritors* as an attack on Leopold's African regime is to substitute "Congo" for "Greenland." The hero, journalist Arthur Granger, helps to expose "the real horrors of the système Groënlandais — flogged, butchered, miserable natives, the famines, the vices, diseases, and the crimes" (280). The authors are not even particular about the color of the Eskimo victims: one character says that the Duc "has the blacks murdered" (246–74).

Hueffer and Conrad write some scorching things in *The Inheritors* about "cruelty to the miserable, helpless, and defenceless" (282). But the facts of exploitation in the Congo are perhaps less distressing to them than the lying idealism which disguises it:

> More revolting to see without a mask was that falsehood which had been hiding under the words which for ages had spurred men to noble deeds, to self-sacrifice, to heroism. What was appalling was . . . that all the traditional ideals of honour, glory, conscience, had been committed to the upholding of a gigantic and atrocious fraud. The falsehood had spread stealthily, had eaten into the very heart of creeds and convictions that we learn upon our passage between the past and the future. The old order of things had to live or perish with a lie. (282)

I will come back to the possibility that the worst feature of imperialism for Conrad may not have been its violence toward the "miserable" and "helpless," but the lying propaganda used to cover its bloody tracks.

As Hawkins and others have pointed out, Conrad did not base his critique of imperialist exploitation in *Heart of Darkness* solely on what he had seen in the Congo. What he witnessed was miserable enough, and he was also made personally miserable and resentful by disease and the conviction that his Belgian employers were exploiting him. But, as he assured Casement, while in the Congo he had not even heard of "the alleged custom of cutting off hands among the natives" (Morel, *Rule* 117). The conclusion that Casement drew from this and other evidence was that most of the cruelties practiced in the Congo were not traditional, but were the recent effects of exploitation. The cutting off of hands was a punishment for noncooperation in Leopold's forced labor system, and probably became frequent only after 1890. And just as Conrad had seen little or no evidence of torture, so, Molly Mahood conjectures, he probably saw little or no evidence of cannibalism, despite the stress upon it in his story (Mahood 12).

It thus seems likely that much of the "horror" either depicted or suggested in *Heart of Darkness* does not represent what Conrad saw, but rather his reading of the literature that exposed Leopold's bloody system between the time of his return to England and the composition of the novella in 1898–99. While Conrad's "Congo Diary" and every facet of his journey to Stanley Falls and back has been scrutinized by Norman Sherry and others, much less attention has been paid to what Conrad learned about the Congo after his sojourn there. The exposé literature undoubtedly confirmed suspicions which Conrad formed in 1890; the bloodiest period in the history of Leopold's regime began about a year later. According to Edmund Morel: "From 1890 onwards the records of the Congo State have been literally blood-soaked. Even at that early date, the real complexion of Congo State philanthropy was beginning to appear, but public opinion in Europe was then in its hoodwinked stage" (*Rule* 103).

The two events that did most to bring Leopold's Congo under public scrutiny after Conrad's time there were the 1891–94 war between Leopold's forces and the Arab slave-traders and the murder of Charles Stokes, English citizen and renegade missionary, by Belgian officials in 1895. The conflict with the Arabs — a "war of extermination," according to Morel — was incredibly cruel and bloody. "The first serious collision with the Arabs occurred in October 27, 1891; the second on May 6, 1892. Battle then succeeded battle; Nyangwe, the Arab stronghold, was captured in January, 1893, and with the surrender of Rumaliza in January, 1894, the campaign came to an end" (*Rule* 23). Conrad undoubtedly read about these events in the press and perhaps also in later accounts, notably Captain Sidney Hinde's *The Fall of the Congo Arabs* (1897). Arthur Hodister, whom Sherry claims as the original of Kurtz, was an early victim of the fighting, having led an expedition to Katanga that was crushed by the Arabs. According to Ian Watt, "*The Times* reported of Hodister and his comrades that 'their heads were stuck on poles and their bodies eaten'" (23). This and many similar episodes during the war are probable sources of Conrad's emphasis upon cannibalism in *Heart of Darkness.*

Cannibalism was practiced by both sides in the war, not just by the Arabs and their Congolese soldiers. According to Hinde, who must also be counted among the possible models for Kurtz, "The fact that both sides were cannibals, or rather that both sides had cannibals in their train, proved a great element in our success" (124–25). Muslims, Hinde points out, believe that they will go to heaven only if their bodies are intact, as opposed to mutilated, chopped up, eaten. So cannibalism was in part a weapon of fear and reprisal on both sides, and in part also a traditional accompaniment of war among some Congolese societies. Hinde speaks of combatants on both sides as "human wolves" and describes numerous "disgusting banquets" (69). A typical passage in his account reads: "What struck me most in these expeditions was the number of partially cut-up bodies I found in every direction for miles around. Some were minus the hands and feet, and some with steaks cut from the thighs or elsewhere; others had the entrails or the head removed, according to the taste of the individual savage . . ." (131). Hinde's descriptions of such atrocities seem to be those of an impartial, external observer, but in fact he was one of six white officers in charge of some four hundred "regulars" and "about 25,000" "cannibal" troops. His expressions of horror seem only what are expected of an Englishman, but they are also those of a participant and contradict more honest expressions of sadistic fascination with every bloodthirsty detail.

While it seems likely that Conrad read Hinde's lurid account, he must have known about the war from earlier accounts such as those in *The Times*. To cite one other example, in a series of journal extracts published in *The Century Magazine* in 1896–97, E. J. Glave documented "cruelty in the Congo Free State." According to Glave, "The state has not suppressed slavery, but established a monopoly by driving out the Arab and Wangwana competitors." Instead of a noble war to end the slave trade, which is how Leopold and his agents justified their actions against the Arabs, a new system of slavery was installed in place of the old. Glave continues: "sometimes the natives are so persecuted that they [take revenge] by killing and eating their tormentors. Recently the state post on the Lomami lost two men killed and eaten by the natives. Arabs were sent to punish the natives; many women and children were taken, and twenty-one heads were brought to [Stanley Falls], and have been used by Captain Rom as a decoration round a flower-bed in front of his house" (706). Captain Rom, no doubt, must also be counted among the possible models for Kurtz. In any event, the practice of seizing Congolese for laborers and chopping off the hands and heads of resisters continued and probably increased after the defeat of the Arabs, as numerous eyewitnesses testify in the grisly quotations that form the bulk of Edmund Morel's exposés. According to a quite typical account by a Swiss observer: "If the chief does not bring the stipulated number of baskets [of raw rubber], soldiers are sent out, and the people are killed without mercy. As proof, parts of the body are brought to the factory. How often have I watched heads and hands being carried into the factory" (Morel, *Rubber* 77).

II

When Marlow declares that "the conquest of the earth . . . is not a pretty thing," he goes on to suggest that imperialism may be "redeemed" by the "idea" that lies behind it. But in the real world idealism is fragile, and in *Heart of Darkness,* except for the illusions maintained by a few womenfolk back in Brussels, it has almost died out. In "going native," Kurtz betrays the "civilizing" ideals with which he supposedly set out from Europe. Among the "faithless pilgrims," there are only false ideals and the false religion of self-seeking. "To tear treasure out of the bowels of the land was their desire," says Marlow, "with no more moral purpose at the back of it than there is in burglars breaking into a safe" (p. 46). The true nature of European philanthropy in the Congo is revealed to Marlow by the chain gang and the "black shadows of disease and starvation," left to die in the "greenish gloom," whom he sees at the Outer Station (p. 32). These miserable "phantoms" are probably accurate depictions of what Conrad saw in 1890; they may also be taken to represent what he later learned about Leopold's forced labor system. In any case, from the moment he sets foot in the Congo, Marlow is clear about the meaning of "the merry dance of death and trade" (p. 29). It thus makes perfect sense to interpret *Heart of Darkness* as an attack on imperialism, at least as it was operative in the Congo.

But in the course of this attack, *all* "ideals" threaten to turn into "idols" — "something," in Marlow's words, that "you can set up, and bow down before, and offer a sacrifice to" (p. 21). Conrad universalizes "darkness" partly by universalizing fetishism. Lenin, Rosa Luxemburg, and other Marxist critics of empire described the era of "the scramble for Africa" — roughly 1880 to 1914 — as one when the "commodity fetishism" of "late capitalism" was most intense, a notion that Edward Said touches upon in analyzing *The Nigger of the "Narcissus"* (142–43). If the "natives" in their darkness set Kurtz up as an idol, the Europeans worship ivory, money, power, reputation. Kurtz joins the "natives" in their "unspeakable rites," worshipping his own unrestrained power and lust. Marlow himself assumes the pose of an idol, sitting on shipdeck with folded legs and outward palms like a Buddha. And Kurtz's Intended is perhaps the greatest fetishist of all, idolizing her image of her fiance. Marlow's lie leaves Kurtz's Intended shrouded in the protective darkness of her illusions, her idol-worship.

But the difficulty with this ingenious inversion, through which "ideals" become "idols," is that Conrad portrays the moral bankruptcy

of imperialism by showing European motives and actions to be no better than African fetishism and savagery. He paints Kurtz and Africa
with the same tarbrush. His version of evil — the form taken by
Kurtz's Satanic behavior — is "going native." In short, evil *is* African
in Conrad's story; if it is also European, that's because some number
of white men in the heart of darkness behave like Africans. Conrad's
stress on cannibalism, his identification of African customs with violence, lust, and madness, his metaphors of bestiality, death, and darkness, his suggestion that traveling in Africa is like traveling backward in
time to primeval, infantile, but also hellish stages of existence — these
features of the story are drawn from the repertoire of Victorian imperialism and racism that painted an entire continent dark.

Achebe is therefore right to call Conrad's portrayal of Africa and
Africans "racist." It is possible to argue, as does Parry, that Conrad
works with the white-and-black, light-and-darkness dichotomies of
racist fantasy in order to subvert them, but she acknowledges that
the subversion is incomplete: "Although the resonances of white are
rendered discordant . . . black and dark do serve in the text as
equivalences for the savage and unredeemed, the corrupt and degraded . . . the cruel and atrocious. Imperialism itself is perceived as
the dark within Europe. . . . Yet despite . . . momentous departures
from traditional European usage . . . the fiction gravitates back to established practice, registering the view of two incompatible orders
within a manichean universe" (23). The "imperialist imagination" itself, Parry suggests, works with the "manichean," irreconcilable polari-
ties common to all racist ideology. Achebe states the issue more succinctly: "Conrad had a problem with niggers. . . . Sometimes his
fixation on blackness is . . . overwhelming" (789).

Identifying specific sources for Conrad's later knowledge of the
horrors of Leopold's regime is less important than recognizing that
there were numerous sources, swelling in number through the 1890s.
Conrad reshaped his firsthand experience of the Congo in the light of
these sources in several ways. As I have already suggested, the emphasis on cannibalism in *Heart of Darkness* probably derives in part from
Conrad's reading about the war between Leopold's agents and the
Arabs. At the same time, the war is not mentioned in the novella —
indeed, the Arab rivals of the Belgians for control of the Congo are
conspicuous only by their absence. The omission has the important effect of sharpening the light-and-dark dichotomies, the staple of European racism; "evil" and "darkness" are parceled out between only two
antithetical sides, European and African, "white" and "black." But

while Conrad/Marlow treats the attribution of "evil" to the European invaders as a paradox, its attribution to Africans he treats as a given. Further, the omission of the Arabs means that Conrad does not treat cannibalism as a result of war, but as an everyday custom of the Congolese, even though he probably saw no evidence of it when he was there. Exaggerating the extent and nature of cannibalism is also standard in racist accounts of Africa.

In simplifying his memories and sources, Conrad arrived at the dichotomous or "manichean" pattern of the imperialist adventure romance, a pattern radically at odds with any realist, exposé intention. Perhaps *Heart of Darkness* expresses two irreconcilable intentions. As Parry says, "to proffer an interpretation of *Heart of Darkness* as a militant denunciation and a reluctant affirmation of imperialist civilisation, as a fiction that [both] exposes and colludes in imperialism's mystifications, is to recognise its immanent contradictions" (39). Moreover, the argument that Conrad was consciously anti-imperialist, but that he unconsciously or carelessly employed the racist terminology current in his day will not stand up, because he was acutely aware of what he was doing. Every white-black and light-dark contrast in the story, whether it corroborates racist assumptions or subverts them, is precisely calculated for its effects both as a unit in a scheme of imagery and as a focal point in a complex web of contradictory political and moral values.

Conrad knew that his story was ambiguous: he stresses that ambiguity at every opportunity, so that labeling it "anti-imperialist" is as unsatisfactory as condemning it for being "racist." The fault-line for all of the contradictions and ambiguities in the text lies between Marlow and Kurtz. Of course it also lies between Conrad and both of his ambivalent characters, not to mention the anonymous primary narrator. Is Marlow Kurtz's antagonist, critic, and potential redeemer? Or is he Kurtz's pale shadow and admirer, his double, and finally one more idolator in a story full of examples of fetishism and devil worship? Conrad poses these questions with great care, but he just as carefully refuses to answer them.

III

In the world of *Heart of Darkness,* there are no clear answers. Ambiguity, perhaps the main form of "darkness" in the story, prevails. Conrad overlays the political and moral content of his novella with symbolic and mythic patterns that divert attention from Kurtz and the Congo to "misty halos" and "moonshine." The anonymous narrator

uses these metaphors to describe the difference between Marlow's stories and those of ordinary sailors:

> The yarns of seamen have a direct simplicity, the whole meaning
> of which lies within the shell of a cracked nut. But Marlow was
> not typical . . . and to him the meaning of an episode was not in-
> side like a kernel but outside, enveloping the tale which brought it
> out only as a glow brings out a haze, in the likeness of one of
> these misty halos that sometimes are made visible by the spectral
> illumination of moonshine. (pp. 19–20)

The passage announces that locating the "meaning" of the story won't
be easy, and in fact may be impossible. It seems almost to be a confession of defeat, or at least of contradiction. Conrad here establishes
as one of his themes the problem of rendering any judgment whatso-
ever — moral, political, metaphysical — about Marlow's narrative. It is
precisely this complexity — a theme that might be labeled the disloca-
tion of meaning or the disorientation of values in the story — that
many critics have treated as its finest feature.

In *The Political Unconscious,* Fredric Jameson argues that Conrad's
stories — *Lord Jim* is his main example — betray a symptomatic split
between a modernist "will to style," leading to an elaborate but essentially hollow "impressionism," and the reified, mass culture tendencies
of romance conventions. In a fairly obvious way, *Heart of Darkness* betrays the same split, moving in one direction toward the "misty halos"
and "moonshine" of a style that seeks to be its own meaning, apart
from any "kernel" or center or embarrassingly clear content, but also
grounding itself in another direction in the conventions of Gothic romance with their devalued mass culture status — conventions that
were readily adapted to the heroic adventure themes of imperialist propaganda. This split almost corresponds to the contradiction of an anti-
imperialist novel which is also racist. In the direction of high style, the
story acquires several serious purposes, apparently including its critique
of empire. In the direction of reified mass culture, it falls into the
stereotypic patterns of race-thinking common to the entire tradition of
the imperialist adventure story or quest romance. This double, contradictory purpose, characteristic perhaps of all of Conrad's fiction, Jameson calls "schizophrenic" (219).

By "the manichaeanism of the imperialist imagination," Parry
means dividing the world between "warring moral forces" — good
versus evil, civilization versus savagery, West versus East, light versus
darkness, white versus black. Such polarizations are the common

property of the racism and authoritarianism that constitute imperialist
political theory and also of the Gothic romance conventions that were
appropriated by numerous writers of imperialist adventure tales —
G. A. Henty, Rider Haggard, Robert Louis Stevenson, Conan Doyle,
John Buchan, Rudyard Kipling, and Conrad among them. As Martin
Green points out, "Conrad of course offers us an ironic view of that
genre. But he affirms its value" (219). Conrad is simultaneously a
critic of the imperialist adventure and its romantic fictions, and one of
the greatest writers of such fictions, his greatness deriving partly from
his critical irony and partly from the complexity of his style — his "impressionism." But the chief difficulty with Jameson's argument, I
think, is that the "will to style" in Conrad's text is also a will to appropriate and remake Gothic romance conventions into high art. On
some level, the "impressionism" of Conrad's novels and their romance
features are identical — Conrad constructs a sophisticated version of
the imperialist romance — and in any case both threaten to submerge
or "derealize" the critique of empire within their own more strictly es-
thetic project. As part of that project, providing much of the substance
of "impressionism," the romance conventions that Conrad reshapes
carry with them the polarizations of racist thought.

In analyzing Conrad's "schizophrenic writing," Jameson notes the
proliferation of often contradictory critical opinions that mark the history of his reception: "The discontinuities objectively present in Conrad's narratives have, as with few other modern writers, projected a bewildering variety of competing and incommensurable interpretive
options. . . ." Jameson proceeds to list nine different critical approaches, from "the 'romance' or mass-cultural reading of Conrad as a
writer of adventure tales [and] the stylistic analysis of Conrad as a practi-
tioner of . . . [an] 'impressionistic' will to style," to the "myth-critical,"
the Freudian, the ethical, the "ego-psychological," the existential, the
Nietzschean, and the structuralist readings. Jameson leaves off of the list
his own Marxist-political reading; what he wishes to suggest is how
often criticism ignores or downplays the contradictory politics of Conrad's fiction (208–09). Raymond Williams voices a similar complaint:

> It is . . . astonishing that a whole school of criticism has succeeded
> in emptying *Heart of Darkness* of its social and historical con-
> tent. . . . The Congo of Leopold follows the sea that Dombey
> and Son traded across, follows it into an endless substitution in
> which no object is itself, no social experience direct, but ev-
> erything is translated into what can be called a metaphysical
> language — the river is Evil; the sea is Love or Death. Yet only

called metaphysical, because there is not even that much guts in it.
No profound and ordinary belief, only a perpetual and sophisticated evasion. . . . (145)

There are wonderfully elaborate readings of Marlow's journey as a descent into hell, playing upon Conrad's frequent allusions to Homer,
Virgil, Dante, Milton, Goethe, and devil worship. And there are just as
many elaborate readings of the story as an "inward voyage" of "self-
discovery," in which its geopolitical language is treated as symbolizing
psychological states and parts of the mind. Conrad, Albert Guerard reminds us, was Freud's contemporary, and in *Heart of Darkness* he produced the quintessential "night journey into the unconscious" (39).
Guerard adds that "it little matters what, in terms of psychological
symbolism, we . . . say [Kurtz] represents: whether the Freudian id or
the Jungian shadow or more vaguely the outlaw" (39). Perhaps it matters just as little whether we say the story takes place in Leopold's
Congo or in some purely imaginary landscape.

The point, however, is not to take issue with Guerard and other
critics who concentrate on the "impressionism" of Conrad's story, but
rather to restore what their readings neglect. In a great deal of contemporary criticism, words themselves have ceased to have external refer-
ents. Williams does not take Jameson's line in accusing Conrad's "will
to style" of emptying *Heart of Darkness* of its "social and historical
content"; instead, he accuses criticism of so emptying it. The "will to
style" — or rather the will to a rarefied critical intelligence — devours
us, too, leaving structuralists and deconstructionists, Althusserians and
Foucauldians, and so forth. And yet Conrad has anticipated his critics
by constructing a story in which the "meaning" does not lie at the center, not even at "the heart of darkness," but elsewhere, in "misty
halos" and "moonshine" — forever beyond some vertiginous horizon
which recedes as the would-be critic-adventurer sails toward it.

IV

The crowds [in one village] were fired into promiscuously, and fifteen were killed, including four women and a babe on its mother's
breast. The heads were cut off and brought to the officer in
charge, who then sent men to cut off the hands also, and these
were pierced, strung, and dried over the camp fire. The heads,
with many others, I saw myself. The town, prosperous once, was
burnt, and what they could not carry off was destroyed. Crowds of
people were caught, mostly . . . women, and three fresh rope

gangs were added. These poor 'prisoner' gangs were mere skeletons of skin and bone. . . . Chiyombo's very large town was next attacked. A lot of people were killed, and heads and hands cut off and taken back to the officers. . . . Shortly after the State caravans, with flags flying and bugles blowing, entered the mission station at Luanza . . . and I shall not soon forget the sickening sight of deep baskets of human heads. (Morel, *Rubber* 49)

While the primary narrator and many critics seem to believe that the meaning of *Heart of Darkness* lies in "the spectral illumination of moonshine," Marlow knows better. "Illumination" proves as false as most white men — as false as white "civilization"; the "truth," or at least the meaning of Conrad's story, lies in "darkness." That is why, once Marlow learns about the shadowy Kurtz, he is so impatient to get to the Central Station. And yet Kurtz seems inadequate as a central character or the goal of Marlow's quest — vacuous, a mere "shade," a "hollow man." That, however, may be part of Conrad's point. Ian Watt has identified at least nine possible models for Kurtz, including Henry Morton Stanley, Arthur Hodister, and Charles Stokes, who left the Church Missionary Society for an African wife and life as a gun-runner and slave-trader (Watt 141–45). In 1895 Stokes was executed in the Congo for selling guns to the Arabs, an event which, close on the heels of the war, provided a focus for British public indignation. To Watt's list of models for Kurtz I have already added Captain Hinde, author of *The Fall of the Congo Arabs*, and Captain Rom, who decorated the borders of his flower garden with skulls. The Belgian officer responsible for Stokes's illegal execution, Captain Lothaire, must also be counted.

But just as Conrad probably drew upon many sources in depicting the horrors of the Congo, so he probably had many models for Kurtz in mind. *All* of the white officers in charge of Leopold's empire were in essence Kurtzes, as the eyewitness testimony published by the Congo Reform Association demonstrates. And what about the eyewitnesses? Were they always so objective or so morally appalled as they claimed to be? What about Conrad himself? Although his role in the building of Leopold's "Congo Free State" was minor and also prior to the worst horrors, Conrad must have recognized his own complicity and seen himself as at least potentially a Kurtz-like figure. In the novella, the African wilderness serves as a mirror, in whose "darkness" Conrad/Marlow sees a death-pale self-image.

The massive evidence of wholesale torture and slaughter under the direction of Leopold's white agents suggests not only that there were numerous Kurtzes in the "heart of darkness," but also that, as Hannah

Arendt contends in *The Origins of Totalitarianism*, nineteenth-century imperialism prepared the ground in which fascism and Nazism took root after World War I. Arendt has Kurtz and other Conrad characters in mind when she describes the appeal of "the phantom world of colonial adventure" to certain types of Europeans:

> Outside all social restraint and hypocrisy, against the backdrop of native life, the gentleman and the criminal felt not only the closeness of men who share the same color of skin, but the impact of a world of infinite possibilities for crimes committed in the spirit of play, for the combination of horror and laughter, that is for the full realization of their own phantom-like existence. Native life lent these ghostlike events a seeming guarantee against all consequences because anyhow it looked to these men like a "mere play of shadows. A play of shadows, the dominant race could walk through unaffected and disregarded in the pursuit of its incomprehensible aims and needs." The world of native savages was a perfect setting for men who had escaped the reality of civilization. (70)

A great many Kurtz-like Europeans "went native" in Africa, often to the extent of practicing genocide as a hobby; some were even rumored to practice cannibalism. According to Sir Harry H. Johnston, first governor of British Central Africa, "I have been increasingly struck with the rapidity with which such members of the white race as are not of the best class, can throw over the restraints of civilization and develop into savages of unbridled lust and abominable cruelty" (68). Kurtz is not a member of the *worst* "class" of the white race, however; Conrad is talking about a quite common pattern of behavior.

One of the most remarkable perversions of the criticism of *Heart of Darkness* has been to see Kurtz not as an abomination — a "hollow man" with a lust for blood and domination — but as a "hero of the spirit." That phrase is Lionel Trilling's. In his well-known essay describing the establishment of the first course in modern literature at Columbia University, Trilling explains why he put Conrad's novella on the reading list:

> Whether or not . . . Conrad read either Blake or Nietzsche I do not know, but his *Heart of Darkness* follows in their line. This very great work has never lacked for the admiration it deserves, and it has been given a . . . canonical place in the legend of modern literature by Eliot's having it so clearly in mind when he wrote *The Waste Land* and his having taken from it the epigraph to "The Hollow Men." ("Modern" 17–18)

Despite the "hollow man" association between Eliot's poem and Conrad's novella, Trilling claims that "no one, to my knowledge, has ever confronted in an explicit way [the latter's] strange and terrible message of ambivalence toward the life of civilization" (17). In *Sincerity and Authenticity* (1981), Trilling adds that Conrad's story is "the paradigmatic literary expression of the modern concern with authenticity," and continues: "This troubling work has no manifest polemical content but it contains in sum the whole of the radical critique of European civilization that has been made by [modern] literature" (106).

Although Trilling mentions the Congolese background of the story, it is less important to him than the larger question of the nature of "European civilization." Marlow's quest for Kurtz becomes a quest for the truth about that civilization. Trilling arrives at his view of Kurtz partly the way Marlow does, because Kurtz at the end of his satanic career seems to confront "the horror, the horror." "For Marlow," says Trilling, "Kurtz is a hero of the spirit whom he cherishes as Theseus at Colonus cherished Oedipus: he sinned for all mankind. By his regression to savagery Kurtz had reached as far down beneath the constructs of civilization as it was possible to do, to the irreducible truth of man, the innermost core of his nature, his heart of darkness. From that Stygian authenticity comes illumination . . ." (108).

Marlow does paradoxically come to admire Kurtz because he has "summed up" or "judged" in his final moments: "He was a remarkable man" (p. 87). Marlow's admiration for Kurtz, however, carries a terrific burden of irony that Trilling seems not to recognize. Kurtz has not merely lost faith in civilization and therefore experimented with "Stygian authenticity" — he is also a murderer, perhaps even a cannibal. He has allowed his idolators to make human sacrifices in his honor and, like Captain Rom, has decorated his corner of hell with the skulls of his victims. I suspect that Trilling arrives at his own evaluation of Kurtz as a "hero of the spirit" in part because he himself does not find "the horror" all that horrible, even though the deaths of 6,000,000 Congolese is a high price to pay for the "illumination" of "Stygian authenticity." But Trilling's interpretation of Kurtz's dying words — "the horror, the horror" — does not take account of what transpired in Leopold's Congo. "For me it is still ambiguous whether Kurtz's famous deathbed cry refers to the approach of death or to his experience of savage life" (Trilling, "Modern" 18).

According to Trilling's view, either Kurtz thinks death "the horror," or Kurtz thinks African "savagery" "the horror." There is another possibility, of course, which is that Kurtz's dying words are an outcry against himself — against his betrayal of civilization and his Intended, against the smash-up of his early hopes, and also against his bloody domination of the people he has been lording it over. No one would ever mistake Conrad's other traitors to civilization as "heroes of the spirit." I am thinking, for example, of Willems who goes wrong and then "goes native" in *An Outcast of the Islands*, or of the ironically sympathetic murderer Leggatt in "The Secret Sharer." Even Lord Jim is no "hero of the spirit," but a moral cripple who manages to regain a semblance of self-respect only after fleeing to Patusan. But how was it possible for Trilling to look past Kurtz's criminal record and identify "the horror" either with the fear of death or with African "savagery"? Achebe gives part of the answer: "white racism against Africa is such a normal way of thinking that its manifestations go completely undetected" — so normal that acts that are condemned as the vilest of crimes when committed in the supposedly civilized West can be linked to a "heroism of the spirit" and to "Stygian authenticity" when committed in Africa against Africans.

But the other part of the answer, it seems to me, is that Trilling is right. Conrad himself identifies with and ironically admires Kurtz. He, too, sees him as a "hero of the spirit," although "the spirit" for Conrad is perhaps not what Trilling thinks it is. For Conrad, Kurtz's heroism consists in staring into an abyss of nihilism so total that the issues of imperialism and racism pale into insignificance. It hardly matters if the abyss is of Kurtz's making. No more than Trilling or perhaps most Western critics, I think, did Conrad concern himself deeply about "unspeakable rites" and skulls on posts. These appear in Marlow's account like so many melodrama props — the evidence of Kurtz's decline and fall, yes — but it is still Kurtz who has center stage, with whom Marlow speaks, who is the goal and farthest point of the journey. Kurtz's black victims and idolators skulking in the bushes are also so many melodrama props.

Kurtz is not only the hero of the melodrama, he is an artist, a "universal genius," and a quite powerful, eloquent "voice" as well. As Achebe points out, the African characters are, in contrast, rendered almost without intelligible language. The headman of Marlow's cannibal crew gets in a few phrases of Pidgin-minstrelese, something about eating some fellow Africans. These are the black Kurtz worshippers, shrieking and groaning incoherently in the foggy shrubbery along the river. Kurtz's "superb and savage" mistress, though described in glowing detail, is given no voice, but in spite of this I like to imagine that she, at least, entertained no illusions about Kurtz or about imperialism, unlike the prim, palefaced knitters of black wool back in Brussels. "It's queer how out of touch with truth women are" (p. 27) says Marlow, but of course he means *white* women. Kurtz's black mistress knows all; it's just unfortunate that Marlow did not ask her for an interview.

The voices that come from the "heart of darkness" are almost exclusively white and male. As a nearly disembodied, pure "voice" emanating from the very center of the story, Kurtz is a figure for the novelist, as is his double Marlow. True, the "voice" that speaks out of the "heart of darkness" is a hollow one, the voice of the abyss; but Marlow still talks of Kurtz's "unextinguishable gift of noble and lofty expression." The "voice" of Kurtz has "electrified large meetings," and through it Kurtz "could get himself to believe anything — anything" (p. 89). Is Conrad questioning or mocking his own "voice," his own talent for fiction-making, for lying? Is he aware that the "will to style," his own tendency to "impressionism," points toward the production of novels that are hollow at the core — that can justify any injustice — that contain, perhaps, only an abyss, a Kurtz, "the horror, the horror"? Yes, I think so. It is just this hollow "voice," so devious and egotistical, so capable of self-deception and lying propaganda, that speaks from the center of "the heart of darkness" to "sum up" and to "judge."

Besides a painter, musician, orator, and "universal genius," Kurtz is also, like Conrad, a writer. What he writes can be seen as an analogue for the story and also its dead center, the kernel of meaning or nonmeaning within its cracked shell. True, Kurtz has not written much, only seventeen pages, but "it was a beautiful piece of writing." This is his pamphlet for the "International Society for the Suppression of Savage Customs," which Marlow describes as "eloquent, vibrating with eloquence, but too high-strung, I think":

> The opening paragraph . . . in the light of later information, strikes me now as ominous. He began with the argument that we whites, from the point of development we had arrived at, "must necessarily appear to them [savages] in the nature of supernatural beings — we approach them with the might as of a deity," and so on, and so on. "By the simple exercise of our will we can exert a power for good practically unbounded," etc., etc. From that point he soared and took me with him. The peroration was magnificent, though difficult to remember, you know. It gave me the notion of an exotic Immensity ruled by an august Benevolence. It made me tingle with enthusiasm. This was the unbounded power of elo-

quence. [And here I will add, "This was the unbounded will to style."] . . . There were no practical hints to interrupt the magic current of phrases, unless a kind of note at the foot of the last page, scrawled evidently much later, in an unsteady hand, may be regarded as the exposition of a method. It was very simple, and at the end of that moving appeal to every altruistic sentiment it blazed at you, luminous and terrifying, like a flash of lightning in a serene sky: "Exterminate all the brutes!" (p. 66)

Viewed one way, Conrad's anti-imperialist story condemns the murderous racism of Kurtz's imperative. Viewed another way, Conrad's racist story voices that very imperative, and Conrad knows it. At the hollow center of *Heart of Darkness,* far from the "misty halos" and "moonshine" where the meaning supposedly resides, Conrad inscribes a text that, like the novel itself, cancels out its own best intentions.

But now Kurtz's dying words can be seen as something more than an outcry of guilt, and certainly more than a mere expression of the fear of death or of loathing for African "savagery." They can be seen as referring to the sort of lying idealism that can rationalize any behavior, to a complete separation between words and meaning, theory and practice — perhaps to the "impressionistic" deviousness of art and language themselves. On this metaphysical level, I think, Conrad ceases to worry about the atrocities committed in the Congo and identifies with Kurtz as a fellow-artist, a "hero of the spirit" of that nihilism that Conrad himself found so attractive.

On several occasions, Conrad compared the artist with the empire builder in a way that obviously runs counter to his critique of imperialism in *Heart of Darkness.* In *A Personal Record,* Conrad writes of "that interior world where [the novelist's] thought and . . . emotions go seeking for . . . imagined adventures," and where "there are no policemen, no law, no pressure of circumstance or dread opinion to keep him within bounds." And in the first manuscript of "The Rescuer," which as John McClure points out contains "by far" Conrad's "most sympathetic" treatment of imperialism, empire-builders are "one of those unknown guides of civilization, who on the advancing edge of progress are administrators, warriors, creators. . . . They are like great artists a mystery to the masses, appreciated only by the uninfluential few" (McClure 89–90). Kurtz is empire-builder, artist, universal genius, and voice crying from the wilderness all in one. But he has lost the faith — vision or illusion — that can alone sustain an empire and produce great art. Nihilism is no basis upon which to found or administer a colony, and it is also no basis on which to write a novel, and again Conrad knows it. In suggesting his affinity to Kurtz, he suggests the moral bankruptcy of his own literary project. But once there were empire-builders and great artists who kept the faith. Conrad frequently expresses his admiration for the great explorers and adventurers, from Sir Walter Raleigh and Sir Francis Drake through James Brooke, the white rajah of Sarawak, and David Livingstone, the greatest of the many great explorers of the "Dark Continent."

Conrad's critique of empire is never strictly anti-imperialist. Instead, in terms that can be construed as conservative rather than nihilistic, he mourns the loss of the truth faith in modern times, the closing down of frontiers, the narrowing of the possibilities for adventure, the commercialization of the world and of art, the death of chivalry and honor. Here the meaning of his emphasis on the lying propaganda of modern imperialism becomes evident. What was once a true, grand, noble, albeit violent enterprise is now "a gigantic and atrocious fraud" — except maybe, Marlow thinks, in the red parts of the map, where "some real work is done." Staring into the abyss of his life, or at least of Kurtz's life, Conrad sees in his disillusionment, his nihilism, the type of the whole — the path of disintegration that is modern history. It is not just Africa or even just Kurtz who possesses a "heart of darkness"; Conrad's story bears that title as well.

But I am not going to end by announcing in "a tone of scathing contempt" the death of Conrad's story as a classic, like the insolent manager's boy announcing: "Mistah Kurtz — he dead." I agree with Trilling that "authenticity," truth-telling, so far from being a negligible literary effect, is the essence of great literature. The fact that there are almost no other works of British fiction written before World War I that are critical of imperialism, and hundreds of imperialist ones that are racist through and through, is a measure of Conrad's achievement. I do not believe, moreover, that the real strength of *Heart of Darkness* lies in what it says about atrocities in King Leopold's Congo, though its documentary impulse is an important counter to its "will to style." As social criticism, its anti-imperialist message is undercut both by its racism and by its impressionism. But I know few novels that so insistently invoke an idealism that they don't seem to contain, and in which the modernist "will to style" is subjected to such powerful self-scrutiny — in which it is suggested that the "voice" at the heart of the novel, the voice of literature, the voice of civilization itself may in its purest, freest form yield only "the horror, the horror."

WORKS CITED

Achebe, Chinua. "An Image of Africa." *Massachusetts Review* 18 (1977): 782–94.

Arendt, Hannah. *Imperialism.* New York: Harcourt, 1968.

Conrad, Joseph. *A Personal Record.* New York: Doubleday, 1924.

Conrad, Joseph, and Ford Madox Hueffer. *The Inheritors: An Extravagant Story.* New York: McClure, 1901.

Cookey, S. J. *Britain and the Congo Question: 1885–1913.* London: Longman, 1968.

Glave, E. J. "Cruelty in the Congo Free State." *Century Magazine* 54 (1897): 706.

Green, Martin. *Dreams of Adventure, Deeds of Empire.* New York: Basic, 1979.

Guerard, Albert J. *Conrad the Novelist.* Cambridge: Harvard UP, 1958. New York: Atheneum, 1967.

Hawkins, Hunt. "Conrad's Critique of Imperialism in *Heart of Darkness.*" *PMLA* 94 (1979): 286–99.

Hinde, Captain Sidney L. *The Fall of the Congo Arabs.* London: Methuen, 1897.

Jameson, Fredric. *The Political Unconscious: Narrative as a Socially Symbolic Act.* Ithaca: Cornell UP, 1981

Johnston, Sir Harry H. *British Central Africa.* London: Methuen, 1897.

Mahood, M. M. *The Colonial Encounter: A Reading of Six Novels.* London: Rex Collings, 1977.

McClure, John A. *Kipling and Conrad: The Colonial Fiction.* Cambridge: Harvard UP, 1981.

Morel, E. D. *King Leopold's Rule in Africa.* Westport: Negro Universities P, 1970.

———. *Red Rubber: The Story of the Rubber Slave Trade on the Congo.* London: Unwin, 1906.

Parry, Benita. *Conrad and Imperialism.* London: Macmillan, 1983.

Said, Edward W. *Joseph Conrad and the Fiction of Autobiography.* Cambridge: Harvard UP, 1966.

Sherry, Norman. *Conrad's Western World.* Cambridge: Cambridge UP, 1971.

Trilling, Lionel. "On the Modern Element in Literature." *Beyond Culture: Essays on Literature and Learning.* New York: Harcourt, 1965.

———. *Sincerity and Authenticity.* Cambridge: Harvard UP, 1981.

Watt, Ian. *Conrad in the Nineteenth Century.* Berkeley: U of California P, 1979.

Watts, Cedric. "'A Bloody Racist': About Achebe's View of Conrad." *Yearbook of English Studies* 13 (1983): 196–209.

Williams, Raymond. *The English Novel from Dickens to Lawrence.* New York: Oxford UP, 1970.

Glossary of Critical
and Theoretical Terms

Most terms have been glossed parenthetically where they first appear in the text. Mainly, the glossary lists terms that are too complex to define in a phrase or a sentence or two. A few of the terms listed are discussed at greater length elsewhere (feminist criticism, for instance); these terms are defined succinctly and a page reference to the longer discussion is provided.

AFFECTIVE FALLACY First used by William K. Wimsatt and Monroe C. Beardsley to refer to what they regarded as the erroneous practice of interpreting texts according to the psychological responses of readers. "The Affective Fallacy," they wrote in a 1946 essay later republished in *The Verbal Icon* (1954), "is a confusion between the poem and its *results* (what it *is* and what it *does*). . . . It begins by trying to derive the standards of criticism from the psychological effects of a poem and ends in impressionism and relativism." The affective fallacy, like the intentional fallacy (confusing the meaning of a work with the author's expressly intended meaning), was one of the main tenets of the New Criticism, or formalism. The affective fallacy has recently been contested by reader-response critics, who have deliberately dedicated their efforts to describing the way individual readers and "interpretive communities" go about "making sense" of texts.

See also: Authorial Intention, Formalism, Reader-Response Criticism.

AUTHORIAL INTENTION Defined narrowly, an author's intention in writing a work, as expressed in letters, diaries, interviews, and conversations. Defined more broadly, "intentionality" involves unexpressed motivations, designs, and purposes, some of which may have remained unconscious.

The debate over whether critics should try to discern an author's intentions (conscious or otherwise) is an old one. William K. Wimsatt and Monroe C. Beardsley, in an essay first published in the 1940s, coined the term "intentional fallacy" to refer to the practice of basing interpretations on the expressed or implied intentions of authors, a practice they judged to be erroneous. As proponents of the New Criticism, or formalism, they argued that a work of literature is an object in itself and should be studied as such. They believed that it is sometimes helpful to learn what an author intended, but the critic's real purpose is to show what is actually in the text, not what an author intended to put there.

See also: Affective Fallacy, Formalism.

BASE *See* Marxist Criticism.

BINARY OPPOSITIONS *See* Oppositions.

BLANKS *See* Gaps.

CANON Since the fourth century, used to refer to those books of the Bible that the Christian church accepts as being Holy Scripture. The term has come to be applied more generally to those literary works given special status, or "privileged," by a culture. Works we tend to think of as "classics" or the "Great Books" produced by Western culture—texts that are found in every anthology of American, British, and world literature—would be among those that constitute the canon.

Recently, Marxist, feminist, minority, and postcolonial critics have argued that, for political reasons, many excellent works never enter the canon. Canonized works, they claim, are those that reflect—and respect—the culture's dominant ideology and/or perform some socially acceptable or even necessary form of "cultural work." Attempts have been made to broaden or redefine the canon by discovering valuable texts, or versions of texts, that were repressed or ignored for political reasons. These have been published both in traditional and in nontraditional anthologies. The most outspoken critics of the canon, especially radical critics practicing cultural criticism, have called into question the whole concept of canon or "canonicity." Privileging no form of artistic expression that reflects and revises the culture, these critics treat cartoons, comics, and soap operas with the same cogency and respect they accord novels, poems, and plays.

See also: Cultural Criticism, Feminist Criticism, Ideology, Marxist Criticism.

CONFLICTS, CONTRADICTIONS *See* Gaps.

CULTURAL CRITICISM A critical approach that is sometimes referred to as "cultural studies" or "cultural critique." Practitioners of cultural criticism oppose "high" definitions of culture and take seriously popular cultural forms. Grounded in a variety of continental European influences, cultural criticism nonetheless gained institutional force in England, in 1964, with the founding of the Centre for Contemporary Cultural Studies at Birmingham University. Broadly interdisciplinary in its scope and approach, cultural criticism views the text as the locus and catalyst of a complex network of political and economic discourses. Cultural critics share with Marxist critics an interest in the ideological contexts of cultural forms. *See* "What Is Cultural Criticism?" pp. 258–71.

DECONSTRUCTION A poststructuralist approach to literature that is strongly influenced by the writings of the French philosopher Jacques Derrida. Deconstruction, partly in response to structuralism and formalism, posits the undecidability of meaning for all texts. In fact, as the deconstructionist critic J. Hillis Miller points out, "deconstruction is not a dismantling of the structure of a text but a demonstration that it has already dismantled itself." *See* "What Is Deconstruction?" pp. 185–201.

DIALECTIC Originally developed by Greek philosophers, mainly Socrates and Plato, as a form and method of logical argumentation; the term later came to denote a philosophical notion of evolution. The German philosopher G. W. F. Hegel described dialectic as a process whereby a thesis, when countered by an antithesis, leads to the synthesis of a new idea. Karl Marx and Friedrich Engels, adapting Hegel's idealist theory, used the phrase "dialectical materialism" to discuss the way in which a revolutionary class war might lead to the synthesis of a new social economic order. The American Marxist critic Fredric Jameson has coined the phrase "dialectical criticism" to refer to a Marxist critical approach that synthesizes structuralist and poststructuralist methodologies.

See also: Marxist Criticism, Poststructuralism, Structuralism.

DIALOGIC *See* Discourse.

DISCOURSE Used specifically, can refer to (1) spoken or written discussion of a subject or area of knowledge; (2) the words in, or text of, a narrative as opposed to its story line; or (3) a "strand" within a given narrative that argues a certain point or defends a given value system.

More generally, "discourse" refers to the language in which a subject or area of knowledge is discussed or a certain kind of business is transacted. Human knowledge is collected and structured in discourses. Theology and medicine are defined by their discourses, as are politics, sexuality, and literary criticism.

A society is generally made up of a number of different discourses or "discourse communities," one or more of which may be dominant or serve the dominant ideology. Each discourse has its own vocabulary, concepts, and rules, knowledge of which constitutes power. The psychoanalyst and psychoanalytic critic Jacques Lacan has treated the unconscious as a form of discourse, the patterns of which are repeated in literature. Cultural critics, following Mikhail Bakhtin, use the word "dialogic" to discuss the dialogue *between* discourses that takes place within language or, more specifically, a literary text.

See also: Cultural Criticism, Ideology, Narrative, Psychoanalytic Criticism.

FEMINIST CRITICISM An aspect of the feminist movement whose primary goals include critiquing masculine-dominated language and literature by showing how they reflect a masculine ideology; writing the history of unknown or undervalued women writers, thereby earning them their rightful place in the literary canon; and helping create a climate in which women's creativity may be fully realized and appreciated. *See* "What Are Feminist and Gender Criticism?" pp. 148–61.

FIGURE *See* Metaphor, Metonymy, Symbol.

FORMALISM Also referred to as the New Criticism, formalism reached its height during the 1940s and 1950s, but it is still practiced today.

Formalists treat a work of literary art as if it were a self-contained, self-referential object. Rather than basing their interpretations of a text on the reader's response, the author's stated intentions, or parallels between the text and historical contexts (such as the author's life), formalists concentrate on the relationships *within* the text that give it its own distinctive character or form. Special attention is paid to repetition, particularly of images or symbols, but also of sound effects and rhythms in poetry.

Because of the importance placed on close analysis and the stress on the text as a carefully crafted, orderly object containing observable formal patterns, formalism has often been seen as an attack on Romanticism and impressionism, particularly impressionistic criticism. It has sometimes even been called an "objective" approach to literature. Formalists are more likely than certain other critics to believe and say that the meaning of a text can be known objectively. For instance, reader-response critics see meaning as a function either of each reader's experience or of the norms that govern a particular "interpretive community," and deconstructors argue that texts mean opposite things at the same time.

Formalism was originally based on essays written during the 1920s and 1930s by T. S. Eliot, I. A. Richards, and William Empson. It was significantly developed later by a group of American poets and critics, including R. P. Blackmur, Cleanth Brooks, John Crowe Ransom, Allen Tate, Robert Penn Warren, and William K. Wimsatt. Although we associate formalism with certain principles and terms (such as the "Affective Fallacy" and the "Intentional Fallacy" as defined by Wimsatt and Monroe C. Beardsley), formalists were trying to make a cultural statement rather than establish a critical dogma. Generally southern, religious, and culturally conservative, they advocated the inherent value of literary works (particularly of literary works regarded as beautiful art objects) because they were sick of the growing ugliness of modern life and contemporary events. Some recent theorists even suggest that the rising popularity of formalism after World War II was a feature of American isolationism, the formalist tendency to isolate literature from biography and history being a manifestation of the American fatigue with wider involvements.

See also: Affective Fallacy, Authorial Intention, Deconstruction, Reader-Response Criticism, Symbol.

GAPS When used by reader-response critics familiar with the theories of Wolfgang Iser, refers to "blanks" in texts that must be filled in by readers. A gap may be said to exist whenever and wherever a reader perceives something to be missing between words, sentences, paragraphs, stanzas, or chapters. Readers respond to gaps actively and creatively, explaining apparent inconsistencies in point of view, accounting for jumps in chronology, speculatively supplying information missing from plots, and resolving problems or issues left ambiguous or "indeterminate" in the text.

Reader-response critics sometimes speak as if a gap actually exists in a text; a gap is, of course, to some extent a product of readers' perceptions. Different readers may find gaps in different texts, and different gaps in the same text. Furthermore, they may fill these gaps in different ways, which is why, a reader-response critic might argue, works are interpreted in different ways.

Although the concept of the gap has been used mainly by reader-response critics, it has also been used by critics taking other theoretical approaches.

Practitioners of deconstruction might use "gap" when speaking of the radical contradictoriness of a text. Marxists have used the term to speak of everything from the gap that opens up between economic base and cultural superstructure to the two kinds of conflicts or contradictions to be found in literary texts. The first of these, they would argue, results from the fact that texts reflect ideology, within which certain subjects cannot be covered, things that cannot be said, contradictory views that cannot be recognized as contradictory. The second kind of conflict, contradiction, or gap within a text results from the fact that works don't just reflect ideology: they are also fictions that, consciously or unconsciously, distance themselves from the same ideology.

See also: Deconstruction, Ideology, Marxist Criticism, Reader-Response Criticism.

GENDER CRITICISM Developing out of feminist criticism in the mid-1980s, this fluid and inclusive movement by its nature defies neat definition. Its practitioners include, but are not limited to, self-identified feminists, gay and lesbian critics, queer and performance theorists, and poststructuralists interested in deconstructing oppositions such as masculine/feminine, heterosexual/homosexual. This diverse group of critics shares an interest in interrogating categories of gender and sexuality and exploring the relationships between them, though it does not necessarily share any central assumptions about the nature of these categories. For example, some gender critics insist that all gender identities are cultural constructions, but others have maintained a belief in essential gender identity. Often gender critics are more interested in examining gender issues through a literary text than a literary text through gender issues. *See* "What Are Feminist and Gender Criticism?" pp. 148–61.

GENRE A French word referring to a kind or type of literature. Individual works within a genre may exhibit a distinctive form, be governed by certain conventions, and/or represent characteristic subjects. Tragedy, epic, and romance are all genres.

Perhaps inevitably, the term *genre* is used loosely. Lyric poetry is a genre, but so are characteristic *types* of the lyric, such as the sonnet, the ode, and the elegy. Fiction is a genre, as are detective fiction and science fiction. The list of genres grows constantly as critics establish new lines of connection between individual works and discern new categories of works with common characteristics. Moreover, some writers form hybrid genres by combining the characteristics of several in a single work.

Knowledge of genres helps critics to understand and explain what is conventional and unconventional, borrowed and original, in a work.

HEGEMONY Given intellectual currency by the Italian communist Antonio Gramsci, the word (a translation of *egemonia*) refers to the pervasive system of assumptions, meanings, and values—the web of ideologies, in other words—that shapes the way things look, what they mean, and therefore what reality *is* for the majority of people within a given culture.

See also: Ideology, Marxist Criticism.

IDEOLOGY A set of beliefs underlying the customs, habits, and/or practices common to a given social group. To members of that group, the beliefs seem obviously true, natural, and even universally applicable. They may seem just as obviously arbitrary, idiosyncratic, and even false to outsiders or members of another group who adhere to another ideology. Within a society, several ideologies may coexist, or one or more may be dominant.

Ideologies may be forcefully imposed or willingly subscribed to. Their component beliefs may be held consciously or unconsciously. In either case, they come to form what Johanna M. Smith has called "the unexamined ground of our experience." Ideology governs our perceptions, judgments, and prejudices—our sense of what is acceptable, normal, and deviant. Ideology may cause a revolution; it may also allow discrimination and even exploitation.

Ideologies are of special interest to sociologically oriented critics of literature because of the way in which authors reflect or resist prevailing views in their texts. Some Marxist critics have argued that literary texts reflect and reproduce the ideologies that produced them; most, however, have shown how ideologies are riven with contradictions that works of literature manage to expose and widen. Still other Marxists have focused on the way in which texts themselves are characterized by gaps, conflicts, and contradictions between their ideological and anti-ideological functions.

Feminist critics have addressed the question of ideology by seeking to expose (and thereby call into question) the patriarchal ideology mirrored or inscribed in works written by men—even men who have sought to counter sexism and break down sexual stereotypes. New historicists have been interested in demonstrating the ideological underpinnings not only of literary representations but also of our interpretations of them. Fredric Jameson, an American Marxist critic, argues that all thought is ideological, but that ideological thought that knows itself as such stands the chance of seeing through and transcending ideology.

See also: Cultural Criticism, Feminist Criticism, Marxist Criticism, New Historicism.

IMAGINARY ORDER One of the three essential orders of the psychoanalytic field (see Real and Symbolic Order), it is most closely associated with the senses (sight, sound, touch, taste, and smell). The infant, who by comparison to other animals is born premature and thus is wholly dependent on others for a prolonged period, enters the Imaginary order when it begins to experience a unity of body parts and motor control that is empowering. This usually occurs between six and eighteen months, and is called by Lacan the "mirror stage" or "mirror phase," in which the child anticipates mastery of its body. It does so by identifying with the *image* of wholeness (that is, seeing its own image in the mirror, experiencing its mother as a whole body, and so on). This sense of oneness, and also difference from others (especially the mother or primary caretaker), is established through an image or a vision of harmony that is both a mirroring and a "mirage of maturation" or false sense of individuality and independence. The Imaginary is a metaphor for unity, is related to the visual order, and is always part of human subjectivity. Because the subject is fundamentally separate from others and also internally divided (conscious/unconscious), the apparent coherence of the Imaginary, its fullness and grandiosity, is always false, a *mis*recognition that the ego (or "me") tries to deny by imagining itself as coherent and empowered. The Imaginary operates in conjunction with the Real and Symbolic and is not a "stage" of development equivalent to Freud's "pre-oedipal stage," nor is it prelinguistic.

See also: Psychoanalytic Criticism, Real, Symbolic Order.

IMPLIED READER   A phrase used by some reader-response critics in place of the phrase "the reader." Whereas "the reader" could refer to any idiosyncratic individual who happens to have read or to be reading the text, "the implied reader" is *the* reader intended, even created, by the text. Other reader-response critics seeking to describe this more generally conceived reader have spoken of the "informed reader" or the "narratee," who is "the necessary counterpart of a given narrator."

See Reader-Response Criticism.

INTENTIONAL FALLACY   *See* Authorial Intention.

INTENTIONALITY   *See* Authorial Intention.

INTERTEXTUALITY   The condition of interconnectedness among texts. Every author has been influenced by others, and every work contains explicit and implicit references to other works. Writers may consciously or unconsciously echo a predecessor or precursor; they may also consciously or unconsciously disguise their indebtedness, making intertextual relationships difficult for the critic to trace.

Reacting against the formalist tendency to view each work as a freestanding object, some poststructuralist critics suggested that the meaning of a work emerges only intertextually, that is, within the context provided by other works. But there has been a reaction, too, against this type of intertextual criticism. Some new historicist critics suggest that literary history is itself too narrow a context and that works should be interpreted in light of a larger set of cultural contexts.

There is, however, a broader definition of intertextuality, one that refers to the relationship between works of literature and a wide range of narratives and discourses that we don't usually consider literary. Thus defined, intertextuality could be used by a new historicist to refer to the significant interconnectedness between a literary text and nonliterary discussions of or discourses about contemporary culture. Or it could be used by a poststructuralist to suggest that a work can only be recognized and read within a vast field of signs and tropes that is *like* a text and that makes any single text self-contradictory and "undecidable."

See also: Discourse, Formalism, Narrative, New Historicism, Poststructuralism, Trope.

MARXIST CRITICISM   An approach that treats literary texts as material products, describing them in broadly historical terms. In Marxist criticism, the text is viewed in terms of its production and consumption, as a product *of* work that does identifiable cultural work of its own. Following Karl Marx, the founder of communism, Marxist critics have used the terms "base" to refer to economic reality and "superstructure" to refer to the corresponding or "homologous" infrastructure consisting of politics, law, philosophy, religion, and the arts. Also following Marx, they have used the word "ideology" to refer to that set of cultural beliefs that literary works at once reproduce, resist, and revise.

METAPHOR   The representation of one thing by another related or similar thing. The image (or activity or concept) used to represent or "figure" something else is known as the "vehicle" of the metaphor; the thing represented is called the "tenor." In other words, the vehicle is what we substitute for the tenor. The relationship between vehicle and tenor can provide much additional meaning. Thus, instead of saying, "Last night I read a book," we might say, "Last night I plowed through a book." "Plowed through" (or the activity of plowing) is the vehicle of our metaphor; "read" (or the act of reading) is the tenor, the thing being figured. The increment in meaning through metaphor is fairly obvious. Our audience knows not only *that* we read but also *how* we read, because to read a book in the way that a plow rips through earth is surely to read in a relentless, unreflective way. Note that in the sentence above, a new metaphor—"rips through"—has been used to explain an old one. This serves (which is a metaphor) as an example of just how thick (another metaphor) language is with metaphors!

Metaphor is a kind of "trope" (literally, a "turning," that is, a figure of speech that alters or "turns" the meaning of a word or phrase). Other tropes include allegory, conceit, metonymy, personification, simile, symbol, and synecdoche. Traditionally, metaphor and symbol have been viewed as the principal tropes; minor tropes have been categorized as *types* of these two major ones. Similes, for instance, are usually defined as simple metaphors that usually employ "like" or "as" and state the tenor outright, as in "My love is like a red, red rose." Synecdoche involves a vehicle that is a *part* of the tenor, as in "I see a sail" meaning "I see a boat." Metonymy is viewed as a metaphor involving two terms commonly if arbitrarily associated with (but not fundamentally or intrinsically related to) each other. Recently, however, deconstructors such as Paul de Man and J. Hillis Miller have questioned the "privilege" granted to metaphor and the metaphor/metonymy distinction or "opposition." They have suggested that all metaphors are really metonyms and that all figuration is arbitrary.

See also: Deconstruction, Metonymy, Oppositions, Symbol.

METONYMY   The representation of one thing by another that is commonly and often physically associated with it. To refer to a writer's handwriting as his or her "hand" is to use a metonymic "figure" or "trope." The image or thing used to represent something else is known as the "vehicle" of the metonym; the thing represented is called the "tenor."

Like other tropes (such as metaphor), metonymy involves the replacement of one word or phrase by another. Liquor may be referred to as "the bottle," a monarch as "the crown." Narrowly defined, the vehicle of a metonym is arbitrarily, not intrinsically, associated with the tenor. In other words, the bottle just happens to be what liquor is stored in and poured from in our culture. The hand may be involved in the production of handwriting, but so are the brain and the pen. There is no special, intrinsic likeness between a crown and a monarch; it's just that crowns traditionally sit on monarchs' heads and not on the heads of university professors. More broadly, "metonym" and "metonymy" have been used by recent critics to refer to a wide range of figures and tropes. Deconstructors have questioned the distinction between metaphor and metonymy.

See also: Deconstruction, Metaphor, Trope.

NARRATIVE   A story or a telling of a story, or an account of a situation or of events. A novel and a biography of a novelist are both narratives, as are Freud's case histories.

Some critics use the word "narrative" even more generally; Brook Thomas, a new historicist, has critiqued "narratives of human history that neglect the role human labor has played."

NEW CRITICISM   *See* Formalism.

NEW HISTORICISM   First practiced and articulated in the late 1970s and early 1980s in the work of critics such as Stephen Greenblatt—who named this movement in contemporary critical theory—and Louis Montrose, its practitioners share certain convictions, primarily that literary critics need to develop a high degree of historical consciousness and that literature should not be viewed apart from other human creations, artistic or otherwise. They share a belief in referentiality—a belief that literature refers to and is referred to by things outside itself—that is fainter in the works of formalist, poststructuralist, and even reader-response critics. Discarding old distinctions between literature, history, and the social sciences, new historicists agree with Greenblatt that the "central concerns" of criticism "should prevent it from permanently sealing off one type of discourse from another, or decisively separating works of art from the minds and lives of their creators and their audiences."

See also: "What Is the New Historicism?" pp. 221–33; Authorial Intention, Deconstruction, Formalism, Ideology, Poststructuralism, Psychoanalytic Criticism.

OPPOSITIONS   A concept highly relevant to linguistics, since linguists maintain that words (such as "black" and "death") have meaning not in themselves but in relation to other words ("white" and "life"). Jacques Derrida, a poststructuralist philosopher of language, has suggested that in the West we think in terms of these "binary oppositions" or dichotomies, which on examination turn out to be evaluative hierarchies. In other words, each opposition—beginning/end, presence/absence, or consciousness/unconsciousness con tains one term that our culture views as superior and one term that we view as negative or inferior.

Derrida has "deconstructed" a number of these binary oppositions, including two—speech/writing and signifier/signified—that he believes to be central to linguistics in particular and Western culture in general. He has concurrently critiqued the "law" of noncontradiction, which is fundamental to Western logic. He and other deconstructors have argued that a text can contain opposed strands of discourse and, therefore, mean opposite things: reason *and* passion, life *and* death, hope *and* despair, black *and* white. Traditionally, criticism has involved choosing between opposed or contradictory meanings and arguing that one is present in the text and the other absent.

French feminists have adopted the ideas of Derrida and other deconstructors, showing not only that we think in terms of such binary oppositions as male/female, reason/emotion, and active/passive, but that we also associate reason and activity with masculinity and emotion and passivity with femininity. Because of this, they have concluded that language is "phallocentric," or masculine-dominated.

See also: Deconstruction, Discourse, Feminist Criticism, Poststructuralism.

PHALLUS   The symbolic value of the penis that organizes libidinal development and which Freud saw as a stage in the process of human subjectivity. Lacan viewed the Phallus as the representative of a fraudulent power (male over female) whose "law" is a principle of psychic division (conscious/unconscious) and sexual difference (masculine/feminine). The Symbolic order (*see* Symbolic Order) is ruled by the Phallus, which of itself has no inherent meaning *apart from* the power and meaning given to it by individual cultures and societies, and represented by the name of the father as lawgiver and namer.

POSTSTRUCTURALISM The general attempt to contest and subvert structuralism initiated by deconstructors and certain other critics associated with psychoanalytic, Marxist, and feminist theory. Structuralists, using linguistics as a model and employing semiotic (sign) theory, posit the possibility of knowing a text systematically and revealing the "grammar" behind its form and meaning. Poststructuralists argue against the possibility of such knowledge and description. They counter that texts can be shown to contradict not only structuralist accounts of them but also themselves. In making their adversarial claims, they rely on close readings of texts and on the work of theorists such as Jacques Derrida and Jacques Lacan.

Poststructuralists have suggested that structuralism rests on distinctions between "signifier" and "signified" (signs and the things they point toward), "self" and "language" (or "text"), texts and other texts, and text and world that are overly simplistic, if not patently inaccurate. Poststructuralists have shown how all signifieds are also signifiers, and they have treated texts as "intertexts." They have viewed the world as if it *were* a text (we desire a certain car because it *symbolizes* achievement) and the self as the subject, as well as the user, of language; for example, we may shape and speak through language, but it also shapes and speaks through us.

See also: Deconstruction, Feminist Criticism, Intertextuality, Psychoanalytic Criticism, Semiotics, Structuralism.

PSYCHOANALYTIC CRITICISM Grounded in the psychoanalytic theories of Sigmund Freud, it is one of the oldest critical methodologies still in use. Freud's view that works of literature, like dreams, express secret, unconscious desires led to criticism and interpreted literary works as manifestations of the authors' neuroses. More recently, psychoanalytic critics have come to see literary works as skillfully crafted artifacts that may appeal to *our* neuroses by tapping into our repressed wishes and fantasies. Other forms of psychological criticism that diverge from Freud, although they ultimately derive from his insights, include those based on the theories of Carl Jung and Jacques Lacan.

READER-RESPONSE CRITICISM An approach to literature that, as its name implies, considers the way readers respond to texts, as they read. Stanley Fish describes the method by saying that it substitutes for one question, "What does this sentence mean?" a more operational question, "What does this sentence do?" Reader-response criticism shares with deconstruction a strong textual orientation and a reluctance to define a single meaning for a work. Along with psychoanalytic criticism, it shares an interest in the dynamics of mental response to textual cues. *See* "What Is Reader-Response Criticism?" pp. 115–27.

REAL One of the three orders of subjectivity (*see* Imaginary Order and Symbolic Order), the Real is the intractable and substantial world that resists and exceeds interpretation. The Real cannot be imagined, symbolized, or known directly. It constantly eludes our efforts to name it (death, gravity, the physicality of objects are examples of the Real), and thus challenges both the Imaginary and the Symbolic orders. The Real is fundamentally "Other," the mark of the divide between conscious and unconscious, and is signaled in language by gaps, slips, speechlessness, and the sense of the uncanny. The Real is not what we call "reality." It is the stumbling block of the Imaginary (which thinks it can "imagine" anything, including the Real) and of the Symbolic, which tries to bring the Real under its laws (the Real exposes the "phallacy" of the Law of the Phallus). The Real is frightening; we try to tame it with laws and language and call it "reality."

See also: Imaginary Order, Psychoanalytic Criticism, Symbolic Order.

SEMIOLOGY, SEMIOTIC *See* Semiotics.

SEMIOTICS The study of signs and sign systems and the way meaning is derived from them. Structuralist anthropologists, psychoanalysts, and literary critics developed semiotics during the decades following 1950, but much of the pioneering work had been done at the turn of the century by the founder of modern linguistics, Ferdinand de Saussure, and the American philosopher Charles Sanders Peirce.

Semiotics is based on several important distinctions, including the distinction between "signifier" and "signified" (the sign and what it points toward) and the distinction between "langue" and "parole." *Langue* (French for "tongue," as in "native tongue," meaning language) refers to the entire system within which individual utterances or usages of language have meaning; *parole* (French for "word") refers to the particular utterances or usages. A principal tenet of semiotics is that signs, like words, are not significant in themselves, but instead have meaning only in relation to other signs and the entire system of signs, or langue.

The affinity between semiotics and structuralist literary criticism derives from this emphasis placed on langue, or system. Structuralist critics, after all, were reacting against formalists and their procedure of focusing on individual words as if meanings didn't depend on anything external to the text.

Poststructuralists have used semiotics but questioned some of its underlying assumptions, including the opposition between signifier and signified. The feminist poststructuralist Julia Kristeva, for instance, has used the word "semiotic" to describe feminine language, a highly figurative, fluid form of discourse that she sets in opposition to rigid, symbolic masculine language.

See also: Deconstruction, Feminist Criticism, Formalism, Oppositions, Poststructuralism, Structuralism, Symbol.

SIMILE *See* Metaphor.

SOCIOHISTORICAL CRITICISM *See* New Historicism.

STRUCTURALISM A science of humankind whose proponents attempted to show that all elements of human culture, including literature, may be understood as parts of a system of signs. Structuralism, according to Robert Scholes, was a reaction to "'modernist' alienation and despair."

Using Ferdinand de Saussure's linguistic theory, European structuralists such as Roman Jakobson, Claude Lévi-Strauss, and Roland Barthes (before his shift toward poststructuralism) attempted to develop a "semiology" or "semiotics" (science of signs). Barthes, among others, sought to recover literature and even language from the isolation in which they had been studied and to show that the laws that govern them govern all signs, from road signs to articles of clothing.

Particularly useful to structuralists were two of Saussure's concepts: the idea of "phoneme" in language and the idea that phonemes exist in two kinds of relationships: "synchronic" and "diachronic." A phoneme is the smallest consistently significant unit in language; thus, both "a" and "an" are phonemes, but "n" is not. A diachronic relationship is that which a phoneme has with those that have preceded it in time and those that will follow it. These "horizontal" relationships produce what we might call discourse or narrative and what Saussure called "parole." The synchronic relationship is the "vertical" one that a word has in a given instant with the entire system of language ("langue") in which it may generate meaning. "An" means what it means in English because those of us who speak the language are using it in the same way at a given time.

Following Saussure, Lévi-Strauss studied hundreds of myths, breaking them into their smallest meaningful units, which he called "mythemes." Removing each from its diachronic relations with other mythemes in a single myth (such as the myth of Oedipus and his mother), he vertically aligned those mythemes that he found to be homologous (structurally correspondent). He then studied the relationships within as well as between vertically aligned columns, in an attempt to understand scientifically, through ratios and proportions, those thoughts and processes that humankind has shared, both at one particular time and across time. One could say, then, that structuralists followed Saussure in preferring to think about the overriding langue or language of myth, in which each mytheme and mytheme-constituted myth fits meaningfully, rather than about isolated individual paroles or narratives. Structuralists followed Saussure's lead in believing what the poststructuralist Jacques Derrida later decided he could not subscribe to—that sign systems must be understood in terms of binary oppositions. In analyzing myths and texts to find basic structures, structuralists tended to find that opposite terms modulate until they are finally resolved or reconciled by some intermediary third term. Thus, a structuralist reading of *Paradise Lost* would show that the war between God and the bad angels becomes a rift between God and sinful, fallen man, the rift then being healed by the Son of God, the mediating third term.

See also: Deconstruction, Discourse, Narrative, Poststructuralism, Semiotics.

SUPERSTRUCTURE   *See* Marxist Criticism.

SYMBOL   A thing, image, or action that, although it is of interest in its own right, stands for or suggests something larger and more complex—often an idea or a range of interrelated ideas, attitudes, and practices.

Within a given culture, some things are understood to be symbols: the flag of the United States is an obvious example. More subtle cultural symbols might be the river as a symbol of time and the journey as a symbol of life and its manifold experiences.

Instead of appropriating symbols generally used and understood within their culture, writers often create symbols by setting up, in their works, a complex but identifiable web of associations. As a result, one object, image, or action suggests others, and often, ultimately, a range of ideas.

A symbol may thus be defined as a metaphor in which the "vehicle," the thing, image, or action used to represent something else, represents many related things (or "tenors") or is broadly suggestive. The urn in Keats's "Ode on a Grecian Urn" suggests many interrelated concepts, including art, truth, beauty, and timelessness.

Symbols have been of particular interest to formalists, who study how meanings emerge from the complex, patterned relationships between images in a work, and psychoanalytic critics, who are interested in how individual authors and the larger culture both disguise and reveal unconscious fears and desires through symbols. Recently, French feminists have also focused on the symbolic. They have suggested that, as wide-ranging as it seems, symbolic language is ultimately rigid and restrictive. They favor semiotic language and writing, which, they contend, is at once more rhythmic, unifying, and feminine.

See also: Feminist Criticism, Metaphor, Psychoanalytic Criticism, Trope.

SYMBOLIC ORDER One of the three orders of subjectivity (see Imaginary Order and Real), it is the realm of law, language, and society; it is the repository of generally held cultural beliefs. Its symbolic system is language, whose agent is the father or lawgiver, the one who has the power of naming. The human subject is commanded into this preestablished order by language (a process that begins long before a child can speak) and must submit to its orders of communication (grammar, syntax, and so on). Entrance into the Symbolic order determines subjectivity according to a primary law of referentiality that takes the male sign (phallus, see Phallus) as its ordering principle. Lacan states that both sexes submit to the Law of the Phallus (the law of order, language, and differentiation) but their individual relation to the law determines whether they see themselves as—and are seen by others to be—either "masculine" or "feminine." The Symbolic institutes repression (of the Imaginary), thus creating the unconscious, which itself is structured like the language of the symbolic. The unconscious, a timeless realm, cannot be known directly, but it can be understood by a kind of translation that takes place in language—psychoanalysis is the "talking cure." The Symbolic is not a "stage" of development (as is Freud's "oedipal stage") nor is it set in place once and for all in human life. We constantly negotiate its threshold (in sleep, in drunkenness) and can "fall out" of it altogether in psychosis.

See also: Imaginary Order, Psychoanalytic Criticism, Real.

SYNECDOCHE *See* Metaphor, Metonymy.

TENOR *See* Metaphor, Metonymy, Symbol.

TROPE A figure, as in "figure of speech." Literally a "turning," that is, a turning or twisting of a word or phrase to make it mean something else. Principal tropes include metaphor, metonymy, personification, simile, and synecdoche.

See also: Metaphor, Metonymy.

VEHICLE *See* Metaphor, Metonymy, Symbol.

About the Contributors

THE VOLUME EDITOR

Ross C Murfin, general editor of Case Studies in Contemporary Criticism, is provost and vice president for Academic Affairs at Southern Methodist University. He has taught at Yale University and the University of Virginia and published scholarly studies on Joseph Conrad, Thomas Hardy, and D. H. Lawrence. He is at work on a glossary of literary and critical terms to be published by Bedford Books.

THE CRITICS

Patrick Brantlinger is professor of English and director of the Victorian Studies Graduate Program at Indiana University, Bloomington. Editor of *Energy and Entropy: Science and Culture in Victorian Britain* (1989) and coeditor of *Modernity and Mass Culture* (1991), he has written several scholarly works, including *Bread and Circuses: Theories of Mass Culture as Social Decay* (1983), *Rule of Darkness: British Literature and Imperialism 1830–1914* (1988), and *Crusoe's Footprints: Cultural Studies in Britain and America* (1990).

J. Hillis Miller, Distinguished Professor of English and Comparative Literature at the University of California, Irvine, is the preeminent American deconstructive critic. Among his many important studies of nineteenth- and twentieth-century literature are *Fiction and Repetition: Seven English Novels* (1982), *The Linguistic Moment: From Wordsworth to Stevens* (1985), and *Versions of Pygmalion* (1990).

Peter J. Rabinowitz, professor of comparative literature at Hamilton College, divides his time between music and narrative theory. Author of *Before Reading: Narrative Conventions and the Politics of Interpretation* (1987) and coeditor of *Understanding Narrative* (1994), he has published articles covering a wide range of subjects, from Dostoyevsky to Mrs. E.D.E.N. Southworth, from detective fiction to the ideology of musical structure. He is also an active music critic and a contributing editor of *Fanfare*.

Johanna M. Smith is assistant professor of English at the University of Texas, Arlington, where she teaches eighteenth- and nineteenth-century literature. She is the author of a book on Mary Shelley in Twayne's British Authors series. The volume editor of another Case Study in Contemporary Criticism, *Frankenstein* (1992), she is currently working on a study of representations of nineteenth-century working-class politics.

Brook Thomas is professor of English at the University of California, Irvine, where he teaches courses in literary criticism and critical theory. He is the author of numerous scholarly articles and several books, including *Cross-Examinations of Law and Literature: Cooper, Hawthorne, Stowe, and Melville* (1987) and *The New Historicism and Other Old-Fashioned Topics* (1991).

"*Heart of Darkness:* Anti-Imperialism, Racism, or Impressionism?" Reprinted from *Criticism,* Volume 27, No. 4 (1985), by Patrick Brantlinger by permission of the Wayne State University Press. © Wayne State University Press, 1985.

"*Heart of Darkness* Revisited" is a revised version of a previously published essay (Copyright © 1983) by J. Hillis Miller.